WAY of the ARGOSI

WAY *of the* ARGOSI

SEBASTIEN DE CASTELL

HOT
KEY
BOOKS

First published in Great Britain in 2019 by
HOT KEY BOOKS
80–81 Wimpole Street, London W1G 9RE
Owned by Bonnier Books
Sveavägen 56, Stockholm, Sweden
www.hotkeybooks.com

A CIP catalogue record for this book is available from the British Library.

HARDBACK ISBN: 978-1-4714-0552-5
TRADE PAPERBACK ISBN: 978-1-4714-1031-4
Also available as an ebook and in audio

1

Typeset by Palimpsest Book Production Ltd, Falkirk, Stirlingshire
Printed and bound by Clays Ltd, Elcograf S.p.A.

MIX
Paper from
responsible sources
FSC® C018072

Hot Key Books is an imprint of Bonnier Books UK
www.bonnierbooks.co.uk

For Heather Adams, the Path of Words and Whimsy:
a true Argosi whose road ever winds to curious
and unexplored places.

A Good Girl

Be a good girl now.

People are always saying that to me. Every time the shabby remnants of our tribe come to a new village or town begging for shelter, some stranger pats me on the head and says, 'Be a good girl now.' Different voices. Different languages. But always that same phrase, like a ghost that follows me wherever I go.

A master contraptioneer in one of Gitabria's gleaming cities said it with a smile in her lilting, musical accent: '*Suvé onta bella jaïda.*'

Be a good girl now.

What she'd really meant was: smile, look pretty, and be quiet.

In the Zhuban territories far to the north, a warrior poet (everybody in Zhuban claims to be a warrior poet) took it much more seriously. His brow furrowed with deep lines as he frowned at me. '*Nanging isang bubutay bamba.*'

Being now a good girl.

But he was really telling me to be wise, to be vigilant and, most of all, to be quiet.

Quiet is the part they all agree on. Even now, as this kind

old woman, thin strands of sooty-grey hair burned to the skin of her forehead where the edge of an ember spell caught her a few minutes ago, arm hanging from her shattered left shoulder where that same mage's iron binding slammed her into the corpses of her neighbours, whispers to me through broken teeth, 'Shh . . . be a good girl now.'

It's hard to be anything else in this dank, dark cave she shoved me into. Outside, in what's left of this dusty, dried-out husk of a town on the edge of the Seven Sands . . . Outside the cave, a septet – that's seven, in case you don't know – of Jan'Tep war mages are busy slaughtering the screaming, pleading vestiges of my own clan one by one. They could probably incinerate all of us with one big spell, but from what I saw, the mages were mostly teenagers. I guess they're showing off for each other. Soon they're going to figure out that I'm in here and come up with an especially nasty spell just for me, but I guess I shouldn't worry because the kindly old woman trying to nudge me further and further into the cave has a plan.

Shh . . . be a good girl now.

Great plan, lady.

I feel like telling her that no Mahdek would ever tell an eleven-year-old to be quiet. They wouldn't call me a girl either, because it's not until we turn thirteen that we stand before our tribe and tell everyone who and what we are inside. At my age, I'm supposed to be searching for my spirit animal – the beast or bird who will be my companion as I make my way in the world, whispering its counsel to me, guiding me through life.

How is a spirit animal supposed to hear you calling if you're quiet all the time?

2

Mahdek children are encouraged to make noise, to speak with our minds and our hearts (even if adults don't exactly listen to us, I've noticed), so that spirit herds passing by will be drawn to our words and songs and one of them will sense a kindred soul whose life they want to share.

But I'm never going to have a spirit animal. I'm never getting out of this cave. No matter how many times the nice old woman mutters, '*Be a good girl*,' it's not going to make a difference. Being good never saved a Mahdek exile from being murdered by a Jan'Tep mage.

Although . . .

It occurs to me now, as I'm lying here curled up in a ball, trying to make myself as small as possible among the smouldering corpses of the townsfolk who crawled in here as iron and ember spells were still tearing them apart, while this dying old woman . . . No, I'm pretty sure she's dead now. The index finger of her good hand is still pressed to her lips as if, even in death, she's reminding me to stay quiet. Anyway, I can't help but wonder if maybe there's a connection between the fact that my people are the only ones on the continent who don't expect their young to be quiet and the fact that there are so few of us left. Maybe our problem is that we just never learned to shut up.

I hear the battle cry of one of our warriors outside. She's attacking the mages, shouting at them in the old way, in our own tongue. We don't even speak it among ourselves any more because it makes the people who give us shelter uncomfortable. The Jan'Tep mages who hunt us tell people that our language is a 'demon-tongue'. They say we use it to awaken infernal beings to slaughter our enemies.

How I wish that were true.

I know our warrior has died when I hear the thunder crack of an ember spell lighting up the air outside the cave. I can picture the shower of gold and blue sparks, followed by the scene of early morning after a storm. Part of me wants to run outside just to behold the wonders of Jan'Tep magic. I know I should hate it, but the colours, the lights, the way they move . . . it's beautiful. And if you're going to die anyway, shouldn't it be while looking at something beautiful?

Too late now. The screams have stopped and everything's gone quiet. I wonder if the warrior who just died was the last of my clan. And was my clan the last of all that remained of the once-great Mahdek tribes?

Am I alone now?

'Burn the bodies, bury the ashes,' I hear one of the mages saying. He's the older one, the one in charge. But he's not the one I hate the most.

The one I hate the most is younger, maybe sixteen. He's as tall as any of them though. His shoulders are broad and unlike the others he looks strong beneath his robes. He doesn't smile when he raises his hands, forms those strange shapes with his fingers and sends lightning and fire to kill us. He doesn't laugh or make jokes when we die.

The others I can hate the way you hate a cold winter or a sharp stone that cuts your foot. They're cruel and ugly on the inside. They're monsters. But this one, he knows – somewhere inside he *knows* – that this is wrong. He's a human being. Like me.

But he does it anyway.

I don't know his name because when the Jan'Tep mages are on a mission they call each other things like 'Iron Asp' or 'Ember Fox'. This young one is 'Shadow Falcon'.

4

I'm going to kill Shadow Falcon one day.

Well, probably not since I'm about to die.

More spells are starting to ignite the air outside the cave. Different ones this time. Not the crack of thunder that passes in an instant but the steady crackle of flames that pour out from the mages' palms as if their hands were volcanoes filled with lava.

Why is it so important to them that no trace of us be left behind?

I can hear some of the mages complaining about the stink of flesh burning from the bones of the dead. A couple of them are vomiting, their spells collapsing from the break in their concentration. Then the older one, their leader, shouts at them and they begin the process all over again. Soon he'll send someone into the caves to search for any stragglers. To find me.

'Please spare us!' a voice cries out. Not one of my people, of course. I'm pretty sure they're all dead now. Also, we know better than to ask a Jan'Tep war coven for mercy. One of the villagers who took us in must be pleading for his life.

'We didn't know what they were!'

Not true. We never lied about who we were. Maybe we should've though.

'They summoned demons to force us to shelter them.'

Complete fabrication. No matter how much the Jan'Tep claim we use demon magic – their excuse when they started killing us off three hundred years ago – you can't 'summon' a demon. I know this because I've tried many, many times.

'We only pretended to hide them so we could come find yo—'

Funny how they kill him right as he's finally saying something true. My clan stayed in this little town in the Seven Sands too long and one of the townsfolk must've gone in search of a Jan'Tep hextracker, who then led the war coven right to us.

Never stay in one place too long. *That's* what the Mahdek tell their children.

It's what my mother and father told me right before they died in the raid that wiped out half our clan three years ago. I still remember the looks on their faces, how scared they were.

Why aren't I scared?

I'm going to die here in this dark cave, seeing nothing but the face of a dead woman with her finger pressed to her lifeless lips, smelling nothing but the stench of the corpses all around me. I should be terrified. I should be angry. Instead I feel almost . . . drunk? Is that the right word? We Mahdek don't drink spirits (stupid name for alcohol since spirits are meant to guide you, not make you act silly). Maybe it's just that once you've watched your parents floating in the air, wrists and ankles wrapped in beautiful bands of yellow and silver light, right before they're torn apart, you know without a shred of doubt that one day some other Jan'Tep mage will do the same to you.

Today's that day, I think.

'There!' I hear a low voice growl. 'Get her!'

I stick out my arms to make it easier for them to drag me from the bodies. I don't pull away or scream. Maybe I really am a good girl?

'Quickly now, while they're still destroying the evidence!'

A pair of big hands wrap around my wrists and yank me backwards, away from the entrance. My bum slides over the dead and then scrapes the cold rocks and dirt. We seem to be going deeper into the cave. I hadn't even realised there *was* a deeper part; it just looked like a shallow grotto before the old woman pulled me in here with her.

Whoever's got me lets go of my wrists and scoops me up in their arms. I look up in the darkness and I can just barely make out two figures. They're crouched over me, and the shadows hang over them, making them look menacing. Like demons.

Maybe my people really are demon worshippers.

Something heavy scratches the cave floor, shifting as the bigger demon shoves it with his shoulder. The two of them bend down even lower as they haul me into a narrow tunnel. Must've been camouflaged by the villagers so they could use it to hide themselves and their valuables whenever they got raided. Probably doesn't work so well when the mages coming for you have sand spells that can track you anywhere. The one they call Shadow Falcon, I heard one of the others say he's the best at it. Maybe he's already coming for us.

'Don't be afraid,' one of my rescuers says. He's speaking Daroman, from a country about two hundred miles from here. The Seven Sands doesn't have its own language, so most folk in these parts learn a simplified form of Daroman. This man speaks it awkwardly though, like he learned it only recently. His voice is deep, his tone gruff in a way that warns me not to argue with him.

'What about the others?' I ask anyway, but all I hear is the shuffling of his boots on the rocky ground. I guess he doesn't want to say that there aren't any.

'Where are you taking me?' I ask then.

The voice that answers belongs to a woman. It's unusual sounding. Smooth. Elegant. I like it, but I feel strange hearing it, like I've snuck into a rich person's home and someone's

7

about to find me. 'To a place far from here,' she says. 'A place where you'll be safe.'

The man speaks up, grunting from the effort of carrying me while having to bend so low. 'No more living on scraps for you, my girl. No more trudging through deserts under the hot sun or icy forests in the frozen winter. You'll live in a big house and eat fine foods and have all the toys you could ever want.' His voice catches on those last words – like he's trying to stop himself from crying.

'The Jan'Tep—' I begin, but the woman cuts me off.

'They will never hurt you again,' she says, louder now because I guess we're pretty far from the cave entrance. 'Ours is a wealthy family, child. An important one. And we are . . .' She struggles as if she doesn't know the right word, which tells me for sure she isn't a native Daroman speaker. After a second the man mumbles something to her and she nods. 'Warriors-of-honour. Yes, we are warriors-of-honour. Do you understand me? Not even the lords magi of the Jan'Tep would dare try to take you from us.'

I'd explain to her that I have no idea what warriors-of-honour are supposed to be and that she's wrong because once a mage has seen a Mahdek they *never* stop coming for us, but I find I'm just so very tired now. I'm not sure how long they've been carrying me when beautiful golden light explodes all around us. Must be a Jan'Tep lightning spell. I feel bad for the man and the woman who came here thinking they could save me. Nobody likes to discover that their world isn't as safe as they believed.

'Quick now,' the man says. 'Get her into the carriage!'

The sun. The light I saw was the sun in the sky above, not magic.

They hide me under a blanket inside a carriage which, from the brief glance I get, is just about the most magnificent thing I've ever seen. Soon I find myself being gently rocked to sleep as four fine horses pull us along, first down a dirt path and then onto a road. My head is on the woman's lap. It's as warm and comfortable a pillow as I've ever known.

'Rest now,' she says, stroking the red tangles of my hair under the blanket. 'The worst has passed – this I swear. Be a good girl now, and stay as quiet as a mouse until we're clear of the territories.'

Be a good girl now.

She was nice. So was her husband. They took me to a lovely home just as big and beautiful as they promised.

I buried their bodies in the garden six months later.

KNIGHT

CONQUEROR

The Knight

A knight meets injustice with force, and when armed with compassion, protects the innocent against the would-be conqueror. To journey as a knight can be a fine thing, for a time. But the knight is too easily turned by rage, by blind loyalty and by the thirst for vengeance, and so becomes the conqueror. The Journey of the Knight is not the Way of the Argosi.

1

The Graves

'Little miss, you'll soil your dress,' Squire Vespan warned. Even the clumsily bandaged burns on his chest and collarbone weren't enough to restrain the 'tut-tut' in his voice that always preceded and followed such scoldings. But I just kept on digging, glad of the rain that soaked my clothes to my skin but made the rich earth a little softer. Squire Vespan tried to reach for my shovel but I shook my head and he stepped back.

A squire used to be a sort of companion to a knight, which was apparently what you called a special sort of soldier from across the sea – what Lord Gervais poorly translated into Daroman as a 'warrior-of-honour'. He used to be such a knight – or so Rosarite (who also used to be a knight apparently) had told me when I'd once asked why they behaved so differently from other nobles in this city.

'We're not Daroman,' Gervais had grunted. 'Shouldn't even be counted among their nobility, but spread a few coins here and there and these crooked magistrates will call you King if the price is right.'

'Don't confuse the girl,' Rosarite (never *Lady* Rosarite, because if I refused to call her Mother then I should just use her name) warned her husband, giving him a playful smack on the belly.

'At school the comportment teacher says proper ladies must be demure and quiet and never engage in barbarous fisticuffs,' I informed her.

I hadn't been at school very long and it seemed important to prove to my *patrons* (because if I wouldn't call them my parents then I should simply refer to them as my patrons) that their money wasn't being wasted, especially given how many times Master Phinus had been forced to repeat that particular lesson to me because I was, as he reminded me often, a very-bad-girl-who-never-learns. However, my demonstration of proper manners failed to produce the desired effect in Rosarite.

'And what is the name of this teacher?' she'd asked casually. By then even I recognised that tone in her voice.

'Rosarite . . .' Gervais had said. 'It was your idea for the girl to—'

His wife held up a hand, then took mine in hers and kissed it as if I were the lady of the house and she merely my attendant. 'Of course, little one, your teacher is quite correct, though I believe what he meant to say was that proper ladies *and* lords should be *kind* and *forbearing* and engage in combat only as a last resort.'

That wasn't at all what Master Phinus had meant. But I wasn't stupid. I understood that Rosarite was telling me to behave one way at school and another everywhere else. Mahdek children learn this early on, as we never get to stay anywhere for long before circumstances force us to find some new place to hide.

'You have a wisdom in you,' Rosarite had said then, her smile warm as fresh-baked bread. 'You listen. You watch. You learn the ways of the world around you. This is a rare and

16

valuable skill, darling one.' Her eyes twinkled as she gave Gervais a sidelong glance. 'One *some* people have yet to master.'

Gervais harrumphed. He did that a lot, even though he wasn't by any means an old man. I guess he was just old at heart. 'This from the woman itching to go remonstrate –'

I should admit here that I don't actually know what the word *remonstrate* means, but I suspect it's something like: *to vigorously engage in the sorts of barbaric fisticuffs avoided by proper ladies.*

' . . . itching to go remonstrate with the girl's comportment teacher because he repeated back to her the same lessons he no doubt was forced to learn at her age. And as for *wisdom* –'

Lord Gervais did that a lot. He'd start with one subject and then switch to another with nothing in between but 'And as for . . .' inevitably accompanied by a grand sweep of his arm and the rising of his voice.

'As for wisdom, if that's what we were seeking, we sailed in the wrong direction! This continent is barbaric. For all their wonders, their Gitabrian contraptions and Jan'Tep spells, these people are like children handed too-sharp blades with too little instruction. The powerful nations wage war on the weak; the weak prey on the weaker. Mages – *mages* like we never had at home – turn their fabulous spells on refugees and innocent . . .'

Rosarite took a deep breath. You'd think she was about to launch into a great deal of shouting, but in fact she did this because – even though it was barely noticeable – it always made Gervais sit back, smile sheepishly and stop talking.

They had a lot of little cues like that: a twitch of a smile to say they loved each other; a subtle nod you could barely see that meant they'd agreed on something terribly important.

17

The smaller the nod, the bigger the decision turned out to be. Winks. Gestures. Even a clucking sound Gervais would do sometimes. It was like they had their own secret language that only the two of them spoke.

I'd asked Squire Vespan about it once. He told me it *was* a secret language. He said all lovers had their own secret language, even if they didn't know it at first, and that there was no greater joy than a life spent learning it together.

Squire Vespan was, Lord Gervais once informed me as if it were a great confidence, a bit of a romantic.

I should get back to Vespan actually, if only to mention that for most of the time I lived in that household I assumed 'Squire' was his first name. But like I said, it turns out that a squire is what you call the person a knight trusts more than any other in the world. The nobles in the city who periodically came by the house to look up (though more often down on) Lord Gervais referred to Vespan as 'the butler'. I don't think Vespan appreciated that at all.

He was technically Rosarite's squire – from back in their country across the water where she was known as 'Sir Rosarite', which is funny, because in the Daroman language the equivalent word for 'sir' is used only to refer to men.

'A knight is a knight is a knight,' Gervais had said. He liked saying things three times, though occasionally he'd only say something twice and wait until I was staring at him, getting frustrated waiting for the third, before finally grinning and making me say it with him.

'Could I be a knight?' I'd asked.

Lord Gervais had been cooking supper. He did that some-times – just to prove he could. He retrieved a long wooden ladle from a drawer that he turned and held out as if it were the greatsword he kept above the mantle. I thought he wanted to play at sword fighting, but he gave me a stern look so I froze.

'Hold out your hands,' he commanded.

I did.

With the end of the ladle he poked each of my palms and then my forehead. Had it been a real sword he would've cut me.

'There,' he said at last.

'There what?' I asked.

'There – you're a knight.'

He went back to stirring the soup.

'But not a proper knight,' I said.

'Oh, a *proper* knight.' He turned his head – barely an inch, but enough that I knew this signal meant I should listen carefully to what he was about to say but never repeat it to anyone. 'No one can make you a knight. You can't even make yourself a knight. A knight exists only for a brief instant, when you do something that is brave and kind and impossible and graceful all in the same moment. In that moment a knight walks the earth, and when the moment is over, the knight is gone, and we silly, awkward, fleshy things remain.'

Then he did something very Gervais-like. His jaw worked like he was chewing on his own tongue, and he looked over at me with that wet-eyed look he sometimes got, and said, 'Of course you're going to be a proper knight, my girl.'

I had never before nor ever would again meet someone as gentle-hearted as Lord Gervais. And he was right too: not long after he said those words I *did* become a knight. Just for a moment though, and not at all in the way he would've wanted.

2

The Knight

'Little miss, your dress,' Squire Vespan said again, bringing
me back to the garden and the storm and the ache in my
shoulders and arms from pushing the shovel into the dirt,
lifting it up and tossing it aside over and over. I don't think
he cared about the dress that much, since it was ruined
anyway from the same ember blast that had burned his chest
and broken his ribs.

'The rain will wash the dirt off,' I said, and went back to
digging the graves for Lord Gervais and Lady Rosarite. No,
wait – I said that wrong. *Sir* Gervais and *Sir* Rosarite. They
died as knights. Proper knights.

I was wrong about dirt too. On its own, soil is easy enough
to clean, sure, but once it's been mashed together with blood
and sweat and the smoke that comes from burnt flesh, the
stains don't want to come out. Maybe they shouldn't.

I put down the shovel and dragged the cloth-covered remains
of Sir Rosarite into her grave. My arms were tired. They'd
been tired long before I'd started digging, tired before I'd had
to drag her and Lord Gervais's bodies from the ruins of the
house using an old wheelbarrow from the garden. Vespan
would've helped, despite his injuries, but I'd insisted on doing

it myself because of something the hextracker had said before he'd run away, holding his belly on account of how Sir Rosarite had cleverly broken off her blade inside so he couldn't heal the wound.

He'd killed her for that. Well, I guess he'd killed her for other things, mostly.

'They died because of you,' he'd croaked, coughing up blood that spattered onto my face, his long, elegant fingers wrapped around my throat, choking me because the pain of his wound kept him from concentrating enough to cast a spell. 'Everything you touch, everyone you ever love, will turn to dust, Mahdek bitch.'

Bitch is a bad word. Lord Gervais would've slapped him across the face for that. 'Unworthy of steel,' he would've said. Me? The word didn't bother me nearly as much as the way my tongue was hanging out of my mouth because I couldn't get any air.

We both heard a *thwip* sound then, and the hextracker's eyes went wide just before he dropped me and screamed. There was a crossbow bolt sticking out of his left arm.

I sucked in all the air I could, my throat so raspy I was reminded of that nice old lady who'd shoved me into the cave with her in that border town in the Seven Sands.

Be a good girl now.

I saw the telltale gleam of magic winding itself around the hextracker's forearms. Jan'Tep mages have six different forms of magic they draw on. I don't remember all the names, but I know that the two worst ones are ember and iron, and that explained the shimmering red and grey emanating from his tattooed bands.

I kicked him, very hard, in a place Master Phinus said no

21

proper young lady should ever kick someone. Behind us I heard the sound of Squire Vespan, still half buried under the ruins of the house, winding the crossbow for a second shot.

The hextracker, bolt hanging from one limp arm, a piece of Sir Rosarite's sword buried in his belly, made a quick calculation and decided not to risk Squire Vespan's aim a second time.

'Let their corpses lie here, in this broken house,' he said to me before he ran. 'Let their bodies rot. Unburied. Untouched, until at last their own neighbours burn these ruins to the ground. Let it be a gravestone for all those who would shelter a Mahdek demon spawn.'

With every word, every curse, the hextracker seemed to be waiting for me to yell at him or curse him right back or maybe pray for mercy. I didn't though; I was coughing too much to be able to speak. Besides, if curses or prayers did any good, he never would've found us in the first place.

Even after he started running away, he stopped for a second and turned back to lock eyes with me, staring as if we were in some kind of contest to see whose hatred was so strong it could stop the other's heart from beating.

We both lost.

When the rain made my hands too slick to hold on any more, a shovelful of dirt went flying and the shovel right along with it, clattering against the wrought-iron fence that circled the garden. Squire Vespan went to retrieve it, but I stopped him.

'Don't touch it,' I warned. 'Don't touch the graves either.' When he turned to look at me, sorrow and despair overpowering even the pain from his wounds, I said, 'Don't touch me.'

'*Everything you touch, everyone you love, will turn to dust.*'

I wasn't stupid; I knew the hextracker's curse wasn't a real spell. Just talk. But somehow it made me feel sick all the same, so maybe it was a different kind of magic.

'We must get you inside soon,' Squire Vespan insisted. 'I'll not be hounded by their lord and ladyship's ghosts for having let you catch a cold.'

'I'm not coming inside,' I replied, picking up the shovel and setting myself back to business.

'You can't stay out in the garden all night, little miss.'

'I won't be doing that either.'

Squire Vespan was a nice man, but he could be thick sometimes. Or maybe he understood me just fine and we were actually having a completely different argument. People here did that sometimes: said one thing but meant something else entirely.

'You're an eleven-year-old girl,' Vespan said.

'Twelve,' I corrected, though I wasn't sure if that was true.

'Eleven or twelve, I don't care!' he shouted. Vespan never shouted. Not at anyone. His voice softened, became almost a plea. 'What kind of man would I be if I let you wander out in the world all alone with mages hunting you?'

'The kind of man who keeps his lord's word, I guess.'

The first time I'd tried running away, Gervais and Rosarite had tracked me down a few miles out of town. When they'd brought me back to the house, I'd asked if I was their prisoner. They said no, I was their charge.

'What's the difference?' I'd asked.

They'd spent the next several hours trying to explain the distinction to me while I kept asking more questions. In the end I think they were as confused as I was. But Rosarite had a pretty ingrained sense of honour – another word I had trouble grasping – so finally she took me by the shoulders and said this: 'Sometimes little boys and little girls run away. They do this because they're angry or sad or scared, but they don't know how to say so to the people who love them. So it's the job of those people to bring them home because those little boys and girls don't really want to run away. They want someone to show they care by coming to find them.'

Okay, so that had been hard to hear because I realised then that she was absolutely right. I'd run because Gervais had been cross with me for getting into a fight with the neighbour's boy. He'd been playing a game with his friends, pretending to be a great war mage of the Jan'Tep. They had on silly costumes made from silk gowns they'd borrowed from their mothers' closets and would each make up these elaborate, ridiculous spells and then burst out laughing. The boy, Phantus, had asked if I wanted to play with them.

'You'll have to be the Mahdek though,' he warned. 'New kid always has to play the Mahdek.'

Nobody in that town knew what I was. Gervais and Rosarite had been very clear about that – despite all their promises about Jan'Tep mages not daring to come here.

'Okay,' I'd said to Phantus. 'What do I do?'

He handed me a lacquer mask too big for my face and a doll that looked like a baby. 'Put on the mask and pretend to be summoning a demon as you torture the baby.'

'Why?'

Phantus and the others just looked at me. 'Because that's what Mahdek do, stupid.'

You can probably guess what happened after that.

Gervais had gotten angry with me, because 'honour' couldn't

24

be taken away by words and because I'd kept hitting Phantus even after he'd fallen down. I tried to explain that the whole point was to make sure he didn't get up again, but I guess that wasn't a 'knightly' way to go about things.

So I'd run away that night, and Rosarite had come to find me. She was a real good tracker for a rich lady.

'You're not our prisoner,' she'd said after they'd brought me home. 'We aren't your parents, much as we'd love nothing more. But we need to know whether you're running off because you're angry with us or running off because you've made a true decision – the kind that changes your life and rarely for the better – which we, by our honour, must respect.'

Honour seemed like a complicated and inconvenient idea. I found it strange that two adults would be talking about having to respect the decision of an eleven-year-old. But I guess wherever they'd come from had different traditions regarding such things.

Gervais, already starting to cry the way he did at such times, grabbed me up in his arms as if I were a much younger child and squeezed me to his chest. 'We will always come find you, my sweet, maddening child. Every time. No matter how fast or how far you go, unless first you say these words to us that I pray never to hear so long as I live.'

I guess he got his wish.

I stuck the shovel in the ground so it would stand up on its own and turned to face Squire Vespan. 'Without ire, without fear, without doubt, without tears, I do now choose to leave this place, forever and all my years.'

Vespan stared at me a long time, the rain pelting down harder and harder all around us. I could hear it hissing off the flames that still hadn't gone out on the east side of the house where the first ember spell had struck. Vespan's face looked as if he was trying to decide what to do next. I don't think he really was though. I think he just wanted me to know that he would've gladly given up his life to protect me if only I'd let him.

'I'll go pack your bag,' he said at last.

I shook my head. 'Just my clothes – the ones I was wearing when I first came here.'

'They were practically rags! How will you—'

'Nothing of this place!' I shouted. I hardly ever did that, and never at Vespan. 'Nothing that a bounty mage or hextracker or anyone else could trace back to here.'

Eventually Vespan did as I asked. Just as I was leaving through the melted remains of the front gates, he said, 'That hextracker won't be casting any spells for a while. He'll need to find a place to hide and heal his wounds. Stay away from the cities as much as you can. The Jan'Tep dislike the hardship of the long roads. Keep hidden, keep quiet, and you'll be safe.'

I nodded soberly, as if paying close attention to his words, because I liked Vespan, even though his advice was hardly any different than if he'd ruffled my hair and said, 'Be a good girl now.'

I was done with being a good girl. In fact, despite what I'd told Squire Vespan, I'd stolen something from the house: the sword whose blade Rosarite had broken off inside the hextracker's belly. What was left was still almost two feet long, light enough that I could carry it, and the point was sharp as a razor.

See, there's only one way to protect yourself from a mage.
Kill him before he kills you.

3

The Huntress

All that night I padded through empty streets, knees bent, head bowed, eyes ever lowered. I must've looked like some sort of wild animal covered in rags rather than fur. A jackal or a hyena maybe. A scavenger, tracking a predator ten times its size. A twelve-year-old girl hunting a war mage.

Few people would've observed me however; ours was a dignified city where civilised folk spent their nights indoors, not wandering the streets like vagrants. Those few whose path I crossed stepped aside and turned their head to gawk at me as I shuffled along, my gaze glued to the ground, searching for the next drop of blood, stopping only to sniff the air like a rat.

Spells leave all kinds of odours in the air. Subtle, like all things magical, but detectable if you know what you're looking for. Most people rarely encounter Jan'Tep magic, and in the presence of such wondrous sights and sounds – not to mention someone likely dying as a result – they'd hardly notice a lingering trace of burnt cinnamon or the faint whiff of desert sand stirred by a hot wind. The Jan'Tep themselves are so accustomed to magic that they're hardly even aware of the scents it leaves behind.

But I noticed them. Even when I'd go entire blocks without

spotting a trace of blood on the sidewalk, I'd stop and lift my chin, inhaling deeply until I once again caught the aroma of strawberries and mint, and knew my quarry had passed that way.

Blood magic, which is one of the six sources of Jan'Tep power, leaves that particular scent in the air. Every time the hextracker – his name was Fe'rius, I think . . . no, wait. That can't be right.

I guess I should mention that by this point in my life I wasn't quite right in the head. I hadn't been for a while, I guess – probably since the day I'd watched my parents get torn apart by those beautiful shimmering golden tendrils coming from a Jan'Tep lightshaper's hands. Rosarite said that when we experience something really big – so big that we're just not ready to hold it all in our head at once – our minds some-times break it apart into little pieces, only showing them to us one part at a time, until the day we're ready to look at the entire experience without reliving it.

'But I remember all of it,' I'd argued. 'I can tell you every minute, like when Father first went springing up into the air and I thought maybe he was flying, but then he screamed and one arm came off and—'

'Remembering is not the same as understanding,' Rosarite had said, gathering me up into her arms even though I wasn't upset at all. She'd snuffled her nose into the red curls of my hair. 'One day, when you're so filled up with love that there's only room inside you for a little pain, you'll see it all, and you'll cry a great deal, brave one, but you'll understand that every tear has made you stronger.'

She kept hugging me then, so I'd patted her back. That made her feel better sometimes.

Sorry. I shouldn't keep on about these little stories since none of them matter any more. But it feels important to remember that there was a moment in my life when I could almost – *almost* – glimpse a future ahead of me that was bright and loving and so very different from the one awaiting me in the darkness around the corner.

Anyway, I guess Rosarite was right, because after she and Gervais were gone I started losing track of things – time especially. I'd forget when something happened and in what order. Sometimes I'd get people's names mixed up.

Met'astice! That was the hextracker's name – and he wasn't just a lowly hextracker, but an actual lord magus. 'Met'astice of the House of Met,' he'd told me. Jan'Tep mages are very big on telling you the name of their houses even though they're right there in their own names.

Okay, where was I?

Right. Blood magic.

Whenever Met'astice stopped in some shadowy corner to try to cast a blood spell to keep his insides from coming apart thanks to the six inches of Rosarite's blade stuck in his guts, he'd leave behind a trace of strawberry and mint. That, along with the fact that he can't have been all that good at healing spells as he was still leaving tiny blood splatters every block or so, was how a twelve-year-old girl with no particular skills was able to track him from one side of the city to the other, and then right out the western gates to the river docks, where massive barges from Gitabria would bring exotic fruits and rare hardwoods and sometimes fascinating mechanical contraptions that Gervais would pick up at the market, harrumph over the price and then tell Rosarite that 'These Gitabrians are all . . .'

No. No more stories about Gervais and Rosarite. I have to stay focused.

The fruits on the barges were the problem. Mix those with the musty air from the river, the stink of blacktail and crab and other hauls brought back on little family boats, and I could no longer track Met'astice's magic.

I felt stupid, out there in the dark, only then becoming aware that it was cold outside – that I was cold. I'd gotten too used to living in a nice warm house at night, eating rich food and wearing nice clothes. As I stood there, staring at the river while dock workers and fishermen walked by, giving dirty looks and muttering bad words at me, it was like I was just waking up from a dream.

Had I really spent all those months with Sir Gervais and Sir Rosarite? Had a nice couple from a land across the ocean really rescued me from a cave and brought me to live with them? I looked down at the rags I was wearing. Why would I have even kept these at all?

Maybe I had just lain there in that cave, among the dead bodies, waiting hour after hour, day after day, until at last I was positive the Jan'Tep war coven had left. Perhaps I'd finally crawled out, all by myself, and begun sleepwalking my way from town to town, village to village, until at last I'd finally come to my senses here on this dock, staring at the river barges. And soon I'd sneak onto one of them and hide in a little corner of the hold, stealing little bits of food whenever I could until the barge tied up somewhere new and I began the process all over again.

What if Gervais and Rosarite had just been a fever dream conjured by my brain to hold itself together, and Met'astice the hextracker was just a nightmare that had finally woken me up?

My fists squeezed tightly at my sides, but my right felt different from the left. When I looked down, I saw that I was holding a broken Tristian smallsword.

That word, 'smallsword', is misleading, because these are actually the most dangerous duelling weapon ever made. They're thin and light and move far faster than other types of sword. A greatsword like Gervais kept above the mantle is very good for fighting soldiers because it can crush steel armour and shatter the links holding chainmail together. A longsword is a little smaller, and very versatile, but still heavier than, say, a rapier, which is a true thrusting weapon and far more effective in a formal duel where opponents aren't allowed to wear armour. But a smallsword is even lighter, faster and sharper. The tip would've shattered instantly against a steel breastplate, but it could easily pierce a duelling vest.

Or a mage's robes.

The wire-wrapped hilt felt solid and real against the skin of my palm – more real than the cold air or the stench of fruits and fishes. More real than the dockworkers or fishermen. How could I be holding that weapon – how could I know it was a smallsword and especially good for duelling – unless someone had taught me?

Sir Rosarite and Sir Gervais were real. They'd saved my life six months ago and they'd died last night defending me from a Jan'Tep lord magus named Met'astice of the House of Met. I really *had* tracked him all the way to these docks, and now I was going to find him. I was going to find him because the boats didn't leave until first light, and because Jan'Tep mages distrust and despise everyone who isn't like them. Met'astice wouldn't risk asking anyone here for help. He'd hide out somewhere and keep trying to cast his pathetic blood healing spell until morning when he could book passage on a river-boat.

On the north side of the docks the hills started, and not far from here were the caves. Rosarite liked to go exploring those caves, searching for bits of pottery and metal from the earliest Daroman settlements established in these parts. She'd taken me with her one time, but when I'd started screaming she had to accept that crawling around in dark caves probably wasn't a good outing for me.

But a wounded mage? Who just needs time and quiet to recover his strength and concentration enough to remove a piece of smallsword from his belly without dying? A Jan'Tep who figured anyone different from him was a barbarian who couldn't be trusted? He'd make for those caves. He'd crawl inside and hide, hoping no one would come find him.

Which was kind of funny, when you think about it.

4

The Cave

Two hundred feet inside the cave, I found Met'astice. The going had been hard at first. The tunnels were tight and pitch black. But all Mahdek know what it's like to have to hide, huddled in shadows, unable to see, imagining a thousand awful things coming for us. Now Met'astice was the one hiding, and I was the monster coming for him.

The deeper I travelled through the winding passages, the stronger the scent of strawberries and mint became. That worried me, because didn't that mean stronger blood magic? Maybe he'd healed himself. Maybe he was just waiting for me to come so he could do to me what he'd wanted to back at the house. But then I noticed something else mixed in with the smell of strawberries and mint: a scent for which I had no name, but which was all too familiar to me. It was the stench that oozes from the pores of someone frightened for their life.

I knew I'd found him when I saw faint light leaking from around a corner. A Jan'Tep glow-glass ball. A smart person would stick to the darkness when they were being hunted. As I approached, the first sound I heard was scurrying. Met'astice was *scurrying* away from me.

I was surprised by how well appointed his little cave was. Two large brass-banded travel chests, a small table with a chair, and even a little cot in the corner. The scurrying sounds I'd heard had been its stubby wooden legs scratching on the rocky floor as he tried to push himself further and further back. On the other side of the room I saw a row of clay flagons, several large wheels of cheese and assorted other delicacies that made my mouth water even over the smell of strawberries, mint and Met'astice's fear. How long had he been here in the city? Had he come all this way from the Jan'Tep territories, set himself up with a lair in which to spend his nights, all to hunt for me?

'You,' he said, as if he'd cast a silk spell to draw the thoughts from my mind and had chosen to answer my unspoken question.

'Me,' I said back.

Stupid. I should've had something memorised, like a speech or a poem or something. The words you speak at moments like these should be good ones. Important ones. The kinds of things Sir Gervais said when he got good and full of himself. But I couldn't think of anything to say. I could barely summon up any feelings about Met'astice at all. He just huddled there on his cot, a shirtless and thoroughly unimpressive middle-aged man with layers of bandages wrapped around his mid-section where Sir Rosarite's blade had broken off. Sweat poured down his forehead, reassuring me that he was too feverish from his wounds to cast any spells. He blinked a great deal, and his lips trembled. When he raised one of his hands – something that would've terrified me just hours before – I barely flinched. He was helpless, and afraid, and became even more so when he saw the broken smallsword in my hand.

34

'I am Met'astice of the House of Met,' he croaked.

'You told me that already,' I reminded him.

He kept talking though. Maybe he couldn't hear me on account of the fever. 'I cannot . . . I *will not* be slain by a pathetic, filthy Mahdek child!'

Seems he hadn't rehearsed any good speeches for this moment either.

That thought made me chuckle nervously – and that Met'astice *did* notice.

'You would mock a lord magus?'

I found myself glancing around his cave, searching for a mirror. I wanted him to see how silly he sounded, talking so pompously, when the man I saw looked so very small just then. I felt sure in that moment that there could be no sight more pathetic than a powerful man whose power has been taken from him. But I also felt as if Gervais was there with me, standing just behind me, his big hand resting on my shoulder.

There is no honour in slaying a fallen foe.

I shrugged off his imaginary hand, pulled my other one out of Sir Rosarite's ghostly one. In the depths of my soul, I was standing at a door. On one side I was a child, fearful but innocent. Once through, I'd be a killer forever. I was very, very eager to walk through that doorway.

With three long, low strides – the kind Rosarite had shown me a fencer makes to bridge the distance without giving up balance – I was standing before Met'astice, and he cowered before me. He *cowered*.

'Don't be afraid,' I said, raising the smallsword above my head, the broken blade aimed at the bandages beneath which the other piece had already done most of the work that I'd

35

come here to finish. 'You won't be killed by a filthy little Mahdek girl. I'm a knight.'

An odd thought tickled at the back of my mind though. If Met'astice was too feverish from his wounds to cast spells, how had he bandaged himself up like that? He would've needed someone else to . . .

I only just caught the fractional darkening of the cave, then the widening smile on Met'astice's face and the relief in his eyes. I heard a whispered invocation, and just for an instant I could smell pine needles and cinnamon. Breath magic and ember.

Winding tendrils of gold and silver light slithered around my wrists, then two more took my ankles. Suddenly I was slammed into the floor, only it couldn't be the floor, because the world was now upside down. I was pressed up against the ceiling so hard my ribs struggled to move when I breathed. The smallsword dropped from my hand, clattering on the cave floor. The ceiling wasn't very high, so when the new arrival stood beneath me and turned his chin up to look me in the eye, our faces were so close it was as if he'd come to kiss me.

Stupidly, my first thought was that *he* looked like a proper knight. Black hair, freshly cut. A light dusting of beard on a smooth, symmetrical face. Handsome, with a jaw so firm it almost hid how young he was. Irises a piercing blue with flecks of green. His was the sort of face that if you saw it once, you'd never forget it. I certainly hadn't.

Shadow Falcon.

He opened his mouth to speak, but it was Met'astice's voice I heard, because the mage was rising unsteadily from his cot. 'My thanks, little one, for saving me the trouble of spending another night in this bland little town with its bland little people, waiting to heal so that I could come get you.'

The boy – man, I suppose. You shouldn't refer to someone as a boy when they're about to kill you. Anyway, he asked, 'What would you have me do with this one, Lord Magus?'

Met'astice walked stiffly to one of his chests. Either he or it groaned as he lifted the lid. After a bit of mucking about inside, he shuffled over to the middle of the cave to stand beneath me. In his hand he held a leather case with brass bindings, almost a miniature of one of his travelling chests. When he opened the lid I saw tiny clay jars, each one a different colour with a different symbol engraved into the cork. Next to these were a set of metal instruments, that glinted even in the dim light of the cave.

'Bind her to the worktable,' Met'astice said. He reached up with his hand, wrapped his fingers around my jaw and squeezed. 'Let us show the world what happens to filthy Mahdek brats who think they can grow up to be knights.'

5

Honour

It took Met'astice three days to prove that he was right: filthy
little Mahdek children can't be knights. A knight has to be
honourable, brave and compassionate. I had tried to stab a
fallen enemy through the belly. Not the heart, which would
have been quicker and less painful, but the belly, so I could
watch him die as slowly as possible.

So, clearly not very honourable.

'She's awake again, master,' said Falcon.

I'd taken to thinking of him simply as 'Falcon' both because
that's what Met'astice called him and because it made him
sound like the mage's familiar rather than a real person.

'Ah,' was all Met'astice said in reply.

I could hear him scrawling in a leather-bound book he
buried himself in while Falcon did his dirty work.

I didn't want to open my eyes – didn't want to look at
the young man's face again. Despite all the things he was
doing to me, with metal needles and burning inks and awful
spells that made me sick inside, whenever I looked up at him
all I saw was thoughtfulness and a deep sense of duty. And
honour of course. Honour was written all over his face.

How was that possible? Does being born with an honourable

nature cause your jaw to grow firm and your eyes resolute? Or is it that those born with square jaws and stern eyes grow up to be honourable because that's what everyone expects of them?

'I'm going to put her to sleep again,' Falcon said.

Met'astice slammed his book closed. 'You waste your strength on silk spells when our work calls for your full prowess.'

'Perhaps you ought to perform the spells, master. I worry my skills aren't—'

'You're doing fine,' Met'astice said, so kindly that I couldn't stop my eyes from opening. He had come to stand next to Falcon and put his hand on his apprentice's shoulder just as Gervais used to do with me when he was teaching me something difficult. 'I'm still too weak from my wounds to attempt the spells myself. But you're doing wonderfully, my boy. You've got a real knack for this work.'

There was so much pride in Met'astice's gaze, and such hopefulness in Falcon's. They didn't look evil at all.

I felt myself begin to cry again.

'Time you moved on to the sand bandings, I think,' Met'astice said. 'Begin with the third glyph.'

I caught a glimpse of the long, thin metal instrument in Falcon's hand. It was like a knitting needle, except there was a tiny channel running along its length, into which Falcon carefully poured a shiny, viscous fluid that crept down towards me until he moved the instrument beneath my line of sight. I felt him press the needle into my neck, piercing my skin, and then the burning metallic ink entering my flesh.

In that moment I forever abandoned any desire I might have to be honourable. Honour never protected anyone from being hurt.

39

6

Bravery

I tried to be brave, I really did.

They kept me awake from then on as they stabbed those long, thin needles into my neck. I'd pass out sometimes, but all too soon oblivion would desert me and I'd awaken, still strapped to the table, all my efforts to free myself futile. I could hear the sizzle of metallic inks burning markings into my skin that I couldn't see and didn't understand. After that first time, I swore to myself I wouldn't scream again, and I'd never, ever beg.

'Please,' I whimpered, squirming against my bonds. My throat couldn't produce anything louder, nor my heart anything more dignified. 'Please, stop.'

'Master . . .' Falcon began deferentially, as he always did. 'The work would be easier if she were asleep.'

Met'astice's face appeared over me once again, his scraggly grey hair hanging down to brush the tip of my nose. He looked healthier now, still old to my eyes, but strong. How long had I been in this cave, strapped to this table?

The lord magus scowled, though I think it was for Falcon more than me. 'Do you know what she would do to you, if she could? Have you any conception of what the Mahdek did to *our* people when they captured us?'

'Master, I know, but—'

'The things they did to us, to our children – our babies! They did them not because war demanded it, nor as we do in pursuit of vital research, but simply for pleasure. They enjoyed hurting us.'

You're a liar! I shouted in my mind, but all that came out of my mouth was, 'Please . . .'

'There now,' Met'astice said, taking my bound hand in his as if to comfort me. His long, smooth fingers wrapped around mine. Sir Rosarite used to do that with me, and now the touch of his fingers was strangling the memory of hers, taking even that away from me.

'I know it's hard,' he said to me, voice as gentle as Lord Gervais's had ever been. 'But we are learning so much here! If you could see how well the inks take to your flesh . . . It's remarkable!'

'But, master,' Falcon said, brow furrowed, 'does this not mean the Mahdek have as natural an aptitude for magic as our own people?'

'Pah!' Met'astice said, pretending to spit. 'What is aptitude? A horse has an aptitude for running, yet without a rider, he knows not where to go. This is why the bridle is far more important than the saddle.'

He traced a line across my throat with his finger, and when it touched one of the places where the metallic ink had burned into the skin, my mouth jerked open to scream, but nothing came out but a wheeze. I couldn't even give voice to my pain any more.

'No,' Met'astice said wistfully. 'All it demonstrates is that the formulas we inherited from our ancestors for the banding inks are not nearly as perfect as we've been raised to believe.'

Falcon's lips parted, as if this was such a miraculous insight that hearing it wasn't enough and he had to breathe it in. 'This proves what you have always said, master. The Jan'Tep clans have grown too complacent with the knowledge gleaned by our ancestors. We must envision new ways, new spells, if we are to keep our people safe.'

'Precisely.' Met'astice's gaze sought out mine. 'You see, little Mahdek, this is not about hatred for your people, no matter how well-earned such hatred would be. It's about love. Love of knowledge, love of one's people.'

He pulled back the sleeve of his robe to show his Jan'Tep bands – as if I'd never seen them before. 'Look here, my brave knight . . .'

It sickened me that now that I was in his power, being used for whatever foul experiment he'd captured me to perform, he viewed me not as an enemy, but as a pet. And when he spoke, it was almost as if he were fond of me.

'The raw fundamental forms of magic are all around us. Iron, ember, breath, blood, silk and sand. But they are like mist over water – everywhere yet nowhere. Insubstantial.' He tapped a sigil on the tattooed band that looked like copper – the one that I'd seen shimmer on other war mages' forearms when they cast ember spells. 'The inks, made from special ores attuned to each of the fundamental forces, enable those with the talent and the will to gather that mist, concentrate it and unleash it in our spells.'

Even to me that sounded simplistic. Maybe he thought I was too stupid to understand the real explanation. But then a curious question came to mind – one I probably would have thought of sooner if I wasn't so scared.

'Are you . . . ? Are you giving me Jan'Tep bands?'

He looked at me then, thoughtfully, as if I'd just made some very impressive suggestion he hadn't considered until that moment. Then he laughed so hard he nearly knocked the brazier heating one of the tiny bowls of metallic ink from the table. Falcon had to snatch it and grunted when a drop – barely a drop – splashed on the skin of his hand.

'Oh, what a silly thing you are,' Met'astice said. He finally let go of my hand and patted my forehead. 'No, my dear, don't think of this as a mage's band. It's really more of a . . . bridle.'

When Falcon brought the needle back to my neck, all my attempts at bravery fled, and I began to cry. 'Please, no. I'll be good, I promise. I'll be a good girl.'

Met'astice's warm, uncalloused hand pressed my head back down to the table. 'Shh . . . don't weep now. A knight must be brave after all.'

7

The Candle

Death is the end of pain. It's the end of a lot of other things too, but after days strapped to a table with hot needles pressed into your neck, it's mostly the pain you think about.

I'd prayed for death a lot during my time with Lord Magus Met'astice and his apprentice. I'd begged for it too. Sometimes when Met'astice slept (he did that a lot, due to his wounds), I'd try to goad Shadow Falcon into killing me. Whenever he gave me food or water or wiped off the table where I'd . . . well, you know. Anyway, I'd say awful things about what I would do to him one day once I'd got free. When that didn't work, I made up stories about horrific crimes my people had done to his.

'Don't you care about all those babies we ate?' I'd ask him. *'Don't you want vengeance for the dead?'*

But he ignored me, never really talking to me except to say, *'It's not your fault. It has to be this way.'*

I'm pretty sure he was talking to himself though.

Over and over I begged for mercy, which I knew by then could only mean death. Then one day – it might've been the third day or the thirtieth, for all I knew – I got my wish.

It began with fingers prying my lips apart. I woke suddenly,

44

eyes wide yet seeing nothing but the blur of the two men standing over me. Falcon was forcing my mouth open.

'Hold her still now,' Met'astice warned.

My vision cleared a little, and I saw the lord magus was holding a red candle as thick as his arm. The flame melted the crimson wax, and as it began to drip he tilted the candle over my mouth.

'No!' I tried to scream, but Falcon gritted his teeth and prised mine apart further.

The first drop of wax hit the back of my tongue. The sudden burn stung, but it cooled almost immediately, and that was worse, because I felt it sticking there. Met'astice turned the candle further, and the drips became a thin stream of wax, clogging my throat.

Reflex forced me to swallow the thick lump, but Falcon kept holding my jaws apart, and Met'astice kept pouring more and more of the molten red wax in my mouth. As consciousness deserted me, I realised all my contemplations about death had been wrong. Death wasn't the end of pain. It's just the beginning of a different kind of suffering.

8

Compassion

I woke to the sensation of wet leaves brushing against my back. Then it stopped, and I lay there, cool air tickling my nose and bare legs. When I opened my eyes, I saw the green-leaved branches above me, all overlapping so you couldn't tell where one tree began and the other ended. Then I heard the sound of shovelling.

I was so weak and my throat hurt so bad I couldn't swallow any more. My tongue was thick, swollen from the coating of wax there, but my hands and wrists were now unbound. I turned my head to try to spit it out onto the ground, and saw the blade of a big shovel methodically digging up heaps of dirt and tossing it aside. Shadow Falcon, stripped to the waist, stopped a moment and wiped the sweat from his brow. When he saw me looking up at him, he said, 'Master, she's awake.'

'Cast another silk spell,' the lord magus called out, then, sounding like he was muttering to himself, added, 'The boy begs me to let him put her to sleep when there's no point and then doesn't want to when it serves a purpose.'

They're going to bury me alive!

'Please,' I said to Falcon, my voice sounding a little stronger than it had before. 'Please don't kill me.'

Falcon's fingers twitched, and an incantation came to his lips. I screamed as loud as I could.

'Damn it!' he swore when the spell fizzled. 'Master, I can't formulate the will for the spell.'

Met'astice emerged from the cave, chuckling to himself. 'Here now we see the flaw in your training, young Falcon. Jan'Tep initiates spend so much time on magic they rarely suffer the aches of the flesh, and when those simple pains come upon them, cannot hold together their will to cast even the simplest spell.'

'My silk band sparks the least of all of them,' Falcon said, as if that was some kind of excuse. 'And I've been casting spells for three days now.'

'Forgive an old man his foibles, my boy,' Met'astice said with a sly grin. 'But those of us for whom weakness is our daily tormentor cannot help but take some small pleasure in finding it in the young now and then.'

Falcon looked down at me, not quite rolling his eyes, as if I was supposed to be commiserating with him.

Anger flared up inside me. It had been a while since I'd felt anything but fear, and I'd forgotten how good it felt to be angry. 'You're filth, both of you!' With strength borne only from fury, I rolled onto my hands and knees and sprang to my feet. 'You prattle on about research and magic and protecting your people's future, but it's all a lie!'

'Little one,' Met'astice began as if he'd just come upon me throwing a tantrum, 'whatever troubles you?'

My eyes, still blurry and filled with tears, searched the forest floor for a stick or rock or any kind of weapon. 'You hurt me over and over for days in your so-called experiments – all for what? So you could bury me alive when you were done?'

47

I spun on Falcon. 'Don't you have the guts to kill me with a knife or choke me to death with your own hands, you coward?'

Met'astice laughed then, and his eyes were so wide it was as if he'd been taken completely by surprise.

'Master,' Falcon said, tapping the ground with his shovel, 'she thinks this is her grave.'

The lord magus only laughed harder then, and had to grab hold of his sides where his bandages had been when I'd first found him in the cave. 'Oh, my. What you must think of us!'

'I think you're murderers, that's what I think. Your kind slaughtered my clan.' I jabbed a finger at Falcon and he actually flinched. 'He was there!'

At last Met'astice stopped laughing, and finally nodded his head soberly. 'That, little one, was war.'

'It was a massacre! We did nothing to you!'

The corners of his lips turned down and his eyes narrowed. 'Your ancestors did a great deal to us, just as those who remain would do, given the chance.' He sighed. 'But here I show myself an old fool, arguing with a child.'

He nodded to Falcon, who went inside the cave and soon returned, dragging one of the big chests. He hefted it up to his hips and then dropped it into the grave.

'You see?' Met'astice said to me. 'We're merely ridding ourselves of the materials we no longer need before we make passage back to our own territories. We're done here, and we're done with you.' He waved dismissively at me. 'Go on now. Go back to that house or wherever you wish. It makes no difference to me.'

'But you . . . you killed Sir Gervais and Sir Rosarite! You

came to kill me, to finish what the war coven had started!'

Met'astice shook his head, seemingly disappointed in my lack of understanding. 'I came searching for you, yes. I needed a subject for my experiments. As to those two Tristian barbarians I found you with, I explained to them what you were, and the crime they were committing by sheltering you, but they mocked me.' His hand came up to his cheek. 'The woman struck me.' His hand fell back to his side. 'What a world, in which such people believe they can lay hands on a Jan'Tep lord magus.'

He seemed oblivious to the irony of our first meeting. 'You tried to choke me to death.'

For once Met'astice looked shamefaced. 'I was wounded, not . . . thinking straight. I lost my temper.' He turned to Falcon, who was dumping the second chest into the grave. 'In this I pray you never to follow my poor example, my boy. A lord magus is always master of his emotions, never the other way around.'

Falcon grunted in acknowledgement and began shovelling dirt into the shallow pit. The skin at my throat felt strange where they'd imprinted the markings on me. I started scratching at them.

'I wouldn't do that if I were you,' Falcon said. 'The inks go deep into the flesh, all the way to the bone. Long after the markings are gone and the scars from your scratching have healed, the bindings will remain.'

'Why?' I asked.

'Think of it as . . . a kind of collar,' Met'astice said, his voice dripping with his usual condescension, as if any more sophisticated explanation would fall on deaf ears. 'When you see a dog with a collar, you know that dog must belong to someone, so you don't take it in. Do you understand?' He stared at me a moment, then threw up his hands. 'You explain it to her,' he ordered Falcon.

'When decent folk encounter you, they will sense what you are. They won't know why, but you'll disgust them. They will shun you, Mahdek.'

Met'astice nodded enthusiastically. 'Shun her. Yes, that's a good word for it. You can live your life now, little knight. Go wherever you like, do whatever you please. But you will never know companionship. Anyone who takes you in now will do so only because they secretly wish you harm, just as your people have always wished harm upon ours.'

'One day all Mahdek will have collars upon them,' Falcon said. 'And then can our two peoples know peace.'

Again I felt at the markings, the metallic texture of the lines and curves of the sigils. Met'astice hadn't been lying when he'd spoken of his outrage over Sir Gervais and Sir Rosarite giving me a home, offering me their love. Now, with the help of his assistant, he had ensured I'd never know such love ever again.

'Run along now.' Met'astice waved dismissively at me as he began tossing items he'd brought out of the cave into the dirt pit. 'It's getting dark and little girls shouldn't be running around alone at night.'

Despite everything, I found myself stumbling back, away from the cave, but even as I did I cried, 'Why? Why didn't you just kill me?'

Met'astice looked up from his disposal of scraps of food and empty wine flagons. 'Kill you? Why would we kill you? You're a child.'

For a moment I stood there, staring at my tormentors who'd

gone back to filling in the pit, having already forgotten I even existed. There hadn't been a trace of sarcasm in Met'astice's last words to me, no hate or bitterness.

Only compassion.

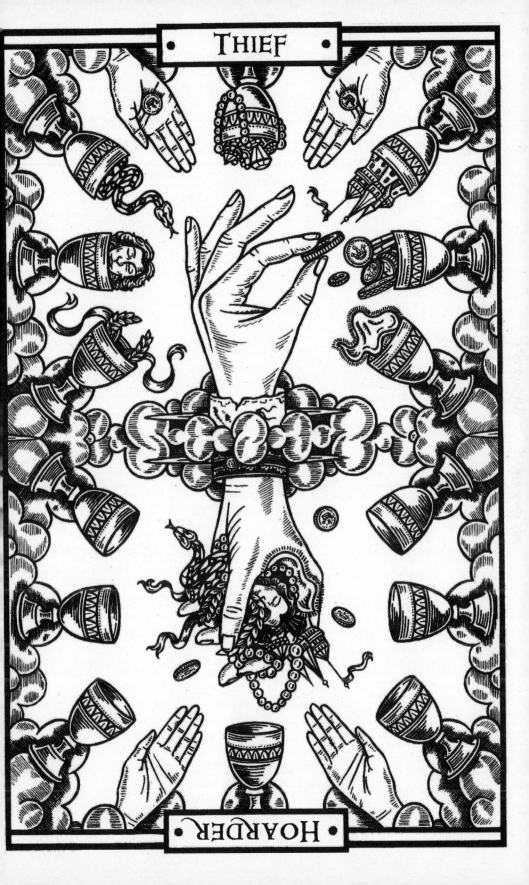

THIEF

HOARDER

The Thief

A thief rectifies inequity by taking from one to give to another. When the world is full of greed, the thief's journey appears a righteous one. But the scales never quite balance, and all too soon they seek to hoard endless wealth for themselves. The Journey of the Thief is not the Way of the Argosi.

9

Shunned

In a town called Domisa Pago I lay huddled beneath piles of refuse in a dead-end alley, listening to the people in the apartments above, sweaty from their day's labours, arguing or laughing. Sometimes they were making love.

This alley stank at the best of times, but now, as darkness settled over the three-storey buildings, the smells of a dozen different meals being cooked and eaten blended to form a thick fog of too many spices, meats and, above all, thick, oily grease. The stench would've made any normal person sick to their stomach. Me? The aroma just made me hungrier.

My thirteenth birthday had come and gone by then, though I couldn't be sure precisely when; keeping track of the passage of time becomes precarious when life has been reduced to its most primal elements. Find food. Seek shelter. Don't get killed. Repeat as many times as you can.

All I knew for certain was that I'd been running a long time. After I'd fled the cave by the docks, I just seemed to keep on running forever. First it was onto a river barge while the owner's back was turned, then, when he caught me hiding among his grain sacks, it was splashing into the water and almost drowning before my feet found the muddy bank on the other side.

I couldn't tell you the name of the first village I trudged to, soaking wet and shivering, but it wasn't long before I was running from shopkeepers who'd spot me stealing their wares. Fruit is best, by the way; there's always someone rummaging through the carts to find the best pieces, and the merchants are so busy frowning at them that they don't notice if you sneak down low and snatch the fallen ones. Of course that only works so long before the local constables see your face one too many times. Fleeing from them means running all the way out of town, and then tramping to the next village, where you turn up even weaker and skinnier than ever because there's not much food to steal on the roads between settlements. Farmers are surprisingly good at chasing thieves.

I heard the groan of a wooden-slatted window being wrenched open and then a grunting complaint as an old man in an apron dumped his cooking scraps out into the alley. I scampered from my pile of rubbish to paw at the pieces of rotting vegetables and bits of gristly, half-chewed meat. I even found a sliver of melon rind for dessert. Practically a feast. Slinking back beneath the heap of refuse in the corner of the alley, I began to devour my banquet.

When I was first learning how to find enough food to survive, I'd had to spend much of my time running from reaver boys – thugs who shake down street urchins even if they don't have anything to take. It's the beatings that give them pleasure. Other times I had to run from dogs who smelled food on me and sensed I was one of those humans they could bite without consequence. There wasn't much to tell the dogs and the reaver boys apart.

As for the nice people? The ones who take pity on filthy girls in rags and offer them food or shelter for the night?

I ran from them fastest of all.

I couldn't tell if Shadow Falcon's boast that the metallic ink sigils around my neck would induce decent folk to shun me was true or not. After my first month alone it hardly mattered; when you look like I looked, it doesn't take magic to make respectable people shy away from you for fear of catching whatever made you this way.

The tattooed collar itched sometimes though. Scratching made it hurt worse, so I kept it covered up with a scrap of sackcloth I'd torn from a big bag of wilted lettuce I found outside a vegetable market. Coming upon those lettuces was like discovering a treasure trove. I ate so many that night I made myself sick, and then I ate the rest of the lettuces even faster. Whatever dignity I'd been born with was soon abandoned, right alongside my sense of honour, bravery and compassion.

Nestled among the warmth of alley debris, I chewed on my bits of gristle. This was a good spot, and I hoped I wouldn't get chased away tonight. Sometimes I could scare people off, by shaking and growling and making my spit look like foam at the corners of my mouth. Most times, though, those who demanded my spots looked as scary as me.

I'd learned early on to avoid mirrors. On those rare occasions when I'd catch my reflection in a puddle, I'd turn away as fast as I could. Never quite fast enough though. Within a year of scraping the bare necessities of life from the hard surface of the world with nothing but my fingernails, I became a truly wretched thing. I was scrawny, filthy, uneducated. I was a beggar – not even a particularly good one. I disgusted all who saw me and no one more than myself. My hair, my clothes, my skin ... every part of me was caked in dirt. I looked like a skeleton, a corpse left in the ground for months and only exhumed when there was no question that I was truly dead.

Sometimes I wished Met'astice and Shadow Falcon had killed me. Sometimes, when I couldn't resist tugging my sackcloth scarf aside and scratching at the tattooed collar around my neck, my nail would catch on the skin, making it bleed. I'd wonder what would happen if I scratched a little deeper, if maybe I could . . .

No. Don't go there. Not yet.

One of the sigils itched again – worse this time than usual. I reached down and picked up a bit of muddy dirt from the alley floor and rubbed it against my neck, hoping to soothe the discomfort, but it didn't work. When one of my fingertips brushed the second sigil, it tingled. A second later I felt sick to my stomach – as if my loneliness had grown into a disease that was eating me from the inside out. This wasn't the first time the sensation had come over me, but it hadn't been this strong before. It was like . . . like being lost in the desert and not knowing where to turn, only you're absolutely sure someone is watching you.

'*I am*,' said a buzzing, stinging voice in my head.

That feeling of sickness became even worse, and I threw up the scraps of food I'd eaten all over myself.

Please, I thought, hoping whatever gods the people who lived in this city prayed to were listening. *Please make it stop.*

'*I wanted to look in on you. I thought you'd be dead by now.*'

The sound was like hundreds of bees squirming inside my ears, fighting with each other, stabbing me with their stingers. But even through all that, I recognised his voice.

Shadow Falcon.

'That's not my name, you know. My master gives us those titles when he sends us out on missions so we can do what must be done, knowing that when we return to our families the acts that we committed were done not as ourselves, but as soldiers acting on behalf of our people.'

I tried to breathe in and out very slowly, hoping to keep the nausea down even a little. *What is your real name then?*

The bees in my ear canals shivered as they laughed.

'And what would you do with my name, Mahdek? Give it to a demon so that he might come to me in my dreams?'

I've seen a lot of horrible things, I said silently to him. But only one that I would ever call a demon. Would you like to see his face?

I pictured Falcon, his lean frame and broad shoulders, his face so perfectly fashioned – as if a sculptor had carved the finest marble into a vision of heroism.

'You mock me?'

Sensing discomfort in the buzzing of his question, I envisioned his face: the strong jaw, the stern brow, the eyes that spoke of duty and honour yet beneath were troubled by the things he'd done.

'Stop. You offend me, little Mahdek.'

I'm showing you what a real demon looks like, Falcon. Not Met'astice. Not a disgusting old man who can't even recognise the evil in his own deeds. A handsome youth, full of promise, full of ideals, who murders families and children and tells himself it's because of a war that ended three hundred years ago. You're the monster, Falcon. Not me. Not my people. You.

'Look at yourself, Mahdek.'

Suddenly he assailed me with a vision, stolen from my own memories of seeing myself in a pool of water just a week ago, but instead of a fleeting glimpse he made me stare at it with perfect clarity.

'Why do you go on living? Look at the filth you're eating. I would rather die than be like you.'

Me too, I said.

Falcon almost sounded sorry for me when he said, 'Then drown yourself. Or go to the top of a precipice and let yourself fall. It will only get worse from here on out. The sigils I inscribed on you are stronger even than Met'astice expected, and there is nothing awaiting you but more suffering. Spare yourself that. I . . . did not set out to harm you this way.'

I would've laughed then, only I felt too sick, and I wasn't sure how long this connection between us could last before it killed me. Falcon seemed aware of that too, because a second later he let me go.

I retched one last time, and lay among the piles of rubbish, shivering, wondering if maybe Falcon was right. Why would anyone want to live this way? And if it was going to get worse . . .

No. They don't get to win like that.

The way Met'astice had dismissed me that day outside the cave had always clung to me like a leech stuck to my skin: 'Why would we kill you? You're a child.'

That hadn't been mercy, I was sure now. What was happening to me – what I was becoming – was by his design: I was a despicable creature, afraid to trust anyone, unworthy of that trust even if anyone was ever stupid enough to offer it to me. A thief. A beggar. A nuisance. This was how Met'astice saw the Mahdek, and that's what he'd made me into.

'One day all Mahdek will have collars upon them,' Falcon had said. 'And then can our two peoples know peace.'

62

No.

No peace.

No easy way out for me, or for you, Falcon.

If the world wants me dead, let it come and kill me.

I reached out with a trembling hand at the scrap of melon rind I'd saved for my dessert, and ignored the bitter taste to find what flecks of sweetness I could. When I was done, I let my fingers run over my torn rags, my soiled hair and grimy skin. Falcon was right: it wasn't worth living like this. Life had stolen every shred of dignity from me.

Tomorrow I would start stealing it back.

10

The Coat

Cleanliness is a luxury that abounds for the rich but is unattainable to the poor. When you live in a nice house with a marble bath filled from aqueducts that flow from private cisterns in the courtyard, fresh water is free. On the streets, however, there's no clean water to be found anywhere. The poor drink a foul concoction called 'small beer' because it's cheap, rarely makes you sick and keeps you a little bit drunk all day long. Craftspersons and merchants make do with spending a few coppers for a weekly trip to the public baths. The rest of us are supposed to get used to the stink.

I wasn't born to this life though. The Mahdek wander the continent, and whether in a forest stream or a desert oasis, we washed our clothes and our bodies. But in Domisa Pago the best I could hope for was a warm rainy night. While others sought shelter, I would look for a dark corner in one of the public parks where I could strip off my clothes and let the rain wash over me. That's a dangerous thing to do when you're small and alone, and even when I could steal a few minutes of privacy, I'd have to put my filthy rags back on and soon I'd smell as bad as before. Only wetter.

But Falcon's mystical violation of my thoughts had ignited

a fire inside me. I was tired of living like a wandering ghost, punished by the sight of the hideous, scrawny, sexless creature I glimpsed in grimy pools of street water. I wanted to be clean again. I wanted to look respectable. The first heist of my burgeoning career as a professional thief, therefore, would require a trip to the garment district.

Even thinking such thoughts – to say nothing of putting them into action – carried a cost. It took most of my waking hours to scrounge enough scraps of food to survive, and the rest to find safe places to sleep at night. Spending an entire day skulking along the backstreets behind rows of clothiers was a risky investment; succeed or fail, I would likely go hungry tonight.

But it would be worth it.

My first instinct was to pull a pilfer-and-run from one of the cheaper stores that catered to the common folk, reasoning that poorer-quality, rough-spun trousers, shirts and under-clothes would be less well guarded than expensive finery. Less than an hour into my mission I learned the reverse was true: cut-rate clothiers were constantly vigilant. They *expected* to be burgled, going so far as to have those who worked in the back of the shop keep watch for potential thieves trying to break in from the alley.

The fancier stores though? With their scarves made from Berabesq silk, embroidered tunics of Gitabrian cotton, and riding trousers cut from Zhubanese leather? Their attention was focused entirely on their wealthy customers. After all, what would a petty thief do with an elegant sapphire gown or richly brocaded burgundy coat?

The twilight hour in the upper-class market district of Domisa Pago was known as *invatio*. During this time, stores were shuttered to all except special guests – nobles mostly – who would be invited into the most fashionable stores to sip expensive wines and nibble on foreign delicacies while the shop owner privately displayed their finest wares. Unfortunately for many a shopkeeper, however, the nobility of Domisa Pago tended to congregate at those establishments where the latest trends could be found, leaving the others empty during that hour.

The good part though – at least as far as my plan was concerned – was that those expensive but less popular stores still closed, to maintain the illusion of exclusivity. As the sun began to set, I watched many a store owner lock their front door, only to sneak out the back to drown their sorrows at the nearest tavern. That was how I picked out a particularly well-appointed coat maker's shop called Tunico Splendira.

The prospect of a coat – a *proper* sheep's wool coat – was enough to make me shiver with excitement. Even better, Tunico Splendira's rear facade featured a little basement window, barely two handspans high, kept open so the workroom below the store would stay cool in the late-afternoon swelter. It was far too narrow for a burglar to slip through – unless you happened to be a small-boned thirteen-year-old who hadn't eaten a decent meal in over a year.

I scraped my ribs on the window casing as I slipped inside, only to then slide down the wall and land awkwardly on my ankle. I had to slam my palm against my mouth to keep myself from crying out. Then my eyes adjusted to the darkness inside Tunica Splendira's basement and I forgot all about the pain.

It was far larger than it appeared from the outside, and filled with work tables and shelves stuffed with bolts of every fabric imaginable. Though my plan had been to sneak upstairs, grab the first thing I saw and then slip back out, I couldn't help but run my fingers along the bolts of silks and linens and wools, each texture like tasting a different but equally delectable cheese.

To touch something so luxurious was . . . I don't know how to explain it. I guess it must've been like how it was for those men and women who stumbled out of smoke taverns after spending a week's wages to suck on pipes filled with concoctions said to bring about a joy and contentment impossible to achieve through any other means. I doubted even their intoxication could've matched mine in that moment. I felt powerful. Special. Always before I'd stolen only such petty things as wormy apples or mouldy bread – the basic necessities of life that no Mahdek would've denied even to their enemies. But now I had *invaded* this store. Walking through that basement workroom made me feel like a conqueror inspecting her new domain.

Coat first, I reminded myself. *Then get out before invatio hour ends and the shopkeeper returns.*

I crept quietly up the stairs to the showroom above. Even with only the dim light sneaking through the partly closed panel windows near the ceiling, I had to squint and blink several times because the polished oak floors and gleaming brass fixtures shone like stars to me. With the sly movements of a hunter I searched for my quarry among the racks of coats of every cut and fashion.

There's too many choices, I began to despair. *How am I supposed to pick . . . ? There!*

Near the back of the showroom stood a mannequin of a young boy posed as if aiming a hunting crossbow at a carved

67

wooden duck suspended from four strings attached to the ceiling to give it the illusion of flight. The mannequin displayed a long leather hunting coat meant for some lordling's son who likely couldn't have aimed that crossbow, never mind wound it after the first shot. But I didn't care because that coat he was wearing was just about the most perfect thing I'd ever seen.

Sleek it was, a brown so dark as to be almost black, which meant it would be hard to see at night-time. The leather was stylishly weathered to give the coat the illusion of being well-used already. Cake on a bit of mud and grime and it wouldn't even draw attention from the constables. I practically glided along the floor to the display, as if the wooden boy and I were about to dance.

Seven buttons, each one hand-carved from a dark mahogany with a reddish tone that made it look like wine, opened smoothly at my touch. I lifted up one of the sleeves and kissed the cuff, breathing in the heady scent of fine leather and expensive oils. As I slid the coat over my shoulders, I found myself embraced in a silk lining that I knew would keep me warm in winter and cool in summer.

I was, quite simply, in love.

Love, they say, makes a fool of wisdom. What then does it do to a stupid little Mahdek who only *thinks* she's a proper thief?

What I heard first was a creak, then a rumble. The creak came from one of the store's front door locks, the rumble from the owner who had returned far too early.

There was nowhere to go. The stairs leading down to the basement were too near the front door and I was at the back of the showroom. I ducked behind one of the racks of thick furs just as the door swung open and the owner entered, walking awkwardly as he genuflected repeatedly to his guests.

'My worthies, such an honour! Such a great honour! So pleased to be of serv—'

He was cut off by one of the other two men, who made a spitting sound then spoke in a language I doubted the Daroman store owner would understand.

'Oh, how they bray, these barbarian sheep.'

My limbs stiffened. My heart froze and a soft moan escaped my lips. The two men who entered the store behind the owner were unknown to me, but I recognised the language they spoke. All Mahdek pick up a few words here and there from those who so often come to kill us.

The other Jan'Tep mage turned in my direction, and though I was well hidden behind the furs, still my soul screamed at me that he could see me.

He smiled.

11

The Pact

'What a funny little display you have there,' the taller of the two mages said to the store owner. 'Are your Daroman clientele stimulated to purchase clothing by the sight of a naked boy shooting at ducks?'

He's looking at the mannequin, not at me!

The store owner's head turned, and his eyes narrowed. 'That ... My assistant was due to change the displays this week, my lords. Fashion changes so quickly in this city, I'm sure you understand. Evidently he left without finishing the task I set him. I will beat the wretch black and blue, of this you can be assured.'

In Jan'Tep, one of the mages said to the other, '*One camel gives a second camel an order and wonders why it isn't properly followed.*'

The owner, worried his guests might be offended by the mannequin's unfortunate nudity, strode across the shop towards the display. The instant he got there he'd see me behind the rack of furs. I started to panic, and the terror that had frozen my limbs before now turned them to jelly.

He's going to find me! He's going to—

'We do not have all day,' the shorter mage said, summoning

the man back. 'Either show us your wares or we will take our custom elsewhere. You'll find yourself poorer in more ways than one, I promise you.'

The store owner rushed to obey, and relief flooded through me. But after only a single step he stopped and sniffed at the air. Again I cursed myself for being so filthy. My breath quickened. I could hear the air rushing in and out between my lips, like the wheeze of a dying animal at the end of its last, desperate flight. I clamped my mouth shut.

Quiet, I commanded my quavering body. *Stay very still. Don't move. Don't breathe.*

Wise words, but fear, like love, makes a fool of wisdom.

It was the acrid smell that caught my attention first – not the usual reek street urchins carry with them everywhere, but familiar nonetheless. One leg felt warmer than the other, and then I, along with the store owner and his guests, heard the trickle sliding down to form a yellow pool at my feet.

The scent reached the two mages waiting at the front of the store. 'What is this foulness?' the taller, hawk-faced one demanded.

With a roar the shopkeeper hurled aside the rack of furs behind which I'd been hiding. He grabbed me by the lapels of my beloved stolen coat and swung me off my feet, hurling me halfway to the front of the store. I landed on my sprained ankle and cried out.

The two mages watched with amusement at first. I was on my knees before them, as if praying for their forgiveness. When I looked up, however, their eyes widened as if they could see the Mahdek blood running through my veins – as if the metallic sigils tattooed on my neck precariously hidden by the collar of the coat, were calling out to them, warning

71

them that their most reviled enemy was here, awaiting their wrath.

The shop owner strode up behind me. This time he grasped me by my hair and hauled me to my feet. I felt his other hand wrap around my jaw, gripping it so tightly I thought he might snap my neck then and there. But my eyes were drawn to the two mages, wondering whether the spell by which they would end my life would be made of ember magic or iron, breath or blood, silk or sand.

Then, in that brief moment between humiliation and death, a miracle happened. The two Jan'Tep mages looked right at me – right *through* me – and began to laugh.

Mahdek don't look any different from the other folk who make their home on this continent. Some of us are dark, some light. Mostly we're sort of beige, I guess. Our hair tends towards bright shades though, and I'd never met anyone else with curls as red as mine and those of the rest of my clan. But now my hair was filthy and matted to my skull, so it looked more like a mop that had been drenched in grease and mud than anything else. Still, these two men in their fine silk robes were Jan'Tep mages. I was their ancient enemy. How could they not recognise me?

'What a disgusting little creature,' the shorter, round-faced one said. His gaze went above my head, to the shopkeeper. 'Your daughter, I take it?'

His companion laughed.

The shopkeeper dropped me to the floor, and when I looked up I saw him grab hold of a metal coat hanger. As he raised it over his head, my treacherous body finally came to my aid. Ignoring the pain in my ankle, I sprang up and raced past the two mages, momentarily feeling the brush of the taller one's robes against my face as I passed by. He lurched away from me, and within seconds I was hopping down the stairs.

The *clomp-clomp-clomp* of the shopkeeper's heavy footfalls chased me all the way through the basement until I threw myself at the wall and grabbed the ledge below the window. With strength born of desperation, I dragged myself through and out into the alley without being hit by that metal coat hanger even once. Panting like a dog, I took a few stumbling steps before I couldn't go any further. The cost of my escape had been the last of my feeble reserves.

In the growing shadows of the alley I listened, expecting to hear the back door of the shop grind open, but there was only silence. My pursuer had made the calculation that the chance of a sale to a pair of wealthy Jan'Tep mages outweighed capturing one scrawny thief in a stolen coat.

Cold, tired, stinking worse than ever, I became aware of a tightness at the corners of my mouth and the cool evening air against my teeth. I was grinning like a fool.

When those two Jan'Tep mages had looked at me, they hadn't seen a Mahdek demon worshipper. They hadn't even seen an enemy. Just a dirty-faced little girl who might've been the shopkeeper's unsanitary daughter. Even with centuries of enmity between us and these cursed sigils around my neck, I was invisible to them.

An unexpected elation filled me. I had stood before the beings of my nightmares and walked away unscathed.

Better than that, I thought, pinching the leather lapel of my new coat.

Ignoring the pain in my ankle, I walked tall as I headed down the alley, whistling to myself as I looked up at all my lucky stars winking at me from the sky above. My first heist had been an unmitigated success, and for almost a full twenty seconds I considered myself the best-dressed thief in all of Domisa Pago.

That's when the hood dropped over my head and the stars were smothered in darkness, and the noose that must've been cleverly attached to the hood tightened around my neck until I couldn't breathe.

12

The Court of Mercy

One thing you learn pretty quick about the Daroman empire: these people really pride themselves on their judiciary. They have entire books (not that I've read any of them – or think most Daromans have either) expounding on the ways in which the mechanisms for administering justice are just as important as the laws themselves. After all, what's the point of allowing arcane legal defences, if many of the accused lack the finances to hire professional advocates or the education to even read the law books on their own behalf? How could any legal system call itself impartial if only the rich can mount a proper defence?

One might think the solution to this would be for the empire to offer all its citizens free legal representation, but that's not in keeping with the Daroman spirit of *nimen optimi altudas* – 'Let the finest ascend' – which is another way of saying, 'the rich are rich because they're better than you'.

The Daroman innovation, therefore, is to have not one, not two, but three entirely distinct sets of courts: one for the nobles represented by expensive advocates; a second for the middle class, whose generally inartful arguments are translated into proper legalese by a court interpreter; and for the poor, who have neither the wealth to afford advocates nor the education to understand the winding machinations of the legal system, you get the *curitas clementia* – the courts merciful.

'The penitent will supplicate as the charges are read.'

Through the black sackcloth hood, the magistrate's chiming command made him sound young. Or maybe he was just overenthusiastic.

An accused brought before a court merciful isn't considered a defendant. How, after all, could a beggar be expected to argue that a constable was lying when he testified to having caught said beggar in the act of stealing another's property – say, a brand-new hunting coat? Besides, if every thief in a city the size of Domisa Pago was allowed to argue their innocence, the courts merciful would collapse under their collective weight in a single day. Therefore, when a thief is dragged before the magistrate, they are deemed a 'penitent' – there not to mount a defence but to abase themselves by kneeling on the ground, arms outstretched with palms up as they plead for the mercy of the court. In most cases, this allows the magistrate to skip right over the trial part and go straight to the verdict.

I didn't have any personal experience with the courts merciful; thus far I'd been able to stay out of them. But you hear things, living on the streets, and I'd never heard anyone say they brought you before a magistrate with a bag over your head.

'The penitent will supplicate as the—'

'I demand the right to plead my case,' I said, cutting him off.

Instinctively I cringed, anticipating somebody punching me in the side of the head. Turns out my instincts were pretty much spot on.

76

'The prosecutor will defer the beating of the penitent until the magistrate has ruled on the objection!'

'Sorry,' said a thicker, grumblier voice.

That set off a chorus of hisses and catcalls all around me, along with a few choice suggestions of dubious legal merit.

'Now then,' the reedy-voiced magistrate went on, 'what is this "plea" the penitent would so boldly put before this hollowed court?'

'I think you mean "hallowed",' I said.

'The prosecutor will admonish the penitent.'

My belligerence got me a second round of jeers and taunts from the gallery – along with another thump to the side of my head. Fortunately, it wasn't nearly so hard this time.

There couldn't have been much light in the room. The sackcloth wasn't very thick yet all I could see were vague shadows all around me.

'The court awaits the penitent's plea,' the magistrate said, though he sounded more excited than impatient.

'First, someone take this damned sack off my he—'

This time the blow sent me reeling. Somebody caught me before I fell and then slammed me down onto my knees. All I could see now were yellow spots.

'Excessive force,' charged the magistrate.

'She deserved it,' countered the prosecutor.

'Objection sustained.'

Laughter erupted from the gallery, and something wet splattered against the back of my coat.

Okay, I thought. *Nothing merciful about this court. Nothing particularly judicial about it either.*

Back when I lived with the two knights, they insisted I learn the basic principles of Daroman law. 'Every citizen must know the system of justice by which they are governed,' Lord Gervais pontificated after I'd returned from school, freshly educated in the specific flowers a proper lady ought to wear during various formal occasions.

'Even when those laws happen to be particularly stupid?' Sir Rosarite had wondered aloud.

'Especially then,' Gervais replied.

So while I was no expert, I knew a thing or two about Daroman law, which I expected made me a legal genius in that roomful of idiots. With my arms outstretched and palms upturned, I declared loudly, 'I plead *tuta a lebat!*'

There was just a hint of a pause before a windstorm's worth of oohs and aahs filled the courtroom – or whatever dank cellar we were actually in.

'The penitent has submitted a plea of tuna halibut!' announced the magistrate, banging what sounded suspiciously like a battered tin cup against . . . well, another tin cup.

'Tuna halibut!' cheered the onlookers. 'Tuna halibut!'

'What's *tuta a lebat?*' asked the gruff-sounding prosecutor – who, impressively, got the pronunciation right. Then he smacked me about the head again. 'You made that up, didn't you?'

The magistrate, however – perhaps persuaded by the rising chorus of 'Tuna halibut! Give us tuna halibut!' – ruled in my favour.

'The penitent will offer their defence. Be warned,' he said, clanging his tin cups again, 'this court is well acquainted – expert, in fact – on all principles of tuna halibut, and will know if the penitent is making things up.'

'Eminently reasonable, your eminence,' I said, and awkwardly rose to my feet. 'As I'm sure this court is well aware, the defence of *tuta* ... tuna halibut ... requires the defendant be free of any hoods, blindfolds or other impairments.'

The rowdy cacophony descended to a sort of steady rumble while the magistrate tried to ascertain whether I was lying or not.

The thing is, there really *is* a legal defence called *tuta a lebat*. It just doesn't happen to exist in *Daroman* law. It originated in the country where the two knights came from. When Lord Gervais had first explained it to me, I'd told him it sounded like a pretty simplistic – not to mention, dumb – way of settling legal disputes. He insisted it was far more complicated than I appreciated, and that little girls who can't even make their bed properly had no business being snooty about a great nation's thousand-year-old legal traditions.

'Hurry up!' someone in the gallery shouted, and it wasn't long before others joined in. At last the magistrate ruled on my request, no doubt reckoning the crowd wanted to see what would happen next.

'Objection sustained,' he announced. 'The prosecutor will remove the penitent's hood.'

'Fine,' the prosecutor grumbled.

Taking a sackcloth off someone's head should not normally require choking, elbowing or punching, yet the prosecutor managed all three.

'You're gonna regret this,' he warned as he finally yanked the hood off my head.

I had to wipe my hair out of my face before I could take in the full majesty of the court merciful, which was, as I'd predicted, some sort of cellar. The floor was mostly dirt and rock, with a few broken pieces of grey stone tile here and there. The walls were made of blocks of the same material, held together with crumbling mortar. The ceiling had to be forty feet high, and was as rough as the roof of a cavern.

'Where are we?' I asked.

'A place rats like you don't never leave,' the prosecutor informed me.

'Well . . . ?' the magistrate asked, clanging together what was indeed a pair of battered tin cups.

He was probably my age, though he looked younger with his spindly arms and boyish cheeks. He was perched on what must've been a stone shelf carved into the rock face, the stumps of his amputated legs sticking out just over the edge. Among the thirty or so onlookers, sitting on assorted wooden chairs or broken slabs of rock, I saw lean faces wearing feral grins. Most were teenagers a couple of years older than me, a few in their early twenties. I saw two or three children though, who couldn't have been older than seven.

Different shapes and sizes, skin colour and hair, yet every single person in that cellar was, without doubt, a thief. As I'd suspected, I hadn't been arrested by constables for stealing; I'd been pinched by a gang for thieving in their territory.

'The penitent will offer their defence,' the boy magistrate commanded, 'or this court will deliver its sentence!'

I let my gaze wander from him to the burly prosecutor, who was probably about sixteen with a shovel-shaped jaw, and then to every other mismatched face in that room. In seconds I had my plan.

Though my formal education had ended the night Met'astice had killed Sir Gervais and Sir Rosarite, my year on the streets had taught me to read faces, postures and clothes the way I used to read books. One grin can mean joy, another intoxication, a third madness. A fine new hat was sometimes worn not by a successful man, but by a merchant whose business was failing and needed to keep up appearances in front of his competitors. A rich woman might dress in plain clothes to keep from getting accosted by beggars like me when she walked through the market. I'd learned an entire language of smiles and scowls – which ones were real and which ones were masks worn to hide the perverse desires underneath.

The thing about being poor – *really* poor – is that beyond all the suffering and sorrow, mostly what you live with is boredom. That's what I saw beneath all the jeering and taunting, the threats and promises of violence aimed in my direction. Even misery becomes tedious when you live with it day after day. My job, then, was to entertain this pack of wild dogs just enough to keep them from tearing me apart.

'I'll need two sticks,' I said to the magistrate. 'Roughly two and a half feet long.'

'Why would you need two sticks?' he asked, then looked suddenly uncomfortable at the possibility he'd just revealed his lack of expertise in the esoteric judicial details of tuna halibut.

I turned to the burly young man looking distinctly disappointed that his role as the prosecutor hadn't afforded him nearly enough opportunities to beat me up yet.

'One for me, one for him.'

Tuta a lebat is a phrase from Sir Gervais and Sir Rosarite's homeland that means 'revealed through battle'. It's the legal basis for trial by combat.

13

Trial by Combat

When I was little, huddled in crowded makeshift tents with the remnants of my clan in the days and weeks after my mother and father had been killed by a Jan'Tep lightshaper, I spent a lot of time thinking about justice. Not the sort of justice my fellow Mahdek looked for when they prayed to various gods (who even then I was pretty sure didn't exist). The elders would sit outside in the cold, wailing with arms outstretched: 'Why, emperors of earth, sovereigns of sky, lords of thunder and ladies of lightning, why do you not protect us from our enemies?'

You'd figure the reply they got back – usually being rained on – would've been a clue as to their answer (though really it's not fair to blame beings who probably don't exist for your troubles). But I wasn't concerned about the gods. My question was much simpler: how can a righteous person who is weak defeat a wicked one who is strong?

The short answer? They can't.

In any fair fight, someone has the advantage, and it almost never has anything to do with their sparkling personality. Righteousness, like pluck, determination or good personal hygiene, offers no defence against an opponent's bigger size, faster speed or better training. It certainly doesn't protect you against spells that can burn you from the inside out.

The prosecutor – whose name I learned from the cheers coming from his fellows in that dank cellar where we would soon do battle – was called Petal. If that sounds like a strange name for a hulking brute of a boy, well, it's possible he had a completely different name, like Grizo or Terberon or Ferius. No, wait – Ferius is my name. I think. It might belong to a dog.

I did warn you, I get confused sometimes.

Anyway, Petal had every advantage you could imagine over me. He was a foot taller, twice my weight, broad in the shoulders with a longer reach, and one look at his steady, deep-set eyes told me he was both a very experienced fighter and one who took violence seriously, even when faced with a scrawny girl in a stolen coat holding a stick.

'On the count of three,' our legless magistrate intoned eagerly. 'Three . . . Two . . .'

'Wait!' I called out.

He rolled his eyes at me. 'What now?'

'It's too late to back out,' Petal grunted at me. He gave his own two-and-a-half-foot stick a few test swings in the air. Not only had I *not* requested the sticks be shaved to a sharp point at the end, but the kids who'd gone in search of our make-shift weapons had given him one thick enough that I was pretty sure he could snap my bones with it.

Unfair? Sure, but that's how these things work.

Back when I used to sit and think about justice a lot, I eventually came to the conclusion that what made the world *un*just was simply the laws of nature themselves. Big is more useful than gentle; quick is better than funny; deviousness

83

wins more fights than honesty. Life, when you get right down to it, isn't designed to be fair. That means justice is an entirely human invention – a violation of the primal laws of nature. So how does that answer my question about a weak, righteous person defeating a strong, wicked one?

'The rules,' I declaimed loudly to the court, with such vehemence that the obvious veracity of my words couldn't possibly be denied. 'As all learned legal scholars know, the strictures of *tuta a lebat* must always be enumerated prior to the battle for the edification of an audience as noble as this one.'

I was probably laying it on a little thick, and I doubted many of them knew what 'edification' meant – to say nothing of 'enumerated'. Still, they liked being referred to as 'noble', and snorted with laughter in response. Poor folk never tire of the joke where you treat them like wealthy lords and ladies.

'Only rule that matters is that I'm gonna beat you to death,' Petal growled at me.

'Obviously, stupid.' I turned away from him and spread my arms wide to the audience. 'But only if you can follow the sacred rules of *tuta a lebat*!'

Before Petal could say anything else, I addressed the magistrate. 'Would your eminence like to inform the court of the rules, or shall I?'

The sly grin that crossed his face – which I reckoned came from the fact that somebody who has to get along in a crappy life like this without the use of his legs knew way more about injustice than I ever would – told me he'd figured out I was up to something, but he was curious to see how this all played out. 'The penitent is hereby ordered to announce the rules of *tuta a lebat* . . . as is traditional, of course.'

Did he just wink at me?

'The rules are simple,' I began, to forestall any accusations from Petal that I might be playing for time. 'First, there is no limit to how hard, how merciless, or how cruel our blows can be . . .'

That got me a rousing chorus of cheers – especially from Petal.

'So long,' I said, holding up my stick, 'as we only strike each other with these weapons provided for us by the gods themselves.'

That sent the audience into perplexed murmurs. Street kids are used to fighting up close and dirty, not with the kinds of restrictions you're forced to adapt to when you learn fencing. Petal looked none too pleased. I'd likely just taken away half his best moves and reduced the advantage of his greater strength. He still had the reach on me, but by specifying that each of our sticks had to be cut to the same two and a half feet, I'd ensured mine was the proper length for my height and his was too short. Usually that wouldn't be a problem for somebody like him, because he could weather a couple of blows and get in close to deliver crippling punches and kicks. Except that . . .

'Whosoever touches their opponent with any part of their body violates the laws of *tuta a lebat* and must suffer the consequences.'

Petal looked like he was about to object to any such rules, but someone from the gallery shouted out, 'And what, pray tell, might those consequences be?'

I spun around, because that was the first time any of the onlookers had said anything more sophisticated than, 'Kill her!' or, 'Tuna halibut!'

Off to one side, leaning against the remnants of a broken stone column, was a tall girl about two years older than me. She was skinny, like me, but lean and wiry rather than bony. Like those of most of her gang of street thieves, her clothes were a mishmash of stolen bits and pieces. The one difference was that everything she wore, from head to toe, was a crimson so dark it looked like dried blood. Crimson blousy trousers that looked like they'd been stolen from an actor in a travelling pirate show; a crimson leather vest that left her arms bare to show off the scars that went up her shoulders to one around her neck that looked like she'd survived a hanging and another on her cheek just below her right eye. The earrings and bracelets were unusual for a thief, but hers had been painted that same dark red so they didn't reflect the light. And atop her head, covering up blonde tresses – the only part of her that *wasn't* crimson – a frontier hat like those worn by Daroman outriders, only in a dusky dark red. That hat was just about the coolest thing I'd ever seen.

Staring at that girl was like looking into a mirage in the desert. I was enthralled. It wasn't love of course – the only thing in this world I loved was my new coat. It was just that. . . I wished that confident, rebellious, ready-for-anything grin plastered on her face were mine. I didn't want her – I wanted to *be* her.

'Well?' Petal demanded behind me. 'What are these so-called consequences if I punch your face in with my fist instead of playing with sticks?'

'Hmm? Oh, right. That's easy.' I slowly turned on my heel to address the entire crowd of dirty, feral, entertainment-starved young thieves in that cellar. 'The penalty is death of course!'

Before Petal could protest – before even the cheers, shouts

86

and whistles had died down – I added, 'And as all in this magnificent court are well aware, the second law of *tuta a lebat* requires that each strike be paired with either an accusation, a denial, or an interrogatory.'

'An inter . . . gory?' Petal asked. 'You made that up!'

The crowd looked inclined to agree.

'An *interrogatory* is a question, you stupid lump of rock,' the tall girl in the crimson hat said.

'You shut your mouth, Arissa!' Petal roared back, jabbing his stick in her direction like it was some kind of magic wand. 'I'm the prosecutor here. I get to crush the little thief.' He then tried to replicate my little performance with the crowd, turning in a slow circle as he proclaimed, 'This little rat stole in our territory. That means she stole from *us*. And *that* means we gotta make it so's she can't never steal from nobody ever again!'

'Objection!' I shouted, before too many of the audience could jump up to show their support for that sophisticated legal argument. 'An accusation of thievery must be made during *tuta a lebat* itself, otherwise it is vile slander, as all know!'

'As all know,' the magistrate agreed with a chuckle.

'Fine,' Petal said, shooting the gangly magistrate a glare that promised payback for this betrayal. 'Don't care if it's with my fist, my feet, or this stupid stick. Either way I'm going to break you into little pieces, Rat Girl.'

I smiled back at him. 'If the world is just, then I've no doubt you're correct.'

The magistrate, eager to ensure he was still running the show, chimed in. 'On my count of three, let *tuta a lebat* begin, and the gods decide your fate! Three . . .'

87

Like I said before: justice is a set of rules human beings create to twist nature into their own vision of what the world should look like.

'Two . . .'

Live on the wrong side of those laws long enough and you come to understand that the society they create is just as cruel and unfair as nature itself.

'One . . .'

But every now and then? If you figure out how to twist those laws just a teensy little bit in the right direction? You get to make up your own rules.

'Fight!' the magistrate commanded.

14

Tuta a Lebat

'She's a dirty thieving rat!'

Petal dashed towards me, his stick held up at shoulder height, poised to smash in my skull. You can spot someone who's never had any fencing training by the way their first instinct is to swing the sword at you like it's a club. I was no expert, of course, and in any real fight – even one with proper rapiers or smallswords – Petal would've killed me within seconds. But I'd set the rules for this duel, and that meant all his instincts were working against him, whereas my admittedly limited skills were still in my favour.

Had Sir Rosarite been in that cavernous cellar watching me, she would've rolled her eyes with disappointment at my clumsy *tei passo*, which was less a diagonal evasion lunge and more of a panicked ducking followed by me scrabbling on all fours beneath Petal's legs while barely hanging on to my own stick.

The crowd laughed at me as Petal crowed, 'Look at the coward! Come take your beating, Rat Girl!'

My concern wasn't over a beating. It was that once he started, he wouldn't stop until he'd crippled me. That's the thing wealthy, refined people don't understand about those of us who live on the streets: we may not read a lot of books, but we're experts on how to hurt each other in ways that don't heal.

Petal turned to the magistrate. 'Are we done with this farce, Rudger? Your stupid trial is embarrassing the whole gang.'

I didn't wait for a ruling. Instead, I leaped to my feet and shouted, 'I deny that accusation and offer *this* as my proof!'

I lunged, aiming straight for his stomach. Petal, of course, knew a sneak attack would come and was ready to parry my blow. What he *wasn't* ready for was that I'd no intention of hitting his belly since it was the most natural thing for a person to protect. At the last instant, I dropped my point and thrust at the top of his unprotected bare foot.

Gervais always called such attacks 'pretender's follies'; while they might look impressive and score you a point on the fencing piste, no true duellist would risk exposing their head just to touch someone's toes. I was inclined to agree, but Rosarite espoused a different philosophy: 'Hit them anywhere you like, my darling. Just make sure they bleed.'

I hadn't fenced since the day I left the broken remnants of her smallsword in Met'astice and Falcon's cave. My lunge was too pronounced, and threw me off balance. Usually that's a fatal error, but in this case my aim was lucky, and all my weight went into that thrust. Even if the points of our sticks hadn't been sharpened, my attack would've stung him hard. As it was, when I withdrew my stick from his foot there was a coating of blood on the tip.

'You little bitch!' he bellowed.

Petal lurched after me, but he wasn't expecting the amount of pain his injured foot would cause him, and stumbled the moment he took his first step. He reached out to grab me, but I was ready now. With a quick, light slash, the tip of my stick nicked his forearm, leaving an angry red scratch. For some reason I couldn't explain, the frequent admonition of Master Phinus, my comportment instructor, emerged – pompous accent intact – from my lips.

'Bitch is not a proper way to address a young lady!'

Stay out of his way, I reminded myself. *The madder he gets, the more he'll try to close the distance.*

I skipped back several feet, but Petal – less a fool than I might've hoped – didn't rush headlong towards me a second time. Instead he stood upright, knees bent as he'd seen me do, and took up what even Sir Rosarite would have considered a passable *garda basa*.

'I declare it again,' he said, gruff baritone rumbling throughout the chamber. 'She is a rat who pilfered from our territory. The penalty is one broken finger for every copper stolen.'

That was regrettable; my coat was worth considerably more than ten coppers.

Sensing my discomfort, Petal grinned as he added, 'And a busted arm for each silver.'

A coat like mine – I adored her so much I felt I should've given her a name before Petal ended up taking her from me once he had beaten me to a pulp – was probably worth twenty silver. Petal was going to run out of limbs to break.

'Seems excessive for a first offence, if you ask me,' I said, twitching my stick at him to try to lure him into attacking. 'Makes me wonder what the penalty is for falsely accusing an innocent street urchin of such a heinous crime.'

The laugh I got from the crowd was muted and restless. They were getting bored. Petal wisely sensed this and reasoned that if he forced me to come to him, his greater reach would once again work to his advantage. If I tried to wait him out, the crowd would get fidgety and all my fancy talk would get thrown out in favour of a good old-fashioned crippling.

Entertain them, I reminded myself. *That's all this is to them: an evening's diversion to help them forget their daily miseries.*

'The prosecutor names me a thief,' I began, taking sly, circling steps to force him to pivot on his heels or risk me flanking him, 'yet what evidence does he submit to substantiate his charge?'

'That coat, obviously,' he replied. 'You stole it from Tunico Splendira off Needle Alley. That's on *our* turf.'

I made a show of being mystified. 'What coat does the prosecutor prattle on about?' I asked, pretending to glance around in dismay. 'I see no coat put in evidence.'

Petal, seizing the opportunity of my head being turned, lunged at me with a thrust to my face. Cruel and, in this case, ineffective. I danced backwards, leaving him to land heavily once again on his wounded foot. I was starting to come to Sir Rosarite's way of thinking on the subject of foot strikes. Petal grimaced from the pain but held steady and stopped himself from crying out a second time.

I countered immediately with my own double-lunge – which probably looked like a rather ungainly rabbit hop followed by an overextended thrust targeting his right thigh. I came up short though; I'd been too cautious, which, in a duel, is almost as bad as being reckless. Petal batted away my stick with his own, nearly knocking it from my hand.

'The objection is overruled,' the magistrate declared, getting himself back into the game. 'This court awaits proof of the charge of thievery on our territory.' To Petal he added, 'Does the prosecution have further evidence to provide regarding this allegedly stolen coat?'

The audience found this much funnier than my previous joke. Petal didn't. 'You idiot, Rudger! The coat's right there! She's wearing it!' He then made a rather terrible mistake: he jabbed his stick in my direction to indicate the purloined coat.

The instant his arm began to extend, I knew where his point would end up, since he was, in fact, pointing at me, thus opening his inside line. Even before he got there, I'd taken a diagonal step on his right flank and thrust my own stick right at his weapon hand. My point came away bloody once again.

Petal roared with pain and rage, switching his stick to his other hand and holding the injured one under his armpit.

'The penitent appears to make a compelling argument,' Rudger declared. 'Does the prosecution wish to withdraw the accusation?'

He's goading him now. He didn't think Petal could lose, but now he's wondering if maybe I might be able to beat him.

Petal again proved himself nowhere near as dumb as he looked, and settled himself into a forward guard. Violence being the first refuge of the brutish, he clearly felt he must now resort to reason. But I could see the crimson flush in his cheeks, and the barely contained fury that would soon be unleashed on me if I didn't wrap this up quickly.

'This is all shite,' he swore. 'She's wearing a Tunica Splendira coat and everyone here knows it.'

Once again snorts of derision rose up from the restless audience.

Time for the third act, I thought.

93

I'd planned for this moment too, because this wasn't a real duel and it most certainly wasn't a proper trial. This was a story that I was telling, hoping to amuse these young thugs and thieves just enough that I could buy my freedom. And as Master Phinus told us in our lessons on how to behave while being entertained by the witty anecdotes of our betters at dinner parties, all stories – even the funny ones – have a moral if you listen carefully.

'What, this old thing?' I asked innocently, pinching the lapel of my beloved leather coat. *Lorica.* That's what I would name her if I survived this trial. 'The prosecutor is mistaken. I didn't *steal* this coat. I merely . . . *reclaimed* it.'

Even Rudger chuckled at that. 'Reclaimed it?' he asked. 'How do you propose to prove that?'

'Easily, your eminence.'

Once again I began to circle Petal, varying my speed, forcing him to keep shifting his weight. The distance between his feet shortened, putting him further and further off balance. I smiled now. This was the final act of my tale, and even as I began to tell it, I felt a savage fury begin to rise up inside me.

'Reclaimed,' I said, taking another circling step.

Petal caught the look in my eyes. I think even he was surprised by the fire he saw there.

'Repayment,' I said, stamping my forward foot, pretending to lunge. Petal lurched back, then angrily took up his guard again.

'This coat is the fine I charge the world for its crimes against me,' I said.

Rudger, the magistrate, said something then, but I didn't hear it. I couldn't hear anything any more – only the rushing of my blood in my ears.

'Hereby do *I* swear my accusation against the world, and this coat is but the first part of the reparations I level for the crimes committed against me.'

One last turning step, but this time my back foot swung around so that I was fully in line to lunge. 'For the murder of my parents!'

With a nimbleness I doubt I'd ever shown on the fencing piste Sir Rosarite and Sir Gervais kept in their upstairs hallway, I thrust at my enemy. Petal tried to parry, but he was too late. My point came over his arm and caught him in the shoulder. He cried out, sounding for the first time like the boy he probably was underneath the armour of his cruelty. I didn't care.

'For the massacre of my clan!'

Without even bothering to recover from my lunge, I dropped my point and drove it into his thigh just above the knee. I twisted a scream out of him and he dropped his stick, trying to grab mine, but I'd already pulled it back out.

'For the slaying of two knights who dared to love me!'

This time a slash – reckless and filled with vicious elation. A thrill came over me as the sharpened end of the stick sliced into Petal's cheek. He crumpled to the ground, covering his face with his hands. Without hesitating even a second, I leaped forward, loomed over him, and aimed the line of my stick right at his throat.

I felt hot. Feverish. My free hand tugged at the collar of the soiled rag of a dress that stunk all the time and gave me rashes, revealing the tattooed metallic sigils forming a collar around my neck that I despised with all my heart and yet was the only perfect, beautiful thing on my entire body.

'For turning me into a filthy little rat who has to sleep in alleys, and scrounge for awful scraps of rotten vegetables. Who can't sleep at night because it's not safe. Who can't have anyone care about her because a Jan'Tep mage took that away from me, just like his kind took everyone I ever loved. Who can't have anything nice unless she steals it, and who hates herself. *Hates* herself! So for that crime above all, damn the world and damn you all!'

My lungs were empty then. I was poised to strike, Petal curled up beneath me, all his size and strength, his experience in fighting and his brutal confidence, vanished. I had bent the laws of nature to my will. Justice was about to be mine for the first time in my life, and all I had to do was . . .

I breathed in deeply, poised to drive the point of that stick into his throat. I don't know what it was that stayed my hand. Not honour, certainly. Not bravery or mercy either. A memory, perhaps? The gentle weight of Sir Gervais's hand on my shoulder? Sir Rosarite's fingers squeezing mine? I hoped that was what it was. An innate revulsion against killing another human being wouldn't bode well for my future.

I looked up, realising the cavernous cellar had gone silent. Everyone there was staring at me. I no longer knew what to do. I'd thought this far and no further. I'd given them their entertainment, and all that was left was for this merciful court to render their verdict.

Rudger coughed, then said – whispered is more like it – 'This court rules that the accused is . . . not guilty.'

If he'd been guessing at the outcome his followers desired, then he'd guessed right. They leaped up to roar with applause and started cheering '*Tuta a lebat! Tuta a lebat!*' as if it were my name.

At least they weren't calling it 'tuna halibut' any more.

I stumbled back, letting the stick fall from my hand, unprepared for the sensation of being bathed in their applause. I suppose in some sense I'd just given voice to their own stories, even if the details were different. I'd shown them their own pain painted on my face and written a tale in which those like us got to win for once.

The problem with making up sagas of great heroes, though, is that you also have to make up the villains. Nobody likes to end the story as the villain.

The wind fled my lungs as Petal barrelled into me, those big, strong arms of his crushing my midsection before I even realised what was happening. He slammed me down onto the cellar floor. My head smashed against the rocky ground. When I could see again, he was on top of me, straddling me. In his eyes I finally saw what true, righteous vengeance looked like.

He's not going to hurt me, I thought. *He's going to kill me.*

I think he knew it too – we'd both somehow, without even intending it, gone too far. Someone had to come out of this broken.

Suddenly his broad shoulders grew a pair of legs clad in blousy dark red trousers that wrapped around his throat. He fell backwards, trying to slam his attacker on the ground as he'd done to me. But Arissa, the girl in crimson, squirmed around his larger frame like a snake. She slid between his flailing limbs and prised his arm away from his side. By the time I sat up, she had wrapped her own arms around his elbow at an odd angle, her long legs holding his head down and back.

The room fell silent. Petal growled in rage, but anyone

could hear the fear in his voice too. He knew what was about to happen.

The crack that came next was like thunder echoing from the cellar walls. I felt sick to my stomach.

Without hesitation, without mercy, the girl in crimson rolled across the screaming Petal and within an instant had his other arm in the same position.

'Yield,' she said simply.

I was on my feet now, so I saw the look on Petal's face. I felt pity for him in that moment. Either his pride or his other arm was about to be broken, and either way the price was too high.

'I . . . I yield,' he said at last.

She let go of his arm and swung her legs up over her head, rolling over backwards to come up onto her feet.

'Somebody set his arm and splint it between two pieces of wood,' she said. She bent down to pick up one of the sticks we'd used to fight our duel. 'These look about the right length.'

A couple of the older kids ran to assist Petal. I guess when you live the life of a thief, you get used to setting broken arms and legs.

'Well, now,' the girl in crimson began as she came to stand before me, appraising me with bold eyes that probably never turned away from anything.

I felt like I should be kneeling before her.

'Thank you for saving me,' I said.

'I didn't do it for you, Rat Girl.' She gave a negligent shrug of her blonde head towards Petal. 'I'd been looking for an excuse to remind everyone not to mess with me. You just happened along to provide a convenient opportunity.'

'I am in your debt all the same,' I said. It's what Sir Gervais would've said.

'You got a place to hole up tonight?'

I shook my head.

'You can bunk in my spot. I've got extra food too. Tonight's free, but tomorrow you start earning your keep.'

'How?' I asked.

She grinned, gesturing to the thirty kids milling about the cellar, a few helping Petal but most of the others surreptitiously watching us, before flicking the collar of my coat. 'Like you, we're in the property-reclamation business.' Her finger drifted to the tattooed sigils around my neck. 'What are these?'

I had a dozen different lies prepared for a moment like this. *Symbols of royalty – I'm a princess from a faraway land. War tattoos – I get one whenever I slay an enemy in battle. Make-up – I'm a famous actress here to perform the 'Play of the Jewelled Spirits', don't you know it?*

I'm not sure why – maybe those unexpected truths I'd uttered at the end of my fight with Petal had deadened my ability to lie – but I couldn't bring myself to say any of those things.

'I'm Mahdek,' I said at last.

She seemed unimpressed. 'Like one of those refugees from the Jan'Tep territories?'

'They were *our* territories first.'

She arched an eyebrow. 'You planning to go all *tuta a lebat* on me now?'

'Sorry.' I pulled up the ragged collar of my dress. 'A mage imprinted these symbols on my skin. They're like a mystical collar that . . . These markings cause decent people to shun me.'

Arissa jutted her lower jaw thoughtfully for a moment, then laughed out loud and threw an arm around my shoulder. As she led me out of the cellar and down a set of stone steps into the shadows below, she said, 'Then you and me should get along fine, Rat Girl. There ain't a decent bone in my body.'

15

The Black Galleon

Thievery, I discovered over the year that followed my recruit-
ment into the crew of the Black Galleon – that's what they
called the ruins of the old sailcloth factory which served as
their lair – was less a business and more an industry.

'Bindle and Leaf, you're on pockets today,' Rudger announced.
Rudger's mother had, apparently, been an actual pirate, which
was in part how the Black Galleon got its name. 'Nice funeral
for her ladyship the Countess of Pluvia out at Noble's Heap
this afternoon. Wear your blacks if they're presentable, otherwise lift a shovey when you get there.'

Bindle, short and round, grinned as he elbowed Leaf, who
was equally short but so slender a stiff wind would've sent
him flying. 'Gonna be a good haul today!'

The hardest part of my apprenticeship was learning the
language and geography of my new profession. Take Noble's
Heap, for example. You won't find it on any map of Domisa
Pago, because its actual name is *Tranqua Regalis* – the Royal
Cemetery. Every city has one, reserved for those deceased
whose bloodline traces back to one of the imperial lines –
which is just about every count, baronet or marquess whose
ancestor ever sneezed in the presence of the Daroman royal

family. They say all six mausoleums in Tranqua Regalis are stacked so high with noble corpses that the cemetery chamberlains advise the aged and infirm to lose weight before they die if they hope to join their aristrocratic brethren in the afterworld. Hence the name 'Noble's Heap'.

Despite Bindle's elation at the Countess Pluvia's imminent internment, I doubt either he or Leaf owned a decent set of blacks – that's what the gang called any type of formal clothes suitable and of sufficient quality to enable one to show up at such an event without attracting undue attention. A shovey, on the other hand, meant a shovel, but could also refer to any other tools, implements or accoutrements that could be used as props to make the thief appear to be a labourer employed by the establishment at which they'd be doing their thievery.

Pockets, of course, was shorthand for pickpocketing duty.

Pickpocketing was both the safest and riskiest of assignments. On the one hand, you had complete control over whose pockets or purses you pilfered, as well as the timing. If too many constables were about or the situation didn't look safe, you'd move on to somewhere else. But waiting for the perfect opportunity could drive you mad with anticipation. Worse, the more you succeeded, the more you wanted another snatch. Hence the phrase, 'Pockets get you picked, the more pockets you pick.'

Not exactly poetry, but these weren't exactly poets.

'Sniff, Veil and Twill,' Rudger called out, nose buried in the big ledger he kept, 'there's a new art gallery gonna open up in the framer's district next week. Very hush-hush. Gonna be a big surprise for the elite collectors in the city.' He looked up from his ledger with a sly grin.

'The surprise's gonna be the best stuff is missing, right?'

102

Veil asked, winding her fingers in her long chestnut tresses. She was pretty enough to be a lady-in-waiting if she weren't so low-born, or, well, the more obvious thing. But Rudger had convinced her a while ago she could put her looks and discretion to better use. Sniff and Twill gave each other the complicated sequence of congratulatory hand slaps that I still hadn't learned.

'Hey,' Rumble objected, the big man's reedy voice so light and thin from a nasty stab to the throat he'd taken when he was younger that you could only barely hear him. 'How come I'm not on the art job, Rudger? You know how I love art.'

Rudger groaned. 'Yeah, Rumble, we all know your taste in art.' He reached behind the rocky shelf where he perched himself when giving out the day's assignments and hoisted up a gilded oak frame around an oil painting of a rather sad-looking puppy. 'Remember this gem you brought back from Lord Gribney's estate the one and only chance we had to get inside? Worth a whole three coppers, the fences told us – that's if we agreed to rip out the painting before we sold 'em the frame.'

There was a general outpouring of laughter and teasing of poor Rumble, whose barely audible defence was, 'I like dogs.'

'Don't be sad,' Veil said in good-natured ribbing. 'You can come visit your puppy painting when I hang it in the Admiral's Berth tonight!'

In keeping with their nautical sensibilities – though so far as I could tell, not one of these people including Rudger had ever been to sea – they referred to the rooms in the old sailcloth factory as 'berths'. Rudger cleverly kept one room so luxurious and well-stocked with pricey food and even wine that everyone salivated at the thought of pulling off so big a score that he granted them the Admiral's Berth for a night or even a whole week sometimes.

That the gangly, legless boy was allowed to captain this crew came down to his remarkable skill at herding thirty ruffians, urchins and delinquents into a functioning operation that brought in good results month after month and whose members rarely got pinched by the constables. Of course, that was also due to Rudger's second skill: knowing precisely how much to pay in rent.

The old sailcloth factory was owned – through a number of intermediaries – by a wealthy Daroman noble whose name only Rudger knew, and who tolerated the gang's activities for a substantial cut of the proceeds. But that was only one of the forms of rent Rudger had to pay. There were rival gangs (he'd pay one to keep the others off our backs and, when they became too weak, switch his patronage), as well as three different precincts of constables. The amount of money that it cost to buy the freedom and safety of his crew ate up almost everything they stole. But so long as they never got caught, they were allowed to live without resorting to prostitution, begging or selling body parts. Nobody in the crew of the Black Galleon ever doubted they were getting the deal of a lifetime.

'No gang of thieves in a city this big survives without paying the rent,' Arissa had explained my first night in the galleon. 'Rich people don't appreciate the fine art of thievery, except when it's employed to their benefit.'

That happened far more often than I would've ever imagined. Priceless, one-of-a-kind jewellery tends to be hard to come by, as are family heirlooms and embarrassing docu-ments that could upset political ambitions. Many a noble was quite certain such knick-knacks would look better on their mantles than on those of their rivals. When a nobleman, through various intermediaries referred through less savoury acquaintances, offered one of these jobs to Rudger, he called it a 'custom'.

'Arissa and Teigriz, you got a custom.'

Rudger was pretty much the only one who called me 'Teigriz'. At first I thought he might fancy me a little and didn't want to call me 'Rat Girl' like everyone else. Then Arissa had explained that Rudger used to keep a pet rat before it died, and its name was – you guessed it – Teigriz.

Everyone on the deck – that's what they called the big basement cellar – turned to gawp at us. Even Rudger, nose buried in the big ledger he kept, looked surprised. 'I don't recall putting that in there.'

'That's because I saved you the trouble,' Arissa said.

There was a hush on deck. Nobody messed with Rudger's ledger.

'You makin' a play?' he asked.

Everybody knew one day somebody was going to try to take over Rudger's position as head of the gang. He wasn't in much of a position to fight back, so it all came down to whether someone recruited enough of us onto their side to take the job from him.

'No play,' Arissa said. 'Just saving you the trouble.'

Now everyone was whispering, asking each other if they knew anything about this 'custom'. Saving Rudger the 'trouble' meant he would have deniability if the job went bad. It meant whatever happened, Arissa was accepting all the consequences personally, and neither Rudger nor anyone else in the Black Galleon gang would come save her.

Or me.

'You took a custom for us and never asked me?'

The tall girl shrugged. 'Nobody said you have to come along.'

That was a lie. Wherever Arissa went, I followed. I was a piss-poor thief, as it turned out. On most jobs I was Arissa's lookout. That's because I wasn't a particularly good pickpocket, second-story girl, clubber, or just about any of the other subspecialties of our profession. Oh, and I was a lousy liar.

I wasn't useless though. I knew mathematics almost as well as Rudger (which meant other gang members would come to me to make sure they weren't getting shorted). I could read and write better than him too. The most useful of my talents, however, was that I could teach the other kids the proper forms of address for the various levels of nobility and how to bow, curtsy or kiss a hand depending on the occasion. Now that I think of it, Master Phinus's lessons in comportment turned out to be remarkably useful training for a thief.

'Okay,' Rudger said, waving the rest of the crew to silence. 'You and Teigriz are on your own with this, right?'

Arissa nodded.

'Then I've got just one question. Is this job a shiver?'

Shiver. Now there was one of the words of this business you rarely heard even around the Black Galleon. That's because shivering isn't usually a job for thieves.

'Did you just sign us up to commit a murder?' I whispered to Arissa.

The tall girl tilted her hat back on her head, looked down on me and grinned. 'What's it going to be, Rat Girl? You in or you out?'

16

The Shiver

'Since when are we assassins?' I hissed at Arissa.

Problem was, her longer legs meant she was already ten feet ahead of me, taking the stairs down to the dormitory two at a time and leaving me in the dusty darkness of the sloping passageway.

'Stop!' I said.

She didn't. Arissa never stopped for anybody. But she did slow down a little so I could catch up. I felt like she was always doing that for me – slowing down so I wouldn't get left behind.

Arissa wasn't necessarily the best thief or fighter in the gang (though, come to think of it, I couldn't name anybody better). What really set her apart was that she didn't *need* anybody. She had the skills and the smarts to get by in just about any situation. What she didn't know, she covered up so well you'd think she was an expert. I once saw her smile and nod her way through an entire conversation with a visiting Berabesq cleric, waiting for me to finally get up the nerve to use one of her short razor-knives to slice his purse, and only later did she reveal she didn't know a word of Berabesq.

The rest of the Black Galleon crew, whether the big, brutish ones like Petal who, without a gang to back him up, was prone to getting roughed up by bigger, more brutal thugs, or the clever ones like Rudger, who kept Petal out of trouble but couldn't protect himself from him, wouldn't last a day without the gang.

Me? I just needed Arissa.

This past year of living outside the law had been one of the safest and most comfortable of my entire life. I got to eat twice a day, every day. I slept in the same room each night, and because Arissa was always in the cot next to mine, it meant I *actually* slept. Best I could tell I was fourteen years old, and while I was still skinny, I no longer looked like a walking skeleton. On one of the upper floors of the old sail-cloth factory, Rudger had gotten some of the crew to bring in a tub. He even managed to convince the building's true owner to arrange for a partial diversion of one of the local aqueducts. That meant we each got to bathe at least once a week. I no longer got rashes all over my chest. Sometimes, when I was passing a mirror, I'd even stop and look.

I guess I'm telling you all this so that you understand why, when I caught up to Arissa and finally answered her question of whether I was in or out on this job, my response was, 'If you're in, I'm in.'

I doubt Sir Gervais and Sir Rosarite would've been proud of me. But my real parents – the ones who'd had to dangle there, trapped in a Jan'Tep lightshaper's spell before he tore them apart? They would've understood.

'So who's the client?' I asked.

Arissa resumed her march down the passageway. 'Let's just say, somebody . . . important.'

Cryptic, but that wasn't unusual.

'What about the target?'

'A scholar of some kind. Probably one of those Gitabrian theoreticians. Convinced our client to pay him to predict the outcome of certain highly speculative investments.'

'The investments failed?'

Arissa grinned. 'Not for the scholar. He bet against the client and made a fortune.'

We came out of the passage into what everyone called the crew deck but was really a tower whose floors had all collapsed to form a single rocky pit in the centre. Galleries with narrow ledges ran the circumference of the tower, each one segmented off into rooms with varying degrees of structural integrity.

The room Arissa and I shared was on what would've been the topmost floor. She liked it because it was private. Years ago, someone had fastened a fifty-foot-long rope to the ceiling. She'd carry the end up the ladder with her and when she left our room in the morning she could swing down from it and come to a skidding stop right at the mouth of the passage leading out of the tower.

In the year I'd lived in the Black Galleon, I'd never once dared swing down from that rope.

'You sure you're up for this job?' she asked after we'd both climbed the ladders to the fourth-level ledge. She hooked the bottom end of the rope to a broken iron ring embedded in the wall outside our chamber.

'I've seen plenty of death,' I replied. 'Probably more than you.'

Arissa dug out her pack from under her cot, so I knelt down to retrieve my own. I was quite proud of it: dark brown leather almost the colour of my coat, with twin shoulder straps – unusual, but convenient when you needed both hands free for climbing. The buckles were hidden under leather flaps, so they didn't reflect any light. I'd bought it the day after I'd received my share of our first take. Oh, and if paying for something with stolen money sounds strange, it turns out thieves are incredibly superstitious about such things, and not even Arissa would've let me work with her if I'd swiped it.

'Big difference between watching someone die and being the one who kills them,' she said, stuffing an eighteen-inch iron pry bar into her pack.

'When Met'astice murdered Sir Gervais and Sir Rosarite, I took her smallsword and hunted him down. I would've killed him if –'

She shook her head and smirked, busying herself with her packing.

'What?'

'Nothing.'

'It's not "nothing". You're snickering at me.'

She stuffed her bandolier of star-shaped steel blades into her pack. She'd had them custom-made. 'Handles on throwing knives are just wasted weight,' she'd told me after I'd sliced my finger just picking one up by the triangular point. 'If you can't throw a proper blade without cutting yourself, get used to carrying a club like every other clumsy thug in town.'

She closed her pack up and lay it on her lap as she sat back on her cot. 'I've listened to you recount the great saga of the little Mahdek girl who stalked a Jan'Tep mage in the rain and came within a hair's breadth of stabbing him through the belly with a broken smallsword more than once. It's a nice story, except you *didn't* stab him through the belly, just like you *didn't* stab Petal in the throat when you had the chance. Now you have to live your life hanging around me just to keep him from throttling you next time nobody's around.'

That's not why I hang around you, I wanted to say, but all that came out was, 'You don't understand.'

'What I understand, Rat Girl, is if you'd wanted to kill him, you would've, just like if you'd truly wanted to kill that Jan'Tep mage of yours, he'd be dead right now.'

'Don't call me that,' I said.

'What?'

'Don't call me Rat Girl.'

I'm not sure why it bothered me so much. I barely even noticed now when other people called me by that name. But when Arissa said it, I felt . . . cold inside.

'Then pick another name,' she said.

'Mahdek don—'

She threw up her hands. 'I know, I know. "A Mahdek doesn't choose their name, their name comes to them, and then they get up in front of the whole clan and declare it, and everybody throws a big party and dances around like idiots."'

'That's not fair.'

She rose from the bed and tossed her pack over her shoulder. 'You know what I think, Rat Girl? I think you haven't chosen your own name because it's safer that way. You *like* being a nobody, because that way you never have to take responsibility for being *somebody*. That's why you didn't kill Petal even though you knew he'd come after you. That's why you didn't kill that Jan'Tep mage when you had the chance.'

'You're wrong,' I said. It was all I could do not to scream at her. 'You weren't there! You don't know what—'

111

She walked out the big hole in the wall that served as the door to our room. 'Maybe not. Guess we'll find out tonight.'

'What? How?'

She unhooked the rope from the loop and wound it around her left arm. 'Don't be scared, Rat Girl. I'll have your back.'

'What's that supposed to mean?'

Her only response was a wink as she stepped back to the very edge of the stone overhang above the pit fifty feet below.

'Wait . . . You're telling me the client expects *me* to murder this Gitabrian scholar who ripped him off?'

'Can't imagine he cares one way or another, so long as the job gets done.'

'So you're putting this on me just to prove I don't have what it takes to kill?'

'Never said you didn't have what it takes. Only that you've waited too long to decide who you are. After tonight, one way or another, you'll be ready to choose your name.'

With only one hand on the rope, she pushed off backwards, waving at me with her free hand as she swung through the air.

'Why are you doing this to me?' I called out to her.

She hadn't even reached the ground when she shouted back, 'Because that scholar? He's not Gitabrian. He's Jan'Tep.'

17

Ill Omens

The elders among my people used to pride themselves on their ability to stand at a crossroads, look one way, then the next, and pronounce which path led to peace and abundance, and which to violence and heartache. Of all the elders in our clan, Old Mamtha was by far the most confident in her prognostications.

'See how the western wind whispers to us?' she'd ask, eyes closed, outstretched hands shaking as if she were caught up in some mystical trance. 'It says, "Come to me, and know solace."'

She'd then spin a hundred and eighty degrees clockwise and gesticulate wildly as if suffering a seizure. She'd fall to her knees, arms flailing this way and that as she moaned, 'The east wind! The east wind warns of blood and fire waiting for us in that direction!'

Okay, first off, you can't have both a west wind *and* an east wind at the same time. Second, it never made sense to me why Old Mamtha had such prominence in our clan, given none of her conversations with the various winds ever provided any warnings of Jan'Tep war covens coming to slaughter us. You'd figure the winds would've considered such details pertinent.

So I never had much respect for Old Mamtha – nor anyone else, really – who claimed insight into which paths led to refuge and which ones to disaster. How then was I so sure the path I was on that night with Arissa was going to ruin everything?

'Keep up,' she said, disappearing into the narrow gap between two old buildings known in these parts as the lawman's lock, because constables never patrolled the impoverished and rundown neighbourhoods on the other side.

My Mahdek ancestors believed all great architecture must weave in and around the natural landscape. It's not like we all slept under trees and foraged for nuts and berries, either; we lived in cities. Beautiful, gleaming cities. But those cities flowed within and around forests and mountains. Instead of building dams, we criss-crossed rivers with bridges. Instead of cutting down ancient trees, we built our houses between them, our courtyards were sheltered by their canopies. And when one of our cities grew as far as the surrounding landscape could accommodate, young clans would leave in search of new places to start new cities.

I sometimes wondered if the Daroman people looked upon their own settlements with that same sense of wonder and pride. Perhaps the wholesale razing of forests, the unearthing of every tree root for miles around, the excavation of every rock that committed the unpardonable sin of rising above the perfectly flat streets and alleys their architects envisioned was, to them, bringing order to a chaotic universe. Perhaps they believed that nature was aware of its own imperfections and had created human beings to shape it according to a formerly hidden magnificence.

If so, somebody had to explain slums to me.

'No Jan'Tep would ever be caught dead in a ghetto like this,' I informed Arissa as we skulked down the unpaved alley known as Weeper's Row, past tenements built over decades, one on top of the other until the whole block appeared to teeter precariously, just waiting for someone to pull out a single brick before the whole mess came tumbling down.

Arissa took a sharp right turn beneath a granny bridge. These were ungainly attachments, made from rows of wood planks and ropes bolted to the outsides of windows to create extra rooms – usually for aging grandparents – that clung like pustules to the sides of buildings. Soon those living in apartments on the other side of the alley would get the same idea, and before long these two unstable extensions would sag against each other, somewhat ingeniously keeping both from collapsing over time.

'The scholar's hiding from our client, stupid,' she said sharply. 'Probably figures he can hole up here awhile until one of his Jan'Tep friends can help sneak him out of the city.'

That sounded reasonable enough, unless you'd ever actually met a Jan'Tep and had even the slightest comprehension of how disgusting they found other nations – and especially the lower classes of what they considered barbaric cultures. Also, like good Old Mamtha with all her shaking and flailing about, I had a bad feeling about this.

We finally stopped at a battered door with rusted hinges at the back of a four-storey tenement whose roof had visibly caved in some time ago. I tried to slow my breathing and steady myself. Arissa was watching me through narrowed eyes.

'Something the matter?'

I shook my head. There was nothing to substantiate my

unease, save that I was afraid I didn't have the nerve to do what we'd come here for.

'Maybe you should skip this job? Head back to the Black Galleon and I'll meet you there when it's done.'

I'd never known Arissa to offer *anyone* the chance to walk away once the job was agreed.

'Are you going soft on me?' I asked. 'Or do you just think I can't handle what happens next?'

I was expecting some clever quip or dismissive snort, but she just held my gaze. She looked serious. Sad, almost. 'Back in our room . . . I shouldn't have said those things. What we're here to do . . . I don't want to see you get hurt, inside or out. That's all.'

More hesitation, more anxiousness, was packed into those two sentences than Arissa had ever shown me in the year I'd known her. She took responsibility for no one but herself. If you tagged along and got hurt, that was your choice and your problem.

'Since when do you concern yourself with other people?' I asked, suddenly suspicious. 'You remind me practically every morning that we're "colleagues in crime", not friends. You've got no use for friends, remember?'

She shrugged, trying to dismiss my accusation, but there was a softness in her gaze when our eyes met again. 'Maybe I just never . . . You know what? Forget it.' She slipped her pack off her shoulder and opened it to retrieve a small tin flask which she uncapped to drip oil on the door's hinges so they wouldn't creak. 'You coming or not?'

18

The Client

Once inside the rundown building we padded through dark corridors and stairwells enveloped in the fog of human stench and decay. Too many people all packed too close together, their respective miseries oozing into those narrow spaces between, like mortar bonding them in place.

The floors were treacherous, with nails sticking out of the planking that no one had bothered to hammer back down, or perhaps left that way intentionally to create a more treacherous landscape for any intruders. The entire hallway sagged in the middle, and sometimes doors to individual apartments wouldn't close properly because the frames were warped by moisture and rot.

Watching Arissa weave her way through those hazards was enthralling. Her creeping steps were like a mysterious and exotic dance, with every crouch, hop or side-skip part of a story she was telling. It wasn't just that she could move so quietly either; sometimes there were people slumped in the corners of those hallways and stairwells who might regard two young women alone as prey. But all it took was a glance – sometimes paired with the gleam of one of her star-shaped throwing blades – to send those who would attack us scurrying back to the shadows.

We made quick progress up to the fourth floor, most of which had been crushed under the collapsed roof. We had to climb over bits of rubble to get to the north-west corner and the door of what had to be the only apartment left intact. Arissa stepped aside to make room for me, and I removed the folded linen cloth that contained my lock picks from my bags.

I was actually a fair hand with locks. Slender fingers are an advantage for holding the steel picks and rakes, of course, but lock-picking is all about sensitivity, and my fingertips could feel the slightest shift in tension inside the mechanisms. The problem with locks like these, though, wasn't opening them, but doing so quietly.

Arissa gave three quick taps on my shoulder to warn that I was taking too long. She was just about the most impatient person I'd ever met. Soon enough I had the bolt turned and I motioned for her to oil the hinges outside the door.

Inside, the apartment was larger than most one finds in a building like this, suggesting the top floor had once been reserved for wealthier denizens of the neighbourhood, back before it had gone to ruin. A long inner hallway connected a kitchen, dining room, two indoor privies, a tiled chamber with an actual bath, and three bedrooms. All of these were shrouded in darkness, lit only by moonlight peeking through the gaps in the plastered slatted ceiling. Only one door was closed, this one at the far end of the hall.

Arissa led the way, our steps slow, silent, careful. But before we reached that door, she stopped and looked down at my fingers that were wrapped around her arm. Her eyes came up to mine, seeking an explanation. I hadn't even realised I'd grabbed her. How could I make her understand that I found myself like one of those elders of my clan, standing at a crossroads, looking at two paths and suddenly knowing that one led to calamity and sorrow?

When I was seven years old, I'd once asked my mother how the elders could possibly make such predictions. Was it magic?

She'd smiled and said it *was* magic, of a sort, just not the kind Mahdek shamans used to perform, nor that of the Jan'Tep.

'See those horse tracks Old Mamtha's staring at on the road headed east? See those peculiar hoofprints in the dirt? Those come from the kind of horseshoes made for the royal Daroman marshals service.'

Young as I was then, even I'd heard about the famed long-riding marshals who would pursue a fugitive even into the depths of other countries. Wherever those grim, grey-coated riders went, violence and bloodshed always followed.

'There are a whole lot of those tracks,' I said.

My mother had nodded. 'And that's how Old Mamtha knows there's a whole lot of trouble waiting down that road.'

Divination, I came to understand, wasn't about seeing into the future the way our elders sometimes liked to make us young ones believe. It came from experience – from having seen enough of the world and its ways that you recognised the signs and patterns that told you what was waiting at the end of a road.

But it wasn't in the shuffling footprints in the dust on the floor of that broken-down apartment that I found the signs foretelling my destruction. It was written in the cloying, damp air, whispered in a faint whiff of strawberries and mint outside that bedroom at the end of the hall.

'Come, my little knight,' said Met'astice from behind the closed door as if he could smell my presence too. 'Time you and I made an end of things at last.'

19

The Target

Of all the forms of Jan'Tep magic, silk was reputed to be the rarest. It was also the one that terrified me the most. Silk spells can be used to violate thoughts, infiltrate the mind with maddening visions that leave the victim tearing at their own eyeballs. Silk spells could make a person do things they didn't want to do.

'Let's go,' Arissa whispered urgently.

She'd heard Met'astice's words from behind the door, and no matter how bold the criminal, when you find out the job's been blighted from the start, you turn and walk away.

Only I couldn't.

A cough emerged from the closed room. To me it was like one of those siren songs Gitabrian sailors talk about, echoing in my head, summoning me. My right foot rose from the floor, drifted forward a few inches, then stepped back down. My left foot followed.

How can you tell that something you're about to do is by your own choice? What's the difference between a thought that's been with you for two entire years – a face you can't forget; a yearning to find yourself within killing distance of them, so strong that it might as well be love – versus one implanted only seconds ago with silk magic? Would it really feel any different?

I didn't know the answer to that question. Not then, not after it was all over. I only knew that I had to enter that room. I had to see my tormentor again.

As I approached, the door swung open of its own accord. It might've been some petty breath or iron cantrip Met'astice had cast or just the result of sagging floorboards that buckled the door frame a fraction when I stepped on them. An eerie glow lit the room, coming from a sphere about the size of an orange set on the small side table next to what would've been a magnificent lord's bed were it not covered in cobwebs and plaster dust. The man who lay beneath the covers was no lord.

'My knight,' he said softly.

There was nothing in his tone to warn me whether his words were mocking or sincere, save that nothing about Met'astice had ever suggested he held someone like me in anything more than dismissive contempt.

'Rat Girl . . .' Arissa warned.

I glanced down at her right hand, which held a pair of her sharpened steel stars. Fast as she was, it was hard to imagine she couldn't have nailed Met'astice right between the eyes before he could've cast a spell, but, like me, she was scanning the room for traps. Jan'Tep mages rarely left themselves so unprotected.

'Did she just call you "Rat Girl"?' Met'astice asked, cheeks bulging as if he were swallowing a frog. Suddenly he burst out laughing. The laughter set him coughing and the coughing became tiny droplets of blood dribbling down the front of his robes.

He didn't seem to notice, or, if he did, to care.

'They call you Rat Girl?' he asked again. 'Truly?'

It struck me as a petty point on which to taunt me, but Met'astice was oddly enthralled by the notion. 'So that aspect worked,' he mused. 'How fascinating. I must make a no—'

His right hand reached out clumsily to the side table as if searching for that massive leather-bound book of his into which he'd written down all his notes during the torments he and Shadow Falcon had performed on me. But there was no book on the table, and instead his arm knocked over the glow-glass ball, which rolled across the floor.

I stopped it with my foot and picked it up.

'The quality and strength of the light is a reflection of the mage's will,' I said to Arissa. 'See how it flickers and dims. He doesn't have long.'

My voice sounded cold. Distant. An observer standing high atop a cliff as a ship ran aground on the rocks below. All the anger I'd kept bottled inside, waiting for the day when at last I might hope to avenge myself upon this all-powerful lord magus of the Jan'Tep, and now all I felt was . . . empty.

Met'astice pounded his bedding with his bony fists. 'Do not speak as if I cannot hear you!' he growled, but that only set him to coughing again.

'You're dying,' I observed.

He wiped at the bloody spittle with the sleeve of his robe. In my life I'd never seen a Jan'Tep mage look so undignified.

'I've been dying since I met you,' he said, bowing his head just slightly as if this were some grand acknowledgement he was bestowing upon me. A knighthood perhaps.

'Sir Rosarite's blade,' I said.

123

He reached down and patted the emaciated stomach beneath his robes. 'The wound never healed properly. It took me too long to get back to my apprentice.' He chuckled softly. 'Like all young lads, he was far more diligent in practising war magic than healing spells.'

My fingers reached up to scratch at the collar of my shirt. 'Where is he?'

Though Met'astice haunted my nightmares, I knew now that Falcon was by far the more dangerous of the two. He'd be at least nineteen now, a full mage, in even greater command of his magical abilities. Probably well on his way to becoming a lord magus himself.

Met'astice spread his hands in helpless surrender. 'My faithful falcon spread his wings and flew away long ago. His commitment to our research was regrettably half-hearted.'

'Half-hearted?'

For three days Shadow Falcon had kept me in that awful cave, strapped to that table. He'd cast spell after spell as he pierced the skin around my neck with needles dripping molten metallic inks. Not once had he refused Met'astice's orders. Not once had he tried to help me, save only to ask if he could use silk magic to put me to sleep so my cries and struggles wouldn't interfere with his concentration.

'I don't blame the boy however,' Met'astice went on, as if Arissa and I were his private secretaries and he was dictating his memoirs. 'The young are obsessed with making themselves powerful, the old with what service that power can deliver to their people.'

Arrogant son of a—

'Rat Girl, let's go,' Arissa said under her breath, grabbing my arm. 'The mage must've paid off the client to hire me, which means he had to have known you were my partner, which means this whole thing was a set-up to get you here.'

She was right of course; we needed to get out of here. I tried to heed her warning, to turn around and walk out the door with her – I really did. And, for just an instant, I almost managed it. I almost walked away from Met'astice, lord magus of the Jan'Tep. But he made me stay, and it didn't even require silk magic, just a simple request.

'Tell me your name.'

I froze.

'What?'

The mage pressed his hands down into the rotting bedclothes, pushing himself up shakily to a seated position. 'Your name. The snarling thief at your side refers to you as Rat Girl.'

'That's just a nickname. It's not my real na—'

'Then you should have no difficulty telling me your real name.'

'Why are you—'

'Come now,' he said, the flicker of a grin creeping up at the corner of his mouth. 'You must be – what? Fourteen by now? Don't all Mahdek take their true name by thirteen?'

'It's not . . . I don't have a clan to stand before an—'

'You think we Jan'Tep are ignorant of the ways of our enemies? A Mahdek chooses their name alone. It matters not one jot whether they present themselves to their clan or not.' His eyes, weak and teary, nonetheless bore into mine. 'Tell me your name.'

'I . . . I haven't chosen one.'

He released his gaze, nodded to himself and smiled. 'How encouraging. I honestly didn't expect such a promising result.'

Arissa's words back in our room at the Black Galleon returned to me.

'I think you haven't chosen your own name because it's safer that way. You like being a nobody.'

But I *didn't* like being nobody.

'You're trying to confuse me,' I said, but Met'astice only shook his head as if I were a disappointing pupil.

'Nonsense. You lived with those two Tristian barbarians for half a year. Half a year! You expect me to believe they called you "Rat Girl" all that time?'

'Of course not – they loved me!'

He snorted. 'They *loved* you? Yet these two so-called knights offered you no name, never encouraged you to choose your own? How did they call you to dinner, or ask you to clean your room? Did they whistle for you the way one summons the family dog?'

'They . . . They called me . . .'

Darling. Sweetheart. Little one. Brave one . . . But those aren't names, are they?

Again Arissa tugged at my arm. 'I'll give you all the names you want, Rat Girl. But let's get out of here.'

But I couldn't move. Met'astice, weak, bedridden, bereft of his magic, held me captive with nothing more than his words. 'Even a Mahdek child younger than thirteen, when taking on the responsibilities of an adult or after suffering some great trauma, will choose their name early. You stalked me through an entire city! Held a Jan'Tep's life in your hands.' He slapped a hand on his belly. 'Aimed your dead foster mother's blade right here. Was that not a feat worthy of something so small as a name?'

'I didn't . . . There wasn't time to—'

126

'You called yourself a knight, do you remember? Knights have names, don't they? Shall I dub you Sir Rat Girl?'

'Don't call me that!' I screamed.

Met'astice laughed as he leaned back against the grime-encrusted headboard of the bed. 'The answer to the question you work so hard never to ask yourself is actually quite simple. You did choose your name, long ago. You just can't remember it.'

All of a sudden I felt so sick, the muscles in my stomach clenching so tightly, that I couldn't even stand up straight.

'Stop whatever you're doing to her,' Arissa warned, showing him the steel stars. 'Or I'll send one of these into each of your eyes.'

'Me?' Met'astice asked innocently. 'I'm just a sick old man who crawled into this bed to die. I'm not doing anything to her . . . any more.'

I looked up from my nauseous dizziness to see him tap a slender finger just at the right side of his throat.

Unbidden, my own hand rose and touched the sigil marking the identical spot on my own neck. It felt cold to the touch.

'We called it a collar,' Met'astice said, as if he were beginning a class and Arissa and I were his dutiful students, 'yet in truth it's so much more. Each sigil constitutes its own experimental procedure, with its own purpose.' Again he tapped that same spot on his neck. 'This one was to see if we could impair aspects of the subject's sense of self, their awareness of who they are. At the time I suspected it was too complex an aspect of the mind to target with magic. I see now that we achieved a partial success, though not in the way we intended.' Again he looked around as if searching for his book.

127

'Why?' Arissa demanded. 'Why would you want to do that to someone? What purpose would it serve?'

Absently Met'astice replied, 'On its own, on a single Mahdek girl? Nothing. Though the curious implications the results suggest are more than sufficient justification for the effort. However, if we could similarly collar enough Mahdek, over time – perhaps as little as a single generation – we could eliminate from human history the very idea of their existence. We wouldn't need to keep risking the lives of our young mages to hunt them down, wouldn't need to fear their blood mixing with that of other nations. They would simply . . . be forgotten.'

Arissa turned to me. 'Either you kill him, or I'm doing it. Now.'

'That's what he wants,' I said, looking at the old man smiling at me from the bed. 'That's what he brought me here to do.'

He smiled warmly, rewarding me with a wagging finger. 'Clever. I knew you were clever right from the start. And brave too. You know, I do believe had things turned out differently, you might very well have become a knight, just like those two barbarians who took you in.'

'You stole that future from me.'

'No, my dear, I stole *every* future from you. Do you understand now? Everything you do, every life you try to build –' he traced a line across his neck with his finger – 'will come apart in your hands. A tapestry whose weaving unravels over and over.'

'You're wrong, old man,' Arissa said. 'She's a thief now, with a crew and a home and . . . and me.'

Had I known, all these months, how badly I'd wanted to hear those words? How much I wanted a family? A place in the world? But Met'astice didn't even acknowledge that she had

128

spoken. 'I brought something for you, Sir Knight.' He pointed to a slender black wooden case, about four feet long and six inches high and wide on the floor at the end of the bed.

'Don't,' Arissa warned. 'It's a trap.'

'No trap,' Met'astice said. 'A gift. Something you left behind.'

I walked slowly over to the black case and knelt down before it. The training I'd learned from Rudger, Arissa and the others in the Black Galleon guided me through the next steps. First I inhaled deeply, searching for any aroma of one of the contact poisons that could be painted onto a box or safe. All I smelled was the moist decay of the room all around me, and the stench of Met'astice, who probably hadn't left his bed for several days. Next my fingers traced the contours of the brass clasp, then the thin line between the lid and the base, searching for any threads or unusual grooves. I opened the clasp slowly, a fraction at a time, listening for the first hint of a coiled spring beginning to release. Nothing. It was a simple, if well made, wooden box. And inside was an equally simple, equally well-crafted smallsword.

Could Met'astice have known that this mockery of a present was, in fact, a gift more precious than I could ever have hoped for? Sir Rosarite's sword. A tangible, real thing that had belonged to her, that her fingers had gripped a thousand times. When I grasped the hilt, it was like she was holding my hand again. Yet for all that, the smallsword was not as I'd left it in that cave.

'It cost a surprising amount of money to have the silly thing repaired,' Met'astice said. Again he patted his belly. 'But at least you'll know both halves of the blade are reunited.'

I stared at the sword, my eyes travelling all the way from the pommel to the tip. Even without touching it, I could see the blade had been sharpened to perfection. How could a mere object, given to me by an enemy, fill me with such . . . longing?

'It's time,' Met'astice said. 'I have given you a gift, and now you will render me a service.'

I walked to the front of the bed, placed the tip of the sword over his belly. He shook his head, took hold of the razor-sharp blade and moved it to his throat. His hands bled where the edge cut into his palms. 'Faster this way.'

'Why?' I asked.

I was more than willing to grant his last wish, if only to be absolutely certain the job was done once and for all, yet a Jan'Tep mage had any number of easier ways to end his own life.

'The experiment must continue,' he replied.

'What does—'

His eyes flared with the summoning of his magic as his right hand came away from the blade, fingers twitching through the somatic form of a spell, then he shouted, 'Falcon! Save me! The girl has come to—'

But he never finished that sentence. The sword in my hand shuddered as the tip slid all the way through his throat and out the back, lodging itself in the bed's wooden headboard. I hadn't even moved. Met'astice had yanked the blade into his own neck.

'Why?' I asked.

I thought he had to be dead, but death isn't so quick even when it's certain. His mouth opened, blood dribbled down his chin. When he tried to speak, no sound came out, but I saw his answer in the trembling movements of his lips.

The experiment must continue.

20

The Experiment

Arissa tried to drag me away from the bed, but I didn't move. It was as if my hand was glued to the hilt of the sword that now pinned Met'astice's corpse to his final resting place. She was shouting at me too, but I couldn't hear anything over the buzzing in my ears, the tickling sensation of bees squirming around inside.

'What have you done?'

I recognised that voice – could almost smell him as if he were standing right next to me. My eyes itched. He was looking through me at Met'astice's corpse.

'You murdered him!'

I didn't. He ki—

I felt a stinging in my cheek as if he'd slapped me. 'You're holding the blade, damn you! He was an old man, no threat to you!'

Despite everything, I almost laughed at that.

'His magic had all but faded.' Falcon's voice thudded in my head. 'I abandoned him, told him I wouldn't help with his experiments any more. All you had to do was leave him be!'

'Rat Girl, we've got to get out of here,' Arissa said, yanking my arm so hard this time that the blade pulled free of

Met'astice's neck with a wet slurp that sent blood spurting over his body.

'I left you alone, Mahdek bitch,' Falcon swore. 'You could've lived your miserable little life, playing the rogue with that band of petulant child thieves, and never seen nor heard from me again. Why did you have to hunt him down?'

Met'astice's words came back to me, as if already he were haunting me.

The experiment must continue.

'You'll pay for this,' Falcon said, his words more than just a buzzing in my head now. They were a promise. Not the idle boast of a boy, but the oath of a man.

One of the sigils on my neck burned – didn't sting, but *burned.* I cried out. The smallsword fell from my hand.

Arissa caught me, and helped me down to my knees. 'Tell me what to do!' she said. 'Tell me how to help you!'

Judging by the way she looked at me, I must've looked pretty terrible. But in her desperate, frightened stare I saw something else too – the tiniest flicker, like a spark that ignites when flint strikes steel in the rain, only to die away again instantly.

She loves me, I thought dully.

Shadow Falcon's voice came to me one last time before he left me there in that room. '*Let my master's experiments continue then, until there is nothing left of you for me to hate.*'

The sigil stopped burning, but I could still feel its presence. My fingers scratched desperately at it, cutting into my skin. Arissa grabbed my wrist, begging me to stop, but it was too late. The curse etched into my flesh that made decent people distrust me had grown into something far, far worse.

Arissa's hand fell away, and the fondness that had been in her eyes an instant before was extinguished.

'Rat Girl,' was all she said.

Always before that name had carried a kind of gentle teasing, a joke between the two of us. Now it dripped with disgust and oozed with hatred.

'Arissa, no . . .'

I wanted to believe she'd changed somehow – that she was under some kind of spell. But she was still Arissa. Confident. Mischievous. Daring. The only difference was that in her entire life she'd never been so close to something that disgusted her this much.

'Get away from me,' she said, not shouting, just letting out a low snarl, the way a dog does before it leaps on a rat.

'Please,' I begged, 'it's me. I'm the same per—'

Her hand shot out, grabbed my throat. She rose to her feet and I was hauled up with her. I could see her eyes moving over the features of my face, as if she were trying to reconcile her fury with her memories of the past year. At last she pulled me close, as if the scent of me both repelled and fascinated her. 'It was a fun game, for a while, pretending to take you under my wing. But I'm bored of it now. *You* bore me.'

She let go, and my legs failed me. I crumpled to the floor, crying, begging, my shaking hands reaching for her ankle to keep her from leaving. She didn't even bother to kick them away.

'You're dead meat in this city,' she said. 'Show up at the Black Galleon again, and I'll string you up by a rope myself – that is if Petal or the others don't get to you first.'

I wailed like a mad girl, knowing I should fight back

somehow, but with no weapons to fight with. For a time, I knelt there, rocking back and forth, listening to the soft pad of Arissa leaving me behind in that filthy room filled with decay and death and the end of my life. Leaving me alone, with no one for company but a dead Jan'Tep mage.

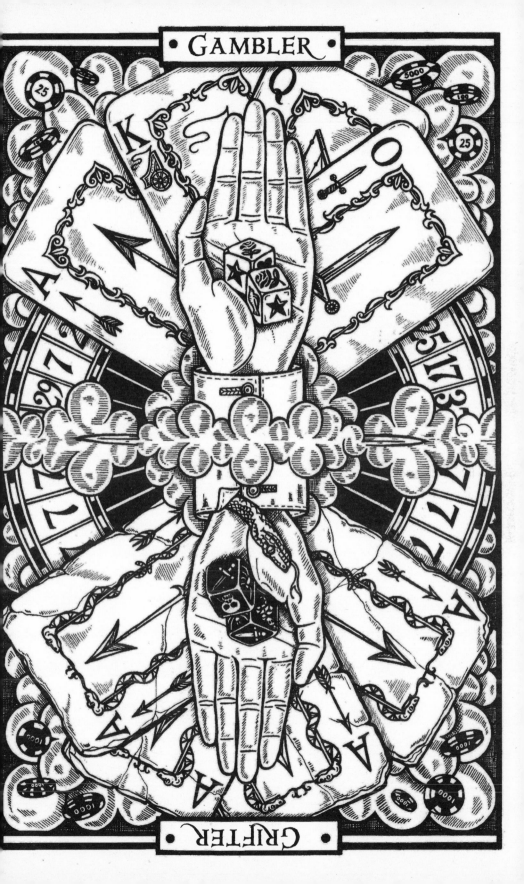

The Gambler

A gambler walks the fine line between risk and recklessness, mastering the rules of each game to alter the odds in their favour. To journey as a gambler enables one to avoid the temptations of the thief's path. But when the desire to win overcomes the joy of doing so justly, the gambler resorts to deception, double-crossing and preying on the gullibility of others. The Journey of the Gambler is not the Way of the Argosi.

21

The Rules

Hours later, once the stench of Met'astice's corpse had overcome my capacity for grief, and the rising sun peeking through broken wood-slat windows had begun to awaken the denizens of that rundown tenement building to their daily groans and grunts and shuffling steps, some lingering sense of self-preservation forced me to my feet. I ran down hallways and stairwells, faster and faster as narrowing eyes all around me took notice of the young girl who'd invaded their territory the night before and was no longer accompanied by her taller and far deadlier companion.

I had a little money on me, some of which I spent on a long, leather tube bag of the sort architects and mapmakers use to hold their precious drawings. It came with a shoulder strap and served as a reasonably inconspicuous case for the smallsword that Met'astice had claimed was a gift, but was, in fact, payment for taking Arissa away from me forever.

'*You're dead meat in this city,*' she had warned me.

I believed her, and knew that, in her own way, that warning had been the last flicker of a friendship extinguished without either of us having a say in its demise.

I fled Domisa Pago forever, only realising as I passed through its gates hours later that the two years I'd spent in this city, first scurrying through its alleys as a beggar and later strutting along its avenues as a professional thief and member of the Black Galleon gang, had been the longest I'd lived in any one place. Had that been why Met'astice sought me out before his death? Was my greatest crime not that I'd once tried to kill him, but that I'd refused to become what he wanted me to be: a filthy Mahdek, consigned to wander through the world like some condemned, restless spirit, never finding a place to call home?

If that was his aim, then in whatever afterworld the Jan'Tep went to, Met'astice of the House of Met, lord magus and dedicated scholar, must have been smiling as he looked down on me, for a ghost is what I became.

Shadow Falcon had promised to make me pay for his former master's death, and the young Jan'Tep mage proved as good as his word. He turned my life into a set of rules for a game I'd never asked to play and could not win.

Rule Number One? You will always be alone.

Until that night in the tenement in Domisa Pago, the mystical sigils he'd so painstakingly inscribed around my neck had fostered a sort of passive distaste in what he'd referred to as 'decent folk'. The more dignified and compassionate a person was, the less they wanted to be around me. This had made a certain amount of sense to me: had such a collar been imprinted on my skin when Sir Rosarite and Sir Gervais had found me in that cave while the Jan'Tep war coven were massacring my clan, the spells in the sigils would surely have caused them to leave me there to be slaughtered with the others.

But since Met'astice's death, Falcon had poured more and more of his own magic into the sigils from afar. Now, the kinder someone's nature, the more intensely they wanted to hurt me. Oh, at first they might take pity on the sad, emaciated girl they found wandering the long roads, but after a day or two – often just a few hours – a fury would ignite in them that had them chasing me away, hurling stones at my head and promising to commit such atrocities upon me that I sometimes felt bad for the shame they would feel once the fever passed and they were left only with the memories of the terrible things they'd said.

And I was left alone, sometimes weeping, sometimes screaming my own foul oaths at the world, but mostly missing Arissa.

I missed her lanky, unselfconscious posture; the mischievous look in her eyes; above all I missed the raw, unquenchable confidence in her smile. Sometimes I'd miss her so much that I'd try to emulate her ways. I'd pretend the sigils around my neck were a badge of honour, and walk down a crowded street as if I'd just bought the entire city. I never behaved that way for long, because it only made people dislike me even more. Life was easier for everybody if I kept my head down.

So that's what I did.

Over those next weeks and months, I learned to play by the rules Falcon had set for me. I made sure never to be around a person for more than a few hours, so that by the time they discovered how badly they wanted to kill me, I'd be long gone. A distasteful memory, soon forgotten. I was then free to make the acquaintance of someone new – a kindly old lady or stern roadside cleric or even a handsome boy taking his lunch in a park. I could get to know them, play on their generosity and then disappear from their lives before the first spark of loathing appeared in their eyes. Life became an endless sequence of con games and ephemeral relationships; of promising friendships begun and ended in a single afternoon; of love affairs that existed only in a few shy glances and my desperate need to imagine the sensation of another's touch that wouldn't end with their hands around my throat.

You can go mad this way.

I'm pretty sure I did.

But then came Rule Number Two: sometimes you'll wish you really were alone.

'Did you love him?' Falcon would ask sometimes with a buzzing in my ears, after I'd once again disappeared around a corner only to hide in the shadows of an alley as some new acquaintance wandered about calling the name I'd made up for myself that day. Marsa, Luvenia, Jubis, Andeja, Feriu—

No, that wasn't one of them, was it?

Falcon's laugh would flutter around my skull like a butterfly before he'd disappear once again.

But survival, I discovered, was a talent that gave birth to other skills. I learned to use Falcon's periodic taunts as a means to uncover the limits of his power over me. For example, sometimes I would hear from him twice in a single night, other times weeks or even months would pass in silence. This told me his visitations were no small matter, requiring either great concentration and solitude or perhaps some particular location, like a mage's sanctum, from which to perform the necessary spell.

142

I further noted that there was no correlation between the intensity or indignity of my own experiences – say, nearly dying at the hands of a healer I'd had to risk visiting when I was injured – and whether Falcon would mock me about the incident or even mention it at all. I inferred therefore that he was only infrequently seeing through my eyes, and thus – despite the implications in his subtle jibes – witnessed only fleeting snatches of my life.

'Did you like it when he asked to kiss you? Did it make your wretched little Mahdek heart beat quicker?'

I almost laughed out loud when he asked that of me, but kept my elation hidden from him. If he couldn't tell that I wasn't attracted to those boys then he didn't know my heart; he could hear those thoughts that took form in my mind when he was there, but not the feelings underneath. He could force me to live as a ghost, day by day losing any sense of connection to other human beings, never able to hold on to so much as a name I tried to give myself, always drifting from one place, one life, to another. But for every lock he would close around me, I would make of myself a new key to open it.

Rules. Games. I hadn't asked for any of them. But I was damned if I was going to let him win.

Rule Number One: you will always be alone.

Really, Falcon? Is that a leash you're holding, tied to the collar around my neck? Or does hatred bind you to me as much as your magic binds me to you? And what will happen when I find a way to follow this chain that links us back to your door?

Rule Number Two: sometimes you'll wish you were alone.

143

Will you even know my face when I walk into your home? Or will I be as a stranger to you, disguised so that recognition will come only when you see the glint of this blade your master returned to me, never expecting it would be your end as it was his?

Rule Number Three: every rule can be broken.

22

The Dog, the Horse
and the Squirrel Cat

The day I truly began to understand how to cheat at life was the day I learned to play poker. I'm not saying I suddenly discovered some supernatural aptitude for the game; in fact, I was a pretty lousy player – all those cards! And each one so pretty I'd get lost just staring at my hand instead of figuring out which one to play. I'd hang on to a card just because I found it prettier than the others, when I should've discarded it while I'd had the chance.

Anyway, I'm getting ahead of myself. One of the consequences of being untethered to other human beings is that the passage of time and the order of events lose any real meaning. During those long stretches when I wouldn't hear from Falcon, there was no one I could talk to who actually knew me. I tried to fill the gaps by talking to myself, but it turns out I'm not that great a conversationalist. I'd get so bored of hearing myself mumble that I'd lose track of what I'd started talking abou—

Wait. I've done it again, haven't I?

Okay, let's do this right: the most important day of my life began with a horse, a dog and a squirrel cat. There. That sounds better.

Have you ever *seen* a squirrel cat? Funny-looking critters. The Daroman call them *felinis arborica*, which sounds way too dignified for something that looks like a slightly tubby wildcat with a big bushy tail and weird furry flaps that extend from their front paws to their back feet. They can glide through the air if they start from a tall perch like a tree or a rooftop, and since they're pretty good climbers, they glide a lot.

Anyway, I was trudging past this roadside tavern in a small town that bordered the azure region of the Seven Sands. That's where the sand is kind of blue, and at night under the stars it's like you're walking on water. I'd been having a rough time of it lately, because never having any relationship that lasted longer than a few hours had taken its toll on my brain. It was getting harder and harder to pretend to be normal, and the last few people whose generosity I'd tried to play on had pretty much chased me away within minutes. Going days without eating a proper meal doesn't help either, and by then I was completely broke.

Anyway, I spied this guy on the other side of the road, walking his horse towards the tavern. A dog was running alongside. The dog wasn't all that big, but he wasn't some puny terrier either. Kind of in-between. He had this short, almost chocolate-and-silver fur that made him look sleek. Professional-like. His head swivelled left and right all the time, like he was keeping watch.

The man himself had a lanky, long-legged stride, and when he stopped to tether his horse to a wooden post outside the tavern I saw that everything about him was brown, from the russet frontier hat with the tan band around

146

the brim to the chestnut hair that tickled the collar of his sandy-beige linen shirt, partly obscured by an almost walnut-coloured suede vest. Gloves? Brown. Trousers? Brown. Well, dirt-coloured, but mostly from the dust and grit you pick up travelling the long roads. He wore brown leather boots without spurs, which told me he liked his horse.

The dog curled up beneath the horse like he was using it for shade from the hot sun. His owner pulled a silver canteen out from the right saddlebag, that he stuffed back inside after taking a drink and giving some to his dog before he sauntered into the tavern. By then I was practically dying of thirst. I wasn't going to try to steal it with the dog right there, just waiting to bark for his owner if anyone got too close. But I didn't know what else to do either, so I just sat underneath the awning of an empty shop on the other side of the street. There were a lot of them in that town. It was pretty poor, which didn't bode well for my chances of wheedling a meal out of anyone.

So I sat there waiting, and waited some more, not even sure what I was waiting for, except that I couldn't stop staring at the dog and the horse. How fine would it be to have your own horse to carry you wherever you wanted to go? And a faithful dog who could warn you anytime someone tried to sneak up on you while you were asleep? And then I started thinking about Rule Number One, and how I was pretty sure none of the sigils Met'astice and Falcon had imprinted around my neck would make animals hate me.

When you've got no family and no friends, a dog and a horse start to look like mighty fine companions.

My more immediate problem, though, was that I hadn't had anything to eat or drink in far too long. Sometimes when that happened, I'd start hallucinating. As I sat there in the dirt on the other side of the dusty street, I found myself imagining that the dog and I were having a conversation. We were negotiating over the terms of a contract in which he and the horse would come with me in exchange for various promises on my part. At least six steak bones per week and three walks per day. I'd have to provide a comfortable blanket for him to sleep on when we were out in the desert and I'd have a maximum of five years to get rich, because by then he'd want to retire and not have to watch over me all the time.

It's a deal, I told him in my dreamy state.

Marked, he said. Actually he woofed.

It was the bark that woke me up. I blinked the sleep and grit out of my eyes and looked across the street to see the dog was on his feet, head tilted to the sky as he barked at something on the roof of the tavern. I'd never seen a squirrel cat before, but during my short time in their lives, Sir Gervais and Sir Rosarite had insisted on me having a proper education, so I'd seen a picture of one in an old zoology book that they'd let me keep in my bedroom.

I really missed that bedroom. It wasn't big, but that made me appreciate it all the more. I felt warm and cocooned inside it, like I was . . .

I'm doing it again. Back to the dog and the squirrel cat.

The squirrel cat – I had a feeling it was a female, even though I had no way of knowing – was chittering and snarling at the dog, her fur a fiery orange with menacing black-and-crimson stripes. The dog, in turn, had the hackles up on the back of his neck and was growling back at her. The horse wasn't paying any attention to either of them.

I was afraid the two of them might get into a fight. I didn't

148

want to see either of them get hurt – not that there was anything I could do about it.

The threats went back and forth a while. Chitter. Bark. Snarl. Growl. After a while it stopped sounding to me like two animals trying to chase each other away and instead resembled two people having a debate. The barks got less agitated, the chitters less . . . *rude* is the only word I can think of. Finally the dog took two steps back, away from the tavern, and sat down on its haunches.

The squirrel cat watched him for a while, like she was making sure this wasn't a set-up, and then she leaped off the rooftop. The furry flaps between her front and back limbs caught the breeze and, just for an instant, she was this elegant flying creature. Noble, almost. Just as quickly, she brought her front and back paws in close to her body and dropped onto the horse's saddle. With her clever little claws she set about unbuckling the saddlebag on the horse's right flank. The dog gave a single bark. The squirrel cat looked over at him, then switched to the other saddlebag and opened that one instead. The zoology book I'd seen had illustrations of squirrel cat paws that showed them stealing things, and of course everyone says they're thieves by nature.

It was funny to watch the little bandit rummaging inside the saddlebag. She dug around until she gave this excited little chitter and pulled out a small package folded in cheesecloth. She laid it out on the horse's back, slow and careful like she was setting out a picnic. Inside was some kind of food. It might've been cheese, I guess, but it looked more like cookies or biscuits of some kind. The squirrel cat picked one up and sniffed at it excitedly. The dog barked and the squirrel cat started on him with the meanest snarl I'd ever heard, then stopped herself and, with obvious reluctance, tossed the first biscuit to the dog, who jumped up into the air to catch it in his teeth and swallowed it down with one gulp. He wagged his tail.

The squirrel cat tried to take a bite of the second one, only to narrowly avoid being shaken off the saddle by the horse, who settled when the squirrel cat ambled over to the top of its head and deposited a biscuit on the horse's tongue. Once the visibly irritated squirrel cat finally had her own biscuit, she tried to take her time, nibbling at the edges and then licking her lips. But soon she ate faster and faster as if she couldn't stop herself, and within seconds the biscuit was gone and she was reaching for another. The dog gave a low growl, not so loud this time but deeper, like he was making sure the squirrel cat knew he was serious. The squirrel cat chittered, almost plaintively, but the dog just growled back.

With an angry sniff, she wrapped the cheesecloth back up and stuffed the package back in the saddlebag, even going to the trouble of buckling the strap again, with more difficulty than she'd had opening it. Then she leaped from the horse's back to one of the outside wooden posts and climbed up, before hopping onto the tavern's roof and skittering away to then jump to the next rooftop, no doubt in search of her next heist.

A strange sound took me by surprise, and it took me a second to realise first that it was somebody laughing, and second, that that somebody was me. I couldn't recall the last time I'd laughed, which is funny when you consider that the Berabesq – they're the people who live in the hottest, southern part of the continent – sometimes referred to the Mahdek as 'the laughing people'.

But I felt so good just then. I'd witnessed something I'd never expected to see. Something I doubt hardly anyone else in history had ever seen: a squirrel cat and a dog negotiating over biscuits. The deal, apparently, had been that the squirrel cat could steal one biscuit – and only one – so long as she gave one to the dog and one to his friend the horse.

Again I found myself imagining just how fine the world might seem if I had a dog, a horse and a squirrel cat as my companions. The next time Shadow Falcon's voice buzzed in my ear to taunt me about how I was destined to suffer alone until the day I finally laid down in the dirt and died, I'd say, 'Who says I'm alone? I've got all the friends I need.'

Childish? Sure. But you think stupid things like that when you're under the hot sun and you haven't had anything to eat or drink for too long. Now I was wondering if maybe I could make a deal with the dog similar to the one he'd made with the squirrel cat. A little water for me, a little water for him? Maybe he'd be willing to toss one of those biscuits into the deal . . .

Slowly, carefully, I got to my feet and half walked, half stumbled across the road towards the tavern. I started talking to the dog in the sweetest, calmest voice I could manage. It didn't sound too good. My throat was pretty hoarse by then.

'Hey, boy,' I said. 'Today's a good day for tradin', don't you think?'

The dog said nothing in reply. Didn't bark. Didn't growl.

'Pretty hot under all this sun,' I observed casually, shading my eyes as I looked up at the sky. By now I was about ten feet from the horse, and still the dog did nothing. I took this as a good sign. 'So here's what we'll do: I'll open up that saddlebag like your friend the squirrel cat did, and take out the canteen real slow. Then I'll take a little drink and after that pour some in my palm for you. Does that sound good?'

The dog just sat there, placidly watching me with barely any interest at all.

'Or if you're not thirsty, how about another of those biscuits?' I suggested.

His head perked up, just a hair. Maybe it was on account of a bird squawking overhead, but I preferred to believe that I'd piqued his interest.

'Or how about *two* biscuits for you and just one for me? That's more than fair, don't you think?'

Still nothing, but by now I was so close that I could've reached out and patted the horse's rump, so I figured we were in business.

I wiggled my finger under the leather strap in the buckle and tugged it open, all the while keeping an eye on the dog. He seemed fine with how our arrangement was proceeding.

Who knows? I thought. *Maybe this is the beginning of a beautiful partnership.*

With the saddlebag now open, I rooted through clothes and tin containers – even a couple of leather-bound books, which surprised me. But I pushed them aside. The canteen was what I needed.

Water. Just a little water and I'll be okay for a while. Don't drink too much. Stick to your promises.

When I found the canteen and the dried-out skin of my fingers wrapped around that cool silver metal, I nearly wept for joy. Would've too, if I could've spared the water for tears. My trembling left hand gripped the stopper, twisting, tugging, fearing I hadn't the strength to accomplish the task. Then, like that first breath after waking from a nightmare, the stopper started to come free . . . and the canteen fell from my hand. A sudden pain in my wrist was followed by my arm being yanked down to my side. The dog was on his hind legs, paws resting on my thigh and jaws wrapped around my wrist. He wasn't biting hard – hadn't even pierced the skin – but it was like having your arm caught in a steel vice that's gradually getting tighter and tighter.

'We had a deal!' I complained.

The dog replied with a low growl. The horse, uninterested in our negotiations until this point, gave a loud whinny. Apparently he was the lookout, not the dog.

'Shh!' I hissed.

The horse responded by whinnying again, this time even louder.

'Well now,' a man's voice said, accompanied by the screech of rusty hinges on the swinging tavern doors. The heels of his boots thumped on the uneven boards of the front porch. 'Ferius, what'd I tell you about picking up strays?'

'Who's Ferius?' I asked.

The man pointed to the mutt now permanently attached to my wrist.

I looked down at the dog. 'Your name is Ferius?'

Through his teeth he growled his assent.

'But my name's Ferius,' I protested.

The man tilted his head back and arched an eyebrow. 'You aiming to steal my dog's name on top of my favourite canteen?'

What little sanity remained to me started to kick in again. 'I wasn't stealin' nothing, mister! I saw somebody going through your saddlebags and thought I should do something, that's all.'

'Man or woman?' he asked. No smile. Deadly serious.

'Um. Woman, I guess.'

He chewed on the inside of his cheek, nodding slowly. 'You chased her away?' he asked.

'Sure did. She was real big too. Mean.'

'Big *and* mean,' he said, then gave a little shiver of his shoulders. 'You must've been powerful scared. I'm shakin' just hearin' the tale.'

I looked down at the dog, Ferius, who despite still having his teeth around my wrist, stared up at me with a sort of sympathetic shrug, to let me know I was being toyed with.

'Please, mister,' I said. 'Just let me go.'

'Let you go?' He pushed up the brim of his frontier hat. 'After you chased off a big, mean woman and saved me from a fate worse than . . . having a scrawny kid steal my favourite canteen?' He shook his head. 'Durral Brown may be a no-good, down-and-dirty rogue, but he don't leave a debt like that hangin' over his fate. No, ma'am.'

'Your name is Brown?'

'Yeah, why?'

I looked at his brown hat, brown hair, brown everything. 'No reason. But if you want to settle the debt, a little water would be much appreciated.'

'Just water?' he asked, frowning. 'Nothing else?'

'Well,' I said, before I could stop myself, 'one of those biscuits would be real . . .'

I saw the smile reach his eyes. Just like that, I'd given up the game. Only maybe a game was all it had ever been. This guy wasn't stupid. He knew I'd tried to steal from him. Now I'd given him proof.

'Please, mister,' I said, going back to my earlier strategy, 'you don't want nothing to do with me. I'm bad luck. Real bad luck.'

'Bad luck?' He bent over and sniffed the top of my head. 'Yeah, reckon you smell like bad luck. Still, we got us a confounding problem now, girl. What fancy folk call a dilemma.' He leaned even closer and whispered, 'Maybe even a paradox.'

'A what?'

'Well, see, by my calculations I owe you a debt for chasing off that big, mean woman what came to steal my stuff.'

'But that—'

'Hang on, hang on. I'm gettin' to it.' He folded his arms across his chest. 'But since we both know you made her up, that means you owe *me* a debt. The Way of Water says we can't take the one without the other.'

'The way of what?'

'Water. You got a hearin' problem, kid?'

I looked down at the canteen on the ground.

Durral Brown reached out a gloved hand and lifted my chin. 'Not *that* water, kid.'

The dog growled – or so I thought at first. Turned out it was me who'd growled.

'Okay, okay,' Durral said, removing his hand and putting them both up like he was surrendering. 'Just tryin' to figure out what the Argosi ways say I gotta do here.'

'What ways? What's an Argosi?'

'An Argosi is, well, me. As for the four ways . . .' He held up one gloved hand, thumb folded across his palm as he counted them off. 'Way of Water says I gotta make a fair trade with you. Way of Thunder says I oughta beat you good for messing with my stuff. Way of Wind though . . .' Again he sniffed at me. 'She says I gotta follow the signs, and you, kid, seem like a sign.'

Okay, sort of good news and bad news. Turns out I wasn't

the only crazy person wandering the desert roads. Durral Brown started muttering to himself as if he'd forgotten all about me. I'd've been fine with that, except the dog still had my wrist in its jaws.

'What about the fourth one?' I asked.

'Hmm?'

'You said there are four Argosi ways – not that you explained what an Argosi's supposed to be.'

He dismissed my question with a wave of his hand. 'Told you, *I'm* an Argosi. And I hate the Way of Stone. Only ever gets me into trouble. No, ma'am, gonna have to follow the Way of Water this time.'

He gave a short, sharp whistle. All of a sudden the dog's jaws opened and he let go of me. I spun on my heel to make a run for it, but I was so weak I would've fallen flat on my face had Durral not grabbed the collar of my coat and held me up.

'Let me go,' I said.

'Not till you and me have settled our debt, kid.'

The second whistle was lower than the first and warbled almost like a birdsong. The dog walked round to look up at me.

Yeah, his expression seemed to be saying, *I'll bite you real good the next time you try to run.*

I turned back to the man in brown, wondering what he had in store for me. He hadn't known me long enough to want to kill me, and he didn't particularly strike me as 'decent folk', which meant it would take longer for the sigils to work on him.

'Look, kid, even I can see you're at the end of your rope. You need a meal like the rest of the world needs a good cause, which is to say, real bad. Now, there's only three ways to get things in this life.' Again he counted off on his fingers. 'Earn it, which you don't seem inclined to do. Steal it, which, no offence, but you ain't so good at. Third . . .'

He looked at me in a way that made me suddenly afraid that I didn't need to worry about the sigils around my neck turning him against me – that there was something he'd wanted from me the moment he'd laid eyes on me. That thing you can always give away even when you don't have anything else and no matter how many times you'd given it up before. That thing I'd seen other girls and boys give to men like him.

'I won't . . .' I blurted. 'I won't go to bed with you.'

Durral Brown's eyes widened like I'd just drawn him a picture of his grandmother naked. 'You think I . . . Talk about the Way of Thunder!' He let out a long, slow breath. 'Kid, you have stabbed me right through the heart and you ain't even got a knife on you.'

'I'm sorry. I didn't mean to—'

Why was I apologising? What difference did it make now? I should've taken advantage of his discomfort, maybe tried to make another run for it and hoped he'd tell the dog to let me go. But under that blazing sun, thirst hit me again, hard as any blow to the stomach. 'Please, mister. I just need a drink of water and maybe a little food.'

'Then why didn't you just ask for them in the first place?' he asked, then glanced around the empty street. 'Come to think of it, why didn't you just walk up to the homes of any of the kind folk in this town and ask for help? Just cos they're poor don't mean they're cruel.'

I felt so stupid. How was I supposed to explain to this

157

stranger that anyone who showed me kindness would soon end up trying to kill me? It sounded ridiculous even to me.

But the man nodded then, like I'd just spouted the wisdom of ancient philosophers. 'You're right, kid. Absolutely right.'

'I didn't say anyth—'

'Scruples. That's what you got. Won't beg cos that makes a person a slave to the whims of others. That's why the gods created a third way for people like you and me to get the things we need without havin' to earn or steal 'em.'

'What's that?' I asked, somehow mesmerised by the sheer confidence with which Durral Brown was spouting nonsense more bizarre than even my own hallucinatory ramblings.

He grinned, and it was one of those grins that reminded me of Arissa – the kind that traps you like the sight of a desert mirage in the distance, convincing you that the world is this big, wondrous place and you just happen to be the luckiest person alive.

'Gambling,' he said.

23

The Game

I'd never been inside a tavern before. It wasn't from being too young; fifteen is a woman grown in the Seven Sands. Marriageable. Old enough to own property. Old enough to hang. But I was so scrawny and filthy that you couldn't have guessed my age if I gave you a dozen tries. Some days I probably looked like a ten-year-old. Others, like some brittle-boned crone wandering the streets, looking for a warm place to die.

'That'll be our table in the back,' Durral Brown said.

I couldn't figure him out. I mean, other than dressing after his own last name, there wasn't anything special about him. He wasn't all that tall, wasn't particularly handsome. But he was just . . . different. Like, when I followed him to the table, I became aware that I was shuffling my feet. I hadn't thought of myself as a shuffler before then, but watching Durral, the way he seemed to strut without putting on a show, the way his boot heels stamped the floorboards with each step like he was announcing his presence to the world, made me feel like a mouse skittering behind a prancing lion. People looked up when he passed, partly to check him out, but it seemed to me that it was more that, deep down, they wanted him to notice *them*.

159

Then they got a look at me, trailing after Durral like I was his dog – like it was my job to keep an eye on anyone who might be trouble for my master, and they snickered or scowled. Funny how you can lose yourself in someone's shadow. Ironic too, given what Durral Brown did to me not long after I followed him into that tavern.

Wait . . . I haven't described the tavern yet, have I?

So hard to get these events straight in my head. One of the ways folks know you're crazy is when you can't keep track of stuff like that.

Okay. Breathe. You can do this.

The reason I'd never been inside a tavern before was that – like restaurants, inns and brothels – taverns were places where a person paid more for things than they were worth. Rickety chairs creaked as rough-necked men and women leaned their elbows on dirt-crusted wooden tables, reaching for clay mugs or copper cups, peering at the swill inside like maybe the answer to all their problems was just one more drink away. I didn't get the appeal.

Maybe being within those draughty walls, crowding together with other sad, lonely drunks, made them feel safe. But I was never safe – and especially not around big groups of people. I never knew when one of them might have a kind heart that would eventually make them want to stick a knife through mine.

'Sit,' Durral Brown instructed, pointing to the chair across the table from his. He gestured to someone behind me.

I jumped out of my skin, convinced someone was about to grab me, but when I turned all I saw was a gangly limbed waiter, probably no older than me, balancing a tray on his shoulder with a red-clay flagon and several mugs.

160

'They charge even for the water in this place,' Durral said, drawing me back to my chair. He winked at me. 'I'll spot you a tenth against your winnings.'

I sank down into the chair, still wanting to flee but no longer able to, like one of those birds up north in Zhuban that get caught in a sudden cold snap, frozen in ice before they can flap their wings.

I'm not being attacked.

He was just calling for the server.

I'm going to have water.

But I have to pay for it.

Or maybe I don't. Was the wink to tell me he was kidding?

Oh, and he's going to spot me – that means loan me – a tenth.

I started with the easy part: a 'tenth' meant a tiny copper coin smaller than a baby's fingernail, valued at a tenth of a Daroman noble – which folks in these parts called a *nob*. A nob was a larger, thicker copper disk with a little silver piece at its centre. Fifty of *those* would get you an imperial sovereign – or *sov* – which was a beautifully engraved silver coin with a disc of actual gold in the middle. The last time I'd seen a whole sovereign was when I ran with the Black Galleon gang. Arissa had held a pair of them up to cover her eyes, asking if they made her pretty.

'You still with me, kid?'

I looked over at the man in the brown frontier hat across the table from me. His own eyes were wide, like he was trying to pretend they were imperial sovs, or maybe he was worried I was close to fainting. Probably I was.

'Your name is Durral,' I said. 'Durral Brown.'

'That's the name they write on the warrants,' he said, shuffling a deck of cards. I'd never held a deck of cards, so I couldn't say for sure, but the way he shuffled them looked like magic to me. How was he keeping them from flying out of his hands?

'How did I know your name?' I asked.

He kept shuffling. 'I told you outside, when we met. See, when civilised folk first make each other's acquaintance, they give each other their names.'

Actually, the Mahdek don't, because a stranger's name doesn't tell you anything useful about them. We give the name of our tribe, unless there are other members of our tribe around, at which point we offer the name of our clan. If someone else from our clan is nearby, we use our family name. So only in the presence of other family members do we give our own individual names. Still, as I was a long way from anything that had ever been Mahdek territory, and this guy was giving me an entire tenth of a noble and a glass of water, I decided it would be prudent to oblige him.

'My name is Ferius,' I said.

'Ferius is the dog's name. Ferius Parfax. It means—'

'You're lying!' I snapped. Maybe barked is a better word. 'Ferius is *my* name.'

Durral arched an eyebrow as he continued effortlessly shuffling the cards. 'Funny thing to lie about, don't you think?'

Hard to argue with that. Also, I remembered now that he'd told me the name of his dog outside, and I was almost positive it was Ferius. So why did I think that was my name? My fingernail scratched at one of the sigils around my neck. It stung.

'Ain't no harm in you bein' Ferius too, I suppose,' Durral said.

There was a gentleness in his tone that should've made

162

me feel grateful, because he was being kind, or maybe scared, because that meant I'd only know him a few more hours before I'd have to run. Instead it just made me angry.

'You don't get to give me a name,' I said. 'I'm supposed to choose my name when I turn thirteen and stand before my clan. I'll tell them things about myself. Important things. Things I've kept secret from everyone until that very moment.'

'How old are you now?' he asked, though he said it in a way that made me think he knew I was older than thirteen.

'Thirteen is the day of *declaration*,' I said, giving the last word so much emphasis it practically burned away all the others. I was talking too fast, the words tumbling out of me like scarabs trying to skitter away from a fire, or maybe more like playing cards flying from a deck when you lose control of your shuffling.

'That so?'

'Yes, *that's so*. You tell the members of your clan what name you've chosen and what spirit animal walks alongside you. It's the day you tell everyone how you're going to live and what service you intend to give to your clan, or if you're going to leave to start a new clan, though that's pretty rare, especially now because—'

'That's enough chatter for now, kid,' he said.

I had no plans to shut up. I still had lots of things I needed to say, even if I had no idea why it was so important to say them. Maybe it was because this was as close to a real conversation as I'd had with anyone in over a year. Yet I couldn't seem to find the breath to speak. It wasn't magic. I've seen magic. But Durral's stare was so hard it just locked up all the air in my lungs and wouldn't let any in. Just when I thought for sure that stare was going to choke me to death,

163

his eyes moved, up and to the right, over my shoulder and behind me. My head, like that of an obedient hound, turned to follow.

They were all staring at me now. Everyone in the whole tavern. I'd been shouting – shouting things that anyone who knew anything about the Mahdek would recognise. Lots of places don't like the Mahdek – have I mentioned that before? Sometimes it's because we bring trouble with us. Sometimes it's just because.

Four men were sitting at a table not far from ours. One of them got to his feet. It was like watching a massive oak tree rising up from the ground. He stomped over to our table, every step a warning to the rest of the folks not to get in his way. When he got close, his gaze washed over me, from the top of my muddy hair to the tips of my filthy shoes. I was a leech, stuck to his leg, waiting to be flicked off with a fingernail so he could crush it under his boot.

He spat on me.

'Got a noose out back.'

That was all he said: 'Got a noose out back'. Five words, and still I was glued to that chair, trying to understand all the things he wanted me to know: he could kill me if he wanted. He was thinking about it. There might be something I could do to make him change his mind, but it wasn't clear what that could be. *Out back*, he'd said. Maybe if I left by the front door, he'd let me live?

'Got me a good strong noose right out the back,' he said, changing the words only slightly, but more than enough to throw out all my carefully considered conclusions as to his meaning.

'How strong?' asked the man in the brown frontier hat.

Durral was his name, though I didn't know it at the ti—
No, wait, I *did* know his name by then. It was getting harder
to think straight.

The man who was maybe planning to hang me looked
over my head at Durral. 'What did you say?'

Durral dealt a card to me and one to himself, face down.
'How strong a noose?'

The big man looked down at the cards on the table as if
there were something there for him to see. 'Strong enough, I
reckon.'

'Has to be real strong,' Durral said, dealing a second card
each. 'Gotta hold two hundred, maybe two hundred and
twenty pounds. Don't forget there'll be a whole lot of shakin''
and strugglin'. Rope's gotta hold until the neck breaks or the
wind stops comin' out of the body.'

The big man snorted. 'This little piece of dust?'

I guess he meant me, because he grabbed me by the back
of my beloved coat and hauled me up until I was balancing
on the tops of my toes.

'Can't weigh more than a sack of wheat,' he said. 'No more
than sixty pounds soaking wet.'

Durral took the rest of the deck of cards and fanned them
out face down on the table. He picked one seemingly at
random, held it up between thumb and forefinger to show
it to the man who was holding me by the scruff of the neck.
The card showed a picture of three arrows piercing a heart
while lightning struck a house in the background.

'Looks unlucky, if you ask me,' Durral said. 'Three of arrows
foretells of pain and sorrow.'

'Just a card,' the noose man countered. 'Don't mean nothing.'

Durral snapped his fingers – or that's what it looked like

to me – and the card went flying from his hand. It whizzed in a diagonal line up past my right ear. I heard a squeal from the man holding me. He let go and I dropped right back down in the chair.

'Son of a bitch!' he bellowed.

'Told you the card was unlucky,' Durral said.

Noose Man reached behind his back and pulled out a knife that must've been nearly ten inches long. The blade looked a little dull, but I could make out splotches of red staining the steel. 'Looks like you're getting the noose first,' he said to Durral. 'Only maybe I'll strip the skin off your bones before I let you dangle.'

Durral didn't look nearly as impressed as someone in his predicament should be. The whole tavern went quiet as a crypt, and a crypt it was, for surely somebody was about to die. Funny thing was, I no longer thought it would be me.

More thudding of boots on the floorboards heralded the arrival of the other men from Noose Man's table. Close up you could see a few differences in their hair and noses and jaws and such, but they were definitely all related.

'Four against one,' the biggest of the bunch said.

Durral sighed. 'Wish that weren't so.'

'I'll bet,' chuckled one of the others.

'Odds ain't that bad,' Durral said, like he was genuinely trying to convince the four men standing behind me to back down. 'More like four against two, actually.'

Noose Man snickered, slapping the back of my head so hard my vision went blurry. 'This little mutt? She ain't gonna do you no good.'

Durral smiled. 'Wrong mutt.'

He gave a short, sharp whistle. At first nothing happened,

but then we all heard the quick clacking of claws on the wooden floor and felt the rush of air as Durral's dog leaped up and bowled over the man who'd first come to hang me.

The dog couldn't have weighed more than forty pounds, but the way he barrelled into the guy's head knocked him over, slammed his face onto the table. The dog immediately spun around and sat on the big man's head as he growled at the other three.

'Get him!' shouted the fellow who was now serving as the dog's seat. He tried to stab him with the knife but couldn't get the angle.

Quick as lightning, Durral snatched the weapon from him, flipped it over and pressed the point into the flesh of the man's hand, pinning him there.

'One push and you never use that hand again, friend.'

The other three were moving now, flanking our table, pulling out knives of their own as they prepared to swarm the dog. I tried kicking one of them – I liked the dog, after all. My kick didn't land, but it did keep the men back long enough for me to reach into the mapmaker's case I kept strapped to my back. A smallsword's not a good weapon for fighting this close, but maybe I could make them hesitate long enough for Durral to get his own weapon out. But when I glanced back, he was leaning in his chair like nothing had happened, except he was still pressing Noose Man's knife against the back of his hand.

'Civilised folk,' he began, his gaze going from one of the fellows to the next, 'introduce themselves when first they meet. How about I start? My name is Durral Brown, and I am the Path of the Rambling Thistle.'

I felt a shiver when he said those words, even though I

didn't understand what they meant. Noose Man's brothers must've though, because all three looked like they badly wanted to be anywhere else but that tavern.

'Now, today is Tearsday,' Durral went on, like he was about to tell a story, 'and Tearsday is my very favourite day of the week for dying.'

His dog growled.

'Pretty good day for killin' too,' Durral translated.

Still holding the first man's wrist, he shifted the point of his knife to just inside the fellow's ear, like he was going to clean it. Leaning in close, he whispered, 'In case you're wonderin', no matter who starts the fight, you'll be dyin' first.'

Durral looked across the table at me. 'You scared, kid?'

I shook my head.

'Really? I'm practically wetting myself over here.'

What was I supposed to say to that?

Durral grinned up at the other three even as he kept the point of the knife right inside Noose Man's ear. 'Ain't life glorious? Bet not one of us woke up this mornin' imagining the day would end like this, did we?'

The brothers snarled louder than the dog had. They said things – curse words mostly. Some I knew, others sounded so silly they almost made me laugh. I didn't laugh though, because right then I wasn't paying attention to them or their threats. I was watching Durral's smile.

He'd admitted he was scared – said it like he wanted them to hear him, but it didn't shake his placid grin. It was like he was goading them into attacking him.

No. Not goading. That's the wrong word.

Daring.

Maybe he wants to die, I thought. *Maybe like me he's*

168

already buried on the inside, just waiting to feel the dirt cover his skin.

Only . . . he didn't look like he wanted to die.

'Time's a-wastin', gentlemen,' Durral said. 'Way I see it, there are only two possible explanations why you ain't made a move on us yet.'

The middle brother tried a sneer on for size. 'Oh yeah?' he asked.

'Sure,' Durral replied amiably. 'First one is, you're a bunch of cowards so accustomed to starin' down other cowards that now that you've found yourself a man – well, a man, a girl and a dog, to be precise – staring right back at you, you're hearin' a little voice inside your head that's sayin' maybe you ain't quite so quick or so tough as you like to believe.'

Now I knew for sure he had a death wish. In a small town like this, someone shows weakness, everyone notices. The brothers, hearing themselves mocked this way, were sure to attack now.

'Course, there is one other possible explanation,' Durral went on almost dreamily, like he was talking to himself. 'Maybe the reason why you ain't killed us yet is that there's a different voice in your head. A nobler one. This voice is tellin' you there ain't no fight worth a good man's time here. Just a loudmouth in a bar with his mangy dog and a child who ain't never done harm to nobody but is payin' the price for a thousand sins anyway. Maybe this other voice is remindin' you that men of honour – *true* men of honour, mind you – don't pick fights they know they can win. Ain't no . . . What's the danged word again?'

He was looking at me. I had no idea what he was talking about. Had he only said a tenth of all that nonsense, I'd still

169

have been hard-pressed to explain an hour later what had happened. Couldn't get any of it straight in my head just then. I kept expecting the cool sting of a knife blade sliding across my throat.

'Darn it now, can't anybody remember that word?' he asked, raising his voice as if to the entire tavern.

Nobody answered at first. Why would they? Only trouble could come of it. But Durral Brown, he held that question up in the air like it was a rattlesnake. You couldn't seem to turn away from it for fear it would bite you.

'Dignity?' one of the brothers suggested at last, the smallest one.

His brothers looked at him like he was soft in the head, but Durral whooped for joy. '*Dignity!* That's the one! Ain't no *dignity* in a fight you know you'll win.'

Then he did something very stupid: very slowly, he removed the point of the blade from Noose Man's ear and set the knife down on the table. He let go of the man's wrist and said, 'These are the moments – and precious few there are in any man's life – when he gets to make a choice that sticks with him forever. He gets to ask himself, "What kind of a soul is inside me?" and then, with one single decision, he gives an answer that lasts all the rest of his days.'

I wondered how this poor idiot had gotten through life this long without a noose around his neck. A person doesn't shed their cruelty just because some lunatic in a tavern spouts nonsense about searching inside yourself. Mean people don't become that way because of a few harsh words, and they aren't cured of it by kind ones. So Durral Brown was about to die, along with his dog, and probably me too. I almost wished Shadow Falcon was there in my head so there'd be someone with me when I died.

A grunt.

Barely even a grunt, really.

Might as well have been a cough or a groan or a fart.

Yet in that piggish exhalation was a tale I'd never heard before. A story of a brave man. A hard man, forged by the troubles that come with a hard life, who comes to a crossroads when any other man – born high or low – would've taken the wrong road. The easy road. But this man? At this precise moment? He takes the other one.

The man who'd strutted over here spitting on me and talking of nooses pressed his hands against the table and pushed himself up, causing Durral's dog to hop down to the floor and sit, wagging his tail.

'C'mon,' the man said to his brothers, grabbing one by the shoulder and turning him around as if *he'd* been the one who'd started the ruckus. 'Plenty of work to do on the farm and the day's gettin' away from us.'

I glanced over at Durral, sure as sure can be that something clever was going to come out of his mouth. But he never uttered a word. Didn't thank the men for their mercy nor mock them for their cravenness, just watched them go without a trace of malice in his eyes.

They left us there, in that dingy little tavern by the road. Durral couldn't have taken on those four men any more than I could've fought off the war coven who'd killed my clan. Yet somehow, with nothing but an arcane mixture of words and smiles and stares, he'd made the impossible happen. Like I said before, it wasn't magic. But Durral Brown had something inside him that defied the rules by which the world as I understood it was constructed.

I didn't know it then, but what he'd shown me was called *arta valar*, and even if I didn't know the name, I knew I had to get me some.

24

The Gambler's Credo

Of all the things you can forget, the most dangerous is forgetting who you are. Back when I was running with the Black Galleon gang, Arissa bragged that a good thief can go their entire lives without once getting pinched by the constables. I'd glanced around at the pack of teenage miscreants in the cellar, regaling each other with their latest heist, and asked why there weren't any thieves over the age of twenty in the gang.

'They're all either in prison or in the ground,' she'd replied, going back to cleaning and sharpening each of her steel stars before moving on to wiping down every single piece of her thief's kit.

'But you just told me th—'

'The ones who lack talent or discipline get caught young. The good ones aim for bigger heists than they've got the skills to pull off, or get some money together and try to go straight – which never works, by the way, because eventually somebody always figures out how you made your money. One way or another, they all make the same mistake.'

'Which is?'

Instead of answering me, she'd looked up from cleaning

173

her tools. 'That collar around your neck – you shouldn't keep picking at it.'

'I hate it,' I'd said. I hadn't even noticed I'd been scratching one of the sigils.

'You should be grateful to those Jan'Tep mages. It's a gift.'

'A gift?' I'd leaped up from my cot, so angry I might've swung at her had she not had one of her sharpened steel stars hidden in the cuff of her shirt. Now one of the spikes was pressed underneath my jaw.

'Those other thieves? The reason they get pinched is because they forget that thieves is what they are. Not master criminals, not noble rogues. Thieves.' The edge of the star drifted down to one of the sigils above my collarbone. 'You're a cursed little Mahdek rat, running from cats whose claws will always be a hundred times sharper than yours. Getting rid of these markings won't change that one bit.' The steel star disappeared back inside her cuff. 'The day you forget who you are, Rat Girl – that's the day you die.'

You'd think a lesson like that would stick with you – that it would be impossible to forget something so simple, so fundamental.

You'd be wrong.

After witnessing what Durral Brown did with those four big men who'd been ready to kill me – seeing first-hand the kinds of abilities these Argosi wanderers possessed, talents that didn't require magic but instead a clever mind – you're damned right I forgot.

'You gonna play?' he asked, moving his own cards around in his hand. 'Or is my face so pretty you can't stop starin' at it?'

For hours we'd been sitting opposite each other at that

uneven table in that seedy tavern – well, I say 'seedy', but it might've been the nicest tavern in the entire Seven Sands for all I knew. If it was, I can't say much for the merits of taverns as a species of business establishment. Anyway, by then I was so obsessed with trying to understand what these Argosi were all about – and Durral so determined not to reveal anything except through vague hints here and there as he taught me one game after another – that eventually I became utterly enthralled with cards.

'Ain't but three laws that determine the outcome of a game,' he'd informed me early on that evening.

'Luck?' I'd suggested.

'Ain't no such thing,' he'd claimed. 'First lesson an Argosi learns to live by: whatever hand you're holding is the winning one if you figure out how to play it.'

In cards, as in life, that was, quite obviously, untrue. In any given game, some cards are valuable and others worthless. Shuffling the deck makes the cards come up at random. Lucky is when you get a good card. Unlucky is when you don't. Lucky is being born a Jan'Tep mage. Unlucky is being born a Mahdek.

Durral, though, insisted that winning or losing the game was first based on what he called *arta precis*, which seemed to me to be a fancy way of saying *paying attention*.

'If you know what's in your hand, you know what *ain't* in mine. Every time they discard, they're showing you both what *used* to be in their hand and what they no longer value. When their fingers linger on that card, when their eyes tighten at the corners, when they lick their lips without thinkin' about it, they're showin' you the shape of their thoughts, the colours of their intentions, the textures of their plans.'

175

Yeah, I didn't really get it either.

The second law was simpler to understand: *arta loquit*, or 'speaking the language of the game'. That's really just a fancy way of saying, 'Don't make stupid mistakes.' See, each game has its own set of rules from which key principles can be derived. Fail to adhere to those principles – say, discarding the queen of trebuchets when it would've given you a benevolent court in a game of Royal Roads – is a miscalculation that can cost you the game.

I made those mistakes a lot.

Durral's third law is a lot harder to explain. He called it *arta tuco*, and when I asked what that meant he said it was the Argosi talent for strategy, which is kind of like your overall approach to the game. It's not about plays or discards, but the path you choose in order to achieve victory. Most of the time this came down to figuring out your opponent's strategy and doing the opposite. For example, if you're playing Seven Sins, a game in which one suit is deemed wicked and the aim of the game is to end with as few 'sins' in your hand as possible, then a common strategy is to try to force your opponent to pick up your discarded sins by dropping them whenever their hand has too few cards, because each player has to draw from the discard pile before they can draw from the deck. But you can also win Seven Sins by achieving a 'perfectly wicked' hand – when all seven of your cards are from the sinful suit. So if you know your opponent is trying to force his sins on you, a good strategy is to seem like you're making mistakes that force you to draw them, while hiding the fact that it's your intent all along.

Simple, right? Only, the more sin cards you are holding at the end of the game *without* having a perfectly wicked hand, the more money you have to pay. So losing a hand when you went for all sins but failed can cost you more than losing a dozen others.

Arta tuco.

So, as any professional player (at least that's what Durral claimed) will tell you, the only three forces that count in a game of cards are arta precis, arta loquit and arta tuco.

Except that there's actually a fourth element – one which didn't need a fancy name – and it turned out to be the only one I was good at: cheating.

Cheating is against the rules, of course, but that only counts if you get caught. Durral, for all his fancy shuffles and the way he could make cards appear and disappear at will, was lousy at spotting a cheater.

I first discovered this during a hand of Spears and Snakes, which is a game where . . . you know what? You really don't need to know how to play Spears and Snakes. Suffice it to say that aces – which are like number-one cards only with a dumb name – are the most important cards in the game.

'There's a card on the floor,' I said, noticing the ace that must've dropped from the deck while he'd been shuffling.

'Hmm?'

Durral wasn't paying much attention by this point in the evening; he was too busy making eyes at the lady serving us food and drink. He kept having her come over with these tiny portions of meats, cheeses, breads and vegetables, all in little blue-glazed clay bowls. He'd let me have a nibble of one, then make me wait to see if I'd puke it back up.

'Scrawny as you are, kid, we can't be sure what your stomach can handle. Just eat a little and see if it sticks.'

Every time he bought me one of these specks of food, he'd

put another coin on the table. Usually it was a copper hundredth, which around there they called a *spit*. At first I thought these were to pay the serving lady, but when I asked why she never took them, Durral informed me the copper spits were to show me how much I owed him for his hospitality, and therefore how much I was going to have to win at cards. This didn't strike me as fair since I had no say over what he purchased – which, when you put it all together, was more than I could ever eat. Also, I was pretty sure he was overpaying because the tavern lady kept smiling at him.

By the time the pile of copper spits was starting to slide off the table, I protested. 'I've no money to gamble with. How am I ever supposed to win it back?'

Durral chuckled as he tossed down the scholar of blades onto the table and ended the game in his favour. 'Free piece of advice, kid: never put your own money on the table until you know what game you're playing.' With that, he placed another copper spit next to the rest.

'What's that for?' I asked. 'I thought you said we weren't playing for money.'

'That's for the advice.'

'But you said it was free! You started with –' here I put on his condescending baritone drawl – '"Frey pace of advass, keed, nevuh puht yow awn mahney on th' tay-bull."'

Durral grinned at my impression, then added *another* copper spit to the pile! 'Second free piece of advice, kid: nothing worth anything is free.'

He dealt the next hand. I fumed, staring at my cards, resenting my lousy luck. 'So we're not playing for anything right now?' I asked.

'You're always playing for something,' he replied, dropping

178

a knight of chariots on the discard pile. 'Even when there ain't no stakes on the table, somethin's always at risk. Maybe it's just your pride, cos you want to win so bad.'

That much was true. I'd lost every single hand since we'd started playing and it was infuriating me, even though I shouldn't have cared. But for the first time in ages, I had good food in my belly, I'd drunk my fill of fresh clean water and even tasted wine – awful, by the way. So who cared if I was losing at a stupid card game?

Me, it turned out.

Which brings us back to that card that had fallen on the floor.

'Hmm?' Durral mumbled after I mentioned it.

'Nothing,' I replied.

I pretended to fumble with my hand and dropped a card on the floor – a lousy two of trebuchets, which is pretty much the worst card you can get in Spears and Snakes.

'Oops,' I said.

I reached down and left the two on the floor, picking up the ace instead. Two minutes later I'd scored my first win at cards.

'Nice work, kid,' Durral said, tapping his frontier hat with his finger and giving me a sideways grin.

I know what you're thinking: he must've seen the ace. Maybe he'd even made sure it had fallen to the floor in the first place. Maybe this was all some lesson about how the world worked, for which I'd owe yet another copper spit. But I didn't think so. He wasn't taking the game as seriously as I was, so he hadn't noticed the way I'd swapped the two for the ace. Just like he missed it when I dealt myself an extra card in our next hand of Royal Court, or when I'd slipped a queen of arrows into the cuff of my torn, filthy shirt as I was collecting the cards to shuffle them for the next hand.

After a while, I was winning more than I was losing. Durral's third law of cards: always have a strategy. My strategy was to learn the rules and then devise a way to cheat.

As the sun went down and the tavern slowly emptied out, Durral kept right on playing with me, smiling up at the serving woman and drinking everything she put in front of him. By the time it was just the three of us, he'd gotten pretty drunk. I worried he might resent me winning so many hands, so I kept suggesting we stop. But every time he shook his head and dealt a new game.

I heard a rustle as the serving woman removed her apron. When I turned to look, I noticed her dress underneath was nicer than I would've expected – dark blue cotton the same colour as the azure sands outside. The neckline was cut low, brought lower by the fact that I was pretty sure she'd pulled it down to show more of her cleavage. I figured she was going to seduce Durral, which suited me just fine, because they could go off and have sex while I made a run for it with whatever coins Durral forgot to pick up off the table. As she approached, his grin widened, and he pulled out his coin purse again to offer her a handful of copper tenths and two silver nobs. He must've overpaid, because her own smile grew. Then something strange happened: she gave me a sideways glance and her expression changed utterly. The smile was still there, but something ugly hid beneath, like she'd just tasted something sour.

'There's a room upstairs you can have for the night,' she informed Durral. 'It's private. Nobody ever goes up there.'

Why had those words sent a chill down my spine? Durral

180

was drunk; it was late; he'd given her plenty of money. The obvious conclusion was that she was either honestly offering him a quiet place to spend the night, or offering him a place to spend the night *with her*. Perfectly reasonable.

Only ... she *was* staring at me funny, and in that look I knew she didn't like me. I didn't blame her. I was filthy and smelled bad and would've absolutely stolen anything in that tavern I could've gotten my hands on. But the way her eyes moved over me, like a rattlesnake searching for the softest vein to sink its fangs into ...

Durral was looking at me funny now too, like he couldn't understand why he'd wasted a whole day playing cards with such a disgusting delinquent. Except that it seemed to me then that he *could* think of a reason to be interested in me.

When you hate someone – when you hate them beyond what hate a body should be able to contain – you don't want to beat them to death or slit their throat. You want to get them someplace you can hurt them as bad as you want, for as long as you want. Someplace no one will hear them scream.

'It's private. Nobody ever goes up there.'

There's a corollary to the lesson Arissa tried to teach me. It goes like this: *Never forget who you are, because sooner or later, the world always remembers.*

25

The Empire

The last time I'd cried had been the night Arissa had fallen under the sway of the mystical sigils around my neck, threatened to kill me and walked away. Plenty of bad things had happened to me since then, but I didn't sit around weeping about them. Grief and misery are for when the danger has passed.

So why could I feel the wet warmth of tears drifting down my cheeks now?

'Private room, eh?' Durral asked the serving woman.

She nodded, her hand resting on my shoulder. I could feel her fingernails pressing into the soiled fabric of my linen shirt. 'Real private.'

'Sounds nice,' he said, his blurry gaze sweeping over me as he bit the inside of his cheek. 'Reckon I might just take you up on that.'

Nothing had changed in his expression or his voice. Not one thing. Durral Brown was still the man who'd saved me from a hanging, given me food and taught me cards. Yet I was so scared of him that I was afraid I'd pee myself like I'd done the day in that tailor shop in Domisa Pago where I'd stolen my coat.

And I *was* grieving too. I'd only known Durral for a few measly hours – had barely begun to make sense of his strange talk of the laws of cards and the ways of the Argosi. Yet I knew – I *knew* – something precious was being taken away from me.

'Don't cry now, little girl,' he said, and his upper lip twitched into a sneer I don't think he even noticed was there. 'We'll get you all sorted out.'

The serving woman was still looming over our table, waiting, I imagined, to be paid extra for the room. Durral fumbled with his purse, but knocked over a half-empty cup of wine. He swore and stumbled down to his hands and knees, grabbing drunkenly at the coins that were falling to the floor. Winking up at the serving woman, he stuffed the coins back into his purse one by one.

All save the one that had quietly rolled next to the leg of my chair.

This coin was gold all the way round, all except for the very centre where a gleaming blue gemstone worth more than this whole town threatened to announce its presence to the world. Until I stuck my foot over it.

If a copper coin with a silver centre is a noble, and a silver coin with a gold centre is a sovereign, what could you possibly name a *gold* coin with a sapphire at its centre? What's bigger than the sovereign?

The empire.

Durral Brown, in his drunken stupor, working his clumsy charm on the serving woman who'd just offered him a private place where he could use me however he saw fit, had dropped a gold-and-sapphire empire on the floor.

How much was it worth?

Never having seen one before, it was hard for my wildest imaginings to encompass its value. Any thief who'd walked into the Black Galleon brandishing such a coin would've immediately become the leader of the crew. Probably soon after, someone would've killed them of course, but for a while it would be glorious. With an empire in my possession, I would never again know hunger or thirst or the lack of a warm place to sleep. I could live in a mansion, hire a dozen of the best-trained, most brutal mercenaries on the continent, whose foulness would keep them from being influenced by my collar and whose greed would keep them loyal to me. Money meant freedom – a kind of freedom I hadn't even known how badly I craved until I saw how much of it could fit on one little golden disc.

Durral climbed back up to his seat, and almost instantly tilted backwards until his chair was leaning against the wall, where he began softly snoring. Watching his sleeping face, I couldn't help but remark at how kind he looked, and wonder whether maybe I'd just panicked at hearing the serving woman's words when all her innuendo really alluded to was the possibility of a sexual liaison between the two of them.

Then again, mountain lions look innocent when they're asleep too.

With the toes of my left foot, I slid the gold coin closer to me, keeping track of the serving woman's movements in the periphery of my vision. We were the only ones in the tavern, so when I saw her turn her back to us to scrub the bar, I reached down to scratch my foot. I'd used the same tactic to good effect during several games of Thieves' Sleeves.

Durral's dog was sitting in the corner by his master's legs, watching me. I wondered if he knew what I was doing, and if dogs recognised the difference between a gold empire and a copper spit. But he just gave a yawn and settled his muzzle down on his paws.

With the coin palmed in my right hand, I turned and asked the tavern woman, bold as brass, 'Where's the privy?'

'Outside in the scrub and dirt,' she replied without sparing me a glance. 'Same place you came from. Same place you belong.'

'Thank you, mistress,' I said as though I were addressing a great and fine lady like Sir Rosarite. It seemed the least I could do, considering I would never see her again, and once Durral woke he might be angry with her for letting me escape. But she – no doubt like him – couldn't imagine a wretch like myself abandoning food and shelter, even if the price for it was to be someone's plaything.

I counted thirteen steps before I reached the swinging tavern doors. Thirteen more before I was on the opposite side of the street. One thousand and forty-two to the edge of town. More than I could keep track of to reach the next town where I would trade in this coin for everything I needed in the world. Food. Lots of it. New clothes and repairs to my coat. A bed in the best inn they had. A good dependable horse, for sure.

Maybe even a dog.

Spirits of the dead, kindly and cruel, what a stupid little girl I was.

26

Priceless Dreams

Priceless.

The coin I carried hidden upon my person – don't ask where, it's not a pretty story – was, in every sense of the word, priceless.

Now, you might assume a coin must always have a predictable value. After all, if ten copper spits make a tenth, and ten tenths make a noble, and fifty nobs make a sovereign, and one hundred sovs make up an empire, then mathematically an empire is worth half a million copper spits.

(You have a lot of time to add things up in your head when you're trudging for three straight days with a gold-and-sapphire coin lodged in your . . . but let's get back to my maths problem).

In most villages, you can buy a half-loaf of bread for a single copper spit. It's more expensive in a city, of course, but that's beside the point. What matters is that, in theory, my empire coin was worth roughly a quarter-million loaves of bread. No baker on the continent can sell you such a quantity, nor will they sell you a few loaves and give you change for your once-shiny empire. In fact, the only place you could tender an empire coin would be a royal Daroman bank, where someone like me could trade it for a fifty-year sentence on charges of – and this is really what they call it – *magnificent larceny*. Alternatively, I could take it to a large criminal organisation, who would gladly exchange my precious coin for a slit throat.

So what you have to do is find a minor country noble – somebody with enough money on hand to buy it from you for, say, one spit on the tenth. In my case, it was a nice, elderly, tremendously corrupt lady by the name of Daldira, Countess of Pluvia. If that name sounds familiar, it's because back in my Black Galleon days, Rudger had sent Bindle and Leaf to pick pockets at her funeral, only Bindle had noticed that the woman in the coffin had all the fingers on her left hand, whereas rumour had it the *real* Countess of Pluvia had once been a duellist who'd . . . you know what? This really isn't the important part of the story.

Suffice it to say, like any savvy negotiator who understands the economics of their crime, I traded my empire for one spit on the tenth, which is to say, the equivalent of ten sovereigns. Did that kindly old countess rip me off? Sure, but the deal had to be so good there was no value in her turning me over to the constables or just paying the ten sovereigns it would've cost to have me killed.

With ten sovereigns I could still live large for a good long while. No more relying on the kindness of strangers for a few short hours before they tried to kill me. When you have money, you don't need friends. Unfortunately, being flush with coin made me forget Rule Number Two.

Sometimes you'll wish you were alone.

'*What's that in your hand, Mahdek?*'

I stuffed the sovereign back in the pocket of my new riding

trousers on the floor beside the bed. I didn't yet own a horse, but I liked the fit and, after all, still planned on buying one.

Nothing.

But it was too late. Falcon had seen the silver coin with the gleaming gold centre. I should never have gotten into the habit of gazing at one of my sovereigns each night before I went to sleep, but I couldn't help myself. I needed . . . I was fifteen years old and had no friends, no family – only an ache I carried inside me for all the people and experiences I would never know. There were times, during those few weeks of knowing I could buy what I wanted, that I'd see a handsome young man or woman standing outside a tavern, the telltale look in their eyes of someone who rented the pleasures of their bodies by the hour, and I'd think about . . .

But then I'd remember Arissa, both the feelings she'd awoken in me without the two of us ever touching like that, and the warning she'd given me so many times.

'The day you forget who you are, Rat Girl – that's the day you die.'

So what was left, as I lay there waiting for slumber to take the place of loneliness, but to stare at one of my sovereigns and hope it would bring me dreams of a different life?

'Where did you get it?' Falcon asked.

I could feel his curiosity tickling the back of my head.

A gift, I replied. *From a legendary Argosi wanderer. He said I was the cleverest, most beautiful person he'd ever met, and that the Way of Water demanded he—*

'An Argosi?' The sudden rage in Falcon's thoughts jerked me up from the bed. *'Where did you find an Argosi? They're liars! Schemers! They are not to be trusted!'*

In the darkness of my room, I found myself padding softly

across the floor to the window. The inn where I was staying was in a quiet part of town, and the night outside looked peaceful. I drew on that quiet to probe carefully at the thick, angry ball of Falcon's presence.

This one seemed harmless enough, I lied, keeping a tight rein on my own thoughts.

'The Argosi play games with the lives of others. They are spies who pretend at being philosophers. They seek to control the fate of nations.'

There was an . . . echo in his words, as if they weren't his own.

You've never even met an Argosi, have you?

I felt a sudden sting as if he'd slapped me.

'Never mock me, Mahdek. You think I can't hurt you more than I already have? You think you've seen the full effects of that collar around your neck?'

Despite my attempts to stay cool, the way he could intrude on my life any time he wanted caused me to lose my temper.

Then why don't you, Falcon? Why don't you kill me, like you keep threatening?

'Because I'm trying to be merciful. Met'astice said . . . He said it wasn't your fault you were born Mahdek.'

When you lie as much as I do, you develop an ear for how it sounds. Falcon was trying to hide something from me, but his outrage at my mention of the Argosi had let some of his own thoughts slip. I caught a flash of other Jan'Tep, maybe ten or twelve of them. They were in one of those ornate one-room marble buildings mages call 'sanctums'. Through Falcon's eyes I saw these robed men and women, and knew they called themselves the Cabal. Met'astice had been one of them, and now they were offering Falcon his place. I felt my own chest swell with pride, as if it was me there being treated as an equal by all these great mages – visionaries of our people. To be included in their number, given my own mission within the great quest to—

'Stop!'

Another slap, so hard this time that when I came to my senses I was on the floor of my room, looking up at the ceiling. But I held on to the memory of that slap, peeling it back in my mind, examining all that lay underneath. Falcon had reacted viciously because he felt . . . violated by me. I almost laughed at that, but set it aside because there was something else there, lurking underneath his aggression. A secret. This Cabal . . . I wasn't the only one they were experimenting on. There had been a few others, perhaps as many as a dozen, scattered throughout the continent, but they'd all died. The Argosi . . . The Cabal feared they would learn of the experiments. But why? Why would the mighty lords magi of the Jan'Tep worry about a few wandering gamblers?

Had I been cunning, I would've hidden those fragments I'd stolen from Falcon's thoughts, waited until he was gone so I could make sense of the information and work out how to use it. But I was so tired of feeling helpless, tired of being mocked and intruded upon by this bullying mage whenever he pleased. Knowing something he didn't want me to know made me feel powerful for the first time in my life. I wanted more of that feeling, and that desperate desire exposed that even what little I now knew of this Jan'Tep Cabal was far too much.

I don't know how far away he was from me. He might have been across the continent or just around the corner from the inn, but the sudden outpouring of his magic brought us

190

together for an instant, and as my tattooed collar burned with a heat greater than that of the needles with which he'd imprinted the sigils onto my neck, for the first time I saw myself through his eyes.

I wished I was half the woman he thought I was.

'Goodbye, Mahdek,' Falcon said, and anyone but me who heard his thoughts would've sworn there was genuine regret beneath them. 'I . . . *hope the end is quick.*'

One last flicker of his presence, like a kiss on my forehead, and he was gone. In his place, the sigils around my neck awakened, more alive than ever before. It was as if each one grew tendrils that reached beyond the walls of my room into the night, searching for other minds, whispering to them of a creature in their midst so foul it had to be hunted and killed.

I rose up quickly, put on my nice new shirt, riding trousers and leather hunting coat. I strapped on the mapmaker's case that held my smallsword, but left the top open. Most residents of this town would be in their beds at this hour, and my existence would be nothing more than a disturbing nightmare to them, but there were always a few drunks wandering the streets after midnight, and if I ran into any of them . . .

I reached into my pocket and let my fingers grasp one of the silver sovereigns that no longer had any value to me at all, because there was now no place I could spend them, and no one who'd take them from me without also trying to take my life.

No more con games, no more playing on the kindness of strangers for however brief a time.

Rule Number One.

You will always be alone.

Only . . . what if I can't stand to be alone any more?

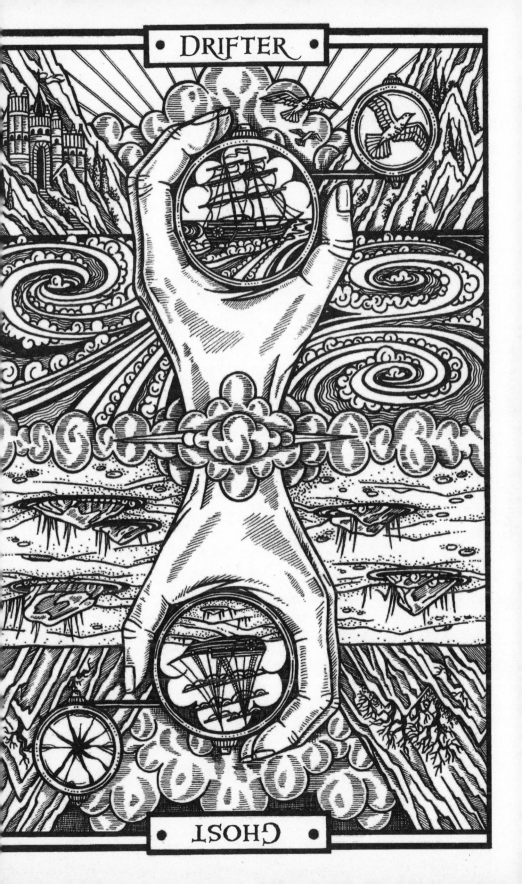

DRIFTER

GHOST

The Drifter

A wanderer journeys far, but has no path, their steps heading wherever the road takes them. To travel untethered can unlock new ways of seeing the world, but eventually the wanderer begins to drift, no longer drawn by possibility but by trudging endlessly to nowhere. The Journey of the Drifter is not the Way of the Argosi.

27

The Gift

A lone scarlet droplet clung to the tip of my smallsword. It was trying to tell me something. It's never a good sign when you think your blood is talking to you.

From the blue sands of the Azurite region, through miles of pale quartz that drifted like an endless field of snow beneath a sweltering sun, and further west into the ruby desert, I ran and ran and ran.

The borderlands don't have much to recommend them: the terrain is harsh, settlements few and far between, and what people you meet don't take too kindly to strangers. In my case, of course, that made little difference.

You will always be alone.

Not much of a curse, when you think about it. Stories abound of hermits living their whole lives without speaking a word to another human being. I liked animals well enough. All I had to do was find some place to hide, learn to live off the land, and keep to myself.

Sure. Sounds great. You try it.

Perhaps it was some hereditary defect of my people. The Mahdek live in clans. We make up stories, dance and sing, fall in and out of love, and . . . well, I guess everybody does those things. Whatever the reason, the further I kept from other people, the more brittle I became. All the problems in my head got worse. I couldn't keep track of time, trudging alone in the desert for days without remembering to sleep, and after a while I couldn't be sure if I was even awake.

My memories manifested as ghosts that haunted me until I could no longer tell where I was or how I'd gotten there. One time I woke up in a cave, huddled there among rocks I thought were corpses, wondering when Sir Rosarite and Sir Gervais would come and save me. Another time I stood unflinching as a sandstorm washed over me, convinced I was inside a Jan'Tep sanctum and the members of the Cabal were testing my abilities before inviting me to join their number. They cast me out after I'd held out my hands for an hour, fingers gesticulating wildly as I mumbled nonsensical incantations that for some reason refused to produce any kind of spell.

How long had it taken for me to get this messed up? Days? Weeks? Months? Was I still a girl, or had I aged into a senile old woman, shuffling along the sands, looking for just the right spot to lie down and die. Most of the time I had no idea who I was or where I was headed.

Worst of all?

I missed Falcon.

How stupid – how *utterly gods-damned pathetic* – was that?

How do you know when you've completely lost your mind? Allow me to suggest that when you find yourself longing to hear the voice of your tormentor because you're so sick of the sound of your own muttering that you're not sure how many more days you can go on like this before you rip out your own tongue – *that's* when you know you've lost it.

Falcon? Are you there?

Idiot.

Out of desperation, I tried to relive my memories of Sir Rosarite and Sir Gervais, and the things they taught me. Honour. Dignity. Kindness. Hope.

Hope.

Hope for what, exactly?

What miracle was I waiting for to get me out of this mess? Not one of the good things that had happened to me had lasted. Any time my life had gotten the least bit better, every effort I made to become someone new – someone who could fight this curse the Jan'Tep had inflicted on me – things fell apart again. Nothing I did, no choice I made, had any chance against the tattooed sigils around my neck.

What was left for me then but death?

From my mapmaker's case I'd taken out Sir Rosarite's small-sword. I hadn't sharpened the blade in ages, but I could still draw blood when I pricked my finger on the tip. I sat down cross-legged on the ground and wondered whether the crimson sand would look any different when I was done.

I'd once read that the Jan'Tep consider suicide to be a crime against the nation. Every citizen owes their lives to their country, their culture. To destroy all the good your life might bring to your people was therefore tantamount to murder.

The Daroman are different; they have all kinds of tragic tales in which the noble thing to do is end your own life rather than face dishonour. Sir Gervais hated those stories. Honour demands service. Death is . . .

'Death is the final gift we have to give others. To die well is to spend that final drop of all of life's wonders to leave the world better than you found it.'

199

I stared at that tiny red droplet clinging to the end of my smallsword. What gift might I make of my death? Surely it benefited no one if I died out here – my blood would do nothing but dull the glittering expanse of crimson sand all around me. When the heat, wind and carrion birds were done stripping my flesh, my bones would only sink deeper and deeper until the last traces of my time in this life disappeared forever.

No.

That's not the way I'm going out.

I got up and gathered my things, holding on to that thought to keep my mind focused. Sharp. There was a town I'd passed two miles back. If I hurried, I could get there while it was still dark, steal a few supplies and begin my journey west to where the Seven Sands finally met the edge of the Jan'Tep territories.

What would I do when I got there? I had no idea. Maybe I would find Falcon and kill him. Maybe he'd kill me. One way or another though, even if it was only to force him to watch me die up close, I would bring him some tiny fraction of the anguish he'd caused me. He would learn that a lowly Mahdek could face death with more courage and dignity than any Jan'Tep mage.

Let that be my gift to the world.

28

That Which Ain't Right

When you consider all the things I had to do to reach the Jan'Tep territories – acts of midnight thievery in villages and farmhouses, crossing sweltering desert, precarious mountain passes, fording raging rivers, and facing off against feral animals and sometimes human beings twice as savage . . . it's a miracle I got as close as I did.

Oatas Jan'Ju. The Oasis of Wise Magic.

This was the name the Jan'Tep had given to their southern-most city – after they'd stolen it from my people three hundred years ago. What had it been called then? No one knows. Ask a half-dozen Mahdek clans and you'll get seven different answers. Some of the younger folk might even tell you, quiet so as not to enrage their elders, that maybe they never were our cities. Perhaps we'd stolen them from someone before us, or perhaps it was all just a myth we'd made up to make ourselves feel better for having no cities of our own.

Sometimes I wondered if my trouble remembering things properly was really so different from the way just about everyone rearranged the past to suit the present. But when I stood there at the edge of the desert, looking across a quarter-mile of flat, lifeless sand to the breathtaking colours emanating from the seven marble columns of their oasis to lend their entire city a kind of swirling, enchanting glow, I understood why the Jan'Tep believed in their own innate superiority.

I almost believed it.

Even from this far away, the aromas that came from their spells combined to become an ocean wave, first crashing over me, then drawing me into the sea itself, seducing me with promises of all the marvels that awaited me beneath the surface.

I guess that's why he took me so easily.

The hand wrapped around the back of my neck squeezed, fingers strong as iron. His grip was tight, but not so much it hurt. He just wanted me to be aware that, out here, in all this empty desert, with the high moon bright enough to light up the sand below, he'd walked right up to me without my noticing.

'Look up at the stars,' he said.

I recognised Durral Brown's voice instantly.

'Are you going to kill me?' I asked.

His thumb and forefinger shuddered, and for a second I thought he might snap my neck with one hand. How long had he been tracking me? Why had he waited until now to make his move?

I stared straight ahead at the lights of Oatas Jan'Ju.

So close. I'd gotten so close.

Maybe that was a lie though. There were at least seven Jan'Tep cities in the territories. I had no way of knowing if Shadow Falcon lived in this one. Still, when you've come so far for nothing, you like to pretend at least you got close.

'Look up at the stars,' Durral growled in my ear.

You'd think, after all I'd gone through, that maybe death

would be a relief. Life so far had been pretty awful. I was tired. I was weak. Everywhere I went, people hated me. Did it really matter whether it was a Jan'Tep mage or an Argosi gambler who finally put an end to me? Yet, for no reason I could explain, in that instant, with death so close I could smell the whisky on its breath, I discovered that life, while perhaps not precious, is decidedly dogged. Just when you try to toss it away, it grabs hold of you so tight you can barely breathe.

'Don't kill me,' I whispered.

Pathetic.

'Look up at the stars.'

It was the third time he'd said it, so I did as I was told. What did he want me to see up there? The beauty of the night sky? The void of eternal darkness? Was this to give me some small comfort before he took my life or to show me the emptiness to which I was headed?

'Where we stand,' he said, the awful warmth of his breath on my ear making me shiver, 'right in this spot is the only place in the world where you can see this exact combination of stars.'

Despite the barely contained rage in his voice, he spoke almost reverentially. Do killers feel reverence? Maybe murder is a spiritual thing to them. A holy thing. I guess that's why I didn't point out that *everywhere* is the only place you can see *some* configuration of stars. There were probably thousands of places where the sky looked just as magnificent.

And it *was* magnificent, I realised then.

'It's breathtaking,' I said, which probably wasn't the best choice of words seeing as how he might choke the life out of me any second.

203

'If you look up at them long enough,' Durral said, one hand on my shoulder and the other shifting higher to squeeze my jaw, 'you stop seeing the beauty. You just . . .' I could hear his teeth grinding, like he was trying to chew through leather. 'You see the sky ain't tryin' to be pretty. It's just . . . right.'

'Right?' I asked, mumbling because his grip on my jaw had tightened.

'As it should be,' he replied, which didn't clarify anything. 'Nothin' bein' forced nor compelled. Nothin' manipulated. The stars are just as they should be.'

Too much confusion and fear started leaking out of me in the form of tears and panicked moans. 'I don't understand! Nothing you're saying makes any sense!'

'It makes perfect sense!' he snarled. There was nothing in that voice of the grinning rogue in the brown frontier hat who'd befriended me in that tavern, who'd stared down four big men to protect me. 'Look at the stars!'

'I am!'

His hand on my jaw forced my head down and around so that I was staring him in the face – into a madness that was both terrifying and yet somehow familiar.

'Look at me!' he demanded. 'Look at me and tell me what you see!'

I did. I looked into the face of a madman, into a perverse, grinding, churning need to hurt me, to hear me scream until there was nothing left but the final sigh of life leaving my body.

'It isn't right,' I wept.

He nodded, sounding almost relieved. 'It ain't right.'

His grip relaxed, just a little, as his gaze drifted back up to the stars overhead. He was staring at them as if he wanted to reach out and hang on to them to keep from being swept out to sea. When his eyes returned to me, he said, 'Somethin' ain't right in me, girl. Ain't been right since I decided to help you back at that tavern. Now it's so bad I gotta . . . I gotta . . .'

'Just let me go,' I pleaded. 'I'll leave you alone and you'll never have to see me again!'

'Can't,' he said, the word coming out almost like a groan. 'I'm too good a tracker and you're too bad a runner. Held out long as I could.'

He hurled me away from him, so hard I went tumbling to the ground. I got back to my hands and knees. Tears slid down my cheeks, dripping from my chin to the sand below.

'Get up,' he said.

Sobbing, I rose to my feet. I reached over my shoulder and drew the smallsword from the mapmaker's case strapped to my back.

'Think that'll do you any good?' Durral asked. 'A fancy little sword like that? Against an Argosi? You never hear of *arta eres*, girl?'

I hadn't. I doubted he was about to teach me either, so I brought my smallsword up into guard and tried to remind myself that the blade was sharp and he was unarmed.

'Come on then,' he said. 'What're you waitin' for?'

Somewhere off in the desert, a dog howled. Durral looked like he wanted to howl too.

'I won't let you hurt me,' I said.

His hands clenched, not into fists, but with his fingers curled like claws. His lower jaw trembled. Whatever Durral had been in life, whatever hopes and dreams for himself, the collar around my neck was stripping them from him. His whole body shook, and I knew that seconds from now he

205

was going to hurl himself at me. I hoped my blade might find his heart before his teeth found my throat.

His eyes went up, and I thought they were rolling back in his head, but instead his gaze locked on the sky above us, and the stars glittering overhead.

'I ain't this way,' he insisted.

'I know,' I said, my own arm shaking as if I'd been holding the sword for hours.

'I am Durral Brown,' he bellowed at the stars. 'I am Argosi! I walk the Path of the Rambling Thistle!'

His shouts became more and more guttural, like he was smashing his head against a rock and losing the power of speech.

'The Way of Water flows through me! My feet follow the Way of Wind!' The fingers of his right hand closed into a fist and he began smashing it repeatedly against his chest. 'When I strike, it ain't clumsy or brutish, but perfect and true as the Way of Thunder.' He stopped hitting himself and took a step towards me, jerkily, as if he were trying to resist ten strong men pushing him from behind. 'When I stand my ground, I am unmovable as the Way of Stone!'

But he was movable, and he kept moving, step by step, to me.

'Please . . .' I begged, weeping now as much from this destruction of the soul I was witnessing as for my own life.

'I am Durral Brown,' he said again. 'I am Argosi. I do not hurt little girls.'

But he was so close, his chest barely two feet from the tip of my blade. My thrust had to come now or I'd never get another chance.

'It ain't in me,' he growled.

206

How many days and nights had he fought against the spells drawing him to me? What had it cost him to hold back so long, to come now to this place and still be fighting against a hatred as real as the sand beneath our feet and as big as the endless night sky?

'I know it ain't in you,' I said softly, my back foot bracing against the ground, the muscles in my calf and thigh propelling my body forward as my arm extended out and I drove the point of my sword towards his heart. 'It's in me.'

One of the first things Sir Rosarite had taught me was not to close my eyes when I lunged. It's a natural instinct because most people don't want to watch a blade pierce another human being's flesh. But I'd never had that problem. Not until that very moment.

'I know it's in you,' Durral Brown said.

I opened my eyes and saw his hand closed around my blade, bending it down so I couldn't push it through, blood dripping from his palm. The madness was still there, in his eyes, but the steel I saw beneath was forged stronger than any sword. He could've yanked the weapon from my hand, but he didn't, and I swear had there really been ten men behind him pushing him towards me, they wouldn't have shifted him an inch.

'I am the Way of Stone,' he said, though it seemed as if he were talking to himself, not me. He let go of my blade, turned on his heel and strode back into the desert, away from Oatas Jan'Ju.

I stood there, only now aware I was covered in sweat, not knowing what to do. I thought that would be the last I ever heard from Durral Brown, but just then he called back: 'Well? You comin' or not?'

I stared at his silhouette, slowly shrinking into the distance.

'What . . . Where?' I stuttered.

The shadow stopped for a moment.

'Like you said, kid. This thing is in you. Been in you far too long, I reckon. Time we get it out.'

29

The Curse

There's something awful about putting your life in another's hands. Even as a child, I resented the way my clan went from town to town, always with our hands out, begging for shelter, offering labour no one wanted in exchange for food and supplies they could barely afford to give us. Living off the kindness – no, the *pity* – of others.

No wonder people look down on the Mahdek. *I* look down on us.

And now my future was entirely dependent on the kindness of a stranger – a stranger from whom I'd stolen a fortune and who hadn't even mentioned it yet – who had to keep his distance and grit his teeth to keep from reaching out with those gentle hands of his and snapping my neck.

'Don't rightly know what it's called,' Durral said, motioning for me to sit across the fire from him. He tossed me the beat-up tin canteen I'd tried to steal from him when we first met. 'Never seen it up close until I met you. Damn if it ain't the most malevolent invention any soul ever came up with.'

My greedy fingers fumbled with the canteen's stopper and soon I was gulping water so fast half of it was dribbling down my chin. 'What do you expect? The Jan'Tep are evil.'

'No, kid. They ain't.'

I wiped my face with my sleeve. 'Are all Argosi idiots?'

A sudden flash of anger passed over his features, and I saw the tension start up in his shoulders. Then he breathed in, long and slow, and closed his eyes as the air came back out in a tiny stream between his lips. At last his gaze found me again. 'Wish you wouldn't do that, kid. This thing you got in you is scratchin' at me hard enough already.'

'Sorry.'

'Ain't your fault. But I'm gonna need you to find a cool breeze inside yourself to soothe that anger of yours.'

'I'll try. I promise.'

He laughed. 'You ever keep a promise in your life, kid?'

I'd never thought about it, but now that he mentioned it, I couldn't think of one.

'Anyway . . .' he went on, scratching the furry head of his dog, who'd trotted out of the shadows to join us. His horse was a little ways off, vastly more interested in a small patch of dried bushes than in our conversation. 'First thing you gotta understand is that the Jan'Tep are just people. Some are kind, some are cruel. They come into the world like the rest of us, knowin' nothin' and only gettin' dumber as they go along. A culture like theirs, obsessed with the wonders of magic, well, it can inspire beauty, exploration, even creation, but it can also—'

Now I had to hold back the rage welling up inside my chest. 'You dare sit there and tell *me* about Jan'Tep culture?' My finger jabbed at the tattoos around my neck. 'You would justify *this*? Because what? It's a product of their *culture*?'

Instead of a reply, he closed his eyes again, and I had to sit there watching him breathe in and out as the fire crackled

210

and the desert blew gusts of red sand all around us. I knew he was going inside himself to protect me – that every time I goaded him I was making it harder for him to fight off the influence of my collar, but I couldn't stop myself. I had a hundred good reasons to hate the Jan'Tep, and I was never, ever going to let even one of them go.

'Kid,' he said.

'What?'

'You're gonna stop doin' that, understand? You're gonna stop lettin' all that righteous fury of yours get the better of you. Rage ain't the Argosi way.'

I took another sip of water from the canteen to give myself something to do while I searched for some fraction of the resolve that was keeping Durral from killing me. But I couldn't find it.

'Does being Argosi mean you can get this thing off me?' I asked, tapping the sigils around my neck. 'Or are you just going to sit there and tell me to contemplate a wild daisy and hope that makes people stop wanting to kill me?'

For no reason I could understand, that brought a smile to his face. 'See, kid? Now you're askin' the right questions.'

Okay, so he really was an idiot, which was unfortunate since he was, at that moment, literally the only person in the world who was on my side.

'You're saying that maybe if I control myself like you're doing now, I can counteract the magic in the sigils?'

He looked up from digging around in his pack. 'What? No, course not. Can't just go around wishing curses away.'

'But you said—'

'I said you were askin' the right questions.'

He tossed me a stick of dried meat. 'Jerky', he called it. Dumb

211

name, but hungry as I was, it tasted delicious, even though it was so chewy I couldn't talk. Maybe that was the point.

'Now, magic's not really my thing,' he began. 'But we Argosi know a fair bit about what lurks inside the human heart. The way this spell they got on you makes me feel tells me there's a . . . a presence to it. Ain't like you just smell bad and that makes people hate you – though a bath wouldn't do you no harm right about now.'

Still gnawing on my stick of jerky, I gestured to the desert around us.

'Good point, kid.' He fed a stick of the dried meat to his dog and then took another for himself. 'Anyhow, the way I reckon it, these feelings that rise up inside me when I look at you, they ain't mine.'

'What do you mean?' I mumbled between chews.

He shook his head as if he weren't sure of his own reply. 'It's like . . . like all these ugly things I'm feeling, they're comin' from you. Doubts about yourself, bitterness over the unfairness in your life, your self-hatred—'

'I don't hate myself. I hate the Jan'Tep. It's not the same thing.'

'Hate is hate, kid. Simple as that.' He held up a hand before I could contradict him. 'What matters is that I'm pretty sure those fancy tattoos around your neck are scoopin' up every ugly thought inside you and scattering them to the world like a handful of seeds. Those seeds start to grow inside the heart of anyone who comes near you.'

I swallowed. 'You're saying this is my fault?'

He didn't catch the sarcasm. 'Reckon so. In part anyways.'

'Because I hate myself?'

'We all got darkness inside us, kid. Wouldn't be any way

212

for us to walk through this world without it. But this curse or spell or whatever it is, I think it attaches itself to very specific pieces of that darkness – to the parts that maybe make you want to hurt yourself.'

I wished what he was saying was wrong, desperately wanted to scream in his face that he was a fool and a bastard and how dare he tell me any of this – *any* of it – was my fault. Only it seemed to me that I *had* wanted to hurt myself. Plenty of times.

'Cruel part of it is,' Durral went on, 'them Jan'Tep mages designed this spell of theirs to feed on a person's altruistic impulses. More somebody wants to help you, more the urge comes on to hurt you instead.'

Those words sunk in deep, and again I sat there staring at this strange man across the fire from me. The Argosi sat cross-legged, hands folded in his lap, but he wasn't still. Not really. Every few seconds you could see the muscles in his neck and shoulders twitch, rebelling against his kinder impulses, trying to force him to get up and leap across the fire to hurt me in a thousand different ways.

'Guess you want to help me pretty bad right now?'

Even through all the tension that made his features look as if they'd been carved in stone, a softness came to his eyes. 'Nobody deserves what they did to you, kid. Nobody. I can't allow it.'

'You can't *allow* it?'

'Nope. I can't allow a thing as foul as what they did to you exist in a world as beautiful as this one.' He opened his right arm out to the desert. 'A world with sand that glitters like a million, million rubies. Or stretches out in blue waves like a calm sea on a clear day.' His other hand pointed up to the

213

sky. 'Under stars so bright each one is like a promise. No, ma'am. Such a curse as you carry offends those stars above. It offends me.'

'It offends you?' I repeated dully.

He nodded, then smiled. 'Sure does. How about you?'

I don't know why, but I started laughing. Durral's description of the magic that had dashed every hope I'd ever allowed myself, as if the sigils around my neck were nothing more than an unsightly vase that didn't suit the surrounding decor, was so ridiculous, so utterly preposterous, that for just a second it shrank the curse down to something that was far too small to encompass my life.

'I . . . Yes,' I said at last. 'It offends me too.'

'Good. So let's you and me do something about it.' He reached into his coat and removed a deck of cards. 'Now, while the Path of the Rambling Thistle rarely travels through such wearisome territory as magic and sorcery and other childish nonsense, we Argosi ain't above a few tricks of our own.'

'You want to play cards again?' I asked, confused.

'You reckon that'll purge the curse from you?'

'No.'

'Me neither.' He motioned for me to join him on the other side of the fire. 'But this ain't a regular deck of cards.'

In spite of the danger I still felt emanating from him like the stench coming off a corpse, I crept closer. The cards he'd fanned out before me were smaller than the ones we'd played with back at the tavern. These were illustrated, but not with the regular Daroman suits of chariots, arrows, blades and trebuchets. The suits on these cards had names like curses, conjurations, abjurations and bindings.

'Spell deck,' Durral offered before I could ask the question.

'Are they magical?'

'Not in the way you're thinking. See, we Argosi like to ramble. Wanderin's in our nature, and when we see somethin' wrong in the world, well . . . some folks would call it meddlin'. The Jan'Tep in particular get ornery when we interfere with their culture.'

Ornery. I almost laughed again. 'Mages torture and kill their enemies. They do that and worse, sometimes just for fun.'

Durral was rifling through the cards, not looking at me. 'Told you before, they ain't as bad as all that – at least not all of them. Most are just folks like you and me, tryin' to make their way through life, carryin' the weight of history on their backs.'

Despite everything that had happened, despite all the things I had to worry about and most of all how much I now found myself dependent on Durral Brown and his Argosi ways, I screamed my next words at the top of my lungs. 'Stop. Saying. That!'

The dog looked up at me and gave a questioning bark. Durral was still nose deep in his cards. I walked right up to him and slapped the cards from his hands. 'The Jan'Tep are evil. They massacred my people. One of them put this curse on me just to make sure I'd die miserable and alone!'

Durral still wasn't looking at me. His hands were shaking with the effort of not reaching out and grabbing me by the throat. 'Ain't no such thing as an evil person, kid,' he said, picking up the cards as best he could, dropping half of them. 'Only evil thoughts and evil deeds, and we all got those. You believe your heart is free of such things? You think I ain't never met no other Mahdek in my time? Seen them commit terrible crimes in the name of vengeance?'

215

'It's not the same thing!'

He didn't speak again until he'd collected every one of the fallen cards. 'No,' he said at last. 'Reckon it's not the same thing.'

I stalked back away from him, staking out my side of the fire, my piece of territory. 'If the cards aren't magic, how can they help?' I asked.

Durral pulled one out, stared at it a while, stuck it back in the deck. 'Like I told you, we Argosi are travellers. We see the world, pieces of it anyway, and when we find somethin' curious, we paint a card to remember it. We share those cards with each other when we meet so that the knowledge we glean isn't lost when it's most needed.' He tossed me one of the cards at random. 'Tell me what you see in this one.'

The card was titled 'Three of Bindings' and depicted a bird wrapped in iron wire, its wings pinned back. 'Iron magic,' I answered. 'Mages use it sometimes to snare their victims.'

'Yep,' he said, but I could tell there was more.

The longer I stared at the card, the more details came to life. The bird didn't look like it was in pain. Instead it looked . . . like it was about to sing. Not a sad song or a happy one, but . . . 'The shape of the bird's beak,' I said aloud. 'It's like he's about to sing a mocking tune, as though the wire weren't binding him at all.'

'And?' Durral encouraged.

I held up the card. 'It's not just a description of the magic, is it? The card is a trick of some kind. A way around the spell.'

When Durral Brown next looked at me, it was as if for the first time I wasn't just some stray he'd met outside a roadside tavern. 'Tell me the trick,' he said.

I went back to the card a third time. 'I think it's saying that if you want to fight an iron binding, you have to pretend it's not working – distract the mage and make him think the spell failed.'

'Got all that from a picture of a bird, did you?'

I nodded.

'Well now,' Durral said slowly, like he had to taste each word before spitting it out, 'that's some pretty good arta precis you got going on, kid.'

'Which one's arta precis again?'

'Spottin' things others miss.' He removed a new card from the deck, started to put it back with the others then stopped himself. 'Yeah, this here's the one we want.'

He tossed me the card. This one was titled 'Six of Conjurations' and depicted a floppy-hatted traveller pulling his own shadow from his mouth while a crowd of men and women armed with knives and clubs crept up behind him.

'The shadow. It represents my curse, right?'

'Reckon so.'

'And pulling it out is the cure? How can you grab hold of a shadow?'

'Cards ain't always literal, kid. Oftentimes – and I'm sorry to say I think this is one of them – the Argosi who first painted the card isn't even sure what it means or how it works. It's just what they gleaned from the events they bore witness to.'

'Then it's useless,' I said, tossing the card back across the fire to him.

He snatched it out of the air even as he stood up and strolled over to my side. 'Maybe you ain't got such good arta precis after all, kid, cos you missed the important part.'

'Which is?'

217

He knelt down next to me and held up the card, pointing a gloved finger at the crowds surrounding the victim. 'If the curse gets stronger the more people want to help you, stands to reason that it gets weaker when—'

'No . . .' I murmured.

''Fraid so.'

I pointed to the man pulling the shadow out of his mouth. 'So I can't draw out the curse until it's weak enough, and the only way to weaken it is . . .'

Durral Brown clapped me on the shoulder. 'Saddle up, kid. We gotta go make a whole bunch of folks want to kill you real bad.'

30

The Noose

There was something unexpectedly reassuring about the feeling of a noose around my neck. My whole life I'd just assumed I'd die from an ember spell. Burned alive in magical flames, struck by lightning on a dry day, one of the real bad ones that eats through your skin one layer at a time before slurping up your internal organs. Iron magic is just as bad. Once a mage has bound his spell to your heart or liver or kidney, he can squeeze as slow as he wants and make you go on living just long enough to wear out your voice begging for death.

Those weren't even the worst options. Blood magic can turn your body against itself. Breath spells can suck the air out of your lungs while you claw at your own throat.

Worse still is silk magic. With his spells slithering around inside your head, a skilled mage can make you tear your own flesh from your bones. Make you eat yourself to death, smiling all the while, convinced you were dining on the finest sweet-meats even as your soul screams for a merciful end.

So, really, hanging by a rope around your neck, betrayed by a fast-talking card player, isn't so bad by comparison.

'Promised y'all I'd find the witch, didn't I?' Durral asked, spreading his arms wide as he strode around the town's gibbet, on which I was now precariously perched.

What kind of town keeps a permanent gibbet in the public square?

I kept my mouth shut. My hands were tied behind my back, the noose around my neck. All I had to stand on was two square feet of plank on a platform five feet off the ground. A brass latch near my feet was connected to a length of rope. Durral had offered to be the one to pull the rope when the time came so as to keep the souls of the good townsfolk untainted. Right now, though, he was too busy being full of himself.

'How many bad harvests you been huntin' the witch that condemns your town to one dyin' crop after another? Calves with two heads and babies with no eyes. How many years you been prayin' and cryin', "Mercy me, mercy me!" until the one and only Durral Brown came to town?'

The word Argosi, I was coming to understand, meant 'scoundrel who can't stop talking about himself'.

Meanwhile the crowd surrounding us just kept getting bigger and bigger. There couldn't be more than two hundred souls in a town this size, but two hundred pairs of eyes is a lot when each one is glaring at you like they might just fight 'the one and only Durral Brown' for the privilege of yanking the rope.

'Too many years now,' he went on, 'suspicion has turned you fine people against each other.' He gave a chuckle and tugged at the collar of his shirt. 'Set you to mistrustin' innocent Argosi wanderers just lookin' for a nice place to sleep and a friendly game of cards.'

So he'd been here before. No doubt cheated them at cards,

and these rubes had figured that was sufficient evidence for a charge of witchcraft.

'Told you then, didn't I?' the Argosi went on, wagging his finger at each area of the crown in turn. 'When you had that rope around my neck? Told you only one of my kind could find the real culprit.' He tapped a gloved finger to his temple. 'Got me the finest arta precis of all the wandering peoples.'

Arta precis again. He seemed to think it very important to make this point, despite the fact that no one in the crowd seemed to have any better idea what *that meant* than I did.

Durral Brown, though, was undaunted. 'Got me some even finer arta tuco. That's subtlety, for those of you ain't familiar with the Argosi ways.'

He started circling even closer to the gibbet, hunching low as if there was a danger I might suddenly break my bonds and leap on him and bite his face off. He wasn't wrong about that, actually.

'She's a wily one, this here witch,' he bragged. 'Tried to use her demon spells to come on me unawares.' He spun on his heels, fingers crooked like curved claws. The crowd gasped, before he stood up straight and smiled, touching a finger to his hat. 'Tried to mess with my head too.'

More murmuring. A young boy – the only one with brains or guts from what I could see – called out, 'Liar! Everybody knows you can't fight a witch's whisper!'

Durral gave the kid a wink. 'That's regular folk. We Argosi got twisty minds. Can't be fooled by warlocks nor witches.' He swung his arm back towards me. 'Not even demons like this one!'

Somebody screamed. Somebody else moaned. Most of the rest started praying to one god or another, pressing their thumbs and forefingers together in the shape of a house to ward off evil magic.

Stupid townies. If that worked, every Mahdek parent would've glued their children's thumbs and forefingers together at birth.

But now other townsfolk – the ones inclined to put their faith in clubs, pitchforks and knives instead of silly hand gestures – began edging closer to the gibbet.

'Yes!' Durral said as if he was the one urging them forward. 'That's right. Time for justice. Time we sent the demon back to whichever hell she came from.'

More and more of them were crowding in now. I could smell them. I could feel the heat coming off their faces, taste the sweat from all their anxious shuffling under the hot sun. In about five seconds somebody was going to put the sharp end of a blade through my heart.

Guess that's quicker than dangling from a rope. Things are really looking up now that I've hooked up with an Argosi.

'Not so fast,' Durral said.

His tone had changed. It wasn't self-righteous or smarmy. It was commanding, like he was a general who'd just conscripted all these people into his battalion. The crowd froze where they stood, watching him.

'Not until I get paid first.'

Son of a bitch.

I rarely swore, even to myself. But this was a special occasion.

There had been a moment there when I'd thought maybe this whole 'hang the witch' thing had been an act – that Durral had needed to rile them up against me so the curse would become tangible and he could pull it out of me like in the picture on the card he'd shown me. The fact that he hadn't

222

told me he'd been to this town before was suspicious, sure, but I figured maybe it was just conveniently out of the way of any Jan'Tep settlements. The fact that he'd also neglected to mention that long before he'd met me he'd already promised to hunt down the witch who'd been plaguing the townspeople's lives for a reward . . . ?

No wonder he'd been so keen to befriend me back at that stupid tavern. And all his vaunted self-control? Resisting the effects of the sigils around my neck? Talking my ear off about the beauty of the stars and how a curse like mine *offended* him? That was just a gambler's way of turning trouble into opportunity.

He had the gall to turn his head in my direction and give me a wink.

'He's a liar!' I shouted to the crowd. 'I'm not a witch!'

Then I realised that was probably exactly what they'd expect a witch to say. 'Actually, I *am* a witch. A terrible witch. My curses make your carrots taste like cauliflower! I cause babies to be born with . . . with six elbows! And that's not all. This man here, he's been working with me for years, helping me find the most decent, gods-fearing towns so I can ruin them for my demon lord. You know what the word Argosi means? It means . . .'

I was running out of ideas and breath at the same time.

'"Person who finds decent, gods-fearing towns for witches"?' Durral suggested.

'Exactly,' I said.

He laughed so big and broad people started snickering right along with him. 'There you have it, folks. Just like the old stories say: when a witch speaks, her every truth is paired with a lie.'

I guessed that the truth in this case was my admission of being a witch and therefore, by claiming Durral as my confederate, I'd just given testimony proving he wasn't.

'If we can get down to business here,' he said, 'I know we'd all like to see this witch hanged . . .' He turned to me. 'Not hanged to death, you understand.'

'What's the point of that?' I asked. Foolishly.

'So that you're softened up but still awake for when you're being drawn, quartered and finally burned.'

That figured.

'Why should we pay?' asked a stalwart fellow holding a wooden staff he was trying unsuccessfully to light with a match. 'We've already got the witch.'

'A pact is a pact,' Durral replied. He reached into his waist-coat and produced a vial of dark viscous fluid that he poured on the end of the man's staff before taking one of the matches and setting the wood ablaze. 'Reckon a town that's seen as much sufferin' as yours wouldn't want to bring down the ill luck the gods send for those who go back on a blood-sworn bargain.'

That initiated debate among the townsfolk. A few raised voices, a great many glares – mostly for me, but some for Durral too – eventually settled into grim nods of assent. Superstition had won out over greed.

'We ain't got much,' a woman said, coming forward with a bag of coin, 'but it's like you said, Argosi: a pact's a pact.'

Durral glanced at the bag and – without even opening it – shook his head. 'This won't do.'

'You aim to bleed us dry, Argosi?' someone else asked.

'Ain't that,' Durral said. 'If we're going to cleanse this place of a witch's influence, then everybody has to pay.' His voice got louder then, addressing the entire town. 'Pay what you want. Pay what you can. A copper spit if that's all you possess, a silver nob if you want to make sure no witch ever returns. But just as each of you has suffered her foulness, so must each of you sacrifice something of your own to end her reign.'

I was surprised by the unexpected formality in his tone and the solemnity of his stance, like something between that of a priest and a king. Not that I'd ever seen a king.

Soon enough the townsfolk fell into a great long line like a snake slithering all the way from the gibbet to clear on out, further than I could see through the dusty haze. One by one they stepped forward, and at Durral's direction, held out whatever they had – or were willing – to offer. Some didn't have anything at all, so someone richer first handed them one of their own coins. Nice people, I guess.

With the coin in hand, each one would spit on it and then throw it at my feet as they locked eyes with me and swore one malediction or another upon my most wretched soul.

You're all a bit late if you were hoping to curse me, I thought.

The way they were looking at me though, as if it were me forcing them to give up those little copper and silver treasures, it was as if their loss fuelled their hate for me even more than their belief in my witchcraft.

Once each person was done, they crowded round again, surrounding me on my gibbet, waiting for the end. The hatred they felt for me was almost like a living thing.

Not almost, I realised with a start. The vicious fury was like thick, sticky oil being poured down my throat, choking me. I was drowning in it, my body so heavy I thought the small wooden platform would collapse under my weight.

'Ready, kid?' Durral whispered.

225

Ready for what? For death? To burn in the fires of some hell my people didn't even believe in?

But Durral Brown was looking at me like the question was genuine.

Spirits of the dead, kind and cruel, I thought. *Is there really some chance he didn't betray me? That this insane situation he set up is actually his idea of helping me?*

'Oh,' I said aloud, not by choice but because something in my belly was moving. It was like there were two of me stuffed in this body, and the other was waking up.

My face felt itchy. The palms of my hands were so slick and clammy I could almost slip out of the ties around my wrists. Though I couldn't move my head much on account of the rope around my neck, I felt the urge to look down, and saw that I was bleeding everywhere.

No. Not blood. Wax. The red wax Falcon and Met'astice had forced down my throat back when I was strapped to that table in the cave, only far more than I'd swallowed, as if over the years it had grown inside my guts until I was more wax than flesh.

There was a scream from the crowd – probably the same idiot who screamed at everything. I couldn't see them though, because I kept having to blink the molten red wax out of my eyes. I was covered in it now. Drenched all the way through. It was like someone had covered me in a slithering, writhing coat of blood-swollen leeches. Now I was the one who wanted to scream, only I couldn't. I was choking as more and more of the wax came out of my mouth, dripping onto my body. Desperate for answers, for reassurance, my eyes sought out Durral Brown.

The look he gave me . . . I couldn't tell what it meant, but I saw his lips moving as he said, 'Time to be brave, kid.'

Brave? How was I supposed to be brave when I couldn't even breathe?

Just when I thought I was going to suffocate, my remains encased in a red wax cocoon, the scarlet coating began to melt, seeping down my face and chest and limbs until it pooled beneath my feet on the wooden platform of the gibbet. The puddle of red wax never settled though. Instead it began to bubble as if it were boiling, though I felt no heat from it. Higher and higher the molten wax rose, becoming a fountain whose oily red secretions froze as they reached their apex a foot above my head. Soon a figure took shape. As his head tilted down to examine his scarlet limbs, cracks in the wax appeared then melted back into smoothness again. A flame flickered to life at the top of his crimson skull as if he were a living candle.

'Fascinating,' he said.

The voice was both brittle and muffled, the age indiscernible, but I recognised it instantly, and however much horror I'd felt before was magnified a hundred times over.

'Met'astice . . .'

Laughter erupted from his mouth as tiny blobs of red wax, that fell to the platform only to be reabsorbed back into his body.

'Hello, my little knight,' he said.

31

The Candle Man

Shouts and wails erupted all around the gibbet as the towns-people finally bore witness to a horror worthy of all their superstitions and folk tales. I hated them in that moment, for all their screaming and moaning and prayers to gods whose existence was surely disproved by the creature standing before me.

'They are rather . . . gullible, aren't they?' Met'astice asked, as if he and I were two sagacious and worldly scholars come to visit this sad little provincial town together.

He reached out a hand towards me, as if to rest it on my shoulder. I flinched away from his touch, and my panicked gyrations tightened the noose around my neck.

'You died!' I wheezed. 'I saw you—'

'Yes,' Met'astice said enthusiastically, flaunting his waxy red arm in the air. 'The experiment turned out rather well, don't you think?'

'We must kill the witch!' someone in the crowd shouted. 'She summons a demon to do her bidding!'

A few brave souls took up the call, aiming their knives and pitchforks in my direction. Durral leaped up the stairs to the gibbet and ran behind me. I didn't see the knife he used to cut my ropes, but two seconds later my hands were free and the noose was off my neck.

'Don't waste your time talkin' to it,' he said quietly. 'That ain't your Jan'Tep mage. That ain't nobody.'

The candle man was unperturbed by this seeming dismissal. Even without discernible features on his face, his contempt was obvious. 'An Argosi. How have we not eliminated all you meddling frontier philosophers yet?'

Durral didn't take the bait. Instead he pulled me closer to him. 'Gonna need you to be strong now, kid. Brave as brave can be.'

'What *is* he?' I asked.

'I am Met'astice of the House of Met,' the candle man declared, rounding on us. 'I am a lord magus of the Jan'Tep.'

Durral smirked. 'You ain't nothin' but a big ol' pile of wax, a spit of magic and the cruelty of a tired old man that grew inside a petrified child's heart.'

Something about those words got all knotted together in my mind. Wax. Magic. Cruelty. And then, the worst part of all: *that grew inside a petrified child's heart.*

I felt so sick I wanted to throw up. People don't come back from the dead. Not even the Jan'Tep can perform such hideous miracles. All the terrors I'd felt all these years, the bitterness, the hatred, all of it was bound up in my memories of Met'astice. That's why he wanted to see me again before he died. He wanted to make sure my darkest thoughts turned always to him; to his voice, his face, so that he would grow inside me, day by day, until at last, when life left my body, it would give rise to this foul testament to his torment of me.

'He's not really Met'astice, is he?' I asked.

229

Durral turned to me, and his hand reached up to cup my cheek. 'No, kid. He ain't.'

'He's . . . He's me.'

Durral shook his head. 'He ain't nearly big enough to contain all of you, girl. Just the tiniest, meanest parts you let him have.'

Even though I now knew the candle man wasn't Met'astice, even though there was no point to it, still I couldn't stop myself from screaming at him, 'Why would you do this to me? I'm nobody! I could never hurt you!'

With that same sickening patience, that . . . tolerance he'd always displayed with me, he replied, 'Because this is how it must be, child. The sheep must be taught to kill the wolves in their midst, that the shepherds might turn to more profitable endeavours.'

Endeavours like experimenting on a frightened, helpless Mahdek girl who never aspired to anything but a safe place to sleep and a chance to be happy. My fingers reached up to the sigils around my neck.

Are you there, Falcon?

Silence, but I knew it for a lie.

You can't hide from me. I can feel you when you're watching me.

Slowly I stepped past Durral to face the candle man.

Are you proud of what you did to me, Falcon? Was the experiment a success?

The candle man answered with Falcon's voice. 'This is war, Mahdek. Like you, I was born to it. Like your kind, I will fight with every weapon at my command in the service of my people.'

I looked past him at the townsfolk, who stared back,

confused, no longer certain which of us was the monster, only knowing for sure that there were, indeed, monsters in this world, and that it was a darker place than in any fable or folk tale.

Durral Brown laughed.

He wielded that laughter like a fine sword, making it so long the blade stretched all the way to wherever Falcon hid behind his spells.

The candle man raised a hand as if to grab Durral by the throat. 'Cease your braying, Argosi, or I will choke the mischief from you. I am a mage of the Jan'Tep, not some backwater farmhand you can cheat at cards.'

But Durral ducked under the arm and came up on the other side to stand even closer to the red wax creature. When he spoke next, the laughter was gone, and his tone was so cold it would've frozen a lake. I'd never heard him talk that way before, and would only ever hear him talk that way once more.

'I am Durral Argos,' he said, 'the Path of the Rambling Thistle. And I see you, boy. *I see you.*'

The candle man's form stiffened, hardened. Red spines appeared all over the surface of his waxy skin like the needles on a porcupine. 'You call me *boy*, Argosi? You would dare?'

But Durral was having none of it. He'd seemingly forgotten about me, about the townsfolk with their clubs and pitchforks, about the whole world. In that instant the rest of us had ceased to exist and all that was left was him and the candle man.

'I call you *boy*, boy, because that's what you are. Using what power you got for mischief. For cruelty. Look around you, fool. Look at the people suffering from hunger and misfortune, driven to superstition and hate. You think the world ain't already bad enough as it is? Find a righteous cause and set your talents to that, *boy*. Dig deep into that bleak heart of yours and scrape up some gods-damned dignity, *boy*, or I swear I *will* come find you one day. I will follow the Way of Wind right to your door, and all your spells won't break the Way of Stone.' He leaned in close. 'If you make me walk the Way of Thunder, I will end you.'

He glanced back at me, just for a moment, and I saw a look of such tenderness in his eyes that it was like he'd known me my whole life. When he turned back to the candle man, he said, 'I offer you the Way of Water, son of the Jan'Tep. Let your path and hers flow past each other, never again to meet unless it is in peace.'

How a creature made from magic, red wax and bitter hatred could be taken aback by an unarmed man in a frontier hat I did not know, but I swear I heard trepidation in Falcon's voice when he said, 'She is Mahdek, and this is war.'

'That war ended a long time ago,' Durral replied. 'Your side won. Whatever is left of her kind are just lookin' to run out their days as best they can. Ain't enough of them to repopulate their nation. Ain't enough to even call themselves a people no more. Tell your lords magi it's enough now. It is *enough*.'

There was a wavering in the candle man's form, as if the quiet, sorrowful Falcon I'd seen when his war coven had first come to massacre my clan was back, considering Durral's words, edging back from evil.

I resented that more than anything.

'They'll never stop!' I shouted. 'They don't know how. All they know is that it feels good when they watch the pain and suffering of others!'

232

Durral shot me an angry glare. 'Kid, this ain't how you win.'

Win? How could someone so wise be so blind? There was no winning for the Mahdek. He'd said it himself: there were too few of us to ever be a nation again. Our history, our culture, our stories would all fade to nothingness, and all that was left to fight over was how many years it would take for us to be forgotten.

'Then explain it to me, Durral Brown,' I said. 'Durral *Argos*. Show me this Path of the Rambling Thistle – whatever that's supposed to be. Show me how to fight an enemy who has all the power when I don't have any!'

His answer was quiet and sad and hopeful all at once.

'By surviving, kid. One day at a time, one foot in front of the other.'

Murmurs and mutters rose up from the crowd of townsfolk, as if they were debating the merits of our relative positions. Most likely they were trying to decide how safe it might be to kill us all.

The candle man, this heinous creation made from pieces of Met'astice and myself and now controlled by Falcon, responded to my rage with cold, unfeeling reason. 'I see now how you meant for this to work, Argosi,' he said to Durral. 'You surmised that at the moment she was about to die, slain by those who rightly despised her, my master's spells would weaken and could be expunged from her body.'

'You talk a great deal, boy,' Durral said. 'But you never say anything.'

The candle man laughed, and I couldn't tell whether it was with Falcon's voice or Met'astice's. 'The ploy had some merit, I admit, but now the ruse is revealed for what it is.

233

You showed your hand too soon, and her summoning my awareness gives me the chance to send the construct back inside of her.' The wax reached out towards me. 'You have given her the briefest taste of freedom only for me to take it away again.'

Again Durral ducked underneath, and yanked me out of the way. 'Ain't lettin' you have her back, boy. From now on this one is under the protection of the Argosi.'

From where I stood I could see the determination in Durral's eyes, and for the first time saw beneath all his bravado and clever words to the man beneath. I understood at last what the Argosi were – or at least what they aspired to be. Noble, idealistic, hopeful fools. Maybe they really did wander the entire continent observing how people lived and died, painting little cards for every dark deed, every vile spell. But they didn't understand any of it.

He must've caught my look, because he gave me a wink paired with one of his smirks. 'You just about done with this chump, kid?'

'Speak to me!' the candle man roared, the flame atop his skull flaring and causing the townsfolk to stumble back from the gibbet. I couldn't tell how much of him was Falcon any more, how much Met'astice and how much was my own self-hatred. 'Address *me*, not the girl. She is ours. Our property, to live in misery and die when *we* say so.'

There's more of them now, I realised then, hearing many voices in one. *The other lords magi. The Cabal. They're taking over from Falcon.*

I wanted to warn Durral, but he just made it worse, still talking to me. 'You hear that? The words of angry old geezers spoken by a callow youth. A frightened boy talkin' tough in

234

an attempt to prove himself worthy of the company of unworthy men. Problem is, none of those grand lessons in magic ever taught one of 'em the first thing about what bein' a man ought to mean.'

'You ruin her,' the candle man said. 'Your insults only serve to ensure that this time we'll make it so much worse for her, knowing that every day of the rest of her miserable life we will be inside her, waiting.'

Durral just laughed like the candle man was a tavern drunk boasting about himself. 'Problem there, friend, is you had it easy the first time you put this inside her.' He glanced at me with a terrible sympathy in his eyes. 'You Jan'Tep have taught her people so much about hate they couldn't help but take some of it on themselves. Hate is the door through which self-destruction enters each of us.'

The barking laugh that burbled out of the candle man was different yet again, and this time it seemed to me that it was a woman's voice. 'You give us too much credit, Argosi. Look at her! Have you ever seen a creature that seeps with so much self-spite? No, she was ours before. She will be ours again.' The candle man oozed closer. 'The experiment continues.'

I shrank back, but Durral grabbed my wrist. 'Can't fight 'em that way, kid.'

Slowly, mesmerisingly, the waxy crimson arm stretched out towards me.

'Then how do I fight them?' I asked, shaking uncontrollably. Only Durral's grip kept me from falling off the back of the gibbet.

'Gotta let go of the anger now,' he said. 'Let go of righteous vengeance. Let go of hatred.'

Of all the stupid things he'd said to me, that had to be the worst – hateful in itself, in fact, because it asked that I give up the only thing I had left that was mine. Lose my anger? Even for a second? Impossible.

Yet through trembling lips my own treasonous voice mumbled, 'How?'

The grin that came to Durral's face exploded with the promise of unforeseeable joy, of impossible daring, of an optimism known only to the most reckless of gamblers. 'Only one way to shed hatred, kid,' he said, spinning on his heel to face me, placing one hand on my waist and taking my right hand with his left. 'We gotta dance it away.'

32

The Dance

I'd never danced before. I mean, sure, as a small child who couldn't yet balance on two feet, I guess I'd probably swayed and stumbled about. The Mahdek, like all peoples except for the Jan'Tep, had our own music and songs and stories. And yeah, sometimes my people danced.

Not me though.

It always made Sir Gervais and Sir Rosarite sad when I'd come home with a note from my comportment instructor, Master Phinus, tattling on me for refusing to participate in dancing lessons and reminding them that *proper young ladies* had to know the five principal dances if they expected to ever join Daroman society.

But dancing doesn't get you fed. It doesn't find you shelter. No mage was ever killed by dancing. So what was the point of learning? To forget for a few minutes or hours that life was one big, panicked race before you finally got too slow and somebody killed you? Might as well hide your head under the covers when they came for you and make out that if you can't see them, they can't see you.

So, no, I never danced.

Durral, gripping both my hands so I couldn't get away, was

giving me exactly two choices: stand there while the candle man slithered his way back inside me, or dance while he no doubt did it anyway.

I guess when you're tumbling down a canyon you might as well enjoy the view before you hit the bottom.

'That's it,' Durral said, twirling me around the tiny gibbet like it was the grand ballroom of a magnificent palace. 'You're gettin' the hang of it.'

My feet were barely touching the wooden planks. Mostly I was just hanging on, trying to keep up with Durral's raucous whirling.

The townsfolk stared at us in horrified fascination. All in one day they'd witnessed a witch, a demon and now a complete lunatic taking over their town square.

And the candle man? He just laughed.

'What fine sport you Argosi make of all things,' he said. 'To prance about, pretending defiance is a spell.'

'Daring,' Durral said as though correcting a student, all the while keeping me turning with him as we danced to a tune only he could hear. To me he said, 'Or as we Argosi like to say, arta-gods-damned-valar. You know what daring is, kid?'

'Being brave?' I asked, almost tripping over my own feet because while being stupid, dancing is harder than you might expect.

Durral shook his head. 'Bravery is just another word for courage, and courage is just holding on – holding on to what's right even when you want to run so bad you have to nail your feet to the floor just to keep you in one place. Daring is different. Daring is letting go.'

I thought back to that day in the tavern when he'd faced down those four men who'd wanted to hang me. He'd seemed

238

courageous enough to me then, but now that I thought about it, maybe he was right. It hadn't looked like courage exactly.

'Letting go of what?' I asked.

'Enough of these games,' the candle man said.

His fingers reached out so close they nearly touched my face, but Durral spun me out of the way. 'Of everything,' he said. 'Fear. Anger. Even joy sometimes. Imagine you're at the top of a cliff above a lake of blue water. You want to jump in, but you know there are rocks below. You might hit one and break your spine. You might hit the water too hard and knock yourself unconscious. You might get caught underneath the surface and drown. The more you think about it, the worse the fear becomes. You start to resent yourself – start to think that maybe you're a coward, because you've seen others make the jump before you.'

'So what do you do?' I asked, stuttering because the candle man had come within a hair's breadth of grabbing me again just before Durral had danced us out of his reach.

'You stop being you, just for a moment.'

'Who do you become?'

'Nobody. For that one instant, you're just a part of the world like the rocks and the trees and the water below. There's no *you* to be scared or angry. You become nothing but a decision.'

'A decision?'

He nodded, smile widening. 'The decision to jump. The decision to . . .'

Suddenly he swung me around just as the candle man made another grab for me. 'To *dare*.'

I guess to anyone else listening, the Argosi's words would've sounded like gibberish. Maybe they would've sounded that

239

way to me too, before that moment. Words have meanings, but they can mean different things to different people at different times. The words Durral had used just then? They *meant* something to me. They were like . . . like a path I could just make out ahead of me in the dark.

'Enough!' roared the candle man again. His wax body slithered along the platform towards me once more, and I knew that this time Durral wasn't going to stop him.

Jan'Tep spells need something to anchor them. The magic has to attach itself to something. This particular piece of magic snagged itself to my hatred – hatred of the Jan'Tep, hatred of myself and hatred of the whole world for allowing both those things to exist at once. Durral wanted me to let go of all that anger in the hope it would somehow cause the spell to break apart. I couldn't stop hating though. Hatred was the only fire I had to keep me warm.

But then, jumping off a cliff doesn't mean you can fly either. It just means that for a few seconds you let go of the ground beneath your feet.

Could I do that? Not forever, but for an instant?

'Durral, now!' I said.

The Argosi let me go. The momentum of our turn sent me spinning right into the arms of the candle man. My enemy. My curse.

The construct's waxy red features twisted into a look of surprise. I don't think the mage controlling him even realised he'd caught hold of me, and that for one brief moment the two of us were dancing.

Dancing. Me and a Jan'Tep mage's spell.

Ain't that a thing?

Something bubbled from my lips. The first astonished

eruption of laughter at how ridiculous all of this was. Not just how crazy it was for me to be dancing with a creature made from magic and red wax, but the sheer preposterousness of the idea that anyone could hate something so small and meaningless as me – and maybe that something as small and meaningless as me could be bothered to hate those I could never harm. In that instant, in the space between the laughter and the awareness of my own mirth, I let go.

I jumped from the top of that imaginary cliff into the waters below.

The candle man stared at me, the two of us frozen together mid-turn, arm in arm. He looked surprised, and in that moment – a moment no bigger than the space between two ticks of a clock – I could see through the red wax all the way to Falcon as he watched me back. He was older now, maybe twenty. Handsome as he'd been when last I'd seen him. I liked the seriousness in his eyes.

Even then I knew I'd hate him again soon. The fire had only been tamped down momentarily, by a gust of wind caused by my laughter. But that brief peace between us was real all the same. I had let go of both him and myself, my spirit hanging in the air above the water. Free.

'Impossible,' he said through the construct. The shape fell apart, collapsing in on itself until I was left standing next to a pool of red wax that couldn't hurt anybody.

Durral came to stand next to me. He stared down at the puddle. 'You asked me how the Argosi dare walk this world so bold without no magic of our own?'

'Yeah?'

'Here endeth the lesson, kid.'

That was how I took my first step on the path of the Argosi.

241

33

The Way of Stone

The second step was a lot harder.

What are you supposed to feel after a terrible curse has been lifted from you?

Joy.

Relief.

Lightness.

Forgiveness.

None of those things?

The sorts of stories the Mahdek tell aren't so different from those of other nations. Terrible tribulations fall upon the shoulders of those blessed with the strength of spirit to face them. Through bravery and sacrifice, they defeat their enemies, and in so doing save their people. Much rejoicing ensues.

Where was my rejoicing?

I stood on that wooden gibbet, stiff as a statue, freed from the foul influence that had haunted me these past years, yet with my own spirit unable to summon the will to take so much as a step. I was aware of the crowd of townsfolk surrounding me, some looking up at me with sad, understanding eyes, others still glaring at me suspiciously. Stand here too long and there could be more trouble.

Move, I commanded my limbs. *Walk to the edge of the platform and climb down the ladder.*

My fingers touched the tattooed collar around my neck. Was it still working its magic on me? There were twelve sigils in all. Surely we hadn't broken all those spells. Was Shadow Falcon even now sitting cross-legged on the polished marble floor of some mage's sanctum, speaking strange words and making shapes with his hands as his will conjured up new torments for me, kept in reserve for just such an occasion, when I'd foolishly allow myself to believe I was free?

My gaze went to Durral Brown. He was so still he might've been carved from an oak tree, save for the warmth in his brown eyes. Was he, too, frozen by some new incantation?

'The Way of Stone is a good thing,' he said softly, as if it were a secret for my ears alone. 'Keeps our steps strong and true even when the storm tries to push us off the path. Stops our backs from bending under the weight the world puts on us when we gotta stand tall.'

He went silent for a moment, as if to give my mind time to swallow each of his words one at a time, so as not to choke on too much frontier wisdom at once.

'The four ways of the Argosi. First thing my *maetri* – that's what we call a teacher – taught me. Water, Wind, Thunder and Stone. Four ways. Four directions of a soul's compass. Four choices for how we face what's before us.'

Again he paused, and again the words milled about in my brain before finally settling down, leaving me to wonder where he was going with all this, and what it had to do with me not being able to move.

'But I reckon the Way of Stone is different from the others,

243

because each step is like puttin' on another piece of armour, each one harder and heavier than the last. Before long . . .'

'You can't move at all,' I finished for him, and instantly realised he'd left that emptiness for me to fill as a way to get me speaking again.

Durral nodded. 'That's the real price of the Way of Stone. After a while, you realise the armour won't come off any more and the only way to take your next step . . .'

He was doing it again – prompting me to answer so that somehow I'd loosen up inside. The problem was, I knew the answer to his riddle, but I didn't want to say it. I didn't want it to be true.

The townsfolk milling around in the dusty square below us were still watching, waiting. I guess they were getting tired of me taking up space on their fine gibbet.

'Is to shatter the armour,' I said to Durral at last.

The sympathy in his expression surprised me. I'd always hated it when people felt pity for me. Mostly that was because soon after, the collar made them try to kill me. But even before I ever encountered Falcon and Met'astice and their experiments, I couldn't stand the way the kindest folk would look at my clan at their town gates with these looks of . . . borrowed sadness over our plight. It was different with Durral. He never looked at me like I was some pathetic creature in need of coddling. He looked at me as if I was an equal. I guess he looked at everybody that way, which made him different from just about everyone I'd ever met.

'The armour's gotta break,' he said. 'Only question is if you want to break it here or someplace else.'

Someplace else, I thought, watching the men, women and children below all staring at me. *Anywhere else.*

244

As if he'd read my thoughts, Durral nodded and walked over to the ladder before making his way down. Without meaning to, I found myself following behind. It seemed that just knowing I was going to fall apart at some point in the near future – accepting that it was inevitable no matter how humiliating that notion was to me – made it so I could get myself moving again.

I climbed down the ladder. Most of the crowd parted before us, their clubs hanging down by their sides and pitchforks aimed up at the sky instead of at me. But not everybody was as sanguine about how things had turned out.

'You lied to us, Durral Brown,' said a big fellow with an even bigger wife, both of whom looked like we'd sold them a ticket to a play and the actors were walking off before the second act. The man gestured at me with a curled forefinger. 'She weren't no witch.'

'Wasn't she?' Durral asked, seemingly shocked by this revelation. 'Well, ain't that a thing? You reckon maybe there ain't no witches in these parts after all, Bentan?'

Bentan didn't like that. He nodded to the scattered pile on the gibbet and the ground below. 'We'll be pickin' up our contributions. So much as a copper spit missin' and we'll come lookin' for you. Best neither you nor the girl show up in these parts ever again.'

It seemed to me this was nothing more than run-of-the-mill chest-beating. An idle threat to send us on our way. But Durral took it personal.

'Really?' he asked, turning slowly to take in the entire town. 'That's what you learned here? You bear witness to such misery and cruelty as would make a dry desert weep, such daring and courage that the trees themselves stand a little taller today, and all you come back with is –' here he took on such a preposterous impersonation of Bentan's rumbling baritone that it was impossible not to laugh – '"*Best'n you not be showin' up heres no mores, mistuh!*"'

He set off a tide of chortling with that, but some others weren't so amused. A woman holding a young boy by her side said, 'You think you're so smooth, Argosi, that because we live simple lives we must be simple ourselves. But we don't set aside the truths our ancestors taught us just because they don't please a travelling card player.'

Durral's propensity for mockery wasn't subdued by her rebuke in the least. 'The "truths of our ancestors"? Is that what you call them, ma'am? Those same truths that set you to chasin' your own kids into the wild if they suffer a malady that gives them seizures? The superstitious nonsense that gives you leave to blame bad harvests that come when you sow the same seeds in the same soil too many seasons in a row on any strangers you meet? Your eyes catch sight of anyone who looks different from you and all you see are witches and demons?' He jerked a thumb back at me. 'Well, there's your witch. You were ready to hang her from your gibbet for no better reason than some slick-talking gambler walked in here and told you to.'

He seemed oblivious to the fact that *he* was the slick-talking gambler in question.

'Go on,' he said to the crowd, again gesturing to me. 'Take a good long look at your witch. What do you see?'

He walked up to Bentan and poked him in the chest. 'Well, big man. What do you see?'

It takes courage to admit you're wrong. I've never been particularly good at it and I certainly didn't expect anyone in this town to be any better. But Bentan must've been made

246

of better stuff than I'd seen in him because after a moment his eyes fell and he said, 'I see a girl.' He looked over at me and added, 'I'm sorry.'

He wasn't the only one. The big woman next to him gave me a long stare before she finally nodded and said, 'I'm sorry, girl. May gods of sea and sky send you finer days than we showed you today.'

Others muttered apologies of varying degrees of eloquence and sincerity. Durral, though, wasn't done. He went back to the woman who'd tried to admonish him earlier, but before she could speak he knelt down to the boy she had with her. 'What do you see, kid?'

The boy peered around Durral, then shook off his mother's grasp and stepped past him to walk right up to me. He couldn't have been more than seven or eight, around the age I'd been when my parents died.

'You look real sad,' he said.

I nodded.

'And lonely.'

I nodded again.

'When I get like that, Momma gives me a big old hug.' He spread his arms wide. 'You want a hug?'

I didn't. I was tired and angry and all I wanted was to get away from this filthy little town and hope that somehow, someday, I'd forget every moment I'd spent here. The last thing I needed was some snot-nosed brat grabbing at me.

'Yeah,' my traitor mouth said as my backstabbing legs knelt down. 'A hug would be okay, I guess.'

The boy wrapped his arms around me with all the awkward enthusiasm of someone who has no idea what they're doing and thinks calamity and heartache can be hugged away.

'It's okay to cry,' he whispered.

'I'm not crying,' I lied.

Durral was right. Sometimes the armour has to shatter before you can take the next step.

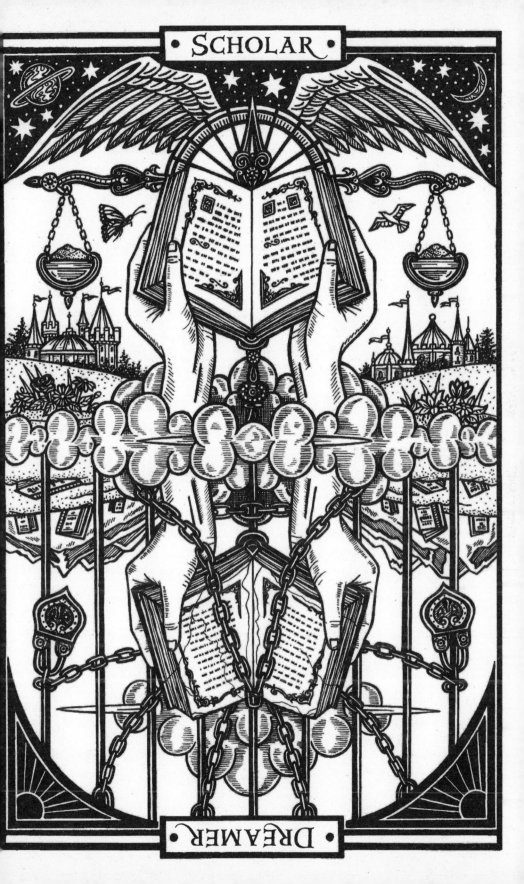

The Scholar

The path of the scholar is tempting. Who wouldn't want to pass all their days in study, unveiling marvellous secrets, gaining new insights? But the scholar who never puts knowledge into action becomes the dreamer, and a dream that never ends is a prison built from the bricks of imagination. The Journey of the Scholar is not the Way of the Argosi.

34

The Argosi Way

'Teach me,' I said.

'Teach you what, kid?'

How many times had the two of us repeated this exact exchange in the past six weeks? A hundred times? A thousand? Let's see . . . The first time was about five minutes after we'd left that little town with its gibbet now covered in red wax.

'Teach me.'

'Teach you what, kid?'

'How to be an Argosi.

'What's an Argosi?'

'A warrior,' I replied. 'Someone who can defeat a mage's spell without any magic of their own, make four strong men back down from a fight. Someone who isn't afraid.'

'Sounds mighty impressive,' he'd said, that first time. 'You ever find such a person, be sure to point 'em out to me.'

Just like that, he shut down the discussion. So every night, after we'd set up our camp, fed, watered and brushed the horse while the dog went off hunting, I tried again. I'd take another crack at Durral while he was placing snares in hopes of catching a fat rabbit or squirrel to go with whatever root vegetables he'd send me to dig up – for him the word 'vegetable', by the way, referred to a disgusting assortment of spiky, unpalatable lumps that bore no resemblance to food.

At the end of each evening, after Durral had laid out his secret traps – none of which he'd let me see – to alert him if anyone tried to sneak up on us unawares, the two of us would sit across the fire from one other, and I'd try a third time.

'I mean it. I want you to teach me.'

'Teach you what, kid?'

'How to be an Argosi.'

'What's an Argosi?'

A trickster. A gambler. A philosopher. A duellist. A holy man. A low-down, dirty, mean-spirited, mocking son of a—

By the second week, I really started losing my temper.

'Stop being an arsehole!' I shouted.

I shouted a lot of other times too. It never got me anywhere. At first I figured it had to be some kind of test – like a philosophical puzzle – and he was waiting for me to come up with the right response. Turns out I'm no good at puzzles. Wasn't for lack of trying though.

'You're supposed to be a teacher, so teach!'

That barely got me half a snicker.

'Stop treating me like a child!'

Durral Brown, I soon learned, was utterly immune to petulance as a form of persuasion.

'You're behaving like a child, Durral!'

He was also unmoved by chastising, cajoling, castigating, debating, negotiating, pleading, wailing and complete silence. Actually he seemed to appreciate that one.

I should've worked out the solution to his puzzle a lot

sooner. I just wanted to be an Argosi so bad – more than anything I'd ever wanted in my life – I guess that blinded me to the obvious answer.

Why would Durral Brown, the Path of the Rambling Thistle, have brought me with him from that town if he'd had no intention of teaching me to be an Argosi like him?

Simple.

'You're taking me to them, aren't you?' I finally asked.

Durral was sitting cross-legged on the other side of the fire, sewing a patch into his other shirt while the dog lay its head in his lap.

'Takin' you where, kid?'

He didn't even acknowledge the fact that not once this past week had I asked him to teach me. Our days and nights had passed in the simple routines of travelling through the stunning desert landscape, our conversations nothing more than little stories and casual observations. Seven entire days it had taken me to build up the courage to ask my question. I'm not sure why I wanted to make him say it out loud; I already knew the answer.

The fading light of the sun dipping below the hills to the west cast a mesmerising glow on the emerald green sand all around us. Over the past six weeks we'd made our way from the southern tip of the Jan'Tep territories up through the mostly unpopulated deserts of the Seven Sands. A few more days of travel would see us into Daroman lands, and from there through the mountains to the desolate region known as the Northern Tribelands. A harsh and unforgiving tundra, but the folk there were known for their kindness, and for never turning away those seeking to share their hard, wild terrain.

I stabbed my finger northward, which momentarily confused the dog, who seemed to think I must be pointing at a rabbit for him to chase. 'Some of the Mahdek clans travel to the Tribelands when there's no place else that'll take them.'

Durral barely showed any sign of having heard me; he just kept right on sewing that leather patch over the hole in his shirt.

'I'm not going back to the Mahdek,' I said.

'That so?' he asked, pushing the needle and thread through the leather. 'You got some better place to go?'

His casual, almost disinterested question hit me like a slap in the face.

'I'm not Mahdek any more,' I declared.

Out the needle came, tugging the thread with it. 'That somethin' you can toss away like an old shoe?'

'I don't care. I'm done running and hiding from the Jan'Tep. I'm sick of it, do you hear me? Sick of it!'

The heat of the fire was far too warm against my shins. Somehow I'd gotten to my feet.

'I hate the Mahdek!' I said, trying not to shout, but failing miserably. 'I hate their weakness! I hate the way they beg and plead and haggle for food and shelter – for *everything*! I wish I'd never been born one! Always fleeing from their enemies. Never fighting back. *Never fighting back!*'

I was screaming now, and tears were streaming down my face. I knew I must sound hysterical, and maybe I was, but I needed to make him understand! I had to make him—

'If you ain't gonna be what you've been,' he began, without a trace of ire in his tone, without a lick of compassion; with nothing to let me know he cared in the slightest about me. 'Reckon you'll have to become somethin' else.'

256

'I told you – I've *been* telling you! I want to be an Argosi!'

'What's an Argosi, kid?'

All the horrors I'd witnessed in my short life, all the different forms of suffering inflicted on me by mages, thugs, constables and just plain, decent folk, I don't think anything ever hurt quite so bad as Durral's simple, innocent-sounding question.

I fled our camp then, running out into the desert. He'd come and find me. Durral knew I couldn't survive out there on my own. Hadn't he found me last time? Risked everything to help me understand the curse Met'astice and Shadow Falcon had put on me? Shown me how to defeat the candle man?

He'd come for me. He'd promise not to make me go live in some cave with the remnants of a clan I didn't know and a people I couldn't stand to be with any more.

And then, after he'd brought me back to our campsite, with our faithful dog wagging his tail and the horse bobbing his head in acknowledgement of our return, Durral would sit me down by the fire and finally agree to teach me the Argosi ways.

Wouldn't he?

35

The Name

For hours and hours I wandered in the desert. First I headed south-west, away from our campsite and away from the border with the Northern Tribelands. When he didn't come, I walked in darkness back the way I'd come. I figured I'd get close enough to spot the fire and then wait it out until he finally came looking for me. Only . . . I never found our campsite. Either I'd gotten turned around in the dark or he'd packed up and left without me.

One night alone in the desert isn't so bad when you've lived through the kinds of things I have. Scary? Sure. But I've been scared plenty of times. Sad? The world's a sad place. Get used to it.

The second night though, after I spent all day just finding the now-deserted campsite? That was harder.

And the third, plodding north, finding and losing and finding again the tracks Durral left in the sand behind him, knowing that one good sandstorm and the trail would be invisible? That's when I remembered what it was like to be alone and afraid again.

You can go three days without water if you're careful. I got lucky and found a type of cactus that hides moisture in its spines. That's how I survived the fourth day. On the fifth, though, I awoke in a daze, my mouth full of emerald-green sand and my head aching from lack of food and water. I was barely able to get on my feet and start walking again, convinced that, between my belligerence and Durral's obstinacy, the two of us had done what even Met'astice and Shadow Falcon had failed to do: end my life without either of them having to lift a finger against me.

I would've trudged right past Durral's camp on the other side of a dune had it not been for his awful singing. I thought I might be imagining it, but you'd think a hallucination could hold a tune.

Climbing the dune took what remained of my strength, and I pretty much just tumbled down the other side. I came to a stop about ten yards from the fire and crawled the rest of the way.

'Thirsty?' he asked, tossing me his canteen before resuming his song.

I looked from him to the dog to the horse – neither of whom showed much enthusiasm for his singing either. I drank the canteen dry.

I would've cried then, but I'd pretty much used up all my tears. So instead I just slumped by the fire and listened to him singing one of those dull, tired tavern songs about pretty girls and flowers and tragic romance. There was a horse in there somewhere too, but even our horse didn't seem to care.

I came to understand then that there's a sort of benevolent cruelty to the Argosi. They want to do right by people, but they know not all suffering can be avoided, and worse, sometimes when you try, all you do is trade momentary discomfort for weakness that makes you even more fragile.

No path, no matter how winding, can evade all the dangers of the world. A girl of fifteen who walks off in a huff in the middle of the Seven Sands when she doesn't know how to survive in the wilds is liable to get herself killed. Maybe even deserves it. So I guess Durral really was teaching me, just not the things I wanted to know.

I wanted to learn to trick my enemies and misdirect them. I wanted to move silently, like Durral did, and to fight like I knew he could, even though he tried hard to avoid violence. With his Argosi skills, I could track down Shadow Falcon. I could put an end to him, and never, ever have to be scared of him again.

Instead Durral had taught me that I was weaker than I knew, tired of fighting against the entire world. And that maybe I'd be better off with the Mahdek after all.

'I'll go,' I said at last.

He stopped singing. 'Go where, kid?'

I wiped my cheeks on my sleeve, smearing dust and grit picked up from sleeping in the sand. There was no point keeping up this game. He always dealt me the same hand. Yet even then, even in the midst of my surrender, some part of my stubbornness refused to stay quiet.

'Stop calling me "kid",' I said.

He took out a cooking pot from one of the saddlebags and filled it with vegetables and water from a second canteen, along with what I assumed was rabbit meat. 'You prefer I call you "girl"?' he asked.

'I'd *prefer* if you call me by my name!'

'What's your name?'

'Ferius. I've told you a hundred times that my name is Ferius!'

260

He set the pot over the fire. 'Ferius is the dog's name,' he said.

The dog looked up, apparently agreeing.

'It is not! You're just saying that to confuse me. My name is Ferius. Ferius Parfax.'

'You keep sayin' that, kid, but you can't tell me where you got the name.'

Whenever the subject came up, I'd run into the same wall, because I honestly couldn't remember. On the night Met'astice had tricked me and Arissa into coming to that tenement, he'd implied that my inability to hold on to a name was caused by one of the sigils around my neck. One of his damnable 'experiments'. But Met'astice was dead now, and I was *not* going through life being called 'girl' or 'kid'.

'Prove to me that Ferius Parfax isn't my name,' I said at last.

Durral stirred the soup. 'Well, for one thing, Ferius isn't a Mahdek word. It's archaic Daroman.'

'What does it mean?'

He smiled. '"Unyielding as iron".'

'Well, that's right,' I said, though I hadn't known that before. 'That's exactly why I picked it.'

'That so?'

'Damn straight.'

'And Parfax?' he asked.

'It means . . . bright spark,' I lied.

He chuckled at that. 'Parfax means "hunting hound",' he said. 'Which is why I named the dog "Ferius Parfax".'

As if on cue, the dog stood up, gave a happy bark, and took on a noble pose as if he were about to leap into action and hunt down a rabbit for us.

Traitor.

261

Maybe it was just how miserable I looked, or maybe Durral felt guilty at letting me wander out there in the desert alone these past days, but when once the soup had finished cooking and he poured it into two tin bowls, he said, 'Look, kid, if you really want to call yourself Ferius Parfax, then fine. Just don't come complainin' to me if you wake up one day barking at squirrels.'

He handed me one of the bowls, only to pull back when I reached for it.

'What now?' I asked.

'To whom am I offering this food and the shelter of my camp?'

Durral hardly ever talked that way, all formal-like. When he did, it *meant* something. He was offering more than just soup. He was telling me that whatever name I chose, it would be mine no matter what. More than that, this name I picked would be a new beginning in our relationship. A chance for me to stop asking him the same stupid question every night and for him to give the same maddening answer.

A name.

My name.

Forever.

'Ferius Parfax,' I answered.

His smile was little more than a smirk, but his laugh was as big as the entire Seven Sands. 'Okay, Ferius,' he said.

The dog looked up and Durral shook his head. 'Not you. You can be Tolvoi Parfax.'

'What does that mean?'

'Dauntless bright spark.'

Damn. I should've chosen that one. And yeah, I know he lied to me about Parfax meaning 'hunting dog'.

'Thank you,' I said.

He handed me the bowl of soup. 'My pleasure, Ferius.'

Something changed in me then. Nothing big – at least nothing grandiose. But I had a name now, and that meant something to me.

'Durral?' I asked.

'Yeah?'

'I'm not going to join any Mahdek tribe.'

He sat back down on his side of the fire and balanced his own bowl on his lap. 'Then what am I going to do with you?' he asked.

I almost couldn't believe he was setting me up *again*.

I sighed. 'Teach me.'

With that absurd, unperturbable patience of his, he asked, 'Teach you what, Ferius?'

I don't know how the answer came to me just then. It wasn't a sudden revelation or flash of insight. In fact, my answer was almost purposely vague and came more from complete exhaustion and having just barely survived five days in the desert than any kind of wisdom. But I guess it was the right one, because after that Durral did take me on as his student, and that changed my life forever.

'Teach me what I need to know,' I said.

36

Arta Precis

The tree was a hundred feet tall, standing alone at the boundary between the Seven Sands and the Northern Tribelands. A solitary sentry rising up from the slope of a hill where emerald-green sand gave way first to dirt and scrub and then to rocky ground.

When Durral had informed me that this would be the first stop on our journey, I'd panicked that he might secretly be planning to drag me across the border where he'd force me to join some refugee Mahdek clan. He'd insisted coming here was the only way I could begin to master the Argosi ways.

'You see that tree?' he asked.

'I'm standing right in front of it, so yes.'

'Standing in front of something isn't the same as seeing it, kid. Looking isn't seeing either. Now, do you *see* the tree?'

I sighed. For a guy who mostly talked like some half-drunken frontier herdsman, he could sure get awfully philosophical.

'I see a tree,' I replied.

He sat down on the cold ground, leaned back against one of Quadlopo's legs. The horse had been nameless until I'd pestered Durral repeatedly to give him one. The Argosi insisted the horse didn't care about such things, but I was obsessed with names, so finally Durral relented. Quadlopo sounded like a rather noble name to me, and suited the horse entirely. Turns out it's Daroman for 'four-legged'.

The dog, apparently sensing this was going to be a long lesson, scampered off up the hill. Durral closed his eyes. 'Tell me about this tree of yours,' he commanded.

'It's a tree. What is there to tell?'

'What's a tree?'

Spirits kind and cruel, not this again . . .

'It's a big plant with a trunk, branches and leaves above the ground and roots below.'

'Go on.'

'It's, uh, mostly brown?'

'And?'

'It's . . . made of wood?'

'Fascinatin'. Continue.'

We went on like this for over an hour, with me reporting on every single part of the tree. I offered my best guess as to its exact height, estimated the number of leaves on each branch and expounded on their texture. When I was done with that, he told me to rap my knuckles against different parts of the trunk and describe the sound. Then he made me smell all the parts of the tree my nose could reach. And yeah, he made me taste the bark too.

'Satisfied?' I asked, wiping a sleeve across my mouth and then my brow. I was sweating, which was unusual given it was pretty cold this far north. Maybe all that concentrating on a big stupid tree had tired me out.

Durral finally opened one eye, stared up at the tree, then closed it again. 'You haven't told me anything.'

'Were you asleep all that time? I went over every inch of your damned tr—'

'All of which I could've discovered just by lookin' at it myself.'

He's trying to goad you into an argument. Don't let him.

Sweetly I said, 'You forgot the part where you had me sniffing and chewing on the bark. That aside, how, precisely, am I supposed to tell you anything that you can't observe yourself?'

He was silent for a second, which stretched into another and another. Just when I was convinced he was about to start snoring, he asked, 'Does the tree exist only in this moment?'

'What's that supposed to . . . ?' Again I stopped myself from losing my temper.

Part of our deal was that, as his *teysan* – what the Argosi call an apprentice (even though Durral denied the word could be so bluntly translated) – I was entitled to ask all the questions I wanted, but outbursts of belligerence, petulance and outrage constituted 'the young teysan informing her maetri that she was very tired, couldn't possibly absorb any more of his great wisdom today and was in need of a nap'.

'No,' I said at last. 'The tree doesn't exist only in this moment.'

The words 'good' or 'well done' being largely absent from Durral's vocabulary, he grunted, before demanding, 'Tell me about some of the other moments in which this tree has existed.'

Seeing no way around this particular lesson, I went on to describe how the tree must've started as an acorn or some other seed or whatever trees are made from. I figured for sure he'd call me out on that – somehow expect me to know

266

precisely what type of tree this was. He didn't. Instead he nodded for me to continue. So I explained that at some point in the past it had been a sapling, then a young tree, and had finally, over many decades – maybe centuries – grown to become a colossal waste of my time.

Come on. That at least deserved a chuckle, right?

Nope.

'Anyone could've told me those things, including people who'd never seen this tree. Look deeper. Find some other moment in the tree's existence.'

It took every ounce of my self-control to keep from screaming with frustration. When I'd lived with Sir Rosarite and Sir Gervais, they'd sent me to an expensive school where teachers taught you things by *explaining* them and then testing you on your recollection of the pertinent facts and techniques. Durral skipped over the whole explaining stage and just expected you to figure everything out on your own.

The sun was getting unpleasantly hot as the afternoon wore on, yet the snows further up on the hill showed no sign of melting, which was weird.

Maybe too much thinking heats up the brain.

My legs were tired from standing for hours on end so I hunched under the branches and leaned my back against the trunk. Having nothing else to offer, I said, 'At some point in this tree's existence, somebody probably used it for shelter.'

'Ah.'

He could load a lot of implied meanings into a simple 'ah'.

'What?' I asked.

'You've discovered something very important, *teysan*.'

'What have I discovered, *maetri*?'

'The tree doesn't exist on its own. It has relationships to

other things – people, for example, who sometimes benefit from the shade it offers.' He gave me the slightest hint of a smirk – as much a reward as I could ever expect for getting something right. 'Tell me more about this tree's relationship to people.'

The sun was starting to set by the time I'd gone through all the things one might do with a tree, all the ways it could be useful to a community, and the effects those uses would have on the tree itself – like how you can burn a tree for warmth, but once you do, the tree is gone forever. You can cut a single branch, however, and use that as firewood without killing the tree.

Brilliantly perceptive, I know. Unfortunately that only launched us into a discussion of all possible uses of a single tree branch. None of this seemed to interest Durral at all until I reached up and bent a thinner branch overhead. 'The wood from this tree is strong and flexible. You could probably make a bow from it.'

'Ah,' Durral said again.

'"Ah" what?'

'See the tree. Not *a* tree this time, and not a tree *like* this one, but this specific tree.'

I paced the circumference of the trunk, examining every inch of the bark that I could see. That's when I found it: the spot where a single branch had been cut down. From the stub that remained, I surmised that the branch must've been some three inches in diameter. I was no expert, of course, but it struck me as a good thickness if you were looking to fashion a bow.

'I think somebody once made a bow from a branch cut from this exact tree.'

'What's a bow?'

Spirits merciful and mad, I would've been better off with the candle man as my teacher.

'A bow. A weapon. A thing for killing people.'

'Hmm . . .' he said, still sitting there with his eyes shut. 'How many people do you think that bow has killed?'

'I don't know.'

Durral opened his eyes at last. 'Me neither, but that seems important, doesn't it?'

He patted the ground next to him, and I sat down, leaning against the horse's front leg. He didn't seem to mind.

For the next several hours and all through the night, Durral and I went back and forth speculating about all the ways the hypothetical bow that had once – *perhaps* – been fashioned from this tree, might be out there affecting the rest of the world. We theorised that whoever controlled this lone tree gained exclusive means for making bows on this barren plateau. We guessed at how other people might feel about that, and what actions they might take to prevent someone else from having dominion over this tree.

'Makes me wonder how no one's ever burned down this tree,' I observed, so tired by this point that I'd started imagining all the moments of joy, anger, comfort and fear this one tree might have caused over its life, just by being a tree.

'That's a proper Argosi question,' Durral said approvingly.

'How so?'

He gestured to the pale green desert we'd journeyed through to reach this tree. 'Seein' the everyday world as strange is the first step to arta precis.'

'Perception,' I said.

He rolled his eyes. 'Why are you always lookin' for small words to describe big things?'

Before I could defend myself, he launched us into an exploration of all the ways this tree might've had an impact on animals in the region. When we'd exhausted that topic, he moved on to the effect the tree had on other nearby plants.

You'd think that such a foolish exercise in philosophical sophistry – I didn't know what 'sophistry' meant at the time, but I sure knew what it felt like listening to it – would never end. Yet somehow, for Durral, it did.

'Good,' he said at last, as the sun peeked out from behind the hills on the horizon. He rose to his feet and offered me a hand up as well. I was so stiff I could barely move. Durral was a lot older than me. How come he looked as limber as if he'd spent all these hours lounging in a warm bath?

'So that's it?' I asked. 'What I did with the tree . . . *that's* arta precis?'

'Not exactly.'

'Then what—'

Durral took me by the shoulders, spun me around and pointed to a rock no bigger than my fist sticking out of the green sand a few yards to the south of us. 'You see that there rock?' he asked.

I nodded.

'How long did it take us to see the tree?'

'A day and a night,' I replied, suddenly aware of just how hungry and tired I was.

'Now see the rock – I mean, *see* it – like you did the tree. But do it in the blink of an eye. *That's* arta precis.'

Despair flooded through me like water rising above my head. 'But . . . I can't! I'd have to spend my entire life just looking at stuff the way we did the tree to get so good I could do it all in a second!'

Durral patted me on the shoulder before turning to go saddle up the horse.

Despite my determination not to lose my temper any more, I couldn't stop myself. 'All that time, all so you could show me that the world is complicated? Is that all you got for me? Did you make up that lesson just to make me feel stupid? Come on, maetri, when are you going to smirk at me and declare, "Here endeth the lesson"?'

Durral whistled for Tolvoi, the dog, then mounted the horse. I started shouting again, but Durral cut me off so quick it was like he'd done it with a sharp blade.

'Quiet yourself, teysan,' he commanded, his voice so hard it banished all my exhaustion and hunger and frustration. When he saw I was calm, he asked, 'Are you ready to understand the purpose of the lesson, Ferius Parfax?'

'Yes, maetri.'

I had no doubt I was about to be handed yet another nonsensical philosophical principle, but at this point *anything* would make me feel better than wasting all this time for nothing.

He extended his left arm and pointed to the tree where we'd passed an entire day and night. 'You see that tree?'

Sighing, I turned. 'Yes, maetri, I *see* the tree.'

'Good. Now, I want you to answer one simple question for me.'

I waited, but he said nothing, so I turned back to him. Durral looked different somehow. Troubled.

'Maetri?'

He shook his head and blinked several times before he finally asked, 'Is that the same tree you saw when we first came here?'

271

I figured for sure I knew the answer this time: that the tree was the same, but *I* had changed. Sounds good, right? Clever even. Only . . . something wasn't right. Yes, it was still a hundred-foot tree, with branches and bark and roots and everything you'd expect, but looking at it now I would swear it was more . . . complete. When I thought back to my memories of the day before, I couldn't remember the tree being exactly like it was now. Then it had just been a big tree.

'Do you see the rock?' Durral asked.

I turned. It was just a rock.

'And the sand?'

I gazed out at the desert, with its faded green minerals that made it . . . sand. But the longer I stared at it, the more detailed everything became. Like before it was just the idea of sand, and now it was *actual* sand.

Only it wasn't.

Something wasn't right.

I thought back to these past weeks, all the time Durral and I had spent travelling together, the routines of riding and walking, setting up camp at night and breaking it down in the morning. I remembered all of it, which seems normal enough.

Arta precis is seeing the everyday as strange.

My mind has never worked in straight lines. I've always had trouble keeping track of the passage of time. I get events mixed up. So why was I remembering everything so clearly now?

The candle man, I thought. *After we left that town, maybe a day or two later, everything just . . . smoothed out.*

But how could that be? Had I suddenly been cured just because I'd thrown up a bunch of red wax? But how come

I didn't feel better in other ways? And all those fights I'd had with Durral – how could we possibly have argued so many nights in a row over the exact same things?

I looked back at the rock, and the longer I stared at it the more it shifted from being an *impression* of a rock to something I could describe. I turned to the tree. When I'd first seen it, it had just been a tree. Now I saw all the hundreds of tiny details, like the nub where a branch had been cut off to make a bow. But had that been there the whole time? Or was it only when Durral kept asking me to describe more things about the tree that it had appeared to me?

Arta precis.

The Argosi talent for perception.

Seeing the strange in the everyday, when others would miss it.

'No,' I said aloud, and now I couldn't hold back the tears. 'Please, no. Please, don't let it be so.'

I understood now why Durral had made me describe the tree to him for hours on end, to keep finding one new detail after another, proving something he himself had begun to suspect.

None of this was real. The Cabal wasn't done with me after all.

I looked up at Durral, and he nodded.

Here endeth the lesson.

37

The Price of Meddling

How do you escape a cage you can't even see? A cage made of Jan'Tep silk magic, with bars constructed from your own thoughts? No idea of where you are or what's being done to you? For all we knew, Durral and I might be stumbling around in the same tiny circle in the desert over and over again, our shuffling steps slowly digging ourselves a grave in the sand. Perhaps we were flat on our backs in some cave, bound to wooden tables, straps holding down our hands and wrists while . . .

No. Don't think like that.

Durral was walking barefoot in the sand as we headed west into a canyon, idly petting the dog and telling himself dirty jokes.

Why west?

'Might as well head somewhere.'

Petting a dog that only existed in our heads?

'Wondered why he was so even-tempered lately.'

That last part, by the way, was how he knew that both he and I were real: we irritated each other far beyond the limits of any mage's imaginings.

Oh, and the dirty jokes?

'Testin' a theory.'

This is who I was stuck with inside a silk spell. *This* is who I was counting on to get me out after being trapped for the past six weeks.

Unless it was a lot longer.

How old was I now? Sixteen? Seventy? Was I a frail old woman wheezing in the corner of some rotten cell, mumbling to myself about travelling through the desert and learning the Argosi ways as my heart was giving out its final beats?

When I raised this possibility with Durral, he said I couldn't be that old because he was twenty years my senior and doubted after all his hard living that he was going to make it to ninety.

'That's not the point!' I shouted – which feels even more pointless when you realise you're probably not really shouting at all. 'I'm saying we might've been in this cage for years without realising it!'

Quadlopo whinnied at my outburst, which was proof none of this was real. Durral's actual horse barely noticed my existence.

'I know, kid,' Durral said, reaching down again to scratch Tolvoi behind the ears. The imaginary dog raised his head in happy acknowledgement. 'Ain't like I relish the idea of gettin' old before my time. Besides, if we've been stuck here for years, I've missed my anniversary, which'll put me in serious trouble with the wife.'

He chuckled at his own joke, which made me want to punch him in his imaginary face, but I was also shocked.

'You're married?'

'Yep.'

I considered that a moment. 'Somebody married you?'

275

He laughed then, a deep, rich rumble that echoed through the canyon.

'It wasn't *that* fun—'

He put a finger to his lips. I spun around, suddenly worried about some hidden presence – which was stupid, because *of course* there was another presence with us. But I saw no one and only heard the fading echoes of Durral's laughter.

His eyes got that look like when he's just pulled an ace out of the deck. I listened more carefully, and realised something strange was happening. Within the reverberations of his outlandish guffaws, I could swear I was hearing the faintest traces of someone else's laughter. Not mine though; a man's baritone, almost as deep as Durral's but sounding considerably younger.

Durral mouthed, 'Got him.'

I wondered at the purpose of trying to communicate surreptitiously, given that the mage was in our minds, but he was right: there was no evidence so far that our captor could actually read our thoughts – at least not the way one reads a book. Either way, when you're in a bad situation, you look for every possible advantage and don't waste any opportunities.

Like when you hear someone laughing whose voice you recognise.

My fingers came up to the sigils around my neck.

Shadow Falcon? I asked silently.

I got no reply at first. I shook my head to Durral, who nodded to me to try again.

I know you're out there. I know you're involved in this dirty business, so you might as well talk to me.

Nothing.

Coward.

The pain that exploded in my head was like a thousand wasps stinging the inside of my skull all at once. I would have collapsed if Durral hadn't caught me.

'Guess you got his attention,' he said.

I pressed my palms against my temples, trying to make the agony go away, but I couldn't.

'No doubt you were your usual diplomatic self,' Durral said drily.

'Make it stop!' I cried out.

Durral leaned in close and whispered into my ear, speaking not to me but to Falcon. 'Torture is a fool's bludgeon. It's how a man shows he ain't a man at all, but a boy so easily frightened by words that he lashes out. No subtlety. No sense of proportion. With every moment of torment you inflict on her, you paint a picture of your own soul. A picture without nobility, without intellect, without worth. Is that the image of yourself you want to see when you close your eyes to sleep tonight, *boy*?'

The pain stopped, just like that, but with relief came a warning.

'Now you see what I can do to you, Mahdek. I could've done it anytime I wanted, as often as I wanted, but I showed you mercy.'

'He says he's been merciful with me up till—'

'Ain't hard to guess that much, kid,' Durral said. 'Now talk some sense into him. Follow the Way of Water.'

The Way of Water. The way of balance. Take nothing from those you pass by, leave nothing behind. If take you must, then a gift must be offered in return.

What can I give you, Falcon, to let us out of this cage?

'Do not attempt to bargain with me, Mahdek. You have nothing we want.'

277

We, not I. He wasn't doing this on his own, which meant the Cabal was involved.

Then why am I here? I asked.

'An amusement. We enjoy watching you stumbling about for weeks on end in this kennel we have built for you, deluding yourself into believing your petty life could have meaning, imagining you might one day become one of these absurd and irrelevant Argosi.

Durral was watching me, waiting for some sign I was getting somewhere.

All Falcon had given me so far were insults – the kind that would usually have sent me into fits of anger and outrage, hurling insults of my own back at him. But even if we were in a cage, I'd spent the last weeks learning Durral's lessons.

Arta precis.

Seeing the strange in the everyday.

Thank you for being so forthcoming with me, I told Falcon.

'*I've told you nothing, Mahdek.*'

Except he'd told me plenty.

The first part: *An amusement . . .*

'This is another experiment,' I informed Durral.

'Makes sense.'

The second part: *We enjoy watching you . . .*

'They're pissed off. Frustrated,' I said aloud.

'How come?' Durral asked.

. . . stumbling about for weeks on end in this kennel we have built for you . . .

'Weeks. He said they've been watching us for weeks. That means time passes at the same rate inside the spell as in the real world. The Cabal must be getting frustrated by how long this is taking.'

You'd think Durral would've questioned how I could be so sure, but he just nodded, as if he trusted me implicitly.

. . . deluding yourself into believing your petty life could have meaning . . .

Yet that delusion was only possible with their help, which meant they *wanted* me to keep trying to change myself. But why?

'This speculation of yours is pathetic, Mahdek,' Falcon said, confirming that I was on the right track.

One piece was missing though.

. . . imagining you might one day become one of these absurd and irrelevant Argosi.

Oh . . .

Now *that* made sense.

'Kid?'

'I'm not the one they want any more. They're just using me as bait to keep you distracted.' I locked eyes with him. 'Durral, it's you they're experimenting on!'

38

The Way of Wind

The Jan'Tep plan was so simple I almost couldn't believe we hadn't figured it out before now.

How had Falcon characterised the Argosi?

Absurd and irrelevant.

When your enemy's entire culture is based on the notion that magic is the most important measure of worth, they can't help but reveal their own anxieties.

Durral was watching me, waiting for me to give him the rest.

'After they saw the way you helped me rid myself of the candle man, the Cabal realised the Argosi were far more dangerous than they'd assumed.'

'Logical enough, I suppose,' he said, scratching his chin. 'Anybody so paranoid they're afraid the ragged remains of the Mahdek tribes will rise up one day to avenge themselves for a three-hundred-year-old war probably gets a might nervous when a little dancin' breaks one of their most convoluted spells.'

Hearing him say it aloud made me even more positive I was right. It explained everything.

'After we left the town, they had Falcon listen in on me,

which is how they knew I was asking you to teach me the Argosi ways.'

'And askin', and askin' and askin' some more,' Durral chuckled.

How he could make fun at a time like this . . .

'So they captured us and put a silk spell on us.' I gestured to the canyon in which we stood. 'Putting us in this imaginary version of the Seven Sands.'

Durral nodded. 'Which made sure we never encountered any other Argosi, so I couldn't let them know what was goin' on in the Jan'Tep territories.'

'Right. So they waited until you agreed to teach me . . .'

Now it was me who laughed, so loud and long I was starting to gasp for breath.

'Kid, you okay?'

I couldn't stop. It was all so ridiculous, so hysterically funny, I had to bend over and lean my hands on my knees.

'All those weeks,' I said, in between breathless giggles. '"Teach me." *Teach you what?* "How to be an Argosi!" *What's an Argosi?*'

I started laughing again, and this time Durral joined in. He too struggled to get words out.

'All that time, this Cabal of great and grand lord maguses, sittin' there, waiting for me to unveil the secrets of the Argosi for 'em, gettin' nothin' but you and me quarrellin' day after day!'

Maybe it really was hysteria. Maybe after weeks of being trapped inside a silk spell, your mind just needs some kind of release. Well, Falcon had given us one.

Thank you, Shadow Falcon, I said silently, not sure if he was listening any more, but honestly grateful for once. *I owe you for this gift of laughter.*

But then a more troubling thought occurred to me: if the Cabal had done all this to uncover the secrets of the Argosi . . .

'You can't teach me any more,' I said to Durral.

He looked back at me quizzically. 'Why not?'

'Because they're listening in.'

'So?'

'So you'll teach them all the Argosi secrets!'

Durral Brown gave one loud 'Ha!' before leading me over to the canyon wall. 'Let 'em! These Jan'Tep mages want to learn the Argosi ways? Well, I for one can't imagine a better way to improve that backwards culture of theirs. Come on, kid.'

He reached up to an outcropping in the rock face and searched with the toe of his boot for a foothold.

'What are you doing?' I asked as he ascended. Somehow I doubted we could escape a silk spell by climbing over it.

He clung to the rock face and gestured for me to follow him up. 'You ever felt the way air moves inside a canyon when you're three hundred feet above the ground?'

'No.'

The Argosi grinned. 'Well, I have.'

Okay, that almost made sense: Durral was theorising that the silk spell required the mage to feed us the sensations of being inside this imaginary world. Maybe he didn't have to paint every rock and tree, so to speak, but he had to induce us to envision the experience of being near it. Only, a sensation the mage had never experienced – like the feel of the wind on your face halfway up a canyon wall – well, he'd have to make something up.

Durral's testing the limits of the spell. He wants to force them to show what they can and can't do with it.

Grabbing a vine root conveniently embedded into the cliffside, I began hauling myself up. I'd never climbed anything taller than a tree in my life.

'Just find a foothold and reach up to a handhold, push up with your feet and repeat,' Durral instructed.

The way was hard. Gruelling even. And yet . . . not nearly as bad as I would've expected, given I had no experience and wasn't all that strong. After a few minutes I caught up to Durral. My fingers ached, my muscles complained and my breathing was laboured. All the things you'd expect to feel while climbing up a cliff for the first time. But while it hurt, it didn't hurt nearly as much as it should've.

Durral gave me a nod like he knew what I was thinking: that whichever Jan'Tep mage was controlling the spell right now had never really experienced true hardship. In his mind, he was feeding us the sensations of intense struggle, but his notion of it wasn't nearly as tough as the things I'd already experienced in my life.

That's one of their weaknesses, I realised then. *When you live in a comfortable society with magic at your beck and call, you risk being unprepared for genuine deprivation.*

'Feel that?' Durral asked.

I hadn't even realised he'd stopped climbing. 'Feel what?'

His eyes were closed. 'The wind on your face.'

I did. It was like any other breeze touching my skin, though maybe a bit cooler and more acute than usual – pretty much what you might imagine a canyon breeze would feel like this high up if, like me, you'd never actually experienced it before.

So Durral was right: the cage the Cabal made for us was limited by their own narrow experience of the world. That meant we always had a way of separating what was real from what they were putting in our minds.

'What now?' I asked.

'No point spendin' the night hanging off a cliff,' he replied. 'Best we get back to the bottom.'

I glanced down, searching for the best foothold.

'Uh-uh, kid,' he said.

'What? You said we had to get back to the bottom.'

The corner of his mouth rose a fraction. 'Never said "climb down".'

His left hand reached out, grabbed me by the back of my collar and yanked me away from the cliff wall. My hands and feet lost their purchase, and I had just enough time to see him giving me a friendly wave as I hurtled to the rocky ground below.

39

The Landing

The folk wisdom that falling to your death in your sleep will cause your heart to stop turned out not to be true. I hadn't actually expected to die when Durral threw me from the cliff face, but that hadn't stopped me from screaming my lungs out the entire way down. One rather expects a fall of several hundred feet to hurt a great deal once you hit solid ground. Roughly as bad as falling from your bed to the floor, as it turned out, which I guess was the closest the mage holding the silk spell together had ever come to such a fate.

I lay there, aching but uninjured, staring up at the strip of sky between the clifftops on either side and contemplating my jailor.

If this is the worst pain you've ever felt, Falcon, then you're in for a nasty surprise when I finally catch up to you.

Durral was right about the Jan'Tep. With all their magic, they rarely fight with their fists, so they don't get bruises and broken bones. They have their Sha'Tep servants to supply their bodily needs, so they never know the raw, soul-crushing experience of genuine hunger, thirst or other forms of deprivation. No doubt all their training in magic costs them tremendous mental fatigue, but the physical hardships that had marked my entire life were probably as unfamiliar to them as the thrill of spellcasting was to me.

I don't think I'd ever understood until that moment just how different my adversaries were from me. I mean, I'd always known they were the enemy. Vicious. Arrogant. Cruel. But still human, like me. Maybe some Jan'Tep had things in common with ordinary folk. Durral insisted people were people. But Shadow Falcon and I? We might as well have been entirely different species.

'You plannin' on gettin' up anytime soon?' Durral asked.

He was looming over me. Something about his casual pose annoyed me. My gaze went to the clifftop from which I'd fallen back to him.

'You climbed down,' I said. 'Why didn't you jump?'

'Reckoned the landing would hurt.'

I bit back an angry retort. When he goaded me like this it was usually because he wanted me to puzzle out the answer myself. So I lay there and made him wait while I figured it out.

'You were watching the canyon as I fell, weren't you?' I asked. 'You wanted to see if any shocks or surprises we created inside this prison would weaken the silk spell.'

He nodded, and maybe – just maybe – offered up the faintest hint of an approving smile.

'Jan'Tep mages,' he said dismissively, reaching down a hand to help me up, 'they reckon that esoteric geometry they have to envision to cast their spells makes 'em more intelligent than the rest of us. But all it makes 'em is predictable.'

Once I was on my feet I glanced around at the world in which we were imprisoned. 'Did you see any breaks in the illusion?'

Durral shook his head. 'It was more like, once you started fallin', everythin' became . . . vague. Like you were tumblin' down the idea of a cliff rather than fallin' from the real thing.'

The idea of a cliff. How are you supposed to escape one of those?

I was about to ask Durral, but then he started talking again, although this time it wasn't to me.

'Best you let us out now, boy,' he bellowed in a friendly voice, then paused to listen to the echoes.

If he was expecting a reply, he got none.

Undaunted he went on, 'That fancy magic of yours makes for a fine parlour trick, but me and the kid here, we've just about got your spell all figured out. You're deep inside our minds now, wrigglin' around, feedin' us your poison.'

'You realise that doesn't sound promising for us, right?' I observed.

Durral went right on lecturing our invisible captor. 'Way you all got it figured, we're trapped inside your thoughts. But see, there's somethin' you don't know about the Argosi ways.' He tapped a finger to his temple. 'They change a person. Our minds are all twisty inside. Yours, on the other hand? Well, I reckon all that magic just makes you soft.'

He winced suddenly and shook his head as if there were a wasp in his ear. I knew that feeling.

'That all you got?' he asked.

Again he was hit, and this time his legs buckled as he grabbed onto me for support. When I looked up at his face, his nose was bleeding. Teeth gritted, a feral grin came over his features.

'Come on,' he baited the mage. 'You can do better, can't ya?'

'Durral, don't—'

Even I felt the sting this time, like sewing needles stabbing into my eyes. I cried out. So did Durral. The pain was so bad it dropped both of us to our knees. I didn't even want to get up again. It was like . . . like my body couldn't understand how something could hurt that bad.

'Heh,' he said, as he pushed himself up.

'Are you crazy?' I demanded, struggling to get back on my feet. 'You've got blood coming out of your eye sockets!'

He wiped it away with the sleeve of his shirt, but more was dripping out, like tears. 'Did you feel it that time?'

'Did I feel it? Of course I felt it! It was like—'

He shook his head. 'No, not our pain. Theirs.'

Oh.

He was right. The first wave was my own agony, but the second one – where I couldn't even think straight because my brain couldn't comprehend the pain – that came from elsewhere.

'It's not Shadow Falcon holding the spell right now,' I said.

'You sure?' Durral asked.

I nodded. 'I've gotten to know the . . . sensation of his mind touching mine.'

Now that's a disgusting thought.

'Whoever's up there,' Durral began, addressing the star-filled sky, 'this is the last chance you're gonna get. The Path of the Rambling Thistle winds towards gentleness, but there are thorns along the road I walk. Now, I offered you the Way of Water, but you refused. I've followed the Way of Wind, and it's taught me the workings of your spell.' He spread his arms wide, then struck a palm against his chest. 'I've got the Way of Stone inside me. When I know the true path, I won't be turned. So you can blast me all you want, but my pain is

288

your pain, and from what I've seen so far, you ain't got the stones to endure it.'

Durral glanced down at me and chuckled. 'Did you see what I did there? With the bit about stones?'

His sense of humour always worked better on himself than anyone else.

'Is that your plan?' I asked. 'Make the mage groan from your bad jokes until they can't concentrate enough to hold the spell together?'

He smiled back at me, but still I saw the change come over him. He was still Durral Brown, still the strange, generous soul for whom kindness guided his every step, but beneath his eyes the seeping blood from the mind-blast had formed thin jagged lines down his cheeks, like red rivers.

Or bolts of scarlet lightning.

'This wasn't the path we chose,' he said quietly, and reached out a hand to me. 'But it is the path we must walk together. To the very end.'

'Where are we going?' I asked.

'Not far. Deeper into the canyon, where the light of the stars doesn't reach.'

'Why?'

'Because underneath all our civilised ways, beneath the scrappin' and the warrin' over one culture bein' better than another, we're all just frightened children. And the thunder scares us most in the dark.'

I took Durral Brown's hand, and it was warm and reassuring, which was odd, because in that moment he was the most terrifying man I'd ever met.

40

The Way of Thunder

How do you break out of an unbreakable prison, with a guard who watches over you every second of every day? Do you try to strike at them through the bars? Wait until their back is turned and grab them by the throat? Do you try to dig your way out, clawing through every inch of stone around you? Do you pray to the gods for mercy? Or just give up?

None of those things, I learned, were the Argosi way.

'You ever seen a trebuchet, kid?'

I shook my head.

We were about a quarter-mile into the canyon pass now, with the cliff walls on either side of us so high they kept out even the light of the imaginary moon that hung overhead in the mind of our captor.

'A trebuchet's a big damned war machine,' Durral said, walking us in a meandering pattern. 'Takes a team of engineers to make one, dozens of soldiers to take it apart, move it to the battlefield, reassemble it and make it work. But when they do, boy, that is a sight to see.' He held up one hand as if it were a wall and pounded it with a fist made from the other, knocking it down. 'A trebuchet can destroy in a couple of hours stone walls that took years to build. Given enough time, one trebuchet can destroy an entire fortress that's stood for centuries.'

Much as his fascination with trebuchets was almost boyishly endearing, I was missing the point.

'How does this break us out of a mind cage conjured by a mage who can probably hear this entire conversation?'

Durral stopped for a moment to reach into his pocket. He took out what looked like a steel pin about the length and thickness of his forefinger. 'Wasn't sure it'd be here, since we're not really anywhere right now, so I'm glad I can show it to you.'

'What is it?' I asked.

'Hinge pin from a Daroman heavy-artillery trebuchet.'

'What are you doing with it?'

He flipped the metal rod in the air. 'Funny thing about the hinge pin on those machines. You can't tell it's missing until you actually fire the trebuchet. Then the beam starts to swing, but with the pin on one side missing, the weight of the boulder meant to be launched at the enemy pulls the swing arm off balance. Whole thing comes down in a heap, pretty much destroying itself.'

'So you—'

He cut me off, and his eyes practically lit up in the darkness. 'An entire Daroman battalion was keepin' an understaffed Zhuban fortress under siege. The defenders' morale was so low they were ready to give up, but the Daroman major wanted to make a point. Figured he'd destroy the keep so that everyone in the region would know never to mess with a Daroman soldier who came demanding their food and gold for his own little crusade.'

Durral held one hand palm down and started wiggling his

fingers as if they were tiny puppets putting on a play. 'Little old Durral wandered into their camp. No magic, no money, no weapons. Didn't even wear a disguise. Just used my arta valar to strut on in like I owned the place. Used my arta loquit to speak to the soldiers – not just in Daroman but in the way a Daroman general's personal engineer talks down to a squad of mere privates so low in the ranks that they're set to guarding the trebuchet all night. Used my arta precis to watch how the real engineers had checked the machine that night. Used all the subtlety of my arta tuco to figure out the exact right time to make my move.'

He held up the pin again. 'And I made them break their precious machine, embarrassed them in front of their enemy, made them lose so much time and effort they had to accept the settlement offered by the Zhuban defenders.' He stuffed the pin back in his pocket. 'All using talents any human being can develop if they're willing. If they believe in themselves. If they can learn to give up all those other kinds of power like spells or military machines or wealth and instead find the kind of magic that belongs to all of us.'

Not so long ago I would've silently derided this kind of romantic idealism about human beings. I would've despised Durral for such wilful self-deception. But now? I was enraptured. Captivated, as if he'd summoned up a mind cage of his own and put me in it.

Which, of course, was the point.

'The world ain't made up of people who fight fair,' Durral said, resuming our winding walk between the canyon walls. 'Them as want to kill you don't stand in front of you, fists cocked, waitin' till you're ready to begin. They get themselves armies with trebuchets, mages with spells, assassins who kill you in your sleep and some souls even more wicked who'll ensure you starve half to death long before they have to see your face. This is why an Argosi must sometimes follow the Way of Thunder.'

'Show me,' I begged, eager for some secret, some new weapon with which to strike at my enemy and hurt them like I'd been hurt my whole life. 'How do we fight people like that?'

'You can't fight 'em, kid. You gotta *defeat* 'em.'

He knelt down to scoop up a handful of dirt and sand, then held out his closed fist. 'A warrior trains her whole life to fight the same battle over and over again. She fights with the same weapons as her enemy, which means her death is assured, because one day she's bound to meet somebody faster. Somebody stronger.' He loosened his fist, and in the darkness I could just make out the tiny granules slipping through his fingers. 'To an Argosi, every battle is unique, each one like a grain of sand in the desert. To win, you have to perceive what makes this one fight different from all the others, never preferring any one means of attack, but instead searching for the one path in each case that leads to victory.' He let the last of the dirt and sand fall back to the ground. 'Do you see our path to victory here, kid?'

A prison of the mind.

Our minds. Their minds. It didn't really matter any more.

Though we were on one side of the bars and our jailors on the other, still we shared the same cold walls all around us, the same dark and dank world that crushed the soul and broke the heart. In such a world the prisoner is free of doubt, for choice has been taken away. They can scream and wail but they will never bend the iron bars that hold them captive. But the jailor? The jailor can walk away, and must devote all their strength of will to keep from fleeing when the screams threaten to drown them in misery.

'I should go first,' I said.

'You sure, kid?'

I nodded. 'I can make it hurt worse.'

He smiled at me, that familiar sadness in his eyes. 'Reckon you can at that.'

Magic is the control by a human being over fundamental energies, moulded by the will and the mind, both of which rely on concentration. Jan'Tep mages spend their entire childhoods learning to concentrate, to envision what they want the spell to accomplish, to guide it with esoteric geometries in their mind's eye. That ability to focus is what makes them powerful, like a sword with an edge so sharp it can slice through stone. But as Durral had proven here, a sword like that cuts both ways. A silk spell binds the victim's mind to that of the mage. By shaping what we saw, they made themselves vulnerable to feeling what we felt.

'Go on, kid,' Durral said softly.

It's a hard thing to do – to relive the worst moments of your life. But over those next hours, as Durral bade me follow his spiralling steps in the darkness, I did precisely that. I summoned up sorrow and conjured despair. I cried for my parents, taken from me so long ago I couldn't even remember their faces. I wept for Gervais and Rosarite and the loss of the woman I might've become had they raised me as they'd hoped. I recalled every moment I'd spent in that cave with Met'astice patiently instructing Shadow Falcon on how to inscribe the sigils into my neck with molten metal inks, screaming just as I had screamed then. I took all my hopes and the moments of joy I'd begun to experience with Arissa

294

and I let the memory of her sudden hatred crush me once again. I went back to every pang of hunger, every second of terror, and I lived them over and over until I feared my own mind would break apart.

Durral's big hand covered my small one. 'Okay, kid,' he said. 'My turn.'

All this time we'd been walking in circles in the canyon, taking a path that had seemed random at first, but after a while we'd followed it so many times that I could recognise the pattern, almost as if our steps were lit up in the darkness. Jan'Tep mages envision esoteric geometries to cast their spells, and now I wondered if maybe Durral was having us deliberately trace one of those patterns in reverse to further weaken our captor's concentration.

When Durral finally spoke, I expected him to recount his own sad tales of suffering. I'm ashamed to say I was almost looking forward to it, as if hearing someone else's sorrows would lessen my own. But he didn't tell me any such stories. He told me joyous ones, of love and laughter and unexpected happiness, and those made my miserable memories hurt all the more.

'First time I ever saw her,' he began, a smile already coming to his lips, 'it was like somebody'd just lifted a blindfold I hadn't realised I was wearing. First words out of her mouth were like the punchline of the best joke you've ever heard.' He chuckled. 'I swear, I've been laughing ever since.'

Her name was Enna, and she was, as Durral put it, 'somethin''. The way she made him feel, not just happy, but surprised – every day, surprised – was like listening to music for the first time. Seeing art, or the leaves in autumn, or . . . well, anything new and wondrous.

The lord and lady knights were in love, of that I'd had no doubt, but it wasn't like Durral and Enna. I ached so bad then – ached to love somebody like Durral loved Enna.

'How did she die?' I asked.

All the while I'd been watching the canyon around us. In the darkness there was so little to see that the mage probably didn't need to concentrate at all because everything was a formless grey-black mist. I suspected Durral had meant for that to be the case, because thunder's always more shocking when you're not expecting it.

'What was that, kid?' Durral asked.

'A while back you said you were going to miss your anniversary, but I guess you meant . . . How did she die?'

I was positive this was the end point. Durral had described his love for Enna with such adoration and joyfulness that now, as he took her away from us, the grief would overwhelm the mage's concentration and the spell would shatter.

Durral stopped walking. He looked off into the grey-black mist as if waiting for her to walk through and into his arms. His face was hardened clay, like he was holding something in that would surely break him apart when it came out. Then he turned to me, utterly expressionless at first. His lips began to tremble. Soon the tremors reached his cheeks, his brow, even the bones of his jaw. The man who'd spoken of following the Way of Stone was about to crack.

And he did.

I thought it was a sob at first, because that's what I'd expected, but when more came, I realised his cries weren't sobs at all. He was laughing.

Huge, rumbling roars. Great, rowdy whoops. It was like he'd gone mad, right before my eyes. I became so frightened for his sanity that I reached out to try to hold him, but then he stopped cold and spoke at last.

'Who said anything about her dyin', kid?'

And the walls of our prison came down around us.

41

The Prison Guard

The first thing that caught my eye as the silk spell that had kept Durral and me trapped for weeks broke apart wasn't the gleaming marble of our pristine surroundings. It wasn't the unusual seven-sided shape of the single-room building, each wall adorned with complex symbols which I assumed were representative of various forms of magic. I glanced briefly up to the domed ceiling, painted blue-black with hundreds of gleaming golden points forming constellations, but was soon drawn back down to the seven burning braziers that circled the two red velvet couches upon which Durral and I found ourselves. None of these things held my notice for more than an instant. Rather it was the face of a woman – a girl really – dressed in shimmering white robes and huddled in the corner, staring up at us as if the monsters of her worst nightmares had descended upon her.

She couldn't have been much older than me.

Her eyes – beneath the blur of tears – shone bright with intelligence. Not all that remarkable. One assumes any Jan'Tep mage capable of maintaining the complex esoteric geometries of a silk spell couldn't be entirely stupid. Her hair was an unusually bright red, almost like my own. Though she was far prettier than I would ever be, still I think we might've passed for sisters had things been different.

She was shaking with fear and confusion, which I attributed to the effects of Durral and I having messed with her mind by reliving memories that I never would've chosen to share. My miseries and tribulations, Durral's tales of love and adoration, all shattered by the unexpected thunderclap of a joke. That's what had broken this mighty tower of the mind in which we'd been trapped, and she'd doubtless been one of our jailors.

Her panic-stricken crying was so apoplectic it was almost as if she were hiccuping sobs. Durral, fool that he was, tried to calm her.

'A girl who can hold an entire world in her head,' he said softly, 'needn't fear a little heartache. Let the feelings come and let them go, just like the tide. You ain't gonna drown, I promise.'

Her breathing came in rushes, but even I could tell his words had brought her a measure of reassurance. Her lips parted, and it seemed to me she was about to thank him, until the fingers of her right hand began to form the somatic shape of a spell.

'Durral! She's—'

But it all happened too fast. Even as the cascade of copper and gold light began to play around the tattooed markings of two Jan'Tep bands around her forearm, a flash of steel slashed the air between us. The girl screamed and grabbed her own wrist. The palm of her outstretched hand had acquired a thin piece of metal, the size and shape of a playing card, buried into the flesh, leaking blood around it.

'Some days,' Durral said with a sigh.

In his hand I saw a deck of cards just like the one embedded in her hand. Durral was looking down at them. 'Surprised they left these on me.' Ignoring the girl's cries, he stretched his arms overhead and tilted his head left and right. 'Don't feel sore. Muscles workin' fine.' He went over and knelt beside the girl. 'Must'a been some kind of spell too, right? To stop time from passin' by the kid and me?'

She wailed, but his closeness and the proximity of his deck of razor-sharp cards induced her to answer. 'Sand magic. Only . . . way to . . . keep you both . . . alive long enough for—'

'Mighty courteous of y'all.' Durral rubbed his chin and smiled up at me. 'Ain't even in need of a shave.' He turned back to the girl. 'What's your name?'

'Ala'tris of the House of—'

'Don't tell me,' Durral said, cutting her off. 'The House of Tris, right?' Before she could answer, he patted her on the shoulder. 'That's enough of your bawlin' now, girl. You're gonna break my heart if you keep on like that. Best we take care of that hand of yours anyway. Gonna need it for castin' spells, right?'

Kindness in a world as cruel as this one was a miracle. Ever since I'd first met Sir Rosarite and Sir Gervais I'd recognised that essential truth. This was the first time I'd learned that kindness could also be a sin.

Barely a minute had passed since we'd emerged from the silk spell, and I'd been in a state of shock, first from waking in this unfamiliar place, then from seeing Durral coddle this Jan'Tep . . . Never before had I so badly wanted to use the nasty word that my old comportment teacher, Master Phinus, always said was unbecoming of proper ladies. Anyway, I mention all this because it was only then that I realised I

300

could move again, and noticed my leather mapmaker's case sitting on top of a chest about six feet away from the cot upon which I'd lain a prisoner of the Cabal, frozen in time by their magic.

I wasn't frozen any more.

Durral was right. My muscles were fine – like I'd lain down for a nap barely an hour ago instead of six or seven weeks. A testament to the wonders of Jan'Tep sand magic, for which I was grateful. Three seconds was all it took for me to leap over the cot, grab the mapmaker's case and draw the small-sword from inside. It would take me two seconds more to end the life of this girl who, despite her youth, despite that we looked a little bit alike and, most of all, despite Durral's stupid, blind compassion for her, had been one of my jailors.

Met'astice had died before I could kill him, and given we had to be in Jan'Tep territory, I'd likely die before I could hunt down Shadow Falcon. That was okay though. I would settle for my first murder being that of Ala'tris of the House of Tris.

Three steps, another leap, one tiny stumble from which I quickly recovered and turned into a long lunge, and the tip of the smallsword was on its way to my enemy's neck. I got to see her eyes go wide as she experienced what I imagined was the first true moment of terror in her life: the sight of a filthy Mahdek's sword about to bury itself in her throat.

When first I felt resistance against the blade, I feared Ala'tris had hit me with another spell – perhaps the same sand magic that had kept us frozen in time all these weeks. But then my eyes opened, and I realised I'd made the same amateur mistake of closing them just before the thrust as I'd made out in the desert weeks ago when Durral had found me. His fist was wrapped around the thinnest part of the blade near the point. He'd twisted his forearm to bend the blade upward, preventing me from pushing it any further forward.

'Don't you dare,' I said with a growl so feral that I almost wondered if someone else had spoken.

'Withdraw your weapon,' Durral said. His voice was as cold as mine.

When I didn't move, he bent the sword even more, arcing the steel blade between us. 'Be a shame to break it,' he said.

I nodded, and he let go, and because I owed him more than just my life I didn't try again. But I hated him in that moment, and turned away because I couldn't bear to see his face.

'Kid,' he said.

I stayed where I was.

'Ferius, look at me.'

But I was too busy choking on rage to follow his orders.

'Teysan.'

'What?' I shouted, gripping the hilt of my smallsword so tight my palm hurt. 'I did what you said, didn't I? Now the rest of the Cabal will come in here any minute and kill us! Are you happy?'

'I need you to look at me, Ferius.'

'Why?'

'Because there's a lesson you need to learn.'

At last I turned back around to face him. He was still kneeling next to the mage. He held up her bleeding right hand, and his own beside it. 'She and I are feeling the same pain right now. Her blood's as red as mine. You understand?'

'She's our enemy.'

He glanced at the girl and smiled. 'She can't be my enemy,' he said. 'I choose who my enemies are.'

There are no words to describe how infuriated I was, knowing that my life – my freedom – would end the moment the Cabal returned to this sanctum. And Durral Brown was still trying to teach me the Way of Water.

'Tell him!' I screamed at the girl, Ala'tris. 'Tell him he's an Argosi and you're a Jan'Tep, and even if you hadn't already kidnapped us and held us captive in a damned silk spell, you'd *still* be our enemy just on principle!'

I don't know why I expected a reply. No doubt to her I was some lunatic Mahdek badly in need of an ember spell to burn her out of existence. Yet when her trembling lips parted, this time she didn't attempt a spell. Instead she said, 'I . . . have a duty to my people.'

Durral stood up and offered her the hand that wasn't bleeding. Surprisingly, she accepted and rose to her feet.

'Reckon you and I have a different notion of duty, Ala'tris,' he said, 'but be that as it may, you followed the orders given to you, kept us inside that silk spell as best you could. When we broke out of your bosses' little prison, even with all the pain and confusion you were suffering, you tried to fight, brave as any soldier. But now your duty's done. By any law in any nation – including this one – me and the kid had the right to kill you for what you done. Instead I offer you the Way of Water once again. Let us pass each other by now, never again our paths to cross, lest it be in peace.'

She looked uncertain. 'The Cabal . . . My masters will—'

'That's between your bosses and us. But I need you to make a choice now. Either say there is peace between us, or we'll have to go on wrestlin' till one of us dies.' He held up his steel deck. 'And right now, girl, I'm holdin' all the cards.'

'Why would you believe me, even if I agreed?' she asked.

He stepped back. 'Because as much as each member of this Cabal you've been workin' for were in our heads, we were in yours too, and the world you painted for us was just a little nicer than theirs.' He gave her a small bow. 'Also, I happen to be an excellent judge of character.'

Ala'tris hesitated, biting her lower lip for a long while as if trying to compose her thoughts. 'I will not betray the Cabal,' she said. 'But . . . I will not attack you again without provocation. If asked to cast a spell upon you, I will refuse, and pay whatever cost such disloyalty demands.'

Durral watched her eyes for a moment, as if he could read the truth in them. The strange thing was, I knew he could. Even more surprising? I was pretty sure I could too. Ala'tris wasn't lying. She meant to keep her word.

Ever since I'd met Durral I'd badgered him to teach me the ways of the Argosi – now that I'd acquired the barest sliver of their talents, I wished I hadn't. Seeing someone through Durral's eyes was like . . . being inside their head. And you couldn't do that for long without coming to understand them.

I turned away, not wanting either of them to see my tears. I should've been happy to be free from the spell, or terrified of what would happen when the Cabal caught us, since there was no way an Argosi and a Mahdek were getting out of a city full of mages without being caught. Yet now all I felt was ashamed for having tried to kill someone I had every right to hate.

'Violence weakens the spirit,' Durral said.

I hadn't even heard him come up behind me. Very gently he put his hands on my arms. 'Vengeance destroys it. Simple as that. An Argosi driven by violence or vengeance can never follow their path and do the things we must do.'

304

I spun on him, hurling the last bitter stones of my anger. 'And what is that, maetri? What do the Argosi do that's so important it means I should be denied any chance at justice?'

Durral pulled me closer. 'We're trying to save the world, kid.'

I don't know if there were words in any language more preposterous, noble, arrogant and beautiful, but if there were, I'd never heard them. I guess I hoped I never would.

'How are we supposed to do that?' I asked.

Gently, he unclasped my arms that were clinging to him, and turned to Ala'tris, who was watching us, mystified and misty-eyed, as Durral might say.

'Where in this town would a fella find the most powerful mages?' he asked her.

'The most . . . This is the testing week for Jan'Tep initiates in our city. The clan prince and the council of lords magi will be at the oasis, watching the students attempt their trials.'

'Much obliged,' Durral said, then walked over to the cots and picked up his pack and frontier hat before heading to the door of the sanctum.

'Wait!' Ala'tris called out. 'You mustn't go to the oasis! Today is the day the initiates face their first spell duels, and my masters will be there to witness!'

'Duellin', eh?' Durral asked.

Ala'tris nodded. 'The leaders of the Cabal seek out the most promising students to recruit them, as they did me, last year.'

Durral set his frontier hat on his head. 'Well now, that sounds just about right.' He winked at me. 'Come on, kid. Let's you and me go show all them impressionable young mages how a proper duel is done.'

The Argosi

The Way of the Argosi is the Way of Water; the Way of Wind; the Way of Thunder. Sometimes it is the Way of Stone. Yet each of these is as incomplete as the journey of the knight, the thief, the drifter or any of the others. The Way of the Argosi is built of all those other journeys, and none of them. It must be crafted one step at a time, knowing that with each footfall the traveller makes a choice and, from all those choices, blazes a path that is theirs alone. This is the Way of the Argosi.

42

City of Mages

The moment we stepped out of the sanctum in which we'd been kept prisoner these past weeks, I found my earlier insight that kindness could be a sin complemented by a new one that equally challenged my faith in Durral's Argosi ways. This one had to do with beauty.

'Takes some gettin' used to, don't it?' he asked.

A wide avenue crossed in front of us, lined with tall slender trees whose pink leaves fluttered in the warm breeze. White stone buildings rose up three storeys, each one adorned with its own architectural curiosities, yet fitting together both with its neighbours and the landscape around it as if the entire city had been designed all those centuries ago not by engineers, but by artists.

Those artists had been Mahdek.

My people.

Fools.

If kindness to those unworthy of it was a sin, then surely such beauty as my ancestors had built for us ought to be a crime. How could I despise the Jan'Tep for waging war against the Mahdek to take such cities away from us? The oasis to which Durral now led us might have been the object of their

311

mages' desire, but surely the glistening avenues and architectural marvels built around them had given our enemies cause to despise us.

Ours had been the most beautiful cities on the continent. Of course the Jan'Tep had hated us. Having lived among the poorest wretches infesting the continent during my short life, I knew that such riches as my enemies now enjoyed were themselves a crime against all of humanity.

The Jan'Tep were right to be paranoid. One day someone would come and take this place, along with all the others like it that dotted their conquered territory.

Then they would be like us.

'Arta precis,' Durral said, taking me by the elbow and leading me down the avenue.

See the strange in the everyday. That was the first part of arta precis, but the second was to see the everyday in that which is strange.

No one screamed when they saw us. These finely dressed lord and lady mages – and even the Sha'Tep servants scurrying about to do the real work of running a city – all strolled by without one of them recoiling at our presence or raising up their hands to cast deadly spells upon us. They took notice of us, sure, and some glared or curled their lips at our dusty clothing and dishevelled appearance. But hey, I would've too, if my hair was as carefully coiffed as theirs, my skin as smooth and flawless. Durral and I were really dirtying the place up.

'They don't care that we're here,' I murmured, almost in awe of their lack of regard.

Durral kept us moving, first down the avenue then onto a smaller street that curved around a glistening tower with gold finials adorning its circular balconies. 'It's a city, kid,' he said.

'People live, work, make love, worry about the future, wonder about the past. They eat, drink, poop, sleep and dream of tomorrows that will never come.'

'Don't,' I warned. 'Don't make them sound like—'

He pointed out a group of four men and women in Gitabrian garb riding along the circular promenade in a fine carriage with chests strapped to the roof. 'Foreigners like us come here to trade goods, negotiate diplomatic relationships . . . sometimes, I reckon, a few come just to see how the Jan'Tep live. All without starting blood feuds or setting off wars.'

I was about to protest again when he turned me towards a family standing across the way who were staring at us. The parents were mages – even from here I could see the tattooed bands peeking out of the wide sleeves of their robes. They had a child with them, a boy of around seven years old, who was pointing at me while clinging to his father's robes.

'There stands your enemy,' Durral said.

'I don't care about the boy. It's his parents I worry about.'

'Oh? Haven't you noticed the kid's arm?'

The markings were faint, no doubt they'd only just begun to tattoo his sigils, but there around the boy's left forearm was the beginning of one of his Jan'Tep bands.

'He'll be an initiate soon, and later a mage. One day he might even grow up to be a war mage like your Shadow Falcon, or a lord magus like that Met'astice fella who started this mess.'

'Don't compare Met'astice to a child, Durral! It's not the same thing and you know it!'

'Why? You think the old coot never walked in a boy's sandals or wore a boy's silly grin?'

'It's not the same thing!' I repeated.

My angry tone had startled the boy across the street, who cringed even further into his father's robes. The parents, however, refused to let their son hide. I guess they wanted him to learn the face of his enemy.

'If you continue down this path you're on,' Durral warned, 'one day, maybe ten, maybe twenty years from now, you might be fightin' that boy. Better for the both of you if you kill him now before he comes into his power.'

'Stop it,' I said, quieter now. 'Just stop it, please.'

Durral leaned down and whispered in my ear. 'Want to see a magic trick, kid?'

No, I thought. *Don't do this to me, Durral. Please don't do this.*

'Smile,' he said.

'No.'

'Smile, or I'll tell you an old Zhubanese joke so dirty your cheeks'll turn a pink brighter than the leaves on one of them tamarisk trees and then you'll end up grinnin' like a drunk.'

Despite my best efforts, an insipid smile had begun creeping onto my face. I could have forced it back, had I tried harder, but by then the boy's eyes had widened with curiosity even as his mother scowled in disgust.

I felt a strange sense of power come over me. Maybe it was because for so long, if someone looked at me too close, Met'astice's foul spells made them hate me. Now at least that part of his influence was gone. Smiling at that kid was like . . . like I could mesmerise him from clear across the street with nothing but the rising corners of my mouth.

The boy raised a hand, and for a second I expected him to try to cast some student's defensive cantrip. But then his palm faced out and he waved at me.

I waved back. The parents dragged him away.

'A wonder to behold,' Durral said, in that way of his where you can't tell if he's making fun of you or being deadly serious.

'What difference does it make? You saw the parents. They'll fill his head with more stories of the vile Mahdek, and he'll grow up in this city – that ought to be *my* city – and learn to hate me.'

'Maybe,' Durral conceded. 'But you can't see the future and neither can I.'

He took out a deck of cards from his coat and fanned it out for me. I'd seen them before. These ones had a suit for each of the cultures on the continent. Shields for Darome. Chalices for Berabesq. Septagrams for the Jan'Tep. There used to be a suit of Leaves for the Mahdek, but the Argosi don't keep those cards in their decks any more because there aren't enough of us to matter.

'These cards can't help me predict nothin',' he said. 'The Argosi don't live in the future, just like we don't dwell on the past. But what I can do with this deck is understand the present, and see when times are changing.'

He put the cards in my hands.

I rifled through them, part of me marvelling at how each card of each suit depicted a different aspect of that culture's ways and how they approached the world. The other part of me only grew more bitter.

I handed the deck back to him. 'Maybe you see the present in these cards, Durral, but all I see – all *my* arta precis shows me – is what's missing.'

'Funny,' he said. 'My arta precis was showin' me the same thing. But then a couple of months back somethin' happened that made me realise my deck was incomplete.'

315

He squared the deck and held it on his palm almost reverentially. 'Care to take a card, kid?'

'We're in a Jan'Tep city, Durral! We're not guests here, we're not tourists, we're escaped prisoners! As soon as the Cabal are done watching whatever stupid initiations are taking place, they're going to find out we broke out of their mind cage. They're going to come hunting us. So you'll forgive me if I'm not interested in any of your stupid card tricks right now!'

He shot me a smirk. 'That so?' He waved a hand over the deck like one of those frontier stage magicians they're so fond of in the Seven Sands. 'Even if this particular card holds the key to outwitting the Cabal, putting an end to their experiments and maybe even you and me gettin' out of this town alive?'

That would have to be one hell of a card.

Frustrated and pissed off, I reached out and took the top card from the deck. The back of it was just like the others, with a hand-painted picture of a compass whose cardinal points were symbols for water, wind, thunder and stone, instead of the directions on a map. When I flipped it over, though, what I saw was completely unlike the rest of the deck.

For one thing, there were no markings for the suit. No shield or chalice or septagram or even leaf. Instead the card was painted with the image of a girl in a long coat with curly red hair. My age. My sharp jawline. My grey-green eyes. Me, in fact, except for two details: first, on her head she had a frontier hat like Durral's, tilted at a jaunty, almost impudent angle. Second, she wore a smile that not once in all the times I'd seen my reflection in a mirror or a puddle of filthy water, or in the glare of an enemy, had ever been on my face. Yet

316

still, the smile was familiar to me. Maybe because when I looked up from the card I found myself staring right into it.

'When did you paint this?' I asked Durral.

'Day after I caught you tryin' to steal the canteen from my saddlebags outside that roadside tavern. Or, to be more accurate, shortly after you pilfered my empire coin.'

'But why? I stole from you. Why would you—'

'That coin was a beauty, sure, but I figured you needed it more'n me. It's like I told you before, kid, Durral Brown's a great judge of character, and I got the best arta precis anybody's ever seen.'

I gazed back at the picture, at the wild, daring girl on the card who almost looked like she was about to wink at me. 'This isn't who I am,' I said.

Durral took the card back and slipped the deck into his coat. 'I'm about to bet a whole lotta people's lives – includin' mine by the way – that you *are* that girl, Ferius Parfax.'

He resumed his march along the curved street, forcing me to follow.

'I'm not like you, Durral. I'm not some wandering pacifist with a knight's honour and a thief's cunning, wandering the world betting my life on a handful of tricks to fight off mages, only to then treat my enemies with infinitely more compassion than they deserve.'

The Argosi paused, just for a second, his right foot waiting to come back down to the sidewalk. 'Why not, kid? Sounds like a pretty fine thing to be, if you ask me.'

'Because I watched my parents get torn apart by a Jan'Tep spell when I was seven, and I watched my clan massacred four years later. Because the two kindest, noblest people I ever met were murdered six months after that, trying to protect me.' I yanked down the top of my coat. 'Because they put this collar on me.'

Durral reached out a finger and tapped one of the sigils. 'Funny,' he said. 'Don't feel like no collar I've ever touched.' He leaned in closer. 'Don't look like one neither. You ask me, it looks more like a necklace.' He stood back up straight. 'A fine necklace too. Never seen one like it.'

He took off down the street, past beautiful homes and shops and all these people smiling and talking to each other as if their hands were clean of the blood spilled in their names. When I caught up to Durral, I grabbed his arm, trying to yank him to a stop, but he shrugged off my hand and kept walking.

'You said the Argosi are fighting to save the world,' I called out. 'But whose world are you fighting for? Theirs –' I swung an arm out towards the Jan'Tep blithely going about their lives – 'or mine? Because you can't fight for both.'

He stopped then, and I saw why. The end of the promenade met another wide avenue, this one even grander than the first. About fifty yards ahead stood the seven marble columns ringing the city's oasis and, within, dozens of Jan'Tep initiates watched by hundreds of their parents, their teachers and, seated atop a golden palanquin, the mystical energies flowing around his tattooed bands which were glowing as if six constellations of multicoloured stars had been wrapped around his forearms, their clan prince.

Durral turned to me, and that gambler's grin of his rose like the sun, so fierce you'd almost think he'd gone feral. When he spoke his voice was so rich with laughter and arta valar – that strange Argosi talent for daring – that I wondered whether I'd truly known him at all.

318

Durral lifted his frontier hat from his head and placed it on mine, tilting it at precisely the same angle as in the picture of me he'd painted on the card.

'Just watch me,' he said.

43

The Oasis

How do you spot a handful of conspirators hidden among a crowd of hundreds of Jan'Tep citizens in their flowing silk robes and sheath-like dresses, patterned with the sigils of their ancestral houses?

Turns out it's not hard at all.

'Mages,' Durral said dismissively. 'Worst poker players you'll ever meet.'

There were six of them. Six pairs of eyes interspersed among the throngs of families watching as teenagers my age displayed their magical abilities in the hope of earning the right to advance in their studies. From where we stood, just outside the stone columns, the members of the Cabal appeared profoundly ordinary to me. Men and women of varying ages and appearance, the features of their faces, their hair and skin colour, so different from one another they might have come from six different nations. The only thing they had in common was the surprise and hatred in their gazes as they glared at us from the ring of elevated benches looking down upon the oasis.

'Where's Shadow Falcon?'

Durral shrugged. 'Who knows? The Cabal probably has suckers like him working for them across the Jan'Tep territories.

The boy might be a hundred miles from here. Besides, he's not the real enemy. He's never been the real enemy.'

He waved at the six members of the Cabal.

'Don't,' I warned. 'They'll blast us with ember spells!'

But the Argosi just grinned. 'Come on, kid. I've been cooped up inside a mind cage for six weeks. Let me have a little fun before we get down to business.'

He turned his attention to one of the members of the Cabal. A tall man with broad shoulders beneath his blue and silver robes. Then Durral did something unbelievably foolish. He delivered an insult that could not be borne. A declaration of war.

Durral Brown blew the mage a kiss.

I saw the glint of copper flare up beneath the man's silk sleeve, and the fingers of his right hand take on a shape I recognised because I'd seen it right before members of my clan had been burned alive. I tried to tackle Durral to the ground, praying we could dodge the first blast. But Durral was too big, and barely noticed my pathetic attempt to grapple him.

His head swivelled towards me, one eyebrow arched. 'What're you up to, kid?'

'Trying to save your dumb life!'

'Much obliged.'

It occurred to me then that we weren't on fire. I turned to the stands and saw that the Cabal mage had set off a commotion, and a dozen people around him had their own hands raised, the tattoos on *their* forearms glinting in the bright sunlight.

'That's the problem with livin' in a city full of mages,' Durral said. 'Folks don't take it too kindly when you start throwin' bolts of fire and lightnin' around willy-nilly.'

'Were you testing him?' I asked. Then I pointed to the angry men and women surrounding the mage, at whom he was shouting as his co-conspirators made their way through the crowds to his aid. 'Or them?'

'Neither.' Durral indicated the palanquin upon which was seated the man whose ornate robes put all the others to shame. 'I was testin' that fella.'

The clan prince wasn't paying any attention to the growing uproar in the stands, however. He was watching us.

'Observant,' Durral noted, waving casually at the sovereign of the city. 'That'll come in handy for what comes next.'

The prince leaned down and spoke to one of the mages in red-and-gold robes standing by the palanquin. Two of them then strode towards us. Unlike everyone else, their hands were still, hanging at their sides without a trace of tension in their fingers.

'War mages,' Durral said as they approached. 'Proper ones. They know the fastest draw comes from the calmest hand.'

'Argosi, you will come with us,' the shorter of the two said once the pair were within eight feet of us.

Close enough to ensure their spells hit us, too far for us to jump them.

Durral bowed low, one hand behind his back. I wondered if he meant for me to see the glint of the steel cards he had palmed there. 'My lords, fearsome and wise,' he said, not a trace of frontier drawl in his voice, 'your merest regard is an honour that shines upon us, illuminating the way ahead. With pride we accept your clan prince's invitation.'

'We don't care for your pride,' the taller mage said, 'and this *isn't* an invitation.'

I saw the slightest twitch in the hand holding the steel

cards, and a hint of a sneer come and go from Durral's lips before he gave them a second, more humble bow. 'You show me the path to greater understanding, my lord. A gift whose value I must spend much time contemplating.'

I doubt anyone else would've noticed, but I was surprised to realise that, for an instant, Durral had been tempted to pick a fight with these two mages just to see if he could win.

Maybe there's a price that comes with all that arta valar of his, I thought.

The shorter mage led the way back to the palanquin and the taller one walked behind us, his looming presence a reminder that we weren't the prince's guests.

'What business does an Argosi have in Oatas Jan'Dal?' the glowing man asked.

Oatas Jan'Dal. Fifty miles north of Oatas Jan'Ju and just across the border from the town where we fought the candle man. We practically delivered ourselves into the Cabal's hands.

When Durral failed to reply, the clan prince gave him a warning glare. 'You will give an answer, Argosi, or—'

Durral held up a finger. 'Wait for it . . .'

I had to squint thanks to the shine coming off the tattooed bands on the clan prince's left arm, but suddenly a new voice called out.

'Spies!' a woman with lustrous golden hair held atop her head with a copper coronet declared as she strode towards the palanquin. She was one of the six who'd registered our arrival earlier, and the rest of the Cabal pushed through the stunned crowds to catch up with her.

'These two come to attack our city,' the big man who'd nearly blasted us said, though I noticed he didn't dare raise his hands now.

323

'Really?' the prince asked. 'And yet it was you, Met'ordan, who came within a hair's breadth of violating our law by casting war magic in my presence.'

Durral elbowed me. 'See, kid? Told you I was just havin' a little fun.'

Met'ordan, I thought. *Of the House of Met. He must be related to Met'astice.*

Met'ordan bowed low. 'I feared they meant to attack you, my prince, and so attempted to—'

'One of the wandering card players?' the prince asked. 'Present a genuine threat to a lord magus?'

His tone was light with humour yet infused with dangerous possibilities at what could happen when one of his subjects implied weakness in him. 'Can you imagine such a thing?'

He'd said this to Durral, who bit his lower lip even through his smile. 'An Argosi take on a Jan'Tep prince? The most powerful mage of his entire clan?' He chuckled. 'Now wouldn't that make for a tale?'

'Indeed,' replied the prince. 'Though it begs the question, what business *do* you have in my city?'

'Just passin' through,' Durral said, before his eyes went to Met'ordan. 'Unless someone here's got business with me.'

If Durral had thought this stand-off might lead to some kind of peaceful parting, he'd severely misjudged the Cabal.

'They assaulted my daughter!' the blonde woman said. She pointed an accusing finger at Durral. 'They snuck into our city and caught her unawares. The things they did to her . . . By our ancestors,' she growled, turning her rage on the clan prince, 'I demand retribution!'

More and more of the Jan'Tep at the oasis were crowding

324

around us, rapt in their attention over these unusual developments. Several began muttering angrily in our direction.

'When?' Durral asked.

'What?' the woman demanded.

'When was it that we supposedly attacked your daughter.'

'What difference could that possibly make? What matters is that you and this Mahdek savage violated the sanctity of our family.' Again she turned her red-faced glare towards her sovereign. 'As *some* of us have warned would happen for many years now!'

Durral shrugged. 'I was just curious on account of, well, I wouldn't want to presume as to your people's ways, but it seems odd that your girl's back home sufferin' from what I've no doubt are many terrible traumas at the hands of me and the filthy Mahdek savage here, while you're sittin' here . . . What is it you all are doin' here again?'

'You do not question our ways, Argosi,' Met'ordan declared. He turned to the prince. 'Give me leave and I will rid our people of two of our adversaries this instant!'

'We've warned you over and over again,' the woman said, taking up the charge. 'Our people have enemies, and here you see two of them. Will you still tell us we should forbear to defend ourselves?'

It was odd standing there, surrounded by all these people I'd despised my whole life, who'd despised me since before I was born, and seeing all the subtle variations drift across their expressions. Most of those watching nodded their heads in agreement, and I saw the fingers of many hands twitch with the urge to blast me from existence. Others looked confused more than outraged and a few even appeared dubious.

The clan prince was one of those.

'I would hear an answer to the Argosi's question, Neva'tris,' he said.

The blonde-haired woman did a great job of looking shocked, offended, wounded and despairing as to how the foundations of civilisation were crumbling before her. She would've made a good actor, or possibly an opera singer, were such vocations not considered beneath the Jan'Tep. 'Do you accuse me of deceit, my prince?'

'More of child neglect, at this point,' he replied with what I felt was remarkable nonchalance.

'The attack occurred in these past hours,' Met'ordan replied. 'While we were here, participating in our civic duty to witness the next generation of mages pass their trials, these two assassins were attacking one of your citizens.'

More mutterings, and even a few vocal accusations of cowardice.

'And you know of this how, Met'ordan?' the clan prince persisted. 'By what means were you informed of the attack on Ala'tris?' One of the bands on the prince's left forearm – my guess was the one for silk magic – glowed brighter than the others. 'For that would be easily verified with a simple spell. I would be happy to perform it myse—'

'Your Highness?' Durral asked.

The clan prince wasn't pleased by the interruption. 'Do you wish to confess, Argosi?'

'No, sir. Just thought – and forgive me for bein' a barbarian who has to go through life figurin' things out without the benefit of spells and such – that maybe an easier way to get at the truth would be to just ask the girl instead of everybody speakin' for her.'

'An interesting point.' The prince glanced around. 'Where

326

is your daughter, Neva'tris? Does she perhaps lack in your sense of civic duty?'

'No,' the blonde-haired woman replied indignantly. 'She is at home, serving our house and our clan in a vital . . . experiment.'

'Nah,' Durral said. 'She's right here.'

Now even I was looking around, along with everyone else. Just when I thought Durral had played the wrong card in this bizarre game he'd got us caught up in, I saw the sheen of red tresses float through the crowd towards us.

'I am here, my prince,' she said, kneeling before him.

Neva'tris shook off whatever anger she felt at her daughter's regrettably timely arrival. 'Tell them, girl. Tell them how these two attacked you.'

Ala'tris turned briefly towards us, her glance passing from Durral to me before returning to the ground beneath the clan prince's palanquin.

'They did not attack me,' she said. 'It was I who attacked them.'

Gasps arose from the crowd, though for the life of me I had no idea why anyone would care. I'd always assumed hunting down Mahdek and torturing them was the Jan'Tep national pastime.

'The child is confused,' Met'ordan declared.

'Tell the prince,' Neva'tris commanded, then indicated the crowds. 'Tell all of them what was done to you. Testify and bring honour to the House of Tris, for we have *always* fought to keep our clan safe.'

Ala'tris was shaking now. 'It is as I've said, Mother. On my own accord, I . . . captured these two foreigners and held them prisoner. They escaped, and I was too ashamed to tell you.'

You'd think Neva'tris would've spotted a good deal when it was put in front of her, but I guess to her this wasn't loyalty, but disobedience. 'No more lies.' She stabbed a finger at us and half the crowd nearly had a heart attack, thinking she was about to send flaming balls of ember magic into the air. 'Tell them!'

Ala'tris was sobbing now, and I almost felt sorry for her.

But Durral whispered, 'Watch this, kid,' and there was wonder in his tone.

'What?' I asked.

'It's all here, right in front of us, in this one moment.'

'Durral, you're not making any sense. What are you talking about?'

He nodded to the Cabal. 'The past.'

His head turned to the clan prince. 'The present.'

With the barest flick of his fingers he gestured to the kneeling girl, who was shaking so badly I thought she might be having some sort of magic-induced seizure. But Durral just smiled. 'The future.'

'I still don't—'

'She's torn between everything she's ever known, between what she's always been taught was duty and loyalty, all her upbringing, set against nothing but a few tales told in a dream.'

Our stories, I realised. *He's talking about the stories we told while we were in the mind cage.*

'Watch close, kid,' he said to me. 'You're about to see magic.'

328

44

Testimony

She told all of it. Right there in the oasis, in front of all those Jan'Tep mages, their Sha'Tep servants and the clan prince who ruled over them. Ala'tris laid out the Cabal's experiments, led first by Met'astice but supported by several of the great houses of lords magi spread across the Jan'Tep territories. She named names. Described the research, the discoveries and every atrocity inflicted on the victims. All had been young Mahdek boys and girls. All had died, except for me.

And when Ala'tris, kneeling in what by now had to be a pool of her own tears, had finished? Her own mother called her a liar.

'And now is my shame laid bare for all to see,' Neva'tris announced, and the shock and sorrow infused into her words was potent as any magical elixir. 'My daughter – my *blood* – betrays her family, her house and her people.'

'Mother, please, let there be an end to—'

But Neva'tris had already turned away from her daughter, appealing instead to her fellow mages. 'Like far too many of our youth, she fell prey to the poisoned words of outsiders. They persuaded her to sneak them into the city, use silk magic to invite them into her mind.'

A gasp erupted from the crowd.

Neva'tris held up a hand. 'We've seen this before, haven't we? This ache our young sometimes have to "understand" the ways of others? Instead of thanking us, their parents, for sheltering them in the most beautiful cities in the world, they complain and question why they cannot leave our territories until their educations are complete.'

Durral's quiet chuckle caught me by surprise.

'What?' I asked.

'Oldest story in the book,' was all he said in reply.

But Neva'tris wasn't done. She spun a tale of a devious Argosi who tricked a gullible young Jan'Tep girl into performing a spell that would give her insights into the lands beyond the borders of her home, but unbeknown to her, Durral had brought a Mahdek with him and used her demon-plagued madness to infect the mind of poor, trusting Ala'tris.

'Funny, ain't it?' Durral said to me as Neva'tris embellished her story with the heroic efforts of her fellow Cabal members to rescue her daughter from the cage in which he and I had imprisoned her.

I wasn't surprised that most of the crowd believed her. Given a choice between what would be a very messy trial for several high-ranking lords magi from powerful houses or blasting an Argosi gambler and a Mahdek demon spawn to ashes, they were choosing the easy path.

'You and I have very different definitions of what's funny, Durral.'

Neva'tris continued her diatribe, spinning one lie after another to make her daughter's claims about the crimes of the Cabal sound preposterous. Neva'tris was, it seemed, a tremendously popular figure in this city. Admired. Respected.

Maybe even adored. She was also a damned good storyteller. Heck, by the time she was done, I half believed that Ala'tris really had been deluded by our cunning manipulations.

Except for one teensy detail.

What was it Falcon had said to me, that day in the cave when he'd finished tattooing the sigils into my neck?

The inks go deep into the flesh, all the way to the bone. Long after the markings are gone and the scars from your scratching have healed, the bindings will remain.

Durral had seen it differently. 'A *fine necklace*,' he'd called it.

My fingers went to my throat, as they so often did, but for once I didn't feel the urge to scrape the skin away. Falcon and Durral had both been wrong. The sigils around my neck were neither a collar nor a necklace. They were my history. I hadn't asked for them, but from now on I would be the only one who got to decide what meaning they held for me.

'A rather . . . elaborate account,' the clan prince said, once Neva'tris had finished making her case. You could see in his face that he badly wanted to summon up all that copper-coloured energy swirling around the ember band on his right forearm and put an end to her, but it turns out politics can be just as powerful a force as magic. 'And we must give due weight to the testimony given by the head of one of our great houses.' He turned to Ala'tris. 'Do you wish to amend the accusations you have made against your mother and these other worthies, child?'

Having already demeaned herself in front of all these people, here in the heart of the only home she'd ever known, Ala'tris paled as horror drained all the colour from her features. She looked to her prince for support, then to her mother for forgiveness; finding none, she turned her gaze elsewhere.

You can't be serious, I thought. *You think you and me are friends now?*

'Don't pretend you weren't goin' to do it anyway,' Durral said to me.

'Doesn't mean I have to like it.'

I walked right up to the clan prince's palanquin and unbuttoned first my coat and then the top of my shirt, tugging them aside until the sigils around my neck glistened beneath the afternoon sun. When those nearby noticed the markings, they gasped. Slowly I turned in a circle, making sure everyone could see, spreading shock and disgust throughout the oasis.

The clan prince descended from his perch and came to tower over me. In the slackening of his jaw and the way his eyebrows rose where they met in the centre of his forehead, I saw in him something akin to pity. There was opportunity to be found in his shame. I could weep now, fall to my knees and kiss his feet. Play the sad little Mahdek girl, confused and tormented, a victim of forces beyond her comprehension.

Be a good girl now.

'If you want to feel sorry for anyone,' I said to him, 'feel sorry for yourself. The way things are going, I get the feeling you might not be big boss around here much longer.'

Anger flashed across his features, but then he chuckled, and smiled at me just for a moment as he asked, very quietly so that only I could hear, 'Do you suppose that when the great and powerful Met'astice went in search of the next subject for his experiments, that he perhaps picked on the wrong Mahdek?'

'Damn straight.'

He held my gaze for a second or two longer, as if he and I were dignitaries of great nations meeting for the first time across the border. I think he wanted me to understand something about him – or at least something he liked to believe about himself. Before I could figure out what that was, his features hardened and he turned to face Neva'tris and her co-conspirators.

'You have banded an outsider,' he said, his clear, precise diction barely hiding the low growl of a dog preparing to clamp its teeth around a rat's throat, 'violated accords signed three centuries ago with Darome, with Gitabria, with Berabesq and Zhuban. Those treaties are all that assure our sovereignty over the oases, the very source of our power.'

'This was merely research,' one of the members of the Cabal – a man older even than Met'astice had been – whined. 'We meant no—'

'You damnable fools! Have none of you any conception of what those other nations would do should they discover the crime you have committed in our name? The Daroman army alone outnumbers every Jan'Tep man, woman and child by ten to one! They've always resented our magic – always feared it could be used to enslave them. In breaching the accords you have legitimised any retaliation they would choose to inflict upon us!'

The crowds were visibly horrified by that prospect. Magic is powerful, but so is a Daroman battalion, complete with their trebuchets, camped outside your city. In laying this out for his people the prince had established the rationale for executing Neva'tris and the rest of the Cabal. Except for one little problem: Neva'tris was smiling.

'Just as you say, my prince.'

333

'Ah, crap,' Durral muttered.

'What?' I asked.

'The prince overplayed his hand.'

Neva'tris turned to the crowds once again. 'Should the Mahdek child leave this place, knowing what she knows, she will surely run to our enemies. She will feed them these same reckless allegations the prince himself now places upon us, his loyal lords magi, naming our researches as treason instead of rejoicing, as he should, for the discoveries which we could surely make, given more time and more . . . subjects.'

Durral's hand clamped on my shoulder to keep me from running at her, which was stupid. My plan was to wait until she wasn't looking and *then* stab her in the back.

'The Daroman empire will come down upon our cities,' she went on. 'With their machines of war they will overwhelm us. They will rain blood and fire upon the heads of every Jan'Tep house, every Jan'Tep family, every Jan'Tep child, until they are satisfied that at last we have been properly cowed as our prince has sought to make us these past years. Unless . . .'

'Here it comes,' Durral said.

Neva'tris held up a finger to forestall the clan prince interrupting her. Then that finger stretched out to point at me. 'Unless we ensure our enemies never find out.'

It wasn't until that moment that I truly understood what all this was about. Met'astice's experiments, the Cabal's nonsense about staving off some imaginary Mahdek threat – it was all part of a game of politics and intrigue, played in the shadows by Neva'tris and her supporters against a clan prince whose passive isolationism they deemed unworthy of a great nation.

This wasn't a war. It wasn't even a coup.

This was a poker game.

And me? Until now I'd been nothing more than a card in someone else's hand, waiting to be played. The two of leaves, lowest card in the deck as far as these Jan'Tep mages were concerned. But in poker, as in magic, any card can be wild.

You just have to bend the rules.

45

The Girl on the Card

Durral had been right about one thing: no nation thinks itself evil. No culture wants to be remembered as tyrants. People don't choose to be cruel. We all want to believe in our own decency.

Cries of outrage followed the Cabal's insistence that Durral and I be executed to keep their own crimes from coming back to haunt the Jan'Tep. Did this righteous indignation erode my prejudices against them? Did the guilt and shame that flickered like candle flames upon the features of so many of them as they gazed at the sad little Mahdek who'd suffered at the hands of unscrupulous mages cause me to question whether, perhaps, the plight of my people was the result of misconception rather than malice?

No.

War isn't a misunderstanding. Massacres aren't accidents. The Jan'Tep had wanted something we had, and they'd taken it. Durral had pointed out to me more than once that my own people had once conquered these lands from those who'd come before us. That the Mahdek language has seven different words for slave hardly paints a virtuous picture of our history.

But my people weren't suffering in the past. They were dying in the present. Already there were too few of us to ever again become a nation. We would fade into the mists of time, becoming nothing more than a myth of devil-worshipping necromancers who ate babies and slaughtered their enemies with forbidden magic.

And the Jan'Tep? Well, the Jan'Tep were a noble people, who fought only when there was no other choice, who meted out violence with the precision of a healer doling out medicine that, though unpleasant to the tongue, was necessary to preserve life. Killing an innocent was beneath them.

'You would add cold-blooded murder to the crimes with which you have stained our people?' the clan prince demanded, rounding on Neva'tris as if one wrong word from her would unleash the storm of mystical fury threatening to explode from the glistening bands around his forearms and the righteous fury in his heart.

Nice of him to summon up such passion for one lowly Mahdek, I thought, given that he surely knew that war covens of young Jan'Tep mages – whether with explicit approval of princes like himself or at least the turning of a blind eye – still hunted us as a means of proving their worth.

Maybe it's just harder to execute someone once you've heard their story.

Neva'tris, however, was undaunted by her ruler's outrage.

'If you're squeamish about euthanising this Mahdek,' she said casually, the serenity in her expression making him seem smaller by comparison, 'then let us do what we'd planned all along.' She gestured to me. 'We will place a mind chain around her memories, create such alterations as are needed to protect our people. The girl will remember her past merely

337

as the wanderings of an orphan, rescued by a noble Argosi who adopted her as his own daughter.'

Had any of the gods my ancestors worshipped been real, surely the heavens would've parted and they would have stepped down from the skies to this sad world of mortals and promptly punched Neva'tris in the face.

'There is . . . merit to this suggestion,' the clan prince was forced to concede.

He turned to me, and with a coward's compassion said, 'For the price of memories that I doubt bring you anything but pain, you would be spared to live out your life. I would further promise to take steps to ban the practices among my clan and the Jan'Tep territories that continue to bring such anguish to the Mahdek. The war ended three hundred years ago. It's past time the hatred died too.'

Meanwhile, I thought, *nobody here has to worry about word getting out about what Met'astice and the Cabal had been up to all this time. Everybody wins.*

'Yes,' the clan prince said, more to himself than to me. 'This is the most humane way forward.'

An ocean's worth of relief washed over the faces of the crowd filling the oasis. It was a miracle their hair didn't get wet.

'One small problem,' Durral said, idly shuffling through his steel deck.

'And what would that be, Argosi?' the clan prince asked.

Durral fanned out the cards, their razor-sharp edges glistening in the afternoon light. He picked one out, seemingly at random, and inspected it. 'First person who so much as utters a syllable's worth of any silk spell to alter our memories is gonna be spitting blood for a month. Messin' with

338

other people's minds is what got you all into this mess. Time you found a new hobby.'

There was a great deal of uproar coming from Met'ordan and the rest of the Cabal, soon spreading to a few of the more militantly minded among the crowd. The clan prince waved them to silence.

'Forgive me, Argosi,' he said to Durral. 'But you will find neither your toys nor your tricks will suffice against a mage of my calibre.' He looked almost grateful for the chance to assert himself, which made me wonder if Durral had put on this show of resistance for his benefit.

'Then it's settled,' Neva'tris said, and stepped forward. 'I will cast the mind chain upon them.' Her gaze settled on me. 'You may find this a trifle . . . uncomfortable.'

I saw Durral sliding the steel card he'd selected from the deck, noticed my own hand reaching over my shoulder to pull the smallsword from its case, and registered the look of regret that passed over the clan prince's face as he prepared to bind us with some spell or other in preparation for the mind chain. But before Durral could throw the card or I could draw my blade or the prince could utter so much as a syllable, a new voice entered the fray.

'No!' Ala'tris screamed.

There was such a fury in her that all of us froze.

She came forward to stand between me and the Cabal. 'Mother, this is wrong!' She turned to the crowd. 'All of you – this isn't who we are!'

Neva'tris looked as if she wanted to put a mind chain on her daughter even more than she did me.

'Child,' the clan prince warned, his precious equitable solution in peril, 'your sense of honour does more credit to the House of Tris than your mother's machinations, but my decisions must be guided by what is best for our people, and if the girl were ever to reveal the sins committed against her – as would be her right – she could ignite a war that would result in unimaginable bloodshed.'

Bizarrely, Ala'tris stepped back to stand beside me. Even more disconcerting, I felt her hand take hold of mine.

What are we now? Sisters?

'Liege,' she said, balancing obeisance and defiance on a knife's edge, 'I have been inside their minds, witnessed for myself some small part of the Argosi ways. It is against their precepts to take any action that could instigate war.'

The clan prince's discomfort was palpable. 'That is a risk my people cannot take.'

Interesting choice of words, I thought, still so distracted by the inexplicable sensation of Ala'tris's hand in mine that I could've almost forgotten that I was moments away from either dying or having my memories stolen from me.

Stick to the plan, I reminded myself.

I turned my head to watch Durral's eyes, and the way they contradicted the ease of his smile.

He's going to challenge the prince to a duel, I knew then. *Draw him into some absurd agreement about letting us go if he wins, which the prince will probably have to accept or wind up looking weak before his people.*

Nice plan, but of course it wouldn't work. Even if Durral could somehow win, there was no way Neva'tris was going to honour any such agreement.

So we'll have to do it my way.

'I accept,' I said, before Durral could issue his challenge.
'Kid?'

'It's the only way,' I said.

The clan prince did a poor job of hiding his relief. 'The girl has spoken. Let her wisdom guide us as we make an end of this dark business. May each of us consign ourselves to look inside and—'

'One condition,' I said.

The clan prince swallowed whatever offence he took at my interrupting what I've no doubt would've been a lovely speech. 'Make your entreaty then,' he said, 'and I will grant it if I can.'

Neat of him to turn it into me begging him for a favour, I thought, but decided not to make a thing of it. Maybe I was growing as a person.

I pointed to Neva'tris. 'She isn't the one to cast the spell.'

'You do not dictate terms to us, Mahdek,' she hissed.

'Agreed,' the clan prince said. 'There are many silk mages with the necessary skills here today. I myself will—'

'I want *her*,' I said.

'Who?'

I nodded to Ala'tris, who was still holding my hand, though now it was like I was the mast of a ship she was clinging on to, to keep from being swept away in the storm.

'Agreed,' the prince repeated before Neva'tris could argue. 'Ala'tris has demonstrated the requisite abilities, as I understand it.' He turned his gaze to Neva'tris and the Cabal. 'One certainly can't doubt the skills of her teachers in these matters.'

For her part, Neva'tris seemed sanguine. 'We must participate in the spell then, to observe and ensure the cages placed around the Mahdek's and the Argosi's thoughts are secure.'

It looked as if the clan prince might object. He was, I decided then, a decent enough fellow after all.

341

'I agree,' I said. Then I turned to the crowds of onlookers, content to be passive participants in this as in so many atrocities carried out in their names. 'I want every single one of you to be part of it too. From this day forward, I want you to carry the weight of my memories, of my story, of all the things the Cabal did to me on your behalf.'

There were murmurs and complaints, but in the end not one of them had the courage to look weak in front of the others.

'A fitting punishment,' the clan prince acknowledged.

'Kid?' Durral asked.

'Yeah, maetri?'

'You sure you want to make this choice? In case you hadn't realised, they'll also be messin' with *my* mind.'

I shrugged. 'Ever since we met, you've been telling me to follow the Way of Water whenever I can. Besides, it's just a few lousy memories, right?'

He opened his mouth to protest, but my smile caught him off guard. Probably because he recognised it from a card he'd once painted of an angry girl who might one day – if she could find the courage, daring, compassion and cunning to leave her past behind – become an Argosi.

Durral Brown was the savviest card player I ever met.

But I was a far better cheat.

46

The Ritual

'I'll try to be gentle,' Ala'tris said as she faced me.

The two of us were standing near the centre of the oasis, right next to the low stone pool inside which silvery waves of something that couldn't be called liquid, but neither was it anything else, rose and fell as if in eager anticipation of being summoned to break the natural laws that ought to govern existence.

Ala'tris had said the spell would be easiest to cast near the raw source of Jan'Tep magic. Her mother had agreed. The more power, the stronger the mind chain.

That suited me just fine.

'Will you be going through my memories one by one?' I asked.

Ala'tris shook her head. 'Memories aren't really made of individual pictures or moments. They're more like . . . like a river we must dam at a particular moment in time and divert the waters to follow a new path. Your mind will create new memories to fill in the gaps on its own, telling and retelling itself these new stories over and over again until it believes them.'

'Okay, but you know that sounds like nonsense, right?'

She smiled shyly. 'I'm sorry, I'm not explaining it very well.'

'You're explaining it just fine,' I said.

'Because I've been in your mind before,' she went on, 'even longer than the others, I will do my best to find the right place to expunge your memories as quickly as possible. You won't suffer long, I promise.'

Durral took his place next to me. 'I'm going to be right there with you, kid. Every step of the way.'

I looked up at Durral Brown, my teacher, my friend, and saw tears in his eyes. If there's a soul in this world who can't love that man then it's a soul not worth saving.

'I think pretty much everybody's going to be with me on this trip,' I said, gesturing to the mass of bodies crowded all around the oasis, all of whom were to be bound in the spell with us.

'Guess that's so.'

I took Durral's hand and squeezed it. 'But I'm glad you're with me,' I said. Then, to try it on for size and because, hey, chances were I wouldn't remember any of this, I added, 'Pappy.'

'Damn straight,' he said, as if it was the most natural thing in the world.

'Enough,' Neva'tris said. 'The hour grows late. Delay will not alter your fate, Mahdek.'

Ala'tris shot her mother a look that said theirs was not going to be a happy home after this. When she turned back to me, she asked more gently, 'Are you ready?'

'Just a sec,' I replied. 'This thing always itches.'

I reached up a finger to tug at my collar and briefly scratched at a particular sigil on the left side of my neck. My eyes locked on those of Ala'tris.

Let's hope I'm right about this.

344

The young mage looked confused for a moment, then nodded almost imperceptibly.

'Let's do this,' I said.

As if those were the words of a magic spell, the world disappeared.

47

The Cave

Be a good girl now.

We crouched inside the cave outside a village where a septet of young mages were murdering the remnants of my clan. It felt so real I had to stop myself from running out there in a desperate bid to fight back. Of course, given I was just eleven and didn't even have a name yet, that would've been difficult.

'We don't have much time,' the old woman who'd dragged me in here moments ago said in a voice that sounded suspiciously like a seventeen-year-old Jan'Tep girl's. 'I've hidden my presence inside the sigil that Shadow Falcon used to watch over you, but soon the others will expect to see the destruction of your memories.'

'Why start here?' I asked. 'I'll remember that the Jan'Tep massacred my clan.'

'We have to begin here, otherwise you'd have no understanding of why your clan disappeared from your life.' There was a fierceness in the old woman's expression that cut through the shadows between us. 'Besides, I never agreed to remove all my people's crimes from your memories.'

'About that . . .' I began.

'You want me to fake the spell,' Ala'tris said. 'But I can't. My mother and the others would know.'

'Oh, I don't want you to fake the spell. I just want you to cast it twice.'

'Twice?'

I nodded. 'The first time you're going to pull out my memories, but project them into everyone with us in the oasis, right?'

'That was the agreement. I promise my people will remember your story, even if—'

'Yeah, I don't care so much about that. What I need you to do is blast their memories of my life back into me after the first spell is cast.'

'That . . . That would be an unusual way to use the spell.'

'Can it work?'

She considered that a moment, as I sat there listening to the screams of the last of my clan and the crackle of ember magic outside the cave.

'After a fashion,' Ala'tris said at last. 'But they wouldn't be your memories any more. They'd be reflections . . . echoes of your experiences. Like thousands of shards from a stained-glass window pieced together from the descriptions of two hundred different people who once saw it. Your recollections would be fragmented, confused. I would fear for your sanity.'

I grinned, partly because I needed to convince her to go ahead with my plan and partly to convince myself I wasn't terrified. 'I've been mostly crazy my whole life. I've gotten used to it.'

'There's another problem,' she said. 'I would be violating the command given me by the clan prince. I know I swore to follow the Way of Water with you and the Argosi, but I warned you both I could not betray my people.'

347

'Oh, I don't think that'll be a problem,' I said, then leaned over towards the deeper section of the cave. 'You can come out now.'

Two figures emerged from the darkness. Foreigners. A big gruff man, and a woman with bright mischievous eyes.

'How did you know I would be here?' Sir Gervais – well, the clan prince of Oatas Jan'Dal – asked.

It was all I could do not to weep at the sight of Sir Gervais and Sir Rosarite, come once again to rescue me from death and despair, even if they weren't quite themselves this time.

'Always wondered what this would feel like,' Durral said, looking down at Rosarite's slender fingers as he crouched in the cave.

To the clan prince I said, 'When Ala'tris suggested letting Durral and me go, trusting that we wouldn't instigate a war by using what was done to me to give your enemies an excuse to invade the Jan'Tep territories, you said, "that is a risk *my people* cannot take."'

'And?'

It was nice seeing Sir Gervais's crooked smile again.

'And you could've said, "*I*" instead, which is how you talk because you're a clan prince and you don't want to show any signs of weakness in front of Neva'tris and the others.'

He turned to Durral, who was admiring himself in Sir Rosarite's body in a way that struck me as entirely inappropriate. 'You've taught her well, Argosi.'

'Right now she's teachin' me.' He looked back at me. 'Okay, kid. How's this going to work?'

I turned back to Ala'tris. 'The moment you finish pulling the memories out of me and Durral, blast those "reflections" you talked about from everyone else back into us.' I turned

348

to him. 'Sorry, but looks like you're going to be a little crazier than usual after this.'

He chuckled. 'Kid, I'm an Argosi. Our minds are so twisty already that I'll be just fine, trust me.'

'We'll need some kind of distraction,' Ala'tris said, sounding ever more dubious about my utterly brilliant plan. 'If even one person notices me casting the second mind chain, they'll close themselves off and know what I tried to do.'

I grinned at her. 'Oh, I'll give them a distraction.'

She looked at me a long while, young eyes growing as old as those of the woman in whose image she'd appeared. 'If this works, if I draw your memories back out of all of us and put them into you, I won't remember any of this. None of us will.' She turned to the clan prince. 'Except perhaps you, my liege, as you've placed yourself outside the spell as well. There will be considerable confusion.'

The clan prince didn't seem to mind that possibility at all. 'That will suit my current needs admirably.'

Ala'tris reached out the old woman's hand and took mine again. She really was a touchy-feely sort. 'May we meet again, Ferius Parfax, and at that meeting, should I remember nothing else, may my ancestors and yours grant that we walk the Way of Water together.'

Not knowing what else to do, I hugged this weird Jan'Tep girl who seemed to insist on pretending we were something other than mortal enemies.

It wasn't so bad really.

After we let go of each other, she took in a long, deep breath, and said, 'When first the spell ignites, you will feel as if you've been plunged to the bottom of a lake too deep to ever swim back to the surface. Count to seven, and as you do, your

349

memories will be pulled out of you, like air. It'll be like . . . like drowning. The more you resist the memories, the worse it will be.'

'No problem,' I said casually. 'You could say I've come to terms with my past recently.'

'So be it.'

I heard only the barest whisper of syllables from her lips, saw nothing but a faint flicker of purple and silver between us, and then . . . and then . . .

Turned out she wasn't kidding about it being like drowning.

48

The Spell

Seven.

My clan. My childhood. The old woman in the cave and her last, futile act of kindness.

Six.

Sir Gervais and Sir Rosarite. A small piece of a life that might have been, with schools and birthdays and a nice house to live in.

Five.

Met'astice. Falcon. A wooden table and a dozen different deaths carved into the skin of my neck.

Four.

Arissa. The Black Galleon. The day-to-day perils and triumphs of a thief. The possibly-maybe-one-day glances exchanged with a girl who didn't have friends but perhaps, just perhaps . . .

Three.

Durral. The dog. The horse. Gambling lessons.

Whatever happened to that squirrel cat?

Two.

Argosi lessons. Seven talents. Four ways. One path.

But which path is mine?

Doesn't matter. You're taking it away from me, aren't you?

All you fine Jan'Tep citizens clothed in elegant robes and the illusions of a glorious past that never was. But with magic you can make people believe anything you want, and you so badly want to believe you can make me disappear.

So go ahead. Try it. I dare you. You want to take these memories from me?

One . . .

Don't resist, Ala'tris had warned me.

Resist? How about I do the opposite?

With every fibre of my being, every shred of my broken soul, I take the stories of my life – the good, the bad and all the ones that defy such blunt and banal definitions – and I hurl them at the crowds in the oasis. I blast them as surely as any ember spell, my incantation encompassing every word I've ever uttered, painting a thousand thousand pictures onto a single card and throwing it through the air so hard and fast it slices through everything it encounters.

I hear Ala'tris gasp and worry for a second that I've hurt her, which is kind of funny, all things considered. But she's strong, and determined, and guided by something that maybe I would've liked to get to know better. Something maybe we could both hang on to, if only I reach out and . . .

Emptiness.

I'm nothing. An eleven-year-old girl alone in a cave, wondering what happened to her people. But when I look down I see a pool, and the face in the water isn't that of a child, is it? She looks older. Fifteen? Sixteen? How is that possible?

Already the explanations concoct themselves. I must've ventured out of the cave, days later, when it was safe. Yes, that makes sense. And then . . . and then I went to the nearest village. That's what we Mahdek do, isn't it? We go from place to place, offering what we can, our meagre labour, asking for what generosity others will give.

Yes. That's it.

From there I searched for another Mahdek clan to take me in, but it was hard. There are so few of us left. So I made my way through the world, alone. Always alo—

'Ferius, I'm casting the second spell!'

I don't even have time to look up before the world flips over on itself and the sea into which I'd sunk before suddenly crashes down upon me, as if the sky had broken apart all at once.

No . . . I cry, unable to hold it all in. *It's too much. No one could hold all these memories, these lives. They can't possibly fit inside one scrawny girl. They're slipping through my fingers!*

I'm about to give up when I remember the one thing, the one tiny detail that, for no reason I can explain, has always been the most important to me.

Ferius Parfax.

My name is Ferius Parfax.

I chose that name. I mean, sure, maybe I kinda stole it from a dog, but still, it's mine now. I've earned it.

That name contains everything about me, every dumb move and ill-considered choice that brought me here. Every piece of bad luck and unimaginable good fortune, deserved and otherwise, that came my way. I've walked the road of a knight, a thief, a gambler, a drifter, a scholar and maybe – just for a second there – I might've even taken a step or two along the path of the Argosi.

Ferius Parfax.

Funny sort of name, when you think about it. Not even

a girl's name really. But it's mine, so I say it out loud just to hear the sound.

Ferius Parfax.

Hmm . . . sounds strange.

'Ferius Parfax!'

That sounds even weirder. It's not my voice.

'Kid, are you gonna stand there all day?'

I open my eyes.

The oasis is gone. The tall marble columns, the low stone pool of silvery water. The clan prince. Ala'tris. All gone.

I'm in a desert. Beneath me the sand is blue from the azurite minerals that give this region its name. I turn around, but there's no Jan'Tep city in sight.

'Damn it,' I swear aloud.

Either Ala'tris failed to cast the second spell properly, or another member of the Cabal stepped in and stuck us back in a mind cage. Only . . . if she screwed up the spell, how come I remember her name? How come I remember mine? How come I remember . . . everything?

Durral's arms are folded across his chest. He's giving me an irritated glare.

'What?' I ask.

'Three days I've been puttin' up with this, kid. Three days of us walkin' through this damned desert with you fallin' into a trance every time we stop to set up camp. I do all the work, and then you start mumbling your name over and over until finally you wake up and we go through this same conversation again.'

'Where are we?' I ask.

He rolls his eyes. 'And here we go.' After a sigh that is far too theatrical for me to be genuinely worried, he rattles off how Ala'tris cast the second spell, and how we came out of it in the oasis but the clan prince used sand magic to freeze everyone else in time so we could leave without making a fuss. Then, after reminding Durral that he'd really appreciate it if the Argosi would stay out of Jan'Tep affairs for a while, he bid us farewell and sent us on our way.

'He warned me you'd be a little confused for a while,' Durral said, giving me a nudge to get us walking deeper into the desert. 'Don't understand why I get these headaches and you just drift off for hours at a time, leavin' me with nothin' to do but listen to you say "Ferius Parfax" over and over like it's some danged magic spell.'

I glance up at the sky. It's still early, the morning sun shining down all sorts of promises it probably won't keep. Then I stare out at the stretch of blue desert in front of us.

'Where are we going?' I ask.

'We're on a mission, kid.'

'A mission?' I stop and grab him by the arm. 'Durral, we fought off a living candle, trudged through an imaginary world that turned out to be a prison, broke out only to then face off with two hundred Jan'Tep mages and get our brains scrambled by not one but *two* different silk spells. You don't think we deserve a bit of a rest in a quiet little town somewhere?'

'After the mission,' he says, and resumes his march into the desert.

'What mission?' I call out after him.

He points to the ground, and only now do I notice the faint tracks he must've been following all this time.

'Gotta find my damned horse and dog,' he says. 'You'd be surprised all the trouble those two get themselves in when I ain't watchin' over 'em.'

Epilogue

The Way of Water

We did eventually find Tolvoi and Quadlopo outside a town called Settler's End, where they'd wound up in even more trouble than Durral had predicted. Through circumstances passing understanding, they'd somehow gotten mixed up with that squirrel cat again, and she'd led them to a wealthy nobleman's country palace where the three of them had nearly . . . You know what? That's a whole other story. Suffice it to say, by the time we rescued them, Tolvoi and Quadlopo were headed for the chopping block, and the squirrel cat had run off with a fortune in gemstones.

There's a lesson there, somewhere.

As for me? Well, that's a little more complicated.

Durral brought me south with him to a dust speck of a town on the border between Darome and Gitabria where he introduced me to his wife, Enna, with his customary blend of diplomacy and tact.

'Sorry I'm late, darlin'. This here's Ferius. Reckon we might want to adopt her.'

Enna, who looked nothing like Durral had described in his stories and yet was all the more beautiful for it, looked

357

me over with a piercing scrutiny that made his arta precis pale by comparison.

'I thought the dog was Ferius,' she said at last.

Durral shrugged, and went off to square away Quadlopo in the barn, leaving me with this strange and frightening woman with whom I'd not exchanged two words until she asked, 'Are you sure you want to stay with us, child? You know what they say: one Argosi is trouble, two is strong evidence the end times are coming.'

I glanced around the foyer of their sparse, two-storey house. It wasn't much to speak of, and it didn't look as if anyone spent much time here. After Sir Gervais and Sir Rosarite's mansion and, heck, even the dank, ruined majesty of the Black Galleon, this place didn't seem special at all. So I can't explain why I was suddenly so nervous, so utterly terrified she might not want me there. And why would she?

My whole body was shaking when I answered, 'Please, ma'am, if you let me stay, I promise I'll be . . . I'll be a good girl.'

Enna watched me again with that penetrating gaze of hers, and then, as if in that one glance she'd drawn a hundred secrets out of me, she reached out a hand and cupped my cheek. 'No,' she said.

I felt all my hopes come crashing down at once. Of course she didn't want me here. Stupid Durral shows up out of the blue after going missing for months, drags some half-starved savage into Enna's house and says he wants them to adopt her? How else was she going to react?

'I'm sorry,' I said.

'You should be.'

She took both my hands in hers and kissed each one, then

the corners of her mouth rose, one just a little higher than the other, and I saw where Durral had stolen his trademark smirk from. Next thing I knew she'd pulled me into a hug that I can still feel to this day. 'We got no use for good girls in this house,' she said.

Yeah, you really can fall in love that fast.

These past six months haven't been all good though. I still get confused sometimes. I forget things. I look at myself in the mirror a lot, which probably isn't good for you, but if I don't, I have trouble remembering what I look like.

Sometimes I open my eyes in the middle of the night to find Durral and Enna standing there in their nightclothes because I've been screaming in my sleep. Other times I hear voices. Met'astice, telling me the experiment continues. Arissa, warning me to get away. Durral, insisting it's up to me to decide whether to allow such apparitions to disturb me. Enna, reminding me that Durral, wise as he is in the ways of the Argosi, can be as blind as any man, sometimes.

The voice I hear most, though, is yours.

The sigils you imprinted around my neck are still there, but they fade a little each day. The clan prince informed Durral that most of the spells had worn out or broken on their own. This one, that lets you see through my eyes and fill my head with your thoughts, is the last. Apparently the clan prince offered to break it for me back at the oasis, but even in my trance I'd refused. Reckon it'll die out soon enough, and you and me still have this one last piece of business before we say goodbye.

The members of the Cabal have all been mind-chained to prevent them from remembering the experiments and what they learned through them. The clan prince assured Durral he was doing the same with you and a couple of others who weren't at the oasis that day. He said that none of you will remember my name, or what you did to me.

Ain't that a thing?

One day, Falcon, I might walk right up to your house. Maybe you'll wonder what an Argosi's doing knocking at your door. Out of curiosity, you'll invite me in, without even knowing that we've met before.

Now that I think on it though, I kinda hope I'll always be there, in your head, just a little bit. Durral says everyone needs a keepsake to remind us of the darkness in our own heart, like a compass that points backwards, showing the road we need never again tread. That's what you'll be to me from now on. For that and only that, Shadow Falcon – whatever your real name is – I offer you the Way of Water. Should our paths cross again one day, let there be peace between us. Because if not . . . ? Well, I've always been just a little bit prone to walking the Way of Thunder.

So you know what they say . . .

Be a good boy now.

Acknowledgements

On 29 January 2020, I called my editor at Hot Key Books, Felicity Alexander, and told her we were going to have to delay publication of *Way of the Argosi*. I'd started the book ages ago, and in fact had written the opening chapter shortly after finishing *Charmcaster*, the third instalment in the Spellslinger series. This book, which set out to reveal the secret origins of one of my favourite characters, Ferius Parfax, should've been easy to write. No sweat. Easy-peasy-lemon-whatever.

'I can't write it,' I told Fliss over our tenuous transatlantic Skype connection. 'I can't find the soul of the book. I need more time. We have to push the publication date to 2022.'

'No chance, punk,' Fliss growled, her six-pack a day cigarette habit turning every word into a hail of wasp stings. 'We gots ways of convincin' lazy-arsed authors to deliver. Ways that would make a pansy-pants like you curl up in a ball and pray for death.'

Okay, maybe that sounds a bit more angry squirrel cat than refined London literary editor. It's possible – just possible – that what she actually said was, 'What's most important to us is to support you as an author and help you do your best work, so if you need more time, we'll do whatever it takes.'

Yeah, most likely her response was along those lines. My version sounds better though.

Anyway, that should've been the end of it. I'd messed up

a book for the first time in my relatively short career and that was that. But then weeks later Fliss was introducing me to her colleague at Hot Key, Maurice Lyon, who would be taking over the book for her while she was off gallivanting about, watching daytime television or something . . . or was she having a baby? I can't remember. Something frivolous, I'm sure.

Regardless, the three of us talked about what was working in the early chapters and what was missing, and the insights that came out of that conversation turned everything around for me. Three months later I delivered the draft *Way of the Argosi – on time.*

And yes, I'd found the soul of the story.

The point of this anecdote isn't to expose my insecurities as a writer (though I have many), nor to highlight how vital editorial intuition can be in helping an author craft the book they're trying to create (though it often is). Instead, this is meant as one more in a long list of examples to remind me that the books I write – and that I hope you enjoy – are the product of many, many people's hard work, passionate dedication and creativity.

Or as Durral Brown might put it, 'You meet a lot of folks on the long roads, kid. Everyone of 'em's got somethin' to teach you if you just learn how to listen.'

The Black Galleon Gang
How many people does it take to transform a finished manuscript into the gorgeous book you now hold in your hands? An entire gang's worth:

The Bosses

Mark Smith: former CEO of Bonnier Zaffre. You still owe me a private jet.

Jane Harris, former MD of Hot Key Books. As Mark left, you'll have to buy me the private . . . Wait, you're leaving too?

Heather Adams and Mike Bryan: Unparalleled Literary Agents Who Would Never Abandon Their Favourite . . . Oh, crap. They've gone off to launch their own successful author careers. Damn it!

Christina de Castell: Aha! I wisely married her and now there's no possible way she could . . . Wait, what's in this suspiciously legal-looking envelope?

The Fixers

Felicity Alexander: Senior Commissioning Editor

Maurice Lyon: Senior Commissioning Editor (Maternity Cover)

Talya Baker: Desk Editor

Melissa Hyder: Proofreader

The Masters of Disguise

Nick Stearn: Art Director

Dominica Clements: Design Manager

Gavin Reece: Cover Artist

Sally Taylor: Interior Artist

Farhad Ejaz: Cartographer

Annie Arnold: Auxiliary

The Muscle

Emma Kidd: Production Controller

Eloise Angeline: Production Assistant

Marina Stavropoulou: Editor, Audio

Laura Makela: Audio Operations Manager
Palimpsest: Stylish Typesetting
Clays: Debonair Printing

The Explosives Experts

Amy Llambias: Senior Marketing Manager
Emma Quick: Senior Marketing Executive
Isobel Taylor: Creative and Marketing Assistant
Molly Holt: Press Officer

The Safe-Crackers

In-House Sales: Kate Manning, Elise Burns, Stacey Hamilton,
   Kirsten Grant, Maddie Hanson, Amanda Percival, Jearl
   Boatswain, Carrie-Ann Pitt
Sales Reps: Alan Scollan, Jeff Jamieson, Jennie Harwood, Robyn
   Haque
Digital Sales: Vincent Kelleher and Sophie Hamilton

The Getaway Drivers

Ruth Logan: Rights Director
Ilaria Tarasconi: Rights Manager
Amy Smith: Rights Assistant
Marc Simonsson: Film and TV Agent

The Lookouts

Lauren Campbell: Freelance Editor and Author's Assistant
   Extraordinaire
Kim Tough, Wil Arndt, Brad Dehnert, Peter Darbyshire, and
   Jim Hull: Kind of like the street toughs you hire to rough
   up your enemies only they roughed *me* up instead. Turns
   out I deserved it.

Nazia Khatoum: Squirrel Cat Expert

Nikki, Moon, and Lis: Pizza Stalkers

Eric Torin: Narrative Mastermind

Twelve-year-old Nicholas Hannington, who spotted a typo in *Shadowblack* and got his dad to let me know. Thanks, Nicholas!

The Argosi

My eternal gratitude to all of the booksellers, librarians, book bloggers and readers who've been so wonderful to correspond with over these past several years. *Spellslinger* never would've had a chance were it not for your kindness in spreading the word about this world of Jan'Tep mages, Argosi wanderers, outcast spellslingers and – most importantly, of course – thieving squirrel cats.

I always appreciate hearing from readers, and you can always reach me at: www.decastell.com/contact

Sebastien de Castell

October 2020

Vancouver, Canada

PS In case you're wondering, the rather devious squirrel cat who suckered Quadlopo (the horse) and Tolvoi (the dog – formerly Ferius) into that daring heist that nearly got them killed? Her name was Chitra. If you read *Spellslinger* you'll find out that thievery runs in the family.

FALL of the ARGOSI

Turn the page for a preview
of Ferius's further adventures . . .

1

The Boy in the Sand

The child raced barefoot across the desert. The cuts on the soles of his feet were staining the sand a madman's scarlet, but the look in his eyes said that was the least of his problems. Though I didn't know it then, he was fleeing his father, who loved him more than anything in the world, and was now intent on his murder. The same could've been said of my father, but I'm not ready to tell that story yet.

At first the boy had been nothing but a puff of dust and blond hair in the distance. The sun was beating down mercilessly that day, reminding all living things who was in charge and that deserts were cursed places at the best of times. I had a horse though, which makes all the difference.

'Reckon that's trouble ahead?' I asked Quadlopo, patting his neck.

The horse showed no signs of giving the matter any thought, just swished his tail to keep the flies away. In the five days since we'd fled to the borderlands, Quadlopo had yet to offer an opinion on anything, except perhaps that he would've preferred that I'd not stolen him in the first place. After all, it wasn't like anyone wanted *him* dead.

The grubby whirl of spindly arms and legs ran up the side

of a dune, then lost his balance and came tumbling down the other. He looked like he couldn't have been more than seven. An unseemly age to be running around the desert alone. His soiled blue tunic was torn to rags, and the skin of his arms and face shone an angry red that spoke of too many days out in the sun with nothing and no one to protect him. He was limping too, but kept on going, which meant whatever was chasing him troubled him more than the pain.

Brave kid.

When he got thirty yards away from me, he stopped and stared as if trying to work out whether I was a mirage. I'm not sure what conclusion he came to, but I guess he'd been running a long time because his legs gave out on him and he dropped to his hands and knees. That's when I saw the two new figures come shambling through the haze towards us. A tall man and a squat woman, whose unnatural, shuffling gaits made me question whether those labels might be too generous in describing whatever had followed the boy.

For the first time since we'd happened upon this unpleasantness, Quadlopo became restless. He blew hot air out of his nostrils, and pawed the sand with his hoofs, trying to turn his head away from the mangled figures lumbering towards the child who was now lying face down in the sand, waiting to die.

Most folk in these parts, should they get lost in the desert and run out of either water or the will to live, choose to meet their end on their backs, so the last thing they see will be the blue sky above. The boy, though, seemed determined to look away from the man and woman coming for him.

Now that I'd gotten a good look at them, I didn't blame him.

Insanity, as I'd learned in my paltry seventeen years, could take all forms, come in all shapes and sizes. I'd witnessed folks of sound mind condemned as lunatics for the crime of being ugly and eccentric at the same time. I'd met well-groomed, erudite gentlemen of means who hid diabolical madness beneath smooth talk and friendly smiles. Then again, when I saw myself in the mirror, I looked sane too, so best not to pass judgement on such matters without strong evidence first.

When two strangers come lurching towards you across the desert, naked as the day they were born except for their hides being caked in blood and dirt and fouler things I preferred not to imagine, when those same souls stare out at the world through eyes opened so wide they look set to fall out of their sockets, jaws hanging open but nothing coming out except for a snake's hiss, well, times like that call for a different sort of prudence.

I reached over my shoulder and uncapped the long black mapmaker's case that held the smallsword I'd sworn five days ago never to draw again so long as I lived. One of the reasons I'd chosen to flee to the Seven Sands had been to smash the blade into seven pieces and bury each one so far from the others that not even the finest tracker in the whole world could unite them.

The hot desert wind shifted. The blood-soaked pair sniffed at the air like hunting hounds. Their heads tilted to the side like they'd just smelled a vixen for the first time and didn't know what to make of her. Some sort of instinct took hold of them, and they stopped heading towards the boy and came for me instead. At first they plodded, so awkward I kept expecting them to trip over themselves like puppets caught in their strings. But with each step their bare, blistered feet found surer footing. Faster and faster they scurried, and the closer they got the more their hisses became a nightmare's worth of whispers that swirled around me like a dust storm.

I drew the sword from its case and slid off the horse's back, knowing that my oath never again to commit an act of violence, sworn while my adoptive mother's blood was still slick on my hands, was about to be broken.

The whispers became howls, and the howls turned to shrieks that sent poor, brave Quadlopo galloping away, abandoning me to whatever fate my bad luck and ill deeds had brought upon us. The two feral, manic creatures that came at me must've once been human beings with hopes and dreams of their own. Now their hands curled into claws, and they showed me teeth that must've clacked so hard and so long against each other that they'd broken down to ragged fangs. Somewhere deep inside their throats, deranged screeches hid words I couldn't understand and didn't want to. Words that proved madness came with its own poetry.

My hand tightened on the grip of my sword, and I breathed in as slow as I could, preparing to make my stand and wondering whether the awful sounds they were making would become the elegy I carried with me into the ground.

My name is Ferius Parfax. I'm seventeen years old. This was the day I first heard the Red Scream.

Thank you for choosing a Hot Key book.

If you want to know more about our authors
and what we publish, you can find us online.

You can start at our website

www.hotkeybooks.com

And you can also find us on:

We hope to see you soon!